William Black

Donald Ross of Heimra

William Black

Donald Ross of Heimra

ISBN/EAN: 9783744686082

Printed in Europe, USA, Canada, Australia, Japan

Cover: Foto ©Raphael Reischuk / pixelio.de

More available books at **www.hansebooks.com**

DONALD ROSS OF HEIMRA

WILLIAM BLACK

NEW AND REVISED EDITION

LONDON
SAMPSON LOW, MARSTON & COMPANY
LIMITED
St. Dunstan's House
1894

LONDON :

PRINTED BY WILLIAM CLOWES AND SONS, LIMITED,

STAMFORD STREET AND CHARING CROSS.

CONTENTS.

DONALD ROSS OF HEIMRA.

CHAPTER I.

GODIVA.

" Well, Mary, it is a pretty plaything to have given you—
a Highland Estate !—and no doubt all your fine schemes
will come right.   But you will have to change three things
first."

" Yes ? "

" And these are human nature and the soil and climate
of Scotland."

" Avaunt, Mephistopheles !—and go and give that porter
a shilling."

The two speakers were on the platform of Invershin
station, on the Highland line of railway.   One of them
was a tall young woman of distinguished presence and
somewhat imperious carriage, as you could gather at a first
glance ; but the next second, if she happened to turn her
face towards you, you would have perceived that her expression meant nothing but a bland gentleness and a prevailing and excellent good-humour.   Perhaps it was the
dimple in her cheek that did it—a dimple that came there
readily whenever she regarded any one, and that seemed
to say she was very willing to be pleased and to please :
at all events, she found it easy, or had hitherto found it
easy, to make friends.   For the rest, she was of an erect
and elegant figure ; her complexion fair ; her eyes grey-
green, and full of light ; her abundant hair of a sunny
brown ; her features regular enough and fine enough for
all practical purposes.   It was of this young woman that

B

her friend and now her travelling companion, Kate Glendinning, was in the habit of saying—

"There's one thing I will confess about Mary Stanley: she's not quite honest. She is too happy. She is so happy in herself that she wants every one she meets to share in her content; and she is apt to say clever and flattering little things that are not quite true. It is for no selfish purpose; quite the reverse: still—you mustn't believe all that Mary says to you."

Thus Kate Glendinning of her dearest friend; but if any one else had ventured to say similar things in her presence—then, and right swiftly, there would have been pretty tempests and flashes of eye-lighting.

And now there came up to Miss Stanley a short, stumpy, red-haired and red-bearded man of extraordinary breadth of shoulder and bulk of frame. He had a massive head despite his diminutive height; his mouth, drawn heavily down at each end, betokened a determined will, not to say a dogged obstinacy; and his small, clear, blue eyes, besides being sharp and intelligent, had a curious kind of cold aggressiveness in them—that is to say, when he was not talking to one whom it was his interest to propitiate, for then he could assume a sort of clumsy humility, both in manner and speech. This was Mr. David Purdie, solicitor, of Inverness. *An Troich Bheag Dhearg*—that is to say, the Little Red Dwarf—the people out at Lochgarra called him; but Mr. Purdie did not know that.

"The carriage is quite ready, Miss Stanley," said he, in his slow deliberate, south-country accent; and therewithal the three of them passed round to the back of the station and entered the waggonette, Mr. Purdie modestly taking a seat by the driver. The two young ladies were well wrapped up, for it was in the beginning of April, and they had fifty miles before them, out to the Atlantic coast. Kate Glendinning, in looking after her companion's abundant furs and rugs, rather affected to play the part of maid; for this shrewd and sensible lass, who was in rather poor circumstances, had consented to accept a salary from her friend who was so much better off; and she performed her various self-imposed duties with a tact and discretion beyond all praise.

And as they drove away on this clear-shining afternoon, Mary Stanley's face was something to study. She was all eagerness and impatience; the colour mantled in her cheeks; her brain was so busy that she had scarcely a word for her neighbour. . For she had heard a good deal and read much more, in Parliamentary debates and elsewhere, of the sufferings of the crofters, of the iniquities that had been practised on them by tyrannical landlords and factors, of the lamentations of the poor homeless ones thrust forth from their native shores; and now, in this little bit of the world that had so unexpectedly become hers, and in as far as she was able, wrong was to be put right, amends were to be made, and peace and amity, and comfort and prosperity were to be established for ever and ever. Perhaps the transcendental vision of the prophet Isaiah was haunting her: "The wilderness and the solitary place shall be glad ... and the desert shall rejoice, and blossom as the rose." And if she were to summon back the poor exiles who had been banished—banished to the slums of Glasgow, perchance, or to the far plains of Manitoba? . . "And the ransomed of the Lord shall return, and come to Zion with songs and everlasting joy upon their heads; they shall obtain joy and gladness, and sorrow and sighing shall flee away." To be sure, as they now drove along the wide and fertile valley that is penetrated by the Kyle of Sutherland, she did not meet with much evidence of the destitution she had been led to expect. She had heard of bleak wastes and sterile altitudes, of ruined huts and dismantled steadings; but here, under the softly-wooded hills, were long and level stretches of arable land, the ploughmen busy at their work; the occasional crofts were very far indeed from being hovels; and the people whom they saw, in the bits of gardens, or tending the cattle, looked well-clothed and well-fed. She ventured to hint something of this to her companion; and Kate, glancing at her, began to giggle.

"I really believe you are disappointed, Mary! Is there not enough misery for you? But never fear. If it's misery you're in search of, you have seldom far to go for it, in this world. Only I must tell you this—if you're so eager to relieve distress—that there is more of wretchedness, and crime, and squalor, and piteous human suffering in a single square mile of the slums of London or New York than you'll find in the whole of the Highlands of Scotland."

"That may be," said Miss Stanley, in her calm and equable fashion. "But you see, Käthchen, I have no call that way. I do not feel a direct responsibility, as I do in this case—"

"It is a responsibility you are making for yourself," her friend said. "You know very well it was not for that your uncle left you the property. It was merely to spite your father and your brothers."

"There was a little more," was the good-natured reply (for she did not seem to resent this reference to her amiable relative). "I think it was to spite the people out there as well. My uncle and they never could get on; and he was not a man who liked to be thwarted. And of course he imagined that I, being a woman, would not interfere; that I would leave the estate to be managed by Mr. Purdie, and simply receive the rents. Well," she continued, and here she lowered her voice somewhat, and there was a touch of colour in her face that was perhaps the expression of some definite resolve, "I may allow Mr. Purdie to manage the estate, or I may not. But if he does continue to manage the estate, it will be under my direction."

Käthchen looked at her, and laughed a little.

"I don't think Mr. Purdie knows whom he has got to deal with," said she, under her breath.

They stopped that night at Oykel Bridge. Miss Stanley invited Mr. Purdie to dine with them; but he declined on the ground that he had business in the neighbourhood—an odd excuse, for the inn and its dependencies constitute the remote little hamlet. The two young women passed the evening by themselves, and talked: the one with generous ardour entering into all her wonderful schemes, the other (who knew the country, and the people) interposing now and again with a little modifying information. But really Käthchen was not unsympathic. Her eyes, which were the attractive feature of her face, sometimes expressed a trifle of demure amusement; but she was not a quarrel-some or argumentative creature; and besides there is something about all fine humanitarian projects that one would rather believe in and welcome.

Next morning they resumed their drive, and very soon entered a much wilder country than that of the preceding day. Wilder but nevertheless beautiful—with its range upon range of russet hills, wine-stained here and there with shadow; its woods of leafless birch of a soft dark rose-lilac; its long undulations of waste moorland, yellow and brown; with now and again the sudden blue scythe-sweep of the river. For now they were traversing the lonely district of upper Strath-Oykel. Far ahead of them rose the giant bulk of Ben More, Assynt its higher shoulders a solid mass of white. The sunlight around them was cheerful no doubt; and yet there was a strange sense of solitariness, of voicelessness; and Mary, who was less concerned about the beauty of the landscape than about certain problems haunting her mind, called out to Mr. Purdie, who was again up beside the driver—

"Mr. Purdie, why are there no people living in this country?"

"Because there's nothing for them to live on," was the laconic answer. "It's fit for nothing but grazing sheep—and for grouse."

"Yes—the hills, perhaps," said she. "But look along the valley—by the side of the river."

"Ay, it's fine land, that," said he, grimly,—"for a wheen pesewepes!" And indeed the plovers were the only visible living things, jerking about in the air, dipping suddenly to the ground and swiftly rising again, with their curious squeaking call, and the soft velvet fluffing of their wings.

However, all that was nothing. By and by they had left the Oykel strath, and had entered upon a far higher and bleaker region, the desolation of which appalled her. There was not even the solitary shepherd's cottage they had seen down in the other valley; here was nothing but a wilderness of brown and ragged moorland, with deep black clefts of peat, and an occasional small tarn, without a bush along its shores, its waters driven a deep blue by the wind. Away in the west they could make out the spectral shapes of the Assynt mountains—Coul Beg, Coul

More, and Suilven—remote and visionary through the universal haze of the heather-burning; but here, all around them, were these endless and featureless and melancholy undulations; and the silence was now unbroken even by the curious bleating of the plovers: once, and once only, they heard the hoarse and distant croak of a raven.

"Käthchen," said Mary, in a sort of piteous dismay, as she looked abroad over those sombre solitudes, "you have been all along the Ross and Cromarty coast; is it like *that* ?"

"Plenty of it worse," was the reply.

"And—and—my place: is it like that ?"

"I have never been into Lochgarra."

"But—but if it is like that—what am I to do for my people ?"

"The best you can," said Käthchen, cheerfully.

It seemed an interminable drive. And then, in the afternoon, a premature darkness came slowly over; the mountains in the north gradually receded out of sight; and heavy, steady rain began to fall. The two girls sat huddled underneath one umbrella, listening to the pattering footfalls of the horses and the grinding of the wheels on the road; and when they ventured to peep forth from their shelter they beheld but the same monotonous features in the landscape: masses of wet rock and dark russet heather, black swamps, low and bare hills, and now and again the grey glimmer of a stream or tarn. It was a cheerless outlook; continually changing, and yet ever the same; and hour after hour the rain came down wearily. There was hardly a word said between those two: whither had fled Mary Stanley's dream of a shining blue sea, a sunny coastline, and a happy peasantry busy in their fields and gardens, their white cottages radiant in the morning light ? Käthchen, on the other hand, was inclined to laugh ruefully.

"Isn't it a good thing, Mary, that duty brought us here ? If it had been pleasure, we should be calling ourselves awful fools."

But quite of a sudden this hopeless resignation vanished, and a wild excitement took its place.

"Miss Stanley," Mr. Purdie called to her, "we've come to the march."

“The what ? ”

“ The march—the boundary of your estate ? ”

Instantly she had the carriage stopped, and nothing would do but that she must get out and set foot on her own land; moreover, when Käthchen took down the umbrella, they found that the rain had ceased, and that the western skies were lightening somewhat.

“That is the march,” said Mr. Purdie, pointing to a low, irregular, moss-grown wall—obviously a very ancient landmark; “and it goes right over the hill and down again to the Garra.”

Leaving the highway, she stepped across the ditch, and stood on the moist, soft peat land.

“And this is mine ! ” she said to Käthchen, with an odd expression of face. “This is absolutely mine. Nobody can dispute my possession of it. This piece of the solid world actually belongs to me.”

“And I suppose your rights extend as deep as ever you like,” said Käthchen. “ You might go all the way through, and have a walk in the streets of Melbourne, and get dry, and come back.”

But Mary’s quick eye had caught sight of what was to her the most important feature of the surrounding landscape. It was a cottage perched on a knoll above a burn—or, rather, it was the ruins of a cottage, the gables standing roofless, the thatch long ago blown away by the winds, the beams and fallen stones lying among the withered nettles, altogether a melancholy sight.

“Now, isn’t it shameful ! ” she exclaimed, in hot indignation. “Look at that ! The very first thing I meet with ! Do you wonder that people should talk about the Highland landlords ? Some poor wretch has been driven away— perhaps at this very moment in Canada or in Australia, he is thinking of the old home, and forgetting all the rain and discomfort there used to be, Mr. Purdie ! ”

“Yes, ma’am ? ” said he, coming a bit nearer; and Käthchen looked on, wondering if his doom was about to be pronounced.

“ Who lived in that house ? ” Miss Stanley demanded.

“ The schoolmaster,” was the reply.

“ The schoolmaster ? And where is he now ? ”

"He's in his own house," the factor said. "We built him a new one and a better one, to be nearer the school and the village; and when he moved it was hardly worth while keeping the old one in repair."

"Oh," said she, a little disconcerted. "Oh, really. Then no one was sent away—from that cottage ?"

"No, no—not at all—not at all," said he ; and he followed her to the waggonette and politely shut the door after her— while Käthchen's face maintained an admirable gravity.

As they drove on again, the afternoon seemed inclined to clear ; the skies were banking up ; and there were faint streaks of lemon-yellow among the heavy purple clouds in the west. And very soon the road made a sweep to the left, bringing them in sight of the Connan, a small but turbulent tributary of the Garra. Here, also, they encountered the first signs of the habitations of men—little clumps of buildings clustered together just over a stretch of flat land that had clearly been recovered from the river-bed. Crofts, no doubt : each slated cottage surrounded by its huddled dependency of thatched barns and byres.

As the waggonette drew near to the first of these rude little settlements, the women disappeared into the out-houses, and the children hid behind the peat-stack; but there remained standing at the door of the cottage an elderly man, who regarded the strangers with a grave and perhaps rather sullen curiosity.

"Mr. Purdie," said Mary, in an undertone, "is that one of my tenants ?"

"Yes, certainly—that is James Macdonald."

"I wish to make his acquaintance," said she ; and she stopped the carriage, and got out.

There was no sort of fear, or unnecessary bashfulness, about this young woman. She walked right up the bank to the door of the cottage. The short thick-set man standing there had something of a Russian cast of countenance, with a heavy grey beard, shaggy eyebrows, and small, suspicious eyes. His clothes were weather-worn as to colour and much mended ; but they were not in the least squalid ; and he had a red woollen comforter round his neck.

"Good evening !" said she, with a most winning smile.

But the propitiating dimple, that had hitherto been all-conquering, was of no avail here. He looked at her. He did not raise his cap.

"*Cha 'n 'eil beurla agam*," said he, with a sort of affected indifference.

She was taken aback only for a moment.

"What does he say?" she asked of Mr. Purdie, who had followed her.

"He says he has no English," the factor answered; and then he added, vindictively: "But he would have plenty of English if he wanted to tell you of his grievances—oh, ay, plenty! Start him on that, and he'll find plenty of English! He's one of the most ill-condeetioned men in the whole place—and I suppose he has enough English to understand that!"

"Tell him who I am," said she, rather disappointedly; for she had set out with the determination to get to know all the circumstances and wants and wishes of her tenants, especially of the poorer ones, without the intervention of any factor.

Hereupon Mr. Purdie, in unnecessarily severe tones, as it seemed to her, addressed a few sentences in Gaelic to the stubborn-looking old man, who, in turn—and with no abatement of his hostile attitude—replied in the same tongue. But to Mary's surprise, he suddenly added— fixing morose eyes upon her—

"She—no my laird! Ross of Heimra—my laird. Young Donald—he my laird. She no my laird at ahl?"

"Oh, but that is absurd, you know," Mary said, eagerly, and with a quick delight that she could enter into direct communication with him. "You forget—you are mistaken —my uncle bought the estate from the late Mr. Ross of Heimra. Surely you understand that? Surely you know that? The whole place was bought in open market. Mr. Ross sold the land, and all the rights belonging to it— yes, and the obligations, too; and my uncle bought it. Don't you understand!"

The man turned away his eyes, and sulkily muttered something in Gaelic.

"What is it?" asked Mary, compelled to appeal once more to the factor.

"Like the scoundrel's impertinence!" said the Little Red Dwarf, darting an angry look at the crofter. "He says the Englishman—that is your uncle, Miss Stanley—the Englishman bought the land but not the hearts of the people."

"And that is quite right!" Mary exclaimed. "That is quite right and true. Tell him I quite agree with him. But tell him this—tell him that if my uncle did not buy the hearts of the people, I mean to win them——"

"Oh, Mary," Käthchen struck in, rather shamefacedly, "don't talk like that! They won't understand you. Be practical. Ask him what complaint he has to make about his farm—ask him what he wants——"

"I can tell ye that beforehand!" said Mr. Purdie in his irascible scorn. "He wants more arable land, and he wants more pasture; and both for nothing. And no doubt he would like a steam plough thrown in, and maybe a score or two o' black-faced wethers——"

But Mary interrupted. She had formed for herself some idea, before she came to this country as to how she meant to proceed.

"Mr. Purdie," said she, in her clear, firm way, "I wish you to ask this man if he has anything to complain of; and I wish you to tell me precisely what he says."

The Troich Bheag Dhearg, being thus ordered, obeyed; but he scowled upon the stubborn crofter—and it was apparent there was no love lost on the other side either. At the end of their brief, and unwilling conversation, the factor made his report.

"Well, there are many things he would like—who could doubt that?—but in especial he wants the pasture of Meall-na-Cruagan divided amongst the crofters of this district, and the tax for the dyke taken off the rent. But Meall-na-Cruagan never did belong to the crofters at any time; and it is part of Mr. Watson's sheep-farm—he has it under lease."

"I will look into that afterwards," said she. "What is the tax you mentioned?"

"Well, when the dyke along there—the embankment," said the factor, "was built to keep the river from flooding the land, the interest of the money expended was added on to the rents of the crofts, as was natural—and that's what they call a tax!"

"How long have they been paying that tax?" she asked.

"It is about thirty years since the dyke was built."

"Thirty years!" she said. "Thirty years! These poor people have been paying a tax all this time for an embankment built to improve the property? Really, Mr. Purdie!——"

"They get the value of it?" he said, as testily as he dared. "The land is no longer flooded——"

"Tell this man," said she, with some colour mounting to her face, "that the tax for the dyke is abolished—here and now!"

"Godiva!" said Käthchen, in an undertone, with a bit of a titter.

And the factor would have protested from his own point of view. But this young woman's heart was all aflame. She cared nothing for ridicule, nor for any sort of more practical opposition. Here was some definite wrong that she could put right. She did not want to hear from Mr. Purdie, or from anybody else, what neighbouring land-lords might think, or what encouragement it might give the crofters to make other and more impossible demands.

"I don't care what other landlords may say!" said she with firm lips: "You tell me that I improve my property —and then charge these poor people with the cost! And for thirty years they have been paying? Well, I wish you to say to this man that the tax no longer exists—from this moment it no longer exists—it is not to be heard of again!"

The factor made a brief communication: the taciturn crofter answered not a word—not a word of recognition, much less of thanks. But Mary Stanley was not to be daunted by this incivility: as she descended to the wag-gonette, her face wore a proud look—right and justice should be done, as far as she was able, in this her small sphere: the rest was with the gods.

And again they drove on; but now was there not some subtle softening of the air, some moist odour as of the sea, some indication of the neighbourhood of the Atlantic shores?

Clearly they were getting down to the coast. And un-happily, as they went on, the land around them seemed to be getting worse and worse—if there could be a worse. A wilderness of crags and knolls — of Hebridean gneiss mostly; patches of swamp, with black gullies of peat; sterile hills that would have threatened a hoodie crow with starvation : such appeared to be Miss Stanley's newly found property. But a very curious incident now occurred to withdraw her attention from these immediate surroundings —an incident the meaning of which she was to learn subsequently. They had come in sight of a level space that had evidently at one time been a lake, but was now a waste of stones, with a touch of green slime and a few withered rushes here and there ; and in the middle of this space, on a mound that had apparently been connected with the mainland, was a heap of scattered blocks that looked like the tumbled-down ruins of some ancient fort.

"What is that, Mr. Purdie ?" she called out, still anxious for all possible information.

A malignant grin came over the face of the Little Red Dwarf.

"That," said he, "was once Castle Heimra ; and then it was Castle Stanley ; and now it is nothing !"

He had scarcely uttered the words when the driver slashed at the neck of one of the horses ; and both animals sprung forward with a jerk—a jerk so sudden and violent that Mr. Purdie was nearly pitched headlong from his seat. He threw a savage glance at the driver ; but he dared not say anything—the two ladies were within hearing. Later on that evening Mary recalled this little incident— and seemed to understand.

Behold, at last, the sea !—a semi-circular bay sheltered by long black headlands ; beyond that the wide grey plain, white-tipped with flashing and hurrying waves ; and out towards the horizon a small but precipitous island, a heavy surge springing high along its southern crags. But she had time only for the briefest glance, for here was the village—her own village !—with its smithy, its schoolroom, its inn, its grocery store that was also a post-office, and thereafter a number of not very picturesque cottages scattered about amid bits of poor garden, just above the shore. Nay, at the same moment she caught sight of Lochgarra House—her home that was to be : an odd-looking building that seemed half a jail and half a baronial castle, but was prettily situated among some larch-woods on a promontory on the other side of the bay. Of course they had driven through the little township almost directly; and now she could turn to the sea again—that looked strangely mournful and distant in the wan twilight.

" But where's the yacht ? " she exclaimed.

" What yacht ? " her companion asked, with some surprise.

" Why, the yacht I saw a minute ago—just before we came to the village : it was out yonder—close to the island——"

" Oh, nonsense, Mary ! " said Kate Glendinning. " You may have seen a fishing-smack, or a lobster-boat—but a yacht at this time of the year !——"

" I declare to you I saw a yacht—for I noticed how white the sails were, even in the twilight," Mary insisted ; and then she appealed to the factor : " Mr. Purdie, didn't you see a yacht out there a minute or two ago ? "

" No, I did not," he made answer ; and then he in his turn addressed the driver : " Did you, John ? "

" No," said the driver, looking straight ahead of him, and with a curiously impassive expression of face—an expression of face that convinced Mr. Purdie, who was prone to suspicion, that the man had lied.

It was a kind of bewilderment to her, this taking possession : the going up the wide stone steps, the gazing round the lofty oak hall, the finding herself waited upon by those shy-eyed soft-spoken Highland maids. But when she was in the retirement of her own room, whither she had been accompanied by the faithful Kate, one thing stood out clear to her mind from amid all the long day's doings.

" Käthchen," said she—and she was pacing up and down the room—or going from window to window without looking out—as was sometimes her habit when she was excited —" I mean to have my own way in this. It is not enough that the tax should be abolished—it is not enough. No doubt those poor people were saved from the risk of floods ; but on the other hand the property was permanently improved; and it is monstrous that they should be expected to go on paying for ever. I tell you they have paid too much already; and I mean to see things made right. What do I care for Mr. Purdie, or the neighbouring landlords? If Mr. Purdie has any business to talk of when he comes along this evening—well, my little piece of business must take precedence. I am going to give Mr. Purdie the first of his instructions." She paused for a second—and then she spoke with rather a proud and determined air: "Fifteen years of that tax to be remitted and returned!"

"Godiva!" said Käthchen, again; but there was not much sarcasm in her smiling eyes.

CHAPTER II.

YOUNG DONALD.

"AND if I am not the laird," said Miss Stanley, as the three of them took their places at table—for Mr. Purdie had accepted an invitation, and had come along from the inn to dine with the two young ladies—"if I am not the laird, I want to know who is the laird: I mean, I want to know all about my rival. What was it the stubborn old crofter called him? Young Donald—Young Ross of Heimra—well, tell me all about him, Mr. Purdie!"

But to Mary's surprise, the Little Red Dwarf remained sternly mute. Yet there was no one in the room besides themselves except the maid who was waiting at table—a tall and good-looking Highland lass, whose pretty way of speech, and gentle manner, and shy eyes had already made a pleasant impression on her young mistress. All the same, the factor remained silent until the girl had gone.

"I would just advise ye, Miss Stanley," said he, rather moderating his voice, which ordinarily was inclined to be aggressive and raucous, "I would just advise ye to have a care what ye say before these people. They're all in a pact; and they're sly and cunning just beyond belief; ay, and ready to do ye a mischief, the thrawn ill-willed creatures!"

"Oh, Mr. Purdie!" Mary protested, in her good-humoured way, "you mustn't try to prejudice me like that! I have already had a little talk with Barbara; and I could not but think of what Dr. Johnson said—that every Highland girl is a gentlewoman."

"And not a word they utter is to be believed—no, not with a Bible in their hands," the factor went on, in spite of her remonstrance. "Miss Stanley, did ye hear me ask the driver as. we came through the village if he had seen the yacht out by Heimra island—the yacht that ye saw with your own eyes? He said no—he had not seen it—and I knew by his face he was lying to me."

"But, Mr. Purdie," said Mary, again, "you did not see the yacht either. And I may have been mistaken."

"Ye were not mistaken," said the factor, with vicious emphasis. "For well I know what that was. That was nothing else than young Ross coming back from one of his smuggling expedeetions—the thieving, poaching scoundrel!—and little thinking that I would be coming out to Lochgarra this very afternoon. But I'll be even with my gentleman yet!—for it's all done to thwart me—it's all done to thwart me——"

The factor's small clear eyes sparkled with malice; but he had perforce to cease speaking, for at this moment Barbara came into the room. When she had gone again, he resumed:

"I will just tell ye how I came to get on his track," Mr. Purdie said, with something of a triumphant air. "And first of all ye must understand, Miss Stanley, I take some little credit to myself for having routed out the illicit stills in this country-side; ay, I'm thinking they're pretty well cleared out now; indeed I'll undertake to say there's not a hidden worm-tub or a mash tun within twenty miles around. There was some trouble; oh, yes; for they're cunning creatures; and they stand by one another in lying and concealment; but I managed to get some information for the Preventive Staff all the same—from time to time, that was—and then I had a good knowledge o' the place—ye see, Miss Stanley, I was factor at Lochgarra before your uncle gave me back my post again; and so, with keeping the gaugers busy, we got at one after another of the black bothies, as they call them, until I doubt whether there's a *bothan dubh* between here and Strathcarron. Yes, I may admit I take some credit for that. I've heard folk maintain that speerits are a necessary of life in a bad climate like this; but what I say is, let people pay their rent before comforting themselves wi' drams. My business is with the rent. I'm not a doctor. Temperance, ay, and even total abstinence, is a fine thing for everybody."

"Won't you help yourself, Mr. Purdie?" said Kate Glendinning, with grave eyes, and she pushed the sherry decanter towards him. Mr. Purdie filled his glass—for the fifth time—and drained it off. Then he proceeded.

"However, this is my story. One day I had finished wi' my business here, and had set out to ride over to Ledmore, when the toothache came into my head just terrible, and I was like to be driven mad. I was passing Cruagan at the time—where ye spoke to James Macdonald, Miss Stanley—indeed, it was at James's house I stopped, and tied up the beast, and went in to see if I could get a drop of whiskey to put in the side of my cheek, for the pain was just fearful. Well, there was nobody in but James's old mother—an old, old woman—she could hardly move away from the fire—and says I, 'For God's sake, woman, give me some whiskey to drive away this pain.' Of course she declared and better declared there was none in the house; but at last, seeing I was near out o' my senses, she hobbled away and brought me—what do ye think?—a glass of brandy—and fine brandy, too. 'Hallo!' says I to the old *cailleach*, when the brandy had burned in my mouth for a while, and the pain was not so bad, 'where did ye get this fine stuff?' Would ye believe it, she declared and better declared that she found it! 'Find it, woman! Where did ye find it?' But no; that was all; she had found it. And then I began to think. Where was an old woman like that to get brandy? So says I ·all of a sudden, 'This is smuggled stuff. Ye need not deny it; and unless ye tell me instantly where ye got it, and how ye got it, the Supervisor will be here to-morrow morning, and in twenty- four hours ye'll be in Dingwall Jail!——'"

"Mr. Purdie," said Käthchen, interrupting—and with

rather a cold manner—"was that your return for the old woman's kindness to you in your trouble?"

But he did not heed the taunt.   He was exulting in his having trapped his enemy.

"She was frightened out of her wits, the wretched old creature.   'Donuil Og,' she says—Young Donald—it was from young Ross that she had got it.   And now the case was clear enough!   I had been suspecting something of the kind.   And here was a fine come-down for the Rosses of Heimra;—the Rosses of Heimra, that in former days made such a flourish at the English court—dancing at Almacks, and skelping about wi' the Prince Regent; and now the last of the family come down to selling smuggled brandy to old women and a parcel of crofters and cottars!   A fine way of earning a living!   But it's all he's fit for—an idle ne'er-do-weell, that never did a turn of work in his life beyond poaching and thieving and stirring up ill-will behind one's back.   But I'll be even with my gentleman!   I'll have the Supervisor of Excise on to him ; his fine little trips to the Channel Islands—I suppose it's the Channel Islands, where you get brandy for next to nothing—we'll soon put a stop to them ; and when he finds himself before the Sheriff at Dingwall, he'll be singing another tune!"

A tap at the door—then Barbara entered ; and the factor looked up quickly and suspiciously.   But if the tall Highland lass had been listening her face said nothing.

"And the young man you speak of," Mary asked, "does he live all by himself—out on that island?"

"It's fit that he should live by himself," said Mr. Purdie, with his eyes beginning to twinkle fiercely again : for any reference to this young man seemed to completely turn his head.   "He's nothing but a savage—brought up as a savage—amongst the rocks and crags—like a wild-goat from his earliest years.   What else could ye expect? There was his mother—a proud woman—proud and vindictive as ever was born—and she hears how her husband is gallivanting from this capital to that—throwing away his money on Italian countesses and riff-raff—indeed there was the one public scandal, but I cannot give ye particulars, Miss Stanley, the story is not for a young lady's ears at all : but the mother, she determines to go away and live in that island, and bring up her only child there; and there the two o' them live, like two savages, the laddie growing up as a wild goat would, clambering about the rocks and the shore and the hills. What could ye expect but that he should turn out a poaching, thieving, smuggling rascal, especially with every man, woman, and child in the place—on the mainland here, I mean—ready to serve him and screen him? Truly it is a debasing thing to think of—such supersteetion; but these poor ignorant creatures —a name's enough for them—any Ross of Heimra, because he's a Ross of Heimra, is a little God Almighty to them; I think they would perjure their immortal souls for that impudent and brazen-faced young scoundrel out there. Brandy! Oh, ay, brandy! And I dare say he gets them tobacco, too; and makes a good profit on't; for what else can he live on? Heimra island is the last of all their possessions; if you go scattering your money among Italian countesses, you've got to cut up the estate, and fling it into the market, bit by bit, until you come to the final solid lump of it—which your uncle bought, Miss Stanley; and then the deserted wife, left to herself on that island out there, can live on whelks and mussels if she likes! Well, a fine lonely place to nurse pride! Plenty of time to think! The great estate gone—her husband at length dead and buried without ever having come near her—and this young whelp to look after—a wild goat among the rocks! No more grandeur now—though at times Lord This or Lord That, or even a Duke or Duchess, would come in their steam-yacht, or send her presents of game in the autumn—"

"Poor woman!" said Mary. "Is she out there still?"

"No, no—her troubles are over," said the factor, with some expression of relief. "There's one the less for these ignorant, supersteetious creatures hereabouts to fall down and worship, as if they were golden images. She died near a year ago; and would ye believe it, this son o' hers, instead of having her put into a Christian graveyard, had her buried on the western coast of the island, up on the top of the cliff, and there's a great white marble slab there, that ye might see for miles off. A nice kind of thing, that! Refusing Christian burial for his own mother!

He's just a Pagan, neither more nor less—a wild savage—
fearing neither God nor man—getting drunk every night,
I'll be bound, on that smuggled brandy ; and I'm no sure
he would scruple to take your life if he found ye in a
convenient place. It's a terrible thing to think of, a
human being brought up like that, in a country of law
and order and releegion. But I've no pity for him, not
one jot ! He and his have done me sufficient harm ; but
I'll be even with him yet—the cheat-the-gallows ! "

Mary Stanley, though not much of a coward, seemed to
shrink back a little in unconscious dismay. She had never
seen such venomous rage working in any human creature's
face ; and it was rather an appalling kind of thing. But
presently Mr. Purdie seemed to recollect himself; this
exhibition of over-mastering hate was not the best means
of propitiating his new mistress; and so, making a determined effort to control himself (and helping himself to
another glass of sherry at the same time) he proceeded to
talk of business, with a certain constrained, matter-of-
fact air.

"You said before we came in to dinner, Miss Stanley,"
he began, in his slow and deliberate way, "that you wished
fifteen years of the dyke tax to be remitted and returned
to the Cruagan crofters. Very well. Whatever is your
pleasure. But have you considered what the result will be?"

"No," said Mary, "I do not wish to consider. I wish
to have the thing done, because I think it is right."

"For one matter," said he, "they will take it and not
thank you."

"I do not care about that," she made answer. "We
will see about the thanks, or no thanks, later on."

"But there's more," said the factor, rousing himself from
his forced restraint of manner. "They'll just begin to
think that the time for the universal getting of everything
for nothing has come at last; and where will there be an
end to their outrageous demands? The ignorant creatures !
—they do not know what they want—they're like children
crying for the moon ; and they're encouraged by a set of
agitators more ignorant than themselves—people in Parliament, and out of it, that never saw a peat-moss, and don't
know the difference between a hog and a stirk——"

"But wait a moment, Mr. Purdie," said she, with some touch of calm authority. "I can hardly tell you yet what I intend to do; I have all kinds of enquiries to make. But every one is well enough aware that, whatever the cause or causes may be, there is great distress among the crofters—great poverty—and, naturally, discontent; and when I hear of them almost starving for want of land— and such immense tracts given over to deer—I know that a great wrong is being done. And that is not going to exist wherever I have a word to say."

"It cannot exist on this estate, Miss Stanley," the factor said, with confidence. "For we have not a single acre of forested land."

"What did I hear my brother say, then, about eleven stags in one season?" she demanded. "Why, he asked me to ask him up here this next autumn for the very purpose of going stalking!"

"Yes, yes, very likely," said the Little Red Dwarf, with the magnanimity born of superior knowledge. "The fact is that when the deer begin to get restless about the end of September and the beginning of October, a few stags and hinds come wandering on to our ground, between the Meall-na-Fearn and the Corrie-Bhreag mostly. But that is not forest; that is all under sheep; that belongs to Mr. Watson's sheep-farm: the stags the gentlemen get in the autumn are mere chance shots; we have not a bit of forested land. Indeed, Miss Stanley, ye'll rarely hear the crofters, in any part of the country, clamouring to have a deer forest split up amongst them; they know well enough what wretched and hopeless kind of stuff it is; they're wiser than the havering folk in Parliament. No, no; it's slices off the big arable and pasture farms they want. And I can tell ye this," he went on, in quite a reasonable way (for young Ross of Heimra was off his mind now), "there's many a proprietor in the Highlands would be willing and even glad to break up his big sheep-farms into small holdings; but where is either landlord or tenant to find the money to pay for the housing, and steading, and fencing; and where is the new tenant to find stock? To change the crofters into small farmers would be a fine thing, no doubt—an excellent thing, a great reform ; and it would pay the landlords well if it were practicable. But how is it practicable? Before the scheme would work, the crofter would have to be given land worth at least £20 a year ; and where is the capital to come from for stock and steading?"

Mary listened, a little uneasily, but not much daunted; for this was merely the professional view ; this was an advocacy of the existing state of things ; and it was the existing state of things, in this small possession of hers, that she hoped to amend, if it was within her power. Nor could she argue with him, seeing she had no facts at her fingers' ends as yet, or, at least, none that she could rely on ; for it was personal inquiry and observation that this young woman meant to trust.

"If they can make the small crofts pay——" said she vaguely.

"But they cannot," said he, with south country bluntness. "The land is too poor ; and there are too many of them wanting to live on it. Over there at Cruagan the crofters manage to earn a little money by serving as gillies in the autumn, and hiring their ponies to the sportsmen ; and along the coast here they eke out a living with the fishing; but they would fairly starve on the crofts, if that was all. And then, besides the poor soil, I do believe they're the idlest and laziest creatures on God's earth ! I'll undertake to say there has not been a boat put off from shore this last week past, though there must be plenty of stenlock in the bay——"

But here Käthchen struck in, a little indignantly. She had Highland blood in her veins ; and she did not like to hear her countrymen and countrywomen traduced by an *Albannach.*

"Stenlock? You mean big lythe?" said she. "But you know very well, Mr. Purdie, there is no market for lythe. They're no use to send away. And even if they were—even if there were a market for them—how could the people get them sent? How often does the steamer call in here ?"

"Oh, well, not very often at this time of the year," he said.

"But how often ?" she persisted

"Once in three weeks," said the factor.

And now it was Mary's turn to interpose, which she did eagerly and gladly, for she was ever on the alert for some actual and definite thing to tackle.

"Oh, really, Mr. Purdie, that is too bad! How can you expect them to be diligent with the fishing, if the steamer only calls in once in three weeks? That must be put right, and at once?" said she, in her generous ardour. "I will appeal to the Government. I will appeal to the Treasury."

"You'd better appeal to Mr. MacBrayne," said Käthchen, drily; and therewithal that subject was laid aside for the moment.

Unfortunately this reasonable mood on the part of the Little Red Dwarf—if he could properly be called little whose great breadth of frame caused him to look like a compressed giant—did not last very long. His half-smothered hatred of the house of Heimra broke into flame again; and it is possible that a glass of whisky which he took at the end of dinner, combined with the previous sherry, may have added fuel to the fire.

"I've warned ye, Miss Stanley, not to say a word about the Ross family, or what I've told ye, or about any of your plans, before that lass Barbara."

"Why all this mystery and suspicion!" said Mary, with a touch of impatience. "The girl seems a very obliging and good-natured girl indeed."

"She's a sister o' the head keeper," said the factor, with a watchful glance towards the door; "and that scoundrel of a young Ross is just hand-in-glove with every man-jack o' them. Do ye think they've got any eyes in their head if my young gentleman is after a salmon on the Garra, or lying in wait for a stag in the Corrie Bhreag? They would swear themselves black in the face that they did not see him if he was standing staring at them within twenty yards!"

"Very well, then; if you cannot trust the keepers, why not get others in their place?" she said, promptly. "Not that I care much about the game. I propose to give the crofters, big and little, free right to trap, or snare, or shoot all the hares and rabbits they can get hold of;

I do not wish their little bits of holdings to be plundered by useless beasts. But grouse do no harm; and whether my own people come here next autumn, or whether I let the shooting, all the same there will be the employment of gillies' labour, and the hiring of the ponies."

"Yes," said the factor. "The only money that ever finds its way into their pocket; and yet you'll find the idjuts declaring amongst themselves that not a single stranger should be allowed to come into the country!"

"That is foolishness," said Mary, calmly. "That is the idle talk of people who are poor and suffering, and do not know why they are poor and suffering. And I, for one, mean to take no heed of it; though, to be sure, it would be pleasanter to think I was a little more welcome. However, about those keepers: if they do not attend to their duty, if they allow poaching, why not get others in their place?"

"That would be worse," said Mr. Purdie, emphatically. "The strange keepers would be helpless; they would be outwitted at every turn. If ye knew the folk about here better, their clannishness, their cunning——"

"But are you sure this poaching goes on, Mr. Purdie," she interposed, "or it is only guesswork on your part? I presume Mr. Ross calls himself a gentleman."

"A gentleman!" said the factor, with that malevolent look coming into his eyes again. "A gentleman that earns his living by selling smuggled brandy to a wheen crofters! A fine gentleman, that! I suppose when the Duke's yacht sails into the bay out there, my gentleman makes haste to hide away the bottles, and takes care to say nothing about the five shillings a gallon profit! Ay, ay, a remarkable change for the great family!—no play-actoring about with the Prince Regent now, but selling contraband speerits to a lot of old women! And snuff maybe? And tobacco? Penny packets! A noble trade!" He laughed aloud, to conceal the vehemence of his hatred. "A fine come down for high birth and ancient gentility—buried alive in an island, not daring to show his head even in Edinburgh, let alone in London, his only companions a wheen thieving gillies and scringe-net fishermen! But plenty of pride all the same. Oh, yes; pride and conceal-ment, they go together in the Highland character: would ye believe it, when he denied his mother Christian burial, and made the grave up there on the hill, would he put up a respectable monument in the ordinary way, so that people could see it? No, no; it's on the sea-ward side of the island. Pride again, ye observe; a scorn of the common people; pride and concealment together."

"I should think it was a great deal more likely," said Käthchen, with some touch of anger, "that the mother chose where her own grave was to be." But Mary, with thoughtful eyes, only said: "Poor woman!"

"Ay, ay, pride enough," continued Mr. Purdie, in a more triumphant strain. "But their pride had a famous fall before your uncle and myself were done with them——"

At this Mary started somewhat.

"My uncle?" said she. "Why, what cause of offence could there have been between him and them? What injury could they possibly have done him?"

"Injury? Plenty of injury: in stirring up ill-will and rebellion among the tenants. It's yourself, Miss Stanley, will find that out ere long; oh, yes, wait till ye come to have dealings with these people, ye'll find out what they are, I'm thinking! A stubborn and stiff-necked race; and cunning as the very mischief; and revengeful and dark. But we broke their obstinacy that time!" He laughed again: a malignant laugh.

"I saw ye noticed it, Miss Stanley, as we came along this afternoon—the dried-up place that was once a loch, and the pile of stones——"

She remembered well enough; and also she recollected the vicious slash the driver had made at his horses when the factor was grinningly answering her question.

"Yes but I did not quite understand what it meant," said she.

"I'll just tell ye."

Mr. Purdie poured himself out a little drop of whiskey—a very little drop—in an inadvertent way. There was quite a happy look on his face when he began his tale.

"Ay; it's a fine story when people of obstinate nature meet their match; and your uncle, Miss Stanley, could hold his own—when there was proper counsel behind his back, if I may say so. And what had Mrs. Ross and her son to do with anything on the land? Heimra island out there had been reserved for them all the way through, as the estate was going bit by bit; and when Lochgarra went as well, there was still the island to preserve the name of the family, as it were. And was not that enough? What did they want—what could any one want—with Loch Heimra and Castle Heimra, when they had been sold into other hands? If they wanted the name kept in perpetuity, there was the island—which undoubtedly belonged to the Rosses; but the loch and the castle on the mainland, they were gone; they had been sold, given up, cut adrift. And so, says your uncle, 'we'll cut adrift the name too. They have their Heimra Island; that is sufficient: the loch and the castle are mine, and that must be understood by all and sundry.' Natural, quite natural. Would ye have people giving themselves a title from things not belonging to them at all, but to you? And what was the castle but a heap of old stones, with about six or seven hundred years of infamy, and bloodshed, and cruelty attached to it? Ay; they could show ye a red patch on the earthen floor of the dungeon that was never dry summer or winter. Many's the queer thing took place in that stronghold in the old days. 'Well, well,' says your uncle, 'if they will call themselves "of Heimra," let it be of Heimra Island. The loch and the castle are not theirs, but mine; and being mine, I am going to give my own name to them. Loch Stanley— Castle Stanley—that's what they are to be. I'm not going to have strangers calling themselves after my property. Let them keep the island if they like——' "

"Why, what did it matter?" said Mary. "They did not claim either the castle or the loch. It was merely the old association—the historical association; and what harm did that do to any one? And an interesting place like that, that has been in possession of the same family for centuries——"

"But, surely, a man has the right to do what he likes with his own?" said the Troich Bheag Dhearg, with the corners of his mouth drawn down, and his small eyes looking forth a challenge. "I can tell ye, Miss Stanley, your uncle was a man not to be thwarted——"

"I dare say!" said Mary, coldly.

"Castle Stanley—Loch Stanley—that was now established : let them take their title from what belonged to them, which was the island. Ay; but do ye think the people about here would follow the change?" Mr. Purdie went on, with something more of vindictiveness coming into his tone. "Would they? Not one o' them, the stubborn deevils! There was not an old bedridden woman, there was not a laddie on his way to school, ye could get to say 'Castle Stanley' or 'Loch Stanley'; it was Loch Heimra and Castle Heimra from every one ; and they held on to it as if it had been the Westminster Confession of Faith—the dour and bigoted animals they are! Even the very game-keepers, that ye might think would be afraid o' losing their situation, they were just like the rest, though they had their plausible and cunning excuses. 'You see, Mr. Stanley,' they would say, 'if we tell the gillies about Castle Stanley they will think it is Lochgarra House we mean ; and if we send them to Loch Stanley, they will be going down to the sea-shore.' But well I know who was at the back of all their stubbornness," the factor continued, with a scowling face. "Well I know : it was that idling, mischievous, thrawn-natured, impudent ne'er-do-weel, egging them on, and egging them on, and keeping himself in the background all the time. The dignity of his family! I suppose that was what he was after—the old castle and the old name; so that strangers might think that his mother and he had still property on the mainland? And I warned your uncle about it. I warned him. I told him that as long as that graceless scoundrel was in the neighbourhood there would be nothing but spite and opposition on the part of the tenantry. 'Well, then,' said he, 'for spite there will be spite, if it comes to that!' Miss Stanley, your uncle was not a man to be defied."

"I know," said Mary, with downcast face : she foresaw what was coming—and did not at all share in the savage glee the factor was beginning to betray.

"'Give them time, Mr. Purdie,' says he. 'If I buy a dog, or a horse, or a house, I can call it by what name I please ; and so I can with a piece of water and an old ruin. But not too much time, Mr. Purdie—not too much time. If they have a will of their own, so have I.   If there's to be neither Loch Stanley nor Castle Stanley, I'll make pretty well sure there will be neither Loch Heimra nor Castle Heimra. I'll put an end to those Rosses calling themself after any part of my property. I'll soon wipe out the last trace of them from the mainland, anyway; and they're welcome to the island out there, for anything I mind.   The seven centuries of history can follow them across the water : I've no room for such things on my estate.' And that's just how it came about, Miss Stanley. Not one creature in the whole of the district but would stick to the old name ; crofter, cottar, shepherd, fisher-laddie, they were all alike. There was no help for it. Your uncle was a determined man. Any one that contended with him was bound to get the worst of it ; and here he was dealing with his own. 'Very well,' said he, 'if there's to be no Castle Stanley, I'll take care there shall be no Castle Heimra. Mr. Purdie, get the loch drained of its last drop of water, and have every stone of the useless old ruin hauled to the ground.' And that's precisely what ye saw this afternoon, Miss Stanley !"

Her reply somewhat astonished the vain-glorious factor, who had perhaps been expecting approval.

"It was shamelessly done ! " said she—but as if she were not addressing him at all.

And then she rose, and Kate Glendinning rose also ; so that Mr. Purdie practically found himself dismissed— or rather he dismissed himself, pleading that it was late. He made some appointment for the next morning, and presently left : no doubt glad enough to get a chance of lighting his pipe and having a comfortable smoke on his way home to the inn.

When the two girls went into the drawing room—which was a large hexagonal room in the tower, with windows looking north, west, and south—they found that the lamps had not yet been brought in, and also perceived, to their surprise, that the night outside had cleared and was now brilliant with its thousands of throbbing stars. They went to one of the windows. The heavily-moaning sea was hardly visible, but the heavens were extraordinarily lustrous; they were even aware of a shimmer of light on the grey stone terrace without; perhaps it was from the gleaming belt of Orion that hung above a dark headland jutting out towards the west; while there, also, was the still more fiery Sirius, that burned and palpitated behind the black birch-woods in the south. And then they turned to seek the island of Heimra—out there on the mystic and sombre plain—under that far-trembling and shining canopy.

"Well," said Käthchen, with some vehemence of indignation (for her Highland blood had mounted to her head), "I know this, Mary: scapegrace or no scapegrace, if I were the young fellow living out there, I know what I should do—I would kill that factor! Isn't it perfectly clear it was he who goaded your uncle into pulling down the old castle and draining the loch?"

Mary was silent for a second or two. Then she said, in an absent kind of way—

"There are wrongs and injuries done that can never be undone. I can never rebuild Castle Heimra."

CHAPTER III.

THE CAVE OF THE CROWING COCK.

MARY STANLEY'S eyes had not deceived her; the boat of which she had caught a momentary glimpse was a smart little yawl of twenty tons or so, that was making in for Heimra Island; and there were three men on deck—two redcaps forward, the master at the helm. This last was a young fellow of about six and twenty, a little, not much, over middle height, of somewhat pale complexion, and with singularly dark eyes and hair. The curious thing was this: though you could not say that any of his features were particularly fine (except, perhaps, his coal black eyes, which were clearly capable of flame, if the occasion demanded) the general effect of them was striking; they seemed to convey an impression of strength—of a certain lazy audacity of strength; while the forehead revealed by the peaked cap being pushed carelessly backward denoted at once intelligence and resolution. But indeed at this moment the young man's attitude was one of merely quiescent indifference—though there was an occasional quick scrutiny of the neighbouring coast; all the graver perils of the voyage were over; they were running easily before a steady wind; and they would get safely to their anchorage ere the light had wholly died out of the western skies.

"Down foresail!" he called to the men. For now they were passing a headland that formed one of two arms encircling a sheltered little bay—a strangely silent and solitary-looking place it seemed in this mysterious light. Sterile, too; tumbled masses of rock with hardly a scrap of vegetation on them; a few clumps of birches here and there; an occasional dark green pine higher up the cliffs. But at all events it was quiet and still; the water lapped clear and crisp along the shingle; while the murmur of the outer sea was still everywhere around, and also, on the northern side of the bay, there was a long out-jutting reef where there was a continuous surge of white foam over the saw-toothed edge.

"Down jib!" The sound of a human voice was so strange in this solitude—far stranger than the mere rattle of blocks and tackle.

"Main sheet!"

The two men came aft: the steersman jammed down his helm; the vessel slowly rounded into the wind—the boom being hauled in meanwhile—the mainsail flapping and shivering in the light breeze.

"Stand by to let go!" was the next order; and the hands went forward again—the vessel gradually losing the way that was on her, until she seemed absolutely motionless.

"Let go!"

There was a splash and a roar that sent a thousand shuddering echoes through the silence. A heron uttered a hoarse croak and rose on heavy and slow-moving wings to make for some distant shelter. A pair of dunlins—unseen in the dusk—added their shrill piping cry. Then all was still again, save for the continual moaning of the surge on the distant reef.

"Give a haul at the topping-lift, lads!" This was the final direction; and then, with another keen look round the little bay, young Ross of Heimra—or Donuil Og Vich Iain Vich Ruari, as some were proud to call him—went

down into the cabin to put a few things together before
going ashore.

Of the two sailors now left on the deck one was a
powerfully built man of about thirty, with a close-clipped
brown beard, bushy brown eyebrows, and eyes of a clear
Celtic grey.   His name was Kenneth Macleod; but he
was more generally known as *Coinneach Breac*—that is
to say, Kenneth of the small-pox marks.   His companion
was younger than himself—a lad of twenty or two-and-
twenty; long and loutish of figure; but with a pleasant
expression of face.   This was Malcolm, or rather, Calum,
as they called him.   Probably he had some other name;
but it was never heard of; the long, lumpish, heavily-
shouldered lad was simply known throughout this neighbourhood as Calum, or Calum-a-bhata, Calum of the Boat.

"It is I who will have a sound sleep this night," said
he, in Gaelic, as he stretched his hands above his head and
yawned.

"And I, too, when the work is over," said his neighbour, pulling out a short black pipe.   "And now you see
what it is to have many friends.   Oh, I know you, Calum ;
you are a young lad; and you are strong: you think of
nothing but fighting, like the other young lads.   But let
me tell you this, Calum ; it is not a good thing, fighting
and quarrelling, and making enemies ; it is easier to make
enemies than to make friends ; and many times you will
be sorry when it is too late, and when that has been put
wrong which you cannot put right.   For you know what
the wise man of Islay said, Calum ; he said—'*He who
killed his mother a few moments ago would fain have her
alive now !*'"

"But who was talking about fighting, Coinneach—tell
me that ?" said the youth, angrily.

"I was giving you advice, Calum, my son," said Coinneach—lighting his pipe and pulling away, though there
appeared to be very little tobacco inside.   "I was telling
you that it was a good thing to have many friends, as the
master has.   Oh, he is the one to make friends, and no
doubt about that !   For look you at this, Calum ; you know
what is stowed in the cabin ; and here we come into the
bay, without waiting for the night at all, and just as if

there was nothing on board but a few tins of meat for our own use and a loaf or two. That is the wisdom of having many friends, as I am telling you. Why, if there was any one after us, if there was any one wishing to put trouble upon us, do you know what would have happened this evening ?—there would have been a bonfire on every headland between Ru-Gobhar and the Black Bay. And that is what I tell you, Calum, that it is a very good thing to have plenty of friends ashore, who are as your own kinspeople to you, and will come between you and the stranger, and will see that the stranger does not harm you. The master, he is the one to make friends with old and young; and believe me as far as that goes, Calum. Ay, you are a young lad; and you do not know what the world is; and you do not know what it is to go sailing with a hard skipper; and if you are an apprentice, a bucket of water in your bunk to wake you in the morning. But the master—oh, well, now, look at this : if there is bad weather, and there is something difficult to be done, and you do it smartly, why, then he calls out to you 'Fhir mo chridhe !' * and that is a far more welcome thing to you than cursing and swearing ; it is a far more welcome thing, and a good thing to comfort you." He shook the ashes out of his pipe, and put it in his pocket. " Well, now, see to the tackle, Calum, and we'll get the boat hoisted out, for the master will be going ashore."

The boat—a twelve-footer or thereabouts—had been stowed on deck ; but they soon had her launched over the side, and everything put ship-shape and in readiness. And presently the young man who had gone down into the cabin re-appeared again ; he threw some things into the boat, and took his place in the stern-sheets ; the men shoved off, and presently they were well on their way to the beach, where there was a rudely-formed slip. By this time the streaks of lemon-hued light that had appeared in the west were dying away ; darkness was coming over land and sea ; already, in the east, one or two stars were visible between the thinning and breaking clouds.

Young Ross landed at the slip, and made his way up to

---

* *Fhir mo chridhe !*—Man of my heart !

a level plateau on which stood a long, rambling, one-storeyed building mostly of timber: a sort of bungalow, with a slated porch, and with some little pretence of a garden round it, though at this time of the year nothing, of course, was visible in it but a few leafless bushes. At the door stood an old woman neatly and smartly dressed, whose eyes were still expressive enough to show how pleased she was.

"Good evening to you, Martha," said he in Gaelic, "and I hope you are well."

"Indeed I am all the better for seeing you back, sir," replied the old woman, with many smiles. "The house is no house at all when you are away."

She followed him obsequiously into the narrow hall. He only glanced at the newspapers and letters on the table. But there was something else there—a brace of grouse.

"Will I cook one of the birds for Mr. Ross's dinner?" she asked, her Highland politeness causing her to address him in the third person.

A quick frown came over his face.

"Who brought these here?" he demanded.

"Oh, well—they were left," said old Martha, evasively.

"Yes, yes, left; but who left them?" he asked again.

"Oh, well; may be it was the Lochgarra keepers," said she.

"The keepers? Nonsense!" he said angrily. "Do you tell me the keepers would shoot grouse at this time of the year, when the birds have paired, and soon will be nesting? It was Gillie Ciotach,* I'll be bound. Now you will tell the Gillie Ciotach, Martha, that if he does not stop his tricks I will have him sent across the land to go before the Sheriff at Dingwall; and how will he like that?"

"Oh, well, indeed, sir," said Martha, in a deprecating way, "the poor young lad meant no harm. He was coming over here anyway, because he lost a dog, and he was wishing to find the dog."

At this the young master burst out laughing.

"The Gillie Ciotach is an excellent one for lies, and that is certain!" said he. "His dog? And how could

---

* *Gillie Ciotach*—the left-handed young man.

his dog swim across from Lochgarra to Eilean Heimra? Tell Gillie Ciotach from me that when he comes over here he may look after the lobsters, but he will be better not to tell lies about a dog, and also he will do well to leave the Lochgarra grouse alone. And now, Martha, if there is any dinner for me, let me have it at once; for I am going back to the yacht by-and-by."

He went into the simply-furnished dining-room, where there was a lamp on the table and likewise a magnificent peat-fire ablaze in the big iron grate—a welcome change from the little stove in the cabin of the *Sirène*. He had brought his letters with him in his hand. He drew in a wickerwork lounging-chair towards the fireplace, and idly began to tear the envelopes open; here were tidings, various hushed voices, as it were, from the busy world that seemed so distant to him, living in these remote solitudes. It is true he had been away for a time from Eilean Heimra; but during that interval there had not been much of human companionship for him; nay, there was for the most part a greater loneliness than ever, especially when he took his watch on deck at night, sending the two men below for much-needed rest. Indeed these letters and newspapers seemed almost to make a stir and noise! —so used had he been to silence and the abstraction of his own thoughts.

Meanwhile Coinneach and Calum had returned to the yacht, had got some supper, and were now up at the bow, contemplatively smoking, and chatting to each other in their native tongue. Night had fallen; but the skies were becoming clearer and more clear; the starlit heavens were gradually revealing themselves. There was not a sound— since the rattle of the anchor had disturbed the quietude of the little bay.

"The work is not over yet," Coinneach was saying, in somewhat low tones, "and it is the part of the work that I have no liking for. Anything else I shrink not back from, when the master wishes; he is the one to follow, and I will go with him wherever he desires; and that in safety, too—for who knows the navigation like himself, yes, and speaking every language that is known upon the earth? I will go with him wherever he wishes; I will do whatever he wishes. But, Calum, I have no liking for the Uamh coilich na glaodhaich." *

"Nor I, Coinneach," said his companion. "Especially in the night-time."

"Day-time or night-time : what is the difference in the Uamh coilich na glaodhaich, when it is so dark that no man has ever been to the end of it, or knows to what it leads ? Nor is any man likely to try to discover, since the one that went on and on, until he heard a cock crowing. Oh, God, that must have been a terrible thing, to be so near the edge of another world that you could hear a cock crowing there. And if the people had caught him and kept him—they would have taken him away to the place where the piper went when he played *Cha till mi tuilich* ; † and that is a tale that is told of many caves; and it may be this, Calum, that all the great caves lead to that other world ; but who can tell about such fearful things ? A cock crowing—that is nothing—when you are in your own home, with the daylight around you ; but to hear the crowing of a cock after you have gone away into the earth, then that tells you of wonderful things, for you know the saying, '*Deep is the low of a cow upon strange pasture.*' Well, well, what the master says must be done ; but many's the time I am wishing that when the kegs have to be hidden, it was some other place we had for the hiding of them than the Cave of the Crowing Cock."

"Coinneach," said the lad, and he also spoke in a hushed kind of way, "how long ago is it since that one heard the cock crowing ?"

"How long ? Who can answer such questions ? Can you tell me when the Macarthurs came into the world ? For you have heard the saying, Calum : '*The hills and the streams and the Macalpines came together ; but who can say when the Macarthurs came ?*' It is a long time ago ; it is not any use asking. Ay, and there was something before all of these." He paused for a second : then he said darkly—"That was—that was when the Woman was in these islands."

<hr>

* *Uamh coilich na glaodhaich*—The Cave of the Crowing Cock.
† *Cha till mi tuilich*—I shall never more return.

" What woman ? " said Calum, with the eager curiosity of youth.

But Coinneach seemed disinclined to answer.

" Have you not heard ? " said he.   " But it is wise not to speak of such things."

" What woman was that, Coinneach ? " his companion persisted, fixing his eyes on Coinneach's face, that was full of a sombre meditation.

" Did you never hear of her—the Woman that was here before there were any people in these islands or in the mainland either ?   But it is not prudent to speak."

" Who was she, Coinneach ? " said Calum.   " Surely she cannot hurt you if she was dead these many thousands of years ? "

" Do not say that," he responded rather gloomily. " Who can tell ?—for there are strange things.   You know I am not a coward, Calum."

" That is what I know well ! " said Calum, confidently. " How many days is it since you stood up against the French skipper, and he with four of them at his back ? "

" Ay, but there are things that are more terrible than blows ; and it is of these that I am afraid.   Or perhaps not quite afraid ; but I think.   And that is the difference between one man and another man, Calum.   There is always ill-luck happening ; but one man will suffer it and not inquire, while the other man will ask what caused it or who it was that did him the harm.   And if it is not always prudent to speak of such affairs, at least the truth is the safest : you know the saying '*Speak the truth as if you were in the presence of kings.*'   And now I will tell you this, Calum, of a strange thing that happened to me when I was a boy."

He abated his voice, as if afraid of being overheard. Calum's eyes ' glowered ' in the dusk.

" I had been over to Ru-Gobhar, where I had a sister married then ; and I was returning home.   It was a moon-light night ; the sea very calm ; there was no wind.   Well, when I was at the highest point of the road, above the Black Bay, do you know what happened ?   But I will tell you what happened.   And this is what I saw : the sea began to move, although there was not a breath of wind, and there was no noise either ; only it moved and heaved in a terrible way ; and there was a line of white, but it was more like white fire than white foam, all along the land, from Ru-Gobhar in to Minard, and all round the headlands to where I was. For I was standing looking, and very much afraid to see so strange a thing ; and then this is what happened : I got to know that there was some one behind me ; and then I got to know it was the Woman, and I durst not look round, for I was shaking with terror. May you never have such an experience in your life, Calum, as was mine that night. I knew that she had come across the sea, from the islands, noticing that I was alone and no one to help me ; and now I knew that she was not only behind me, but in front of me, and all around me, though I could not see anything, for I was in such terror. She did not speak to me, nor touch me ; but I felt myself choking at the throat as if she had a grip of me ; and I gave myself up for dead—for I could not run away from her—and I knew it was the Woman who had a grip of my throat. Well, well, I gave myself up for dead ; but all of a sudden it entered my mind that she would carry me away out to the islands and bury me in one of the caves ; and with that I made a great effort, and cried out 'God on the cross, save me, save me !' That was the last I knew of it ; when I came to myself I was lying in the road, cold as a stone ; and the sea was quite smooth again. May you never have an experience like my experience of that night, Calum ! "

Calum was silent for a little while. Then he said, slowly—

" Coinneach, do you suppose the Woman came from the cave where the cock was heard crowing ? "

" How can I tell ? " was the answer. " Perhaps I have said too much. But what I have said to you, that is the least part of what happened to me that night, for it is not to be spoken of." And then he rose ; and put his pipe in his pocket. "Come, Calum, my son, we must take the boat ashore now, for the master will be coming down to the slip. But do not you speak of such things as I have told you ; for it is not good to speak of them."

And to this Calum merely replied—

" What the master wishes is enough for you and me, Coinneach ; but I would rather not be going into the Uamh coilich na glaodhaich this night."

They rowed the boat in to the shore—they could see their way well enough, for now the heavens were quite clear, and a universe of white worlds was shining down on them ; and there they ran her bow into the soft seaweed by the side of the slip. They had not long to wait. There was a sound of footsteps on the gravel-path ; then from out of the shadow emerged a figure into the open space above the beach ; they knew who this was. Young Ross of Heimra seemed to be in no great hurry ; his hands were in his pockets ; he came down towards the boat with long, lounging, leisurely strides ; and he was whistling a gay air that was unfamiliar to them—for Coinneach and Calum could hardly be expected to recognise ' *La Noce de Jeanne.*'

"It is the master who is not afraid of anything," said the elder of the two men, under his breath.

"Indeed you may say that," rejoined Calum, as he, too, put his pipe in his pocket. "I think he would face old Donas* himself, and not ask for any allowance."

Young Ross came down the beach.

" Lend a hand here, lads," he sung out, "and we'll take the other boat with us. Maybe we'll be able to do it in one trip ; and I'm sure it's a good long sleep both of you will be wanting this night."

They speedily had the second boat launched and shoved along to the slip ; then they attached the painter to the one in which they had come ashore ; and presently they were pulling both boats quietly out to the *Sirène.* The gangway was open. Ross and the elder of the two men stepped on board ; and proceeded to remove the skylight of the chief cabin—Calum securing the boats by the side of the yacht. And then began the final business of the expedition—the hoisting up on deck and the transferring to the boats alongside of a considerable number of kegs that were small enough to be handled with comparative ease. Young Ross, who was down in the cabin, worked just like the others : slim as his figure seemed, there was

* *Donas*—the Devil.

plenty of strength about his arms and shoulders. There was no lamp in the cabin, nor yet on deck; nor was there need of any; the black figures labouring away there did very well with the faint illumination shed by those thousands of tremulous stars. And in course of time the operation was complete; the casks that had been skilfully stowed in the main cabin of the *Sirène* were now ranged as tightly as might be in the boats alongside; then the men stepped in and took to the oars; while the young master went to the tiller. Calum had been told to put a couple of candles in his pocket; and he was not likely to forget that—for they were going to the Cave of the Crowing Cock.

It was a long and laborious pull—the boat astern acting as a heavy drag; moreover, even with this clear starlight, they dared not go anywhere near that saw-toothed reef that guarded the next small bay whither they were bound. They could hear each successive thud of the surge, and the long-receding roar; and they could even descry in a kind of way the line of white foam that boiled and churned incessantly along the almost invisible rocks. But once they were round this dangerous point—giving it a significantly wide berth—they found themselves in smooth water again. Not a word was spoken. The two men toiled away at the oars—most likely thinking of the welcome sleep awaiting them when all was done. The land ahead seemed to grow darker as they approached, even as the black precipitous cliffs appeared to soar higher and higher into the clear starlit skies. Then there was a whispering of water: the beach was near. Young Ross bade them pull more gently now: he was trying to make out the most suitable landing-place—in amongst those mysterious shadows.

Eventually the two boats were grounded, and dragged up to be secure from the tide; while the work of getting the kegs out began.

"Calum," said the young master, "take the candles now and get them lighted; and mind you do not light them until you are well inside the cave."

Calum appeared to receive this commission very unwillingly; at all events he hesitated.

"It is asking for your pardon I am, sir," said he; "but—I have brought a pistol with me."

"A pistol? And why so?" said Donald Ross.

"It is the pistol that I would like to be firing into the cave," said Calum, rather timidly, "before any of us went into it."

"And what is your reason for that, Calum?"

Calum rather hung his head; but he said all the same—

"If there would be wild beasts in the cave, it will scare them before we go in."

"Wild beasts? And what wild beasts are there in Eilean Heimra?" Then the young man laughed. "Calum, is it a badger, or a wild cat, or an otter that you fear? Or is it not rather the Dark Person you are afraid of, who used to come every night to Lochgarra to ask Mr. Stanley if he was not ready yet? Did you believe that story, Calum; and did you not think the Dark Person very foolish to talk Gaelic to Mr. Stanley, when he was not understanding a word of it?"

Calum did not answer: he was shamefacedly awaiting permission to fire into that dreaded place.

"Well, well, Calum," young Ross said good-naturedly, "you are not long from your mother's apron-string: if you are afraid, give me the candles, and keep the pistol in your pocket. Give me the candles—and lend Coinneach here a hand with the kegs."

But at this Calum raised his head.

"Indeed that will I not do," said he, "for it is not Mr. Ross that must go first into the cave, when I am here, or when Coinneach is here. If I am not to fire the pistol, then I will not fire the pistol. But it's myself that am going to light the candles in the cave."

"And a lucifer-match, Calum," said the young master, turning away from him, "will frighten wild beasts as well as any pistol—besides making a great deal less noise."

The Uamh coilich na glaodhaich was only a few yards distant; but the entrance to it was concealed by a huge mass—a perpendicular pinnacle—of rock; and when Calum had got behind this gigantic natural screen, there were no more cheerful stars to guide him; he was confronted by darkness and unknown terrors. And yet he scrupulously obeyed his instructions. His trembling fingers, it is true, grasped the pistol, but he kept it in his pocket nevertheless; while with his left hand he groped his way well into the cave—dreading at every moment to see two fiery eyes glaring on him—before he set to work to light the candles. And how feeble and ineffectual were the small red flames in this vast cavern! Their flickering hardly showed the roof at all; but it was not the roof that Calum was regarding; it was the far-reaching and black abyss in front of him, that led—whither? Perhaps the inhabitants of that other world could see better than himself, and were now regarding him?—that other world in which the dawn began in the middle of the night, and where there were cocks crowing when all the natural universe was asleep. He had to fasten each lighted candle into the neck of a bottle that had been left there for the purpose; but all the while he did so he was staring into that vague and awful space that the feeble, dull red glow did not seem to penetrate at all—staring into it as if he expected to find two white eyes and a ghastly countenance suddenly become visible. And then again, when he had placed the bottles on a shelf of rock that ran along one side of the cave, a few feet from the ground, he did not instantly turn and go. He retreated backward—cautiously, for the shelving shingle was loose and slippery—keeping his face towards that hollow darkness, so that he might guard himself against any strange thing, or be warned by hearing any strange noise. Then a colder stirring of air told him that he was outside; he made his way past the over-looming rock and into the clear star-light again; and with a beating heart—but a thankful heart withal—he went quickly along the beach and rejoined his companions.

By this time the kegs had been all got out; so that in case of any sudden danger, of which they appeared to have but little dread, the three of them could have jumped into one of the boats and made off. There remained, therefore, only the task of carrying along the casks and stowing them in the cave; and this work young Ross left to the two men. He remained on watch—if watch were needed—pacing up and down the shingle, looking at the far resplendent heavens and the darker sea, and listening to the continuous murmur of the distant surf. He had lit his pipe, too ; he did not seem to have much apprehension of being interfered with. And indeed all went well ; and in due course of time the two dark figures came along the beach with the intelligence that all the kegs had been safely stowed, and that they were now ready to row the master back to his own home.·

"Coinneach," said Donald Ross, seated at the helm, when they were some way out on the black and tumbling water, that glanced and quivered here and there with the reflections of the stars, "they were telling me before we left in the yacht that the lady was shortly coming to Lochgarra House."

"And indeed I heard the same thing myself," said Coinneach, "and they were making ready at the big house for the coming of the Englishwoman." *

"And I have no doubt," the master continued, "that Purdie will come with her, to show her the property, and introduce her to the people."

"The Little Red Dwarf," said Coinneach ; and then he muttered to himself : "It is the lowermost floor of hell that I am wishing for him, and for every one of his accursed house !"

Young Ross of Heimra took no notice of this pious ejaculation.

"Now listen," said he. "This is what I wish to say to you, Coinneach. When Purdie comes to Lochgarra with the lady who is the new proprietor, that would be a very good time indeed for widow Mac Vean to ask them to give her a cow in place of the one that she lost in the Meall-na-Fearn bog. Maybe they will give the poor woman a cow ; and she will pay them back bit by bit if they allow her time."

"It is of no use asking the Little Red Dwarf for any-thing," said Coinneach, sullenly. "There is no goodwill in his heart towards the people. Nor is there any goodwill in their hearts towards him—God forbid that there should be any such thing. Indeed, now, there is something I

* *Ban-sassunnach* was the term he used. But young Ross had referred to her as *Baintighearna*, or lady-proprietor—a much more respectful appellation.

could say about the Little Red Dwarf—But it does not serve to talk."

"What were you going to say, Coinneach?" the young master demanded—knowing Coinneach's ways.

"Oh, perhaps Mr. Ross would not like to hear," said Coinneach, evasively.

"Indeed, but I wish to hear. Now what is it you have to tell me about the Troich Bheag Dhearg?"

Coinneach was silent for a second or two.

"Well," said he, slowly, "it was some of the young lads they were saying that it only wanted a word from Mr. Ross. Yes; they were saying that. It was just a word from Mr. Ross; and they would see that the Little Red Devil did not trouble any one any more, neither in this nor in any other country."

"Oh, indeed," said the master, placidly. "Then it is a murder the Gillie Ciotach and the rest of them are for planning—is that what you have to tell me?"

"I would not give a thing a bad name," said Coinneach, as he laboured at the oar. "No, no; they were not talking of a murder, or any bad thing like that. But—but there might be an accident; and a very good thing, too, if an accident happened to the Little Red Dwarf!"

"And what kind of an accident?"

"Oh well," said Coinneach, looking away out to the horizon as if the suggestion might come from any quarter. "Maybe he would be riding home on a dark night; and maybe there might be a wire stretched across the road; and if he was to break his neck, who could help that? And it is I who would laugh to hear that he had broken his neck; indeed I would laugh!" said Coinneach, though there was little laughter in his sombre tones.

"And that is what you call an accident, Coinneach? It is an accident that might end in your finding yourself with a hempen collar round your neck. And what was it set the young men talking like that?"

"Oh well, indeed, they were talking about the draining of the loch and the pulling down of Castle Heimra; and they were saying that nowadays the law was being altered by the people themselves, and that right and justice could be done without waiting for the courts. They were saying that. And they were saying that we have come into a new time, which is the truth. They were speaking of the people over there in the Lews; and the last that was heard was that the people would not wait any longer for more pasture to be given them; they would not wait for the courts; they were going to take the deer-forest to themselves, and hamstring every one of the stags—them that they could not eat; and they had got their tents and baggage ready, to go into the forest and take possession. In former times they would not have dared to do so; but times are different now; and people have not to wait for justice; it is they themselves who must say what is right, whether about the Little Red Dwarf, or anything else. They were telling me that. And who was to put the crofters and cottars out of the deer-forest over there in the Lews? Not all the policemen in the island: there are not enough. And if they were to send soldiers, the Queen's soldiers dare not fire on the Queen's subjects, or the officer would be hanged. That was what they were telling me."

"Coinneach," said the young master, "if the Gillie Ciotach and his companions are talking like that, they will be getting themselves into trouble one of these days. They'd better let the Little Red Dwarf alone; for one thing, I dare say he is safe enough; the devil looks after his own brats. But do not forget what I am telling you now—about Mrs. Mac Vean. Old Martha will be wanting you to go over to the mainland to-morrow; and when you are there, you can seek out Mrs. Mac Vean, and bid her tell the factor how her cow was lost in the Meall-na-Fearn bog. She can do no harm by asking."

"It's very little she will get from the Troich Bheag Dhearg," said Coinneach, gloomily, "whether by asking or any other way."

At last the long pull was over; and the men, having landed the master at the slip, set out again for the yacht. Young Ross of Heimra went up to the house. But before going in, he paused at the porch, to have a final look at the wonderful glories of that vast firmament—the throbbing Sirius low down in the south, the gleaming belt and sword of Orion, the powdered diamond-dust of the Pleiades, the jewelled head of Medusa, Cassiopeia's silver throne.   And perhaps he was not thinking so much of those distant and shining worlds as of her who had first taught him their various names—of the worse than widowed woman who had shut herself up here in proud isolation, himself her only care.   Well, she was at peace now ; her wrongs and sufferings and bitter memories all come to an end ; surely there was nothing but quiet and sweet slumber around that white grave-stone, far up there on the top of the cliff, overlooking the wide and lonely western seas.

CHAPTER IV.

THE BAINTIGHEARNA.

NEXT morning Mary went eagerly and joyously to the window, for here indeed was a welcome change : no more louring heavens and streaming roads, but a vast expanse of wind-driven sea, blue as the very heart of a sapphire, and yet with innumerable sudden flashes of white from the crest of its swift-hurrying waves.   The sky cloudless ; the fresh breeze blowing straight in from the Atlantic ; the world all shining around her ; even those long spurs and headlands, sterile as they were, looked quite cheerful in the prevailing sunlight.   And out yonder, too, was the island of Heimra, to which her eyes would go back again and again with a curious interest.   She thought of the lone mother, and of the boy brought up like a wild goat among the rocks.   And if he had turned out a reckless and unscrupulous ne'er-do-well, an Ishmael with his hand against every man, well, that was a deplorable thing, though perhaps not to be wondered at ; moreover, it could matter little to her what such an outcast might think of her or of her family ; but, nevertheless, deep down in her heart there was an odd and ever recurring feeling of compunction.   She wished to be able to say " I am sorry." Certainly it was not she who had destroyed the last relic and monument of the ancient name—who had drained the loch and levelled the old stronghold with the ground ; and he must know that ; but she wished him to know more ; she wished him to know how indignant she had been when

she first heard of that monstrous and iniquitous act of
vandalism. And then again (as she still stood gazing at
the island out there in the wide blue waters, with the
white foam springing high in the sunlight along its southern
coasts) it seemed to her that she rather feared meeting
this man. Rude and lawless and mannerless, might he not
laugh at her stumbling apologies? Or in his Highland
pride he might scorn her southern birth, and vouchsafe
no word in reply? Well, being sorry was all that remained
for her; what was done could not be undone; it was not
within her power to bring back Castle Heimra from
that waste of ruin.

She had got up very early, but she did not care to
waken Kate, who was no doubt tired with the long drive
of yesterday; she thought instead she would quietly slip
outside and have some little investigation of her surroundings. So she quickly finished dressing; went down and
through the lofty oak hall; passed out upon the stone
terrace, and from thence descended into the garden, where
she found herself quite alone. The air was sweet and soft;
there was a pleasant scent of newly-delved earth; and
everywhere there was abundant evidence that the Spring
had already come to this sheltered space—for there were
masses of daffodils and primroses and wallflower all aglow
in the warm sunlight, and there were bunches of blossom
on the cherry-trees trained up the high stone wall. She
went away down to the end of the garden, opened a door
she found there, and, passing through, entered the wilder
solitude of the woods. And ever as she wandered idly
and carelessly along, the sense that she was the mistress
and owner of all these beautiful things around her seemed
to grow on her and produce a certain not unnatural joy
and pride. For the moment she had forgotten all the
problems in human nature and in economics that lay ahead
of her; here she had all the world to herself—this picturesque world of silver-grey rock, and golden gorse, and
taller larch and spruce, all dappled with sun and shadow,
while the fresh odours of the Spring were everywhere
around, and a stirring of the new life of the year. And
then, when she had fought her way through the thick
underwood to the summit of one of the westward-looking

cliffs—behold! the dark blue sea, and the sunny headlands, and Eilean Heimra, with its thunder-shocks of foam. Heimra island again; it seemed to be always confronting her; but however long she might gaze in that direction, there was no sign of any white-winged yacht coming sailing out into the blue.

And then she scrambled down from this height to the water's edge; and here she discovered a most sequestered little haven—a small, semicircular bay sheltered from the landwinds by rocks and trees, while the pellucid green sea broke in ripples of silver along the cream-white and lilac pebbles. A most solitary spot — quiet, and sunny, and peaceful: she began to think that whatever might be done with other portions of her property, she would keep this little bit of picturesque seclusion entirely for herself. This, surely, could be of no use to anybody—the pebbly beach, the rocks purple-black with mussels or olive-green with seaweed, the clear water whispering along the shore. Political economy should not follow her hither; here would be her place of rest—her place of dreaming—when she was done with studying the wants of others, and wished to commune with her own soul.

But all of a sudden she found she was not alone: an apparition had become visible—a solitary figure that had quietly come round the rocky point, and was now regarding her with dumb apprehension. This was a girl of about five-and-twenty, who had something of an Irish cast of face; fair-complexioned, freckled, a tilted nose, grey eyes wide apart and startled-looking, and curly light-brown hair that was mostly concealed by the scarlet shawl she wore round her head and shoulders. She regarded Miss Stanley with obvious fear, and did not advance; her eyes, that had the timidity of a wild animal in them, had something more than that; they seemed to say that the poor creature was but half-witted. Nevertheless the young proprietress instantly concluded that this was one of "her people," and that, therefore, she was bound to make friends.

"Good morning!" said Mary, and she brought her wonder-working smile and dimple into play, as well she knew how.

A quick light, of wonder and pleasure, sprang into the

girl's eyes. She came forward a little way, timidly. She smiled, in a pleading sort of fashion. And then she ventured to hold out her hand, timidly. Mary went forward at once.

"I am very glad to make your acquaintance," she said, in her bland tones, "and you must tell me who you are."

But the girl, taking the hand that was offered to her, bent one knee and made a humble and profound curtsy (where she could have learnt this trick it is hard to say), and then she uplifted her smiling and beseeching eyes to the great lady (who was considerably taller than she), and still held her hand, and repeated several times something that sounded like *Bentyurna veen—Bentyurna veen.**

"I am very sorry I don't know Gaelic," said Mary, rather disappointedly. "Don't you know a little English?"

The girl still held her hand, and patted it; and looked into her face with pleased and wistful eyes; and again she was addressed as *Bentyurna veen.* And then, in this unknown tongue, something more was said, of which Mary could only make out the single word Heimra.

"Oh, do you come from Heimra island?" she asked, quickly.

But of the girl's further and rapid speech she could make nothing at all. So she said—

"I am really very sorry; but I don't know any Gaelic. Come with me to the house, and I will get some one to speak between us. Come with me, to Lochgarra House; do you understand?"

The girl smiled, as if in assent; and thereupon the two of them set out, following a winding path through the woods that eventually brought them to the garden gate. But here a curious incident occurred. Mary opened the gate, and held it for her unknown friend to follow; but at the same moment the girl caught sight of Mr. Purdie, who had come along for instructions, and was now in the garden awaiting Miss Stanley's return. The instant that this stranger girl beheld the Little Red Dwarf, she uttered a quick cry of terror, and turned and fled; in a moment she was out of sight in the thick underwood. Mary

---

* *Baintighearna mhin*—the gentle lady.

stood still, astounded.   It was no use her trying to follow.
And so, after a second or two of bewilderment, she turned
and went on to the house, saying a few words to Mr. Purdie
in passing, but not with reference to this encounter. Some
instinct suggested that she ought to seek for information
elsewhere.

When she went into the dining-room she found that
Käthchen had come down, and also that Barbara was
bringing in breakfast.

"Barbara," said she, "do you know of a girl about here
who seems to be not quite in her right mind, poor thing?
A fair-complexioned girl, who wears a red shawl round
her head and shoulders——"

"Oh, that was just Anna Chlannach* that Miss Stanley
would be seeing," said Barbara, in her soft-spoken way.

"And does she come from Heimra island?" Was the
next question.

"Oh, no, she is not from Eilean Heimra," said Barbara.
"Maybe she would be speaking to Miss Stanley, and it is
about her mother she would be speaking. Her mother
died about two years ago; but Anna thinks she has been
changed into one of the white sea-birds that fly about
Eilean Heimra, and that she is coming back, and so she
goes along the shore and watches for her. That is what
she would be saying to Miss Stanley."

"Barbara, can you tell me why the girl should be afraid
of Mr. Purdie?"

"Oh, well, indeed, ma'am, they were saying that
Mr. Purdie was for having her sent away to an asylum;
and it is no doubt Anna would rather be among her own
people."

"To an asylum?" Mary demanded sharply. "For what
reason? She does no harm?"

"There is no harm about Anna Chlannach," said Barbara, simply and seriously, as she busied herself with the
table things. "There is no harm at all about Anna
Chlannach, poor girl. But when Mr. Purdie wishes a
thing to be done, then it has to be done."

The hot blood mounted to Mary Stanley's face.

* *Anna Chlannach*—Anne of the many curls.

"Oh, do you think so?" said she. "For I do not think so—not at all! It is not Mr. Purdie who is to be the master here—when I am here. I will let Mr. Purdie understand that he is not to—to interfere with my people——"

"Mary!" said Kate Glendinning in an undertone.

Mary was silent; she knew she had been indiscreet. But presently she said—

"Well, Käthchen, I see I must learn Gaelic."

"Gaelic," observed Kate, sententiously, "is a very intricate key; and then when you've got it, and put it in the lock, and turned it, you find the cupboard empty."

"Perhaps so with regard to literature—I do not know; but I want to be able to talk to the people here, without the intervention of an interpreter. Barbara," said she, to the parlour-maid, who had come into the room again, "do you know what *bentyurna veen* is?"

"*Baintighearna mhin?*" said Barbara, with a smile. "Oh, that is 'the gentle lady.' And that is what Anna Chlannach would be calling Miss Stanley. I have no doubt of that."

"Well, now, Barbara," Mary continued, "you must tell me how to say this in Gaelic—'*Am I welcome?*' What is that in Gaelic?"

But here Barbara became very much embarrassed.

"I am sure it is not necessary that Miss Stanley should say that—oh no, indeed," she answered with averted eyes.

"I am not so sure," said Mary, in her direct way. "I hope the time will come when I shall not have to ask such a question in going into any one's cottage; but at present I am a stranger, and I must make my way gradually. Now, Barbara, what is the Gaelic for 'Am I welcome?'"

But still Barbara hesitated.

"If you would ask Mr. Purdie, ma'am, he would give you the good Gaelic."

"No, I will not," said the imperative young mistress. "I dare say your Gaelic is quite as good as Mr. Purdie's."

"And you would be saying 'Am I welcome?' in going into a house?" said Barbara, slowly—for translation is a serious difficulty to the untutored mind. "Oh, I think you would just say '*An e mo bheatha?*'; but why would Miss Stanley be saying such a thing as that?"

"'*An e mo bheatha?*'—is that right? Very well!"

"And how will you understand their answer, Mamie?" Kate Glendinning asked.

"I will read that in their faces," was the reply.

It was quite clear that the young proprietress had in no wise been disheartened by that first interview with one of her tenants on the previous evening. This fair-shining morning found her as full of ardent enthusiasm, of generous aspirations, as ever; and here was the carriage awaiting them; and here was Mr. Purdie, obsequious; and even Käthchen looked forward with eagerness to getting a general view of the estate. Then their setting forth was entirely cheerful; the Spring air was sweet around them; the sunlight lay warm on the larches and on the tall and thick-stemmed bushes of gorse that were all a blaze of gold. But it was not of landscape that Mary Stanley was thinking; it was of human beings; and the first human being she saw was a little old woman who was patiently trudging along with a heavy creel of peats strapped on her back.

"The poor old woman!" she exclaimed, with an infinite compassion in her eyes. "Doesn't it seem hard she should have to work at her time of life?"

"She's a good deal better off than if she were in Seven Dials or the Bowery," said Käthchen. "But perhaps you would like to give her a seat in the carriage?"

"You may laugh if you like," said Mary, quite simply, "but it seems to me it would be more becoming if that poor old woman were sitting here and I were carrying the creel. However, I suppose we shall have to begin with something more practicable."

But was it more practicable?—that was the question she had speedily to put to herself. For no sooner had they left the wooded 'policies' and surroundings of Lochgarra House than they entered upon a stretch of country the sterility of which might have appalled her if only she had fully comprehended it. Land such as the poorest of Galway peasants would have shunned—an Arabia Petræa —rocks, stones, and heather—wave upon wave of Hebridean gneiss, the ruddy-grey knolls and dips and heights showing hardly a trace of vegetation or of soil. And yet there were human beings here, busy on their small patches; and there were hovels, some of them thatched, others covered over with turf tied down by ropes; while now and again there appeared a smarter cottage, with a slated roof, and lozenge-panes of glass in the window. Moreover, they had now come in sight of the sea again; yonder was a far-stretching bay of silvery sand; and out at the margin of the water, which was at lowest ebb, there were a number of people, mostly women and young lads and girls, stooping at work; while an occasional small dark figure, with a hump on its back, was seen to be crossing the expanse of white.

"What are they doing, Mr. Purdie?" Mary asked.

"They're cutting seaware for manure to put on their crofts," was the answer.

And at the same moment her attention was drawn to a man not far from the roadside who, in his little bit of rocky ground, was making use of an implement the like of which she had never seen or heard of.

"What is that, Mr. Purdie? Is it some kind of spade?"

"Oh, just a foot-plough—there's no other kind of plough would be of any use in this district."

And nothing would do but that she must descend and examine this novel method of tillage. She went boldly up to the man: he was a tall, lean, swarthy person, severe of aspect, who kept a pair of hawk-like eyes fixed on the factor all the time he rather unwillingly answered her questions. For Mary, to her great delight, discovered that this man could speak English; and she wanted information at first hand; and indeed she immediately showed a very definite knowledge of what she was after. The man clearly did not like being cross-examined; again and aga n he resumed his delving operations with that long-coultered instrument that he worked with foot and arms; but she would take no heed of his sullen humour. What stock had he?—two cows, two stirks, eight sheep up on the common pasture, and a pony. What potatoes did he raise!—well, he would plant about two barrels, and maybe get ten or twelve barrels. Did he make any meal?—

hardly any; the cows and stirks did not let his crops come to the threshing. And so forth, until Mary said—

"But I don't see where you get any capital to work the croft, or to increase the stock if we could give you more land. You don't seem to be getting any money."

"No, no money at ahl," said the crofter.

"Listen to him!" interposed Mr. Purdie, with an angry frown. "Let me tell you this, Miss Stanley: that man gets twenty-five shillings a week, gillie's wages, when the gentlemen are here for the shooting, and besides that he hires his pony to them at twenty-three shillings a week; and I suppose he's just the one to cry out that not a sportsman should be allowed to come into the country."

"Is it true that you get that money?" said Mary calmly.

"Ay, that is true," he admitted, in rather a sulky fashion; "but it is not from the croft I get the money."

"Well, I am only making enquiries at present," said Miss Stanley. "I wish to know what improvements are possible—I wish to know what the people want——"

But here, to her surprise, she was interrupted.

"A railway," said the tall, black-a-vised crofter.

"A railway?" she repeated.

"Ay—a railway to Bonar."

"A railway to Bonar Bridge?" she said, staring at the man. "Why, what good would that do you? Take your own case. You say you have nothing to sell. Even if there were a railway to Bonar Bridge—and there couldn't be, for the cost would be enormous, and there would be no traffic to speak of—but supposing there were a railway, how would that benefit you?"

He made no reply; he merely worked away with the long and narrow coulter, turning up the poor soil. So she saw it was no use arguing with him; she bade him a cheerful "Good-morning!" and came away again.

And with a right gallant courage did she continue her house-to-house visitation, desperately trying to win friends for herself, and wondering more and more that she was so ill received. She was not accustomed to sour looks and sullen manners; and in casting about for some possible reason for this strange behaviour she began to ask herself whether she might not get on better with these people if

Mr. Purdie were well away back in his office in Inverness. One point struck her as being very peculiar; not a single man or woman of them asked for a reduction of rent. She thought that would have been the first thing for them to demand, and the simplest for her to consider; but it was never mentioned. They asked for all kinds of other things — when they would speak at all. They wanted herring-nets from the Government; they wanted more boats from the Government—and the instalments of repayment to be made smaller; they wanted the steamer to call in thrice a week, during the ling season; they wanted their arrears of debt to the curers to be wiped off; they wanted more pasture land; they wanted more arable land.

"As for pasture land," said Käthchen, in an undertone, as they were leaving one of these poor steadings, "I don't know whether you will be able to persuade Mr. Watson to give up a slice of his sheep-farm; but as regards arable land, Mary, you should tell those people they have made a mistake about you. You are not the Creator of the Universe; you can't make arable land out of nothing."

"Don't be profane," said Mary, severely. "And mind, I'm not going to have any giggling disparagement of my work: I can tell you, it promises to be very serious."

Serious enough! When they got back to Lochgarra House in the afternoon, her head was fairly in a whirl with conflicting statements and conflicting demands. She knew not how or where to begin; the future seemed all in a maze; while the personal reception accorded her (though she tried to think nothing of that for the moment) had been distinctly repellent. And yet, not satisfied with this long day's work, she would go down to the village in the evening, to see what was expected of her there.

"I suppose I can interfere!" she said, to Mr. Purdie, who was having tea with them.

"Beg pardon?"

"I suppose I can interfere? The village belongs to me, does it not?" she demanded.

"In a measure it does," said the factor. "Of course you are the Superior; but where feus have been granted, they have the land in perpetuity, while you have only the rent——"

"Oh, I can't interfere then?" said she, with some disappointment that her sphere of activity seemed limited in that direction.

"You can step in to see that the conditions of the leases have been respected——"

"But I can't do things?"

"They'll let you do whatever ye like—so long as it means spending money on them," said Mr. Purdie, with grim sarcasm.

"The inn, for example?"

"The inn is different. We built the inn. The landlord is only a yearly tenant."

"We will go down and see him at once, if you please, Mr. Purdie," said Mary, with promptitude. "I have a scheme in my head. Käthchen, are you tired?"

Kate laughed, and dragged herself from her chair. Indeed, she was dead tired; but none the less she was determined to see this thing out. So the three of them proceeded along to the village as far as the inn—which was a plain little two-storeyed building, with not even a sign hanging over the door; and there they went into the stuffy little parlour, and sate down, Mr. Purdie ringing the bell and sending for the landlord.

"Aren't those things dreadful?" said Mary, glancing around at the hideous stone and china ornaments on the mantelshelf and elsewhere—pink greyhounds chasing a yellow hare; bronze stags that could only have been designed in wild delirium; impossible white poodles on a ground of cobalt blue, and the like; while on the walls were two gaudy lithographs—German-looking nymphs with actual spangles in their hair and bits of gold and crimson tinsel round their neck. "I must have all this altered throughout the cottages——"

"Oh, yes, Mamie," said Käthchen; "Broussa silks—Lindos plates—a series of etchings——"

But here was the landlord, a rather youngish and shortish man, who seemed depressed and dismal, and also a little apprehensive.

"Well, Peter," said Mr. Purdie, in his merry way, "what are ye frightened for? Ye've got a face as if ye'd murdered somebody. We're not going to raise your rent."

"It would be little use that—for I could not pay it," said the sad-looking young man with the cadaverous grey face and grey eyes.

"Won't you take a seat?" said Miss Stanley, interposing. "I have a proposal to make to you."

Peter Grant did not answer: he remained standing, stolidly and in silence.

"It seems to me," she went on, "that something should be done to bring visitors here in the spring, as well as the few that come through this way in the autumn. It would be a benefit all round—to the inn, and to the gillies who would be required, I mean for the salmon-fishing in the Garra. Now I don't particularly want the salmon-fishing in the spring months; and it seems to me if you were enterprising you would rent it from me, and advertise it, and let it to two or three gentlemen, who would come and live in your house, and give you a good profit. Do you see?"

He answered not a word; he kept his eyes mostly fixed on the carpet; so she continued—

"Gentlemen will go very far for salmon-fishing now-a-days, so I am told; and you might give them quiet quarters here, and make them comfortable, and every year they would come back. And I should not be hard upon you in fixing the rent. Indeed, I would rather the proposal came from you. What do you think you could afford to give me for the spring fishing in the Garra?"

"Oh, as for that," said the young landlord, rather un-civilly, "I do not see that there should be any rent. For the people about here were saying that no one has a right to the salmon more than anyone else."

"Now you know you're talking nonsense," said Mary, with decision. "For if everyone had a right to the salmon, in a fortnight's time there would not be a single fish left in the river. And besides, do you forget that there is the law?"

"Oh, yes, Peter knows there is the law," interposed Mr. Purdie, who seemed to be in a most facetious mood. "Not more than two months ago Peter found that out when the Sheriff at Dingwall fined him ten shillings and ten shillings expenses for having carried and used a gun without a license. There is quite sufficient of law in the land, as Peter has just found out."

The young man's eyes were filled with a sullen fire; but he said nothing.

"However," continued Miss Stanley, not heeding this interruption, "I would not insist much on rent: I might even give you the spring fishing for nothing, if you thought it would induce the gentlemen to come and occupy the inn. It is an out of-the-way place; but perhaps you would not be charging them very much either—not very much—I don't quite know what would be a fair rent to ask—"

"I would charge them £30 a month," said he. She looked up, a trifle indignant.

"Oh, I see. The fishing is worth nothing while I have it; but it's worth £30 a month when you have it: is that how the matter stands? Do you call that fair dealing? Well, I haven't given you the fishing yet—not on those terms." She rose—rather proudly. "Come, Käthchen, I think we might go and have a look at this fishing that seems to alter in value so remarkably the moment it changes hands. We need not trouble you, Mr. Purdie. Good evening!" This last salutation was addressed to the landlord, who seemed to have no word of explanation to offer: then the two girls went out from the inn, and walked off in the direction of the river, which they had seen in passing on the previous evening.

Mary was no doubt considerably hurt and offended; and there were still further trials in store for her before the end of this arduous and disappointing day. She had proposed this excursion to the river chiefly in order to get rid of Mr. Purdie; but when she and Käthchen found themselves by the side of the Garra, a vague curiosity drew them on, until they had penetrated into solitudes where the stream for the most part lay still and dark under the gloom of the steep overhanging banks. There was something strangely impressive in the silence and in the dusk; for while a distant range of hill flamed russet in the western light—an unimaginable glory—the stealthily creeping river was here almost black in shadow, under the thick birch-woods. And then suddenly she caught Käthchen by the arm. Surely there was some one there—a figure out in

the stream—a faint grey ghost in the mysterious twilight?
And then a startling thing occurred. The figure moved;
and instantly, on the black and oily surface of the water
there was a series of vivid blue-white circles widening out
and out, and slowly subsiding into the dark again. Each
time the grey ghost moved onward (and the two girls stood
motionless, watching this strange phenomenon) there was
this sudden gleam (the reflection of the clear-shining heavens
overhead) that lasted for a moment or two; then the vague
obscurity once more encompassed the unknown person, and
he became but an almost imperceptible phantom. And was
there not some sound in the all-pervading stillness?—an
occasional silken 'swish' through the air? Mary understood what this was well enough.

"That man is poaching," said she, calmly—and she took
no pains to prevent herself being overheard. "And I
suppose you and I, Käthchen, have no means of arresting
him, and finding out who he is."

Her voice was clear, and no doubt carried a considerable distance in this perfect silence. Immediately after
she had spoken there were two or three further series of
those flashing rings—nearing the opposite bank: then
darkness again, and stillness; the spectral fisherman, whoever he was, had vanished into the thick birchwood.

But Mary Stanley made no doubt as to who this was.

"Now I understand," she said, bitterly, as she and her
companion set out for home again, "why the salmon fishing
isn't worth £30 a month to me—when it does not belong
to me! And now I understand what Mr. Purdie said
about the poaching—and the connivance of everybody
around. And yet I suppose Mr. Ross of Heimra calls
himself a gentleman? I suppose he would not like to be
called a thief? Well, I call him a thief! I call poaching
thieving—and nothing but thieving—whatever the people
about here may think. And I say it is not the conduct
of a gentleman."

She was very angry and indignant; and the moment
she got back to Lochgarra House she sent for the head-
keeper. In a few minutes the tall and bushy-bearded Hector
presented himself at the door of the room, cap in hand—
a handsome man he was, with a grave and serious face.

"Is any one allowed to fish in that river who pleases?" she demanded.

"I was not aware of any one fishing, ma'am," said the keeper, very respectfully.

"But is there no one watching?" she demanded, again. "Can any poacher who chooses have the run of the stream? Does it belong to everybody? Is it common property? Because—because I merely wish to know."

She was somewhat perturbed and excited; she did not think she was being dealt with justly; and she saw in the grave and reticent manner of the head-keeper only an intention of screening the culprit whom she herself had by accident detected a little while before.

"The fishing in the Garra is not very good in the spring," said the weather-browned Hector, "and we were not thinking it was much use to have a water-bailiff whatever."

"But surely it is your business to see that no poaching goes on, either on the river or anywhere else? Surely that is your duty? And if there were no fishing, would anyone fish?—you may trust a poacher to know! I'm sure," she went on, with something of a hurt manner, "it is very little I ask. I only want to be treated fairly. I am trying to do my best for every one in the place—I wish to do what is right by every one. But then I want to be treated fairly in return. And poaching is not fair; nor do I think it fair that you, as a keeper, should make excuses for it, or try to screen anyone, whoever he may be."

The man's face became rather pale—even under the weather tan.

"If Miss Stanley would be wanting to get another gamekeeper," he said, slowly and respectfully, "I would not be asking to stay."

"Oh, you would rather leave than interfere with Mr. ——." She did not complete the sentence. She turned away and walked to the window. The fact is, it had been a long and harassing day; her nerves had got unstrung; and all of a sudden a fit of helplessness and despair came over her; it seemed impossible she could ever struggle against this misconstruction and opposition and dislike.

Kate Glendinning turned to the keeper.

"You need not wait, Hector," said she, in an undertone.

Then she went to her friend. Mary had broken down completely—and was sobbing bitterly.

"Mamie!"

"I—I am not used to it," she said, between her sobs. "All day long, it has been nothing but hatred—and—and I am not used to being hated. What have I done to deserve it? I wish to—to do what is right by every one—and—and I tried my—my very hardest to make friends with every one. It is not fair—"

"No, it is not," said Käthchen, and she took her companion by the hand and led her back into the room. "But you must not be disheartened all at once. Give them time. They don't understand you yet. And I will back you to win over people against any one I ever knew : the fact is, Mary, you have always found it so easy, that when you meet with a little trouble you are terribly disappointed. They don't hate you, those people; they don't know you—that is all."

And indeed the girl's naturally sunny temperament soon broke through these bitter mortifications.

"After all, Käthchen," she said, "I have not quite lost a day : I was forgetting that I made one friend." There was an odd smile shining from behind her tears. "It is true she is half-witted ; but all the same I am glad that Anna Chlannach seemed to approve of me."

CHAPTER V.

THE MEALL-NA-FEARN BOG.

AND once again a wild, clear, breezy morning; the sea a· more brilliant blue than ever; the heavy surge bursting like a bomb-shell on the rocks of Eilean Heimra, and springing some sixty or seventy feet in the air. Altogether a joyous and gladdening sight—from the several windows of this spacious room in the tower ; but nevertheless Kate, who was far from being a foolish virgin, observed that the wind must have backed during the night to the south, and therefore she began to talk about waterproofs. For

Mr. Purdie was leaving to-day; and the two girls, thrown upon their own resources, had planned an excursion to those portions of the estate they had not yet visited—the higher moorland districts; and of course that had to be accomplished on foot. They did not propose to take a guide with them: they would simply go along to the 'march' beyond the little hamlet of Cruagan, and follow the boundary line across the hills. Sooner or later they would strike either the Corrie Bhreag or Glen Orme, with the lower parts of which they were acquainted.

And so, with some snack of luncheon in their pocket and a leather drinking-cup, and with their waterproofs over their arm, they set out—the sunlight pleasant around them, and odour of seaweed in the air. This was to be a little bit of a holiday: for this one day, at least, there were to be no persistent and patient questions met by sullen replies, no timid proffers of friendship answered by obdurate silence. And yet as they neared the village, Mary was reminded of her perplexities, and griefs, and disappointments; for here was the solitary policeman of the place, standing outside the small building that served him for both police-office and dwelling-house. John, as he was simply called—or more generally, Iain—was not at all a terrible-looking person; on the contrary he was quite a young man, very sleek and fat and roseate, with rather a merry blue eye, and a general appearance of good-nature: a stout, wholesome-complexioned, good humoured young man, who was evidently largely acquainted with the virtues of porridge and fresh milk. When Mary saw him, she said,—

"Well, Käthchen, if they're all in league against me, even my own gamekeepers, to screen the poaching that is going on, I will appeal to the policeman. He is bound to put down thieving of every kind."

"You'd better not, Mamie," was the instant rejoinder. "It would be very awkward if a question were asked in the House of Commons—about a Highland proprietor who had the shameless audacity to ask Her Majesty's own representative to watch a salmon-river in place of the ordinary keepers."

However, this project came to nothing in the present case; for as they drew near they found that the belted guardian of the peace was himself in dire trouble. An elderly woman—no doubt his mother—had opened an upper window in the small two-storeyed building; and she was haranguing and scolding him with an unheard-of volubility. What it was all about, neither Käthchen nor Mary had the least idea, for the old woman was rating him in Gaelic; but John, seeing the young ladies approach, grew more and more roseate and embarrassed. Of course he pretended not to hear. He gazed out towards Heimra Island. Then with his stick he prodded at the mass of seaweed by the roadside that was waiting there to be carted away. And then he smiled in a tolerant manner, as if all this tempest were rather amusing; and finally, not being able, in such humiliating circumstances, to face the two ladies, the upholder of the majesty of the law turned and beat a speedy retreat, hiding himself in the lower floor of the house until they should pass. So that on this occasion Mary had no chance of asking Iain whether he would catch poachers for her.

"I am sure," said she, as they were passing through the town, and over the Garra bridge, and up into the country beyond, "I do not care to preserve the game, if it were for myself alone. If I thought it would be really for the good of the people here, I would have every head of game on the estate destroyed, and every salmon netted out of the river. But you hear what they say themselves—many of them would never see money at all if it weren't for the gillies' wages, and the hiring of the ponies, and so on, in the autumn. Then the few deer that stray on to the ground, from the Glen Orme forest, they don't come near the crofts—they do no harm whatever, except, perhaps, to Mr. Watson's pasture, and he can easily get rid of them, if he likes, by saying a word to his shepherds. So that the shooting and the fishing are nothing but an advantage, and a very great advantage, to the people; and I tell you this, Käthchen, that I mean to preserve them as well as ever I can. And really it seems shameful that a gentleman in Mr. Ross's position should have so little self-respect as to become a common poacher——"

"You forget how he has been brought up—according to Mr. Purdie's account," Käthchen put in.

But Mary did not heed the interruption.   She was very indignant on this point.

"It is quite excusable," said she, "for the poor, ignorant people about here to believe that the Rosses of Heimra are still the rightful owners of the land.   They know nothing about the law courts and agent's offices in London. They only know that as far back as they have heard of, and down to their own day, the land has belonged to the Rosses; and their Highland loyalty remains staunch and true; it is not to be bought over by the stranger; and perhaps it is not even to be acquired by kindness—but we'll see about that in time.   However, what I say is this, that I don't complain of these poor people having such mistaken ideas; but Mr. Ross knows better; he knows well enough that he has not the least shadow of right to anything belonging to the Lochgarra estate; and that if he takes a grouse, or a hare, or a salmon, he is constituting himself a common thief."

But now, and for an instant, she was stricken dumb. They had come in sight of the dried-up loch and the waste heap of stones that once was Castle Heimra; and this sad spectacle seemed to put some strange fancies into her head.

"Käthchen," said she, "do you think he does it out of revenge?"

Now Kate Glendinning herself was of Highland blood; and she made answer boldly—

"I have told you already, Mary, that if I were young Ross of Heimra, and such an injury had been done to me and mine—well, I should not like to say what I should be inclined to do in return.   A sentimental grievance!—yes; but it is sentimental grievances that go deepest down into the Highland nature, and that are longest remembered. But then on the other hand it seems to me that shooting game or killing salmon is a very paltry form of revenge. That is not how I should try to have it out with Mr. Purdie—for who can doubt that it was Mr. Purdie destroyed the loch and the castle?—I saw his air of triumph when he told the story.   No; poaching wouldn't be my revenge—"

"There is more than that, Käthchen," Mary said, absently.   "It isn't merely defying the keepers, or being in league with them. There is more than that. I wonder, now, if it is he who has set those people against us, so that they will never regard us but as strangers and enemies? It is not natural, their sullen refusal of kindness. There is something hidden—something behind—that I don't understand." She was silent for a second or two: then she said—"I wonder if he thinks he can drive me out of the place by stirring up this bitter ill-will."

"There is one way to get over the difficulty," said Käthchen, lightly. "Ask him to Lochgarra House. He is a Highlander: if he has once sate down at your table, he cannot be your enemy afterwards."

A touch of colour rose to Mary's face.

"You forget the character he bears," she said, somewhat proudly.

And here they were at the Cruagan crofts; and the people were all busy in the wide stretch of land enclosed by a dilapidated fence of posts and wire. James Macdonald, the elderly crofter who had complained of the dyke-tax, was ploughing drills for potatoes; two or three women and girls were planting; and a white-haired old man was bringing out the seed-potatoes in a pail. The plough was being drawn by two horses wearing huge black collars—what these were for the two visitors could not imagine.

"Are you going to speak to him, Mary?" Kate asked in an undertone—as the plough was coming towards the end of the field.

"Yes, I am," said the young lady. "I want to see if the remission of the tax has had no effect on him. Perhaps he will have a little more English now."

There was no time to be lost—the horses were turning. She stepped across from the road.

"May I interrupt you for a moment? I want to ask you—"

Well, the grey-bearded man with the shaggy eyebrows did check the horses—perhaps he had meant to give them a rest at the end of the drill.

"Oh, thank you," said Mary, in her most gracious and friendly way. "I only wished to ask you whether Mr. Purdie had told you that there was to be no more tax for the dyke, and that there was to be fifteen years' of it given back."

The Russian-looking crofter regarded the shafts of the plough without removing his hands ; and then he said—

"Yes—he was saying that."

Not a word of thanks, but perhaps—she generously thought—his English did not go so far.

"It is good dry weather for ploughing, is it not? she remarked at a venture.

There was no reply.

"That very old man," she asked, "who is he—is he your father?"

"Yes."

"It seems a pity he should be working at his age," she went on, wishing to show sympathy. "He ought to be sitting at the cottage door, smoking his pipe."

"Every one will have to work," said the elderly crofter, in a morose sort of way ; and then he looked at his horses.

"Oh well," said Mary, blithely, "I hope to be able to make it a little easier for you all. This land, now, how much do you pay for it? What is your rent?"

"It—thirty shillings an acre."

"Thirty shillings an acre? That is too much," said she, without a moment's hesitation. "Surely thirty shillings an acre is too much for indifferent land like that!"

The small, suspicious eyes glanced at her furtively.

"I not saying it too mich," he made answer, slowly.

"Oh, but I will consult Mr. Purdie about it," said she, in her pleasantest way. "My own impression is that thirty shillings an acre is only asked for good land. But I will inquire ; and see what can be done. Well, good morning !— I mustn't take up your time."

She was coming away when he looked after her.

"I not saying—it—too mich rent," said he ; and then he turned to his plough ; and his laborious task was resumed.

"Isn't that odd?" said Mary, as they were going along the highway again. "None of them seem anxious to have their rents reduced. All day yesterday—not a single complaint !"

"Well, Mamie," said Käthchen, "I don't know ; but I can guess at a reason—perhaps they are afraid to complain."

This set Mary thinking; and they went on in silence. She wished she knew Gaelic.

When they came within sight of the ancient boundary line, they left the road, struck across a swampy piece of land where there were a few straggling sheep, and then set to work to climb the bare and rocky hill-side. It was an arduous climb; but both the young women were active and lithe and agile; and they made very fair progress—stopping now and again to recover their breath. Indeed, it was not the difficulty of the ascent that was present to their mind; it was the terribly bleak and lonely character of this domain they were entering. Higher and higher as they got, they seemed to be leaving the living world behind them; and then, when they reached a level plateau, and could look away across this new world, there was nothing but an endless monotony of brown and purple knolls and slopes, covered with heather and withered grass, and then a series of hills along the horizon, with one or two lofty mountain-peaks, dark and precipitous, and streaked here and there with snow. There was no sign of life; nor any sound. As they advanced further and further into this wilderness, a strange sense of intrusion came over them; it was as if they had come into a land peopled by the dead—who yet might be regarding them; they looked and listened, as if expecting something, they knew not what. They did not speak the one to the other; indeed, they were some little way apart—those two small figures in this vast moorland solitude. Then they came to a tarn—the water black as night—not a bush nor the stump of a tree along its melancholy shores. Nor even here was there the call of a curlew, or the sudden whirr of a wild-duck's wings. At this point the girls had come together again.

"Who can wonder at the superstitions of the Highlanders?" said Käthchen, half absently.

Mary's answer was a curious one. She was looking at the black and oozy soil around her, with its scattered knobs of yellow grass.

"I suppose," she said, meditatively, "they send the sheep up here later on? But it must be wretched pasture even at its best."

All this time they had been shut out of sight of the sea by the higher ranges on their right; but by and by, when they had surmounted the ridge in front of them, they came in view of at least one new feature in the landscape—the river Garra, lying far below them, in a wide and empty valley. No hanging birchwoods here, or deep pools sheltered by lofty banks, as in the neighbourhood where they had surprised the ghostly fisherman; but a treeless expanse of rather swampy-looking ground, with the river for the most part rushing over stony shallows.

"Did it occur to you, Käthchen, that we should have to cross that stream?" Mary asked, as they were descending the hill.

"Where is the difficulty?" said Käthchen, coolly. "We shall simply have to do as the country girls do,. take off our shoes and stockings, wade over, and put them on again on the other side."

However, this undertaking they postponed for the present; for it was now midday; and they thought they might as well have luncheon when they got down to the side of the Garra. They chose out a rock wide enough to afford them seats; opened their small packages, and filled the leather drinking-cups at the stream. Up in these altitudes the water was not at all of a peaty-brown; it was quite clear, with something of a pale greenish hue; it had come from rocky regions, and from melting snow.

"It seems very odd to me," said Mary, as they contentedly munched their biscuits and sliced hard-boiled eggs, "that I should find myself in a place like this—a place that looks as if no human being had ever been here before—and yet be the actual owner of it. I suppose there never were any people living here?"

"They must have been clever if they did," said Käthchen. "To tell you the truth, Mary, the most part of the Lochgarra estate that I have seen is only fit for one thing, and that is to make heather brooms for sweeping kitchens."

"Ah, but wait," said the young proprietress, confidently. "Wait a little while, and you will see. Wait till you hear of all the improvements——"

"A railway to Bonar Bridge?" said Kate Glendinning, carefully lifting the leather cup.

" Now look here, Mephistopheles," said Mary, seriously.
" I could murder you, without the least trouble. I am
stronger than you ; I could kill you, and hide you in a hole
in the rocks, and you'd never be heard of again. So you'd
better have a little discretion in flouting at my schemes.
Ah, if you only knew ! Why, listen to this, now : are
you aware that there is a far greater demand for the
Harris homespun cloth than the people can supply ? I
discovered that at Inverness. I was told that half the
homespun sold in London is imitation, made in Manchester.
Well, I propose to let them have the real homespun—yes,
and plenty of it ! And more than that ; I'm going to
have homespun druggets, and homespun plaids ; and
blankets, and shawls, and patch-work quilts ; and all the
carding and spinning and weaving, and all the knitting of
the stockings, to be done by my own people. And I'll have
a sale-room in London ; and advertise in the papers—that
they're the real things, and not sham at all ; and if I have
any friends in the South, well, let them show themselves
my friends by coming forward and helping us ! No charity
—far from it ; they get value, and more than value for
their money ; why, where is there any such stuff as homespun for gentlemen's shooting costumes or for ladies' ulsters ;
and where can you get such warmth in winter from any
other kind of stockings ? I don't like to see so many
women working in the fields—especially the old women—
and carrying those heavy creels of seaweed ; I'm going
to get them lighter work—that will pay them better ;
and when their sons or husbands are away at the East
Coast fishing, they will be earning almost as much at
home. What do you think of this now ? For a good web
of homespun I can get 5*s.* a yard from the clothiers themselves ; and they will do very well when they get 1*s.* or
1*s.* 6*d.* a yard profit ; but when I sell in my own store at
6*s.* 6*d.* a yard, then that is all the more coming back to us
here at home. Oh, I tell you, you will soon hear plenty of
spinning-wheels going, and shuttles clacking, at Lochgarra ! "

It was a pretty enthusiasm ; and Käthchen did not like
to say anything. Indeed it was Mary herself who paused
in this dithyrambic forecast. She had chanced to look at
the gathering skies overhead.

"Käthchen," said she, "it was a good thing we brought our waterproofs."

Kate Glendinning followed the direction of her glance.

"Yes," she answered, "and I think we'd better be getting on."

Then here was the business of getting over the stream. Mary went down to the edge of the river; pulled off her shoes and stockings covertly (covertly, in this solitude, where there was not even a hawk poised on wing!) and then put one foot cautiously into the swift-running water.   The consequence was a shrill shriek.

"No," she said, "I can't do it.   It's like ice, Käthchen! I'm going to put my shoes and stockings on again; and find some stones or rocks somewhere that I can get across."

"You'll fall in, then," said the matter-of-fact Käthchen, who was by this time over the ankles, and making good progress—with her teeth clenched.

But Mary did not fall in.   She sought out shallows; and made zig-zag experiments with the shingle and with bigger stones; and if she did get her feet wet before reaching the other side, it was gradually.   Very soon it was not of wet feet they were thinking.

For when they ascended the opposite hill—entering upon a still wilder region than any they had as yet traversed —they became aware that all the world had grown much darker; and when at length they beheld the far line of the sea, it was of a curiously livid, or leaden, hue.   The wind was blowing hard up on these heights; now and again there was a sting of moisture in it—the flying precursor of the rain.   But the most ominous thing that met their gaze was a series of sickly-looking, formless clouds that seemed rising all along the western horizon; while the sea underneath was growing unnaturally black.   Rising and spreading those clouds were, and swiftly; with a strange and alarming appearance—as if the earth were about to be overwhelmed: they looked close and near, moreover, though necessarily they must have been miles away.   At first the two girls did not mind very much; all their strength was needed to withstand the buffetings of the wind; indeed, there was a kind of joyance in driving forward against the ever-increasing gale, though it told on their panting chests. They had to shout to each other, if they wished to be heard.

"Where is the 'march,' Mary?"

"I haven't seen any trace of it . . . this side of the Garra . . . But of course we're in the right direction . . . We must get into the Corrie Bhreag sooner or later."

Then came the rain—at first in flying showers, but very soon in thin gauze veils that swept along between them and the distant hills. Waterproofs were donned now; but they proved to be of little use—they were blown every kind of way, with an immensity of ballooning and flapping and clapping; while they materially impeded progress. But nevertheless the two wanderers struggled on bravely, hurling themselves, as it were, against these rude shocks and gusts, until their wet hair was flying all about their faces, and their eyes were smarting with the rain. Sometimes they paused to take breath—and to laugh, in a rueful way.

"There's nothing so horrid as wet wrists!" Mary called to her companion, on one of these occasions, as she shook her arms and hands.

"It won't be wrists only, very soon," said Käthchen, in reply, as they started on again.

The gale increased in violence, so that on the higher slopes ahead of them the heather was beaten and driven into long waves of motion; while even through those whirling veils of rain they could see the torn shreads and tatters of lurid cloud that crossed the greyer sky. The moaning of the wind rose and fell in remote and plaintive cadence; and then again it would mount up into a shrill and long-continued scream, that struck terror to the heart. For there was no more laughter now. All their dogged, half-blind struggle against the storm did not seem to lead them any nearer to any practicable way of getting down to the coast; and they were afraid to leave the line they had conceived to be the march—the imaginary line which they had hoped would bring them to the Corrie Bhreag, or, at furthest and worst, to some portion of Glen Orme. And if the dusk were to come down and find them in these trackless solitudes! During one of their pauses to recover breath, and to get their wet hair out of their eyes and lips, Mary took off her waterproof, and her companion followed her example ; the worse than useless garments were secured by a lump of rock, and left to be searched for by a shepherd on the following day. Then forward again—with the wind moaning and howling across these desert wastes—with the driving rain at once blinding and stifling them—and a dim unspoken fear of the coming darkness gradually taking possession of their mind.

One odd thing was that though Mary Stanley was the taller and much the more strongly built of the two, she could not hold on as well as her smaller companion, who was in a measure familiar with the work of getting over heather-tufts and across peat-hags. Mary complained that the wind and the rain choked her—she could not breathe. And at last she stopped, panting, breathless, entirely exhausted with the terrible strain.

"Käthchen," she said, in a despairing sort of way, "I'm done. But don't mind me. I will stay here, until the storm goes over. If you think you can push on until you find some valley to take you down to the coast, then you will be able to get home——"

"Mamie, what are you talking about ?" said Käthchen, indignantly. "I am going to keep by you, if both of us stay here all night. But we musn't do that. Come, have courage !"

"Oh, I've a fearful amount of courage, but no strength," said Mary, with a very dolorous sort of smile. "Whenever I begin, I get caught by the throat. Well, here goes once more !"

And again they set forth with a desperate resolution, forcing themselves against the gale, though their own saturated clothes were dragging heavily upon them. But they had not gone on thus for many minutes when it somehow seemed as though this laborious stepping from one heather-tuft to another was becoming easier. Surely the land was trending down ?

"Käthchen," Mary called out, brushing away the rain from her eyelashes, "here is a valley, and surely it must lead down to the sea. I don't know which it is——"

"Oh, never mind ; we must take our chance," said Kate ; "if we can get down to the coast-line anywhere, we shall be all right."

And so, notwithstanding their dire fatigue, they kept on now with lighter hearts ; their progress becoming more and more easy, being all down hill. Not that this valley was anything in the nature of a chasm, but rather a hollow plain gradually sloping down to the west. And then again, the further they got away from the wild heights they had left behind them, the violence of the storm seemed to diminish ; they were better able to breathe ; and if the rain did continue to fall, they were about as wet as they well could be, so that did not matter.

Suddenly Kate Glendinning uttered a joyful cry.

"Look ! Look ! "

Far away down the wide valley, and through the mists of the rain, they could make out a small cottage or hut ; and there were signs of life, too—wavering smoke that the wind blew level as it left the chimney. This welcome sight put new animation into their exhausted frames ; and they pushed forward right cheerfully now, little thinking that they were walking into a far more deadly peril than any they had encountered among the hills.

For when they got further down the valley, they found that there intervened between them and the cottage a circular plain : and although it certainly looked marshy, it never occurred to them that they ought to go round by the side of it. How could their feet be wetter ? So they made straight across, Käthchen leading the way, and jumping from clump to clump of heather, so as to avoid the little channels where the black ooze and water might be deep.

But by and by she was forced to go more cautiously ; and had to hesitate before choosing her course. For those oozy channels had grown broader ; and not only that, but the land she had reached was very far from being solid—it trembled in a mysterious way. She still held on, nevertheless, hoping to reach securer foundation ; and now she was not following any straight line whatever, but seeking anywhere and everywhere for a safe resting-place for her foot. Matters speedily grew worse and worse. She could not make the slightest movement without seeing the earth vibrate for twenty yards around her — an appalling phenomenon ; and at last she dared hardly stir, for a sickening feeling had come over her that a single step might plunge her into an unfathomable abyss.

"Käthchen," said Mary, in a low voice (she was close behind), "don't you think we should try to go back?"

But the girl seemed absolutely paralyzed with terror. She turned an inch or two, and looked helplessly around.

"I—I don't know the way we came," she said—and her eyeballs were contracted as if with pain. "Will you try, Mary?"

And then she made a strenuous effort to pull herself together.

"No, no!—let me go first!" she said in a kind of desperation, "I am lighter than you."

"No," Mary made answer, quite calmly, "I will go first."

Yes, outwardly she was quite calm; but dismay had possession of her too. For the whole world underneath felt so strangely unstable; it shivered even as she stood; and as for going back the way they came—why, it seemed to her that the smallest movement in any one direction must necessarily cause this quaking morass to open like the sea and engulf them for ever. She had undertaken to go first; but whither was she to go? When she put out a foot tentatively, the solid earth seemed to slide away from her in billows. Again and again she tried; and again and again she instinctively drew back—her whole frame trembling like the trembling soil beneath her; until at last she stood speechless and motionless, turning strange eyes towards Käthchen—eyes that asked a question her white lips could not utter. And the dusk was now coming over the world.

But help was near. They were suddenly startled by a sound—a distant cry—and at the same moment they caught sight of a man who had come running from the direction of the cottage. As soon as he perceived he was seen, he held up both arms: it was a signal to them not to move—as if movement were possible to them in this prostration of fear! He came along with an incredible rapidity, by the outskirts of the morass, until he was opposite them, and then he ventured in a little distance. But he did not attempt to approach them; with his hand he directed them which way to go; and they—their heart in their mouth the while—obeyed him as well as they could. By the time they got near to where he was waiting, they found themselves with some firmer consistency under their feet; and then, without a word, he turned and led the way off the morass, they following. There he paused for a second, to give them a brief direction.

"You must keep along the side; it is very dangerous," he said, in a somewhat cold manner.

But in an instant Mary had divined who this was. The young man with the pale, clear-cut features and coal-black eyes belonged to no shepherd's hut.

"I—I want to thank you, sir," she said, breathlessly (he had raised his cap to them slightly, and was going away). "If it had not been for you, what should we have done? It is a dreadful place—we were afraid to move——"

He glanced at her and her companion with some swift scrutiny.

"You are wet," said he, in the same distant and reserved fashion. "You will find a fire in the widow's cottage."

"You might show us the way," said Käthchen, half-piteously. "We are frightened."

After that he could not well leave them; though, to be sure, the way to the cottage was plain and easy enough, so long as they kept back from the dangerous Meall-na-Fearn bog. He walked ahead of them, slowly; he did not attempt to speak to them. His demeanour had not been unfriendly; on the contrary, it had been courteous; but it was courtesy of a curiously formal and reticent kind. Perhaps he had not known who these strangers were when he came so quickly to their help.

And in truth the two girls could hardly follow him; for now all the enfeeblement of the terror they had suffered had come upon them; they were no longer strung up by a shuddering apprehension of being entombed in that hideous morass; and the previous fatigue, physical and nervous, that they had fought against so heroically, was beginning to tell now, especially upon Mary. At length she did stop; she said, "Käthchen! Käthchen!" in a low voice; her figure swayed, as if she would fall to the earth; and then she sank to her knees, and burst into a wild fit of hysterical weeping, covering her face with her hands. Their guide did not happen to notice: he was going on: and it was becoming dark.

"Stay a moment, sir!" said Käthchen, in tones of indignant remonstrance. "My friend is tired out."

He came back at once.

"I beg your pardon," said he, gravely. "Tell her it is only a little way further. I am going on to get something ready for you."

And he did go on; so that it was left for Käthchen to encourage her companion, and subdue this nervous agitation.

"It is only the cold, Käthchen," said Mary, who was trembling from head to foot. "I suppose you are wet through, too."

But indeed the cottage was quite close by now; they made their way slowly; when they reached it, the door was open; and here was the young man, with his sailor's cap in his hand, giving a few further directions, in Gaelic, to an old woman and a young girl of thirteen or fourteen, who appeared to be the sole occupants of the earthen-floored hut. There was a peat-fire burning, and a pannikin slung over it. The old woman went into the other apartment—the "ben" of the cottage—and returned with a black bottle, and some sugar; and presently she had brewed a most potent liquor which, in two tea-cups, she presented to the young ladies, and insisted on their swallowing. They were seated on a rude bench by the grateful warmth of the peat; they were made to finish this fiery draught; and here were oat-cakes and milk besides. Life seemed slowly to come back to them—to stir in their veins. But the young man who had guided them hither? Well, he had disappeared.

After some little time Käthchen happened to turn and look round.

"Where has the gentleman gone?" she asked.

It was the young girl with the jet-black hair and the wild, timid eyes who made answer.

"I was told to take the ladies to Lochgarra House," said she, in excellent English, and with a very pretty pronunciation.

"You ? It is nearly dark !" Käthchen exclaimed.
" Why did he leave us ? "

But here Mary interposed in her mild, suave fashion ;
and she regarded the girl with kindly eyes.

"Yes, I am sure you will be able to show us the way
very well," said she. "Only you must tell your mother—
is she your mother ?"

" My grandmother, lady," was the answer.

" Well, tell your grandmother that you must stay the
night at Lochgarra House ; you cannot come back here so
late. We will send you along in the morning ; or I will
come with you myself."

But the old grandmother knew a little English too.

"Yes, yes, indeed, indeed," said she. "Whatever the
ladies will be pleased."

And by and by they set out ; the sure-footed young
mountaineer acting as their guide. Night had fallen now,
and there were no stars ; but after they had gone on some
time they could make out the sound of the sea—and it was
a welcome sound, for it told them they were nearing the
road that here runs all along the coast. And indeed it
was not until they were actually in the highway that it
occurred to Kate Glendinning to ask how far they had
still to go before they got to Lochgarra.

" It will be about seex miles, or more than five miles
whatever," was the answer.

" Six miles !" said Käthchen, faintly. "I wish we had
stayed at your grandmother's cottage. Mamie, shall you
ever be able to manage it ? "

"I hope so, Käthchen," Mary said, though not very
joyfully. "I am a little warmer now ; and there is less
wind blowing."

And so they went on—the unseen sea thundering
beneath them in the dark, along the iron-bound coast—
the wind sometimes rising into a mournful moan, but
bringing no rain with it now. It was a long and weary
tramp ; but they were on a good road ; and their brave
little guide, whatever she may have thought of the
darkness, went forward unhesitatingly.

Then of a sudden they beheld two points of fire away
ahead of them ; and presently there was a sound of wheels.

"I will give £20 for the loan of that carriage," said Mary, "whosesoever it is !"

"Why," said Käthchen joyfully, "in this neighbourhood, whose can it be but your own ?"

And indeed it was. And not only that, but here was the gentle-spoken Barbara, profuse of compassion and pretty speeches; and she had brought with her an abundance of blankets—not shawls and wraps, or any feminine knick-nackery—but substantial and capacious blankets, along with many smaller comforts and cordials. And when they had all four got into the shut landau (for the girls would not allow their young guide to go on the box) Mary said—

"But who took the news to Lochgarra House, Barbara ? Who told you to bring the carriage ?"

"Oh, just the young master himself," said Barbara, with miling eyes, as she was busy with her ministrations. And then she corrected herself. "It was just young Mr. Ross of Heimra. And did Miss Stanley not know who he was ?"

But Miss Stanley had known very well. And Käthchen had guessed.

CHAPTER VI

GILLEASBUIG MÒR.

KÄTHCHEN was standing at the window, looking out upon the wild and wayward sea, that was all brilliantly dappled with sun and cloud, while Mary was at her dressing-table, preparing to go down to breakfast. It was a blowy and blusterous morning, after the storm; but the welcome sunlight was abroad again; and the heavens shone serene and fair.

"Never no more," Käthchen was solemnly remarking, as she regarded the wide plain of hurrying waves and the white sea-birds that dipped and sailed and circled in the light, "never no more shall I have a word to say against smuggled brandy. By rights, Mary, you and I ought both to be in a raging fever this morning; and you look as well as ever you did in your life, and I have only a

little bit of a headache. Nor against poaching : I have
nothing to say against poaching—when it suddenly produces
somebody to get you out of a hideous and horrible morass,
worse than any quicksand that ever I heard of. Do you
know, I hardly dared put my foot to the floor this morning :
I was afraid that frightful sensation would come back,
as if I were standing on nothing, and just about to sink.
Wasn't it terrible ? I know I shall dream about it to my
dying day." And then she said : "I wonder what took
young Ross of Heimra up to that out-of-the-way place ?
Not poaching ; for he had neither rod nor gun."

"More likely selling brandy to that old woman," said
Mary ; and then she added, with a touch of scorn : "A
pretty occupation for a Highland gentleman ? "

"Well, Mary," said Käthchen, reflectively, "I confess
that story does not sound to me true. I should like to
have some proof before believing it. No doubt it is just
possible he may have wanted to make up to these poor
people for Mr. Purdie having banished the illicit stills ;
and perhaps he could not afford to get them spirits for
nothing ; and so he may charge them what he himself has
paid. But it is not like what a Highland laird would do,
however poor he might be—and in a kind of way he still
stands in the position of laird towards these people. No,
it does not sound probable ; but anyhow I mean to find
out—if we are going along to-day to thank the old woman
for her kindness of last night. And whether it was
poaching, or smuggling, or whatever it was, that took
young Mr. Ross up to that hut, it was a very lucky
thing for us : we should never have seen the morning if
we had been left there."

"That is true enough," Mary admitted ; but then she
went on to say, with some asperity : "At the same time, a
favour is twice a favour when it is graciously conferred.
He seemed to me a most ill-mannered young man. I
doubt whether he would have come near us at all if he had
known who we were."

"Oh, I don't agree with you—not in the least ! " said
Käthchen, warmly. "I thought he was most courteous, and
—and respectful. Remember, we were entirely strangers
to him. And just think of his going all the way to

Lochgarra to get the carriage sent for us—and very quickly he must have done it, too."

But Mary had not a word in favour of this young man whom she suspected of far worse offences (in her eyes) than killing salmon or bringing smuggled brandy into the district : she suspected him, in truth, of stirring up wrath and ill-will, and setting these people against her.

"I suppose," she said, rather coldly, "we must thank him, if we should see him."

"I, for one, mean to do so, and very heartily," Käthchen said at once. "I think he was most kind and considerate —if—if a little—a little reserved. And not at all the wild savage I had expected—most distinguished-looking I should call him——"

"Come away down to breakfast, Käthchen," said Mary, taking her friend by the arm : she would hear no more on that subject.

In the hall they encountered the little Highland lass who had been their guide on the previous night; and she, looking up with timid eyes towards this tall and beautiful lady whose smile was so gracious and winning, said—

"Am I to be going home now ? "

"Home ?" said Mary. "Have you had your breakfast ?"

"Oh, yes, indeed."

"Very well, you need not go yet; you may as well wait and come with us in the carriage—for we want to thank your grandmother for her kindness to us. You can amuse yourself in the garden, if you like, until we are ready."

She was obediently going away, but Käthchen stopped her.

"I don't think you ever told us your name."

"Just Isabel," said the little maid, in her pretty fashion.

"Of course you know Mr. Ross ?" was the next question.

"Oh, yes."

"What was he doing up at your cottage last night ? "

"Käthchen ! " said Mary ; but the little girl did not notice the interruption : she answered quite simply—

"He came up to ask about the cow."

"What cow ? "

But here Isabel did begin to look a little frightened ; and she glanced anxiously at Miss Stanley.

"Perhaps the lady will be angry," she said, with shrinking eyes.

"Oh, no, she won't be angry," Käthchen interposed at once. "What about the cow? Tell me about the cow."

"It was my mother's cow that got into the bog and was drowned."

"The bog we strayed into?" Käthchen exclaimed. "Do you mean to say that cattle have been swallowed up in that place?"

"Ay, many and many a one," said the little girl.

"I'll have it fenced round at once," said Mary, in her usual prompt and emphatic way, "no matter what it costs!"

"And the cow?" said Käthchen, encouragingly, to the little Highland lass. "What did Mr. Ross want to know about the cow?"

"Mr. Ross," continued Isabel, "he was sending a message that my mother would ask Mr. Purdie and the lady for a cow in place of that one, and the money to be paid back bit by bit as we could do it; yes, and Mr. Purdie was to be asked for the cow; and Mr. Ross he came up last night to see if we were to get the cow. But we were not hearing about it from any one."

Mary's face flushed with vexation.

"Why was I not told about this?" she said, turning indignantly to Käthchen. "What right had Mr. Purdie to decide—and go away without saying a word? I suppose he refused?—and that was to be all of it!"

But the little girl, hearing the lady talk in these altered tones, grew frightened; and tears started to her eyes.

"Please, I was not asking for the cow," she said, piteously; for she knew not what terrible mischief she had done. "I was not intending to make the lady angry——"

Mary turned to the girl, and put her hand in a kindly way on the raven-black hair.

"Don't you be alarmed, Isabel," she said, with a reassuring smile. "You have done no harm; you were quite right to tell me the story. And you need not be afraid; your mother shall have the cow; perhaps even two of them, if the byre is big enough. Now go into the garden and amuse yourself, until you hear the carriage come round."

However, it may here be said that in this instance Mr. Purdie was in no wise culpable. It appeared that the widow MacVean had two days before gone over to Cruagan, where she had a married daughter, in order to help in the fields; and her only chance of presenting the petition was by intercepting the factor on his way homeward. Whether she did or did not present the petition was of no immediate consequence: Mary had resolved upon offering up this cow, or perhaps even two cows, as a sort of sacrificial thanksgiving for her deliverance from the Meall-na-Fearn bog.

After breakfast they set out, Isabel seated beside the driver. And once again they came in sight of the Minard township, with its poor little crofts on the rocky soil, and the long sweep of white sand where, the tide being out, the people were busy with their sickles cutting the seaweed from the rocks.

"I wonder," said Mary, meditatively, "if I couldn't revive the kelp-burning?"

"Oh, no," said Käthchen (who did not quite understand how indefatigable the young proprietress had been in qualifying herself for her new position). "That is all over now. Those were the grand days for the Highlands —for both the landlords and the people; but modern chemistry has spoiled all that."

"You don't know, then," said Mary, quietly, "that kelp-burning is carried on in some places at this moment? It is, though. Over in South Uist the crofters get from £2 10s. to £3 a ton for kelp. But perhaps they need all the seaweed they can get here for their crofts, or perhaps it isn't the right kind of tangle: I must find out about that."

They drove as far as they could along the road; and they had to descend from the carriage, to make the rest of their way on foot. And strange it was that the moment the two girls left the highway and found themselves upon the yielding heather, they betrayed an unmistakable alarm —looking all around them as if they feared to be betrayed into some hidden quagmire. But indeed at this point the land consisted chiefly of rocks and peat and stones; and gradually they got accustomed to following their surefooted young guide who was going up the hill-side with the lightest of steps. Long before they had climbed to the cottage, they saw the old woman come out to scatter some remains of porridge to the hens : a pleasant-looking old dame she was, with silvery-grey hair and a rennet complexion ; moreover (whether she had expected them or not) she was very tidily dressed—a clean white " mutch," a short-skirted blue gown, a white apron, and red stockings. When she saw the strangers, she remained outside ; and when they came toiling up she saluted them with a grave and gentle " good moarning ! " But beyond returning that salutation, Mary did not enter into further talk just then. Her eyes were drawn with a morbid fascination to the black morass that had so nearly proved fatal to her and her companion. She seemed to feel herself once more standing on that trembling soil, unable to move in any one direction, the darkness coming down. And had the darkness fallen, what would the morning have seen ? The morning would have dawned upon that level waste just as it was now—silent, empty, all its secrets sucked down and buried for ever and ever. A hideous and lingering death : the slow torture of the long and sombre hours, before utter exhaustion came, and despair, and a swooning into the unknown. She shivered a little : then she turned to the old grandmother, who was talking to Käthchen with such English as she could muster.

" Yes," she was saying, " my daughter, she over at Cruagan——"

" And so perhaps she did not speak to Mr. Purdie about the cow ? " Mary interposed. " Very well. That's all right. Little Isabel was telling me about the cow that was lost. Well, I will see that you have one in its place."

The old woman could not speak ; the withered, weather-wrinkled face wore a pained look, as if she were trying not to cry ; and she furtively wiped her hand on her apron and timidly held it out—it was by shaking hands that she could best express her thanks. And here was an extraordinary thing !—here was actual gratitude, the very first symptom of it that Mary Stanley had encountered since she came to the place. But the next moment she was saying to herself bitterly :

" Why ? Why is this old woman friendly ? Because

she saw that Mr. Ross of Heimra condescended to be civil to me yesterday evening. If he throws a word to me, then I am to be tolerated! But if I had come here by myself, I might have offered to double the size of her byre, and give her two cows instead of one, and there would have been nothing but sullen looks and silence. Was I not warned the moment I set foot in the place? It's Donald Ross of Heimra who is their laird. I am a stranger, and an enemy."

And now it was Kate Glendinning's turn to make a few discreet inquiries : for the allegation that a Highland gentleman would condescend to sale and barter was still rankling in her soul.

"Well, Mrs. MacVean," said she pleasantly, "that was very excellent brandy you gave us last night, and very welcome, too : I suppose we should have died of the cold and wet if you had not given us the hot drink. But where did you get brandy in an out-of-the-world place like this?"

An alarmed expression came into the old woman's face, though she endeavoured to conceal it. She looked away down the hillside, and said vaguely :

"It was—in the house. Oh, ay—in the house."

"Yes ; but where did you get it?" Kate asked.

There was a moment of silence—and distress.

"The brandy?—Mr. Ross—he ordering me to give it to you."

"Oh, yes," said the young lady, in the same off-hand sort of way, "and it was very thoughtful of him—and very kind of you. It seemed to bring us back to life again. I don't know what we should have done without it. I was only wondering where you got such good brandy in this part of the Highlands."

The old woman looked anxiously from the one to the other : were they trying to entrap her ?—even after their generous promise that she should have the cow.

"Oh, ay," she said, still clinging desperately to those evasive phrases, "the brandy—it in the house—and—and Mr. Ross, he ordering me to give it—and any one very pleased, whatever he wishes. And the ladies—very, very wet and cold—and a long weh home to Lochgarra—"

"Come, come Mrs. MacVean," Käthchen said, "you

ought to know that we don't want to make any trouble—
is it likely, just after Miss Stanley has promised to give
you the cow? I am asking only out of curiosity; and I
can keep a secret as well as any one. And of course we
are quite aware that it is Mr. Ross who brings the brandy
into the neighbourhood—and very properly, too, for good
brandy is better than bad whisky, and you must have
something in the house in case of sickness. Very well:
tell me what he charges you for it."

"Charges?" the old woman repeated, with a puzzled
air.

"Yes," said Käthchen, encouragingly. "I only want to
know for—for information; and I am not likely to tell any
one. What do you pay him for it?"

Then the old grandmother understood; and though she
did not say much, there was something in her tone that
showed how keenly she resented this imputation.

"Pay—Mr. Ross of Heimra—for the brandy?" said she,
as if it was herself who had been insulted; and she was
turning angrily away. "You think—the young master—
tekkin money from the like of me?"

"Then he gives you the brandy for nothing?" said Kate,
—and this question at once arrested the old dame, who
made answer somewhat sulkily—

"I not saying that—I not saying that at ahl."

"Of course not," said Käthchen, with cheerful good
humour. "It is not necessary for you to say anything.
But now I understand; and I am glad of it; for I have
Highland blood in my veins, myself, and I did not like
to think of a Highland gentleman taking money for little
kindnesses of that sort. And indeed I did not believe it;
and I am very pleased indeed that you have made it possible for me to contradict such a ridiculous story."

Shortly thereafter—the old grandmother having been
won into something of a more conciliatory mood by re-
iterated expressions of thanks and a circumstantial promise
with regard to the cow—the two young women left; and
as they descended the hill, Kate Glendinning was most
triumphant about this refutation of what she considered a
malignant slander. Mary, on the other hand, was inclined
to be coldly severe in her judgment wherever young Ross of

Heimra was concerned—though neither coldness nor severity formed part of her ordinary temperament.

"I don't see anything to be proud of, Käthchen" said she. "He is cheating the revenue, for one thing."

"Cheating the revenue," said Käthchen, in her matter-of-fact way, "is not likely to trouble a Highlander's conscience much. But I dare say he thinks the Government can get along well enough without taking any more taxation from these poor people; and I have no doubt he says to himself that if he pays for a bottle of good brandy for some poor woman with ague or rheumatism in her old joints, the Government can afford to let her have it without the duty. In a climate like this you must have spirits of some kind; and as I was saying to Mrs. MacVean, good brandy is better than bad whisky filled with fusel oil."

"I know perfectly well what his object is," Mary said, proudly and indignantly. "His object is simply to steal away the hearts of the people—and to stir up ill-will between them and whoever happens to be at Lochgarra House. They are all his friends—and my enemies. He can shoot and fish wherever he pleases; he has the run of the whole estate; he is welcome at every fireside; whilst I, when I want to lower the rents, and better the condition of the people in every way, and be their friend—well, I am kept outside at the door, and if I say 'Am I welcome?' there is no answer. For him—everything: for me—nothing. And I think it is hardly fair."

She spoke in a proud and hurt way, and her lips trembled for an instant: it was clear that she considered she had not deserved this ill-usage.

. "No, no, no, Mary," her friend protested. "You are unjust, as far as Mr. Ross is concerned anyway. For one thing it is very likely that the poor people about here were accustomed to look to his mother for little comforts when they fell ill; and he may be trying to carry out the same kind of thing, in the only way that would occur to a man." Then a demure smile came into Käthchen's eyes. "But I will be honest with you, Mary. I don't think it is done to spite you at all: although your family have wrought him and his sufficient wrong. But if you were to ask me if it wasn't done with a determination to spite Mr. Purdie

—in return for the destruction of the illicit stills—well, you see, people may act from various motives, and I shouldn't be surprised if that had something to do with it. As for stealing the hearts of the people—if you knew the curious loyalty and devotion of the Highlanders towards the old families, you would hardly think it necessary that Mr. Ross should have to make use of any bribe—— "

"But why should they hate *me*?" Mary exclaimed —and Käthchen had no answer.

However, if Miss Stanley had on one or two occasions suspected that the presence of the detested factor might have something to do with the failure of her efforts to cultivate amicable relations with her tenants, here was an opportunity of seeing what she could do by herself; for on their way back they again came to the small township of Minard, where the amphibious population were busy in the crofts and along the shore. She dismissed the carriage; and proceeded to make a few friendly little calls—guarding carefully against any appearance of intrusion, and, indeed, almost humbly begging for something of consideration and good-will. And she was resolved to take no heed of any surly manners or uncivil speech; for she was of a large, bland, magnanimous nature; and she had a considerable fund of patience, and gentleness, and sweetness, to draw upon. Then she had to remember that her uncle had been unpopular, and had no doubt amply earned his unpopularity. Moreover, a factor who stands between a wilful and domineering landlord and a tenantry not in the happiest condition, is most invidiously situated: he is the universal scapegoat, and is bound to be hated as well as feared. But here was she willing to make what atonement was possible; ready to sacrifice her own interests for the general good; and above all things anxious to make friends. With gifts in both hands, ought she not to have been welcome at every door? Then she was pleasant to look upon; her manner was gracious and winning; her eyes were kind. With the small children she could get on well enough: they knew nothing of any deep-slumbering feud.

But her charm of manner, her wonder-working smile, her unfailing good-humour, that had made life easy for her elsewhere, seemed to be of no avail here—with the grown-up folk, at all events. Not that they were rude : they were merely obdurate and silent. Of course, when she got this one or that pinned by a direct question, he did not absolutely refuse to reply ; but their answers were so contradictory, and their demands in most cases so impossible, that no practical enlightenment was possible. One man wanted more boats from the Government ; another said that more boats were of no use unless the Government supplied nets as well ; a third said boats and nets were valueless unless they had a steamer calling daily. There was also a demand that the Government should build more harbours ; and when Mary said, in reply to this, that she understood the harbours they had got—Lochgarra, that is to say, and Camus Bheag—to be about as excellent as any in the West Highlands, she was answered that the harbours were perhaps good enough—if there was a railway. Then there were some who did not seem to have any occupation at all.

"Don't you have anything to work at ? " she said, to one tall and rather good-looking young fellow, who was standing looking on at the women and girls gathering the sea-tangle.

"My father has a croft," he made answer, in a listless way.

"But wouldn't you," she said, in a very gentle and hesitating manner, so as not to seem impertinent, "wouldn't you rather go away and find some work for yourself ? "

"Aw, well, I was at Glasgow, and I was getting twenty shillings a week there."

"And you did not stay ? "

"Well, I could not live there," he said, simply enough. "It is no use getting twenty shillings a week if you cannot live in a place ; and in a few years I would be dead, if I was living in Glasgow. I am better to be alive here than dead in Glasgow."

"Then perhaps you go to the East Coast fishing ? " she suggested.

"No, I am not going there now. I was there one or two years, but it did not pay me."

"And don't you do anything ? " she asked again.

"Well, in January I am in the Naval Reserve."

"And the rest of the year you don't do anything ? "

"Well, my father has a croft"—and that was about all the information she could extract from him.

As a final attempt she said to him, timidly—

"If I were to try to get you a boat and nets from the Government, would it be of service to you ?"

"It would need eight of a crew," said he, with an obvious lack of interest, "and I would not be knowing where to find them."

However, a great surprise was in store for her : before getting back to Lochgarra on this occasion she actually encountered a human being who received her proffered friendliness and good-will with cheerful and unhesitating gratitude, and responded with a frank comradeship that quite won her heart. It is true the man was drunk ; but at first she did not perceive that ; and indeed she was ready to make ample allowances in her eager desire to establish pleasant relations with anybody, after the disheartening coldness she had just experienced at Minard. This man whom she and Käthchen overtook on their homeward way was a huge, lumbering, heavy-shouldered giant, with a prodigious brown beard and thick eyebrows, whose deep-set grey eyes (though a little bemused) looked at once intelligent and amiable. On his shoulder he had hoisted a rough wooden box ; and as he trudged along he smoked a small black clay pipe.

"Good-day to you !" said Mary to the giant.

"Aw, good-deh, good-deh, mem !" said he, with a broad grin of welcome, and he instantly put the pipe in his pocket.

"That is a heavy box you are carrying," said she ; "I wish I were driving, and I would take it along for you."

"Aw, it's glad I am I hef something to carry," said he, in a strong Argyllshire accent, "and I wass thinking that mebbe Miss Stanley herself would be for tekkin a lobster or two from me, for the house. Aw, I'll not be charging Miss Stanley mich for them—no, nor anything at ahl, if Miss Stanley would be for tekkin a lobster or two from me——"

"Oh, these are lobsters ?" said she, with the most friendly interest.

"Ay, chist that," said the giant.

"And you will be sending them away by the mail-cart?" she asked.

"Ay, chist that—it's to London I am sending them."

"Oh, really," she said. "All the way to London? Well, now, I wonder if you would think me inquisitive or impertinent if I asked you how much you get for them?"

"How much? Aw, chist two-and-sixpence the dissen," said he, in a good-natured fashion, as if he hardly expected to get anything.

But Mary was most indignant.

"What?" she said. "Two-and-sixpence the dozen? It's monstrous! Why, it's downright robbery! I will write to the London papers. Two-and-sixpence a dozen?—and a single lobster selling in London for eighteenpence or two shillings, and that a small one, too. Isn't it too bad, Käthchen? I will write to the newspapers—I will not allow such robbery."

"It is a long weh of communigation," said the big, heavy-shouldered, good-humoured-looking man; "and Mr. Corstorphine he paying ahl the carriage, and sending me the boxes."

"I will get you twice as much as that for the lobsters," said Mary with decision, "if I sell them among my own friends. I will guarantee you twice as much as that, and I will pay the carriage, and get you the boxes. What is your name?"

"Archie MacNicol, mem," said he; but the whisky had made him talkative, and he went on: "I am from Tarbert on Loch Fyne; I am not from among these people here at ahl. These people, they are not proper fishermen—aw, they are afraid of the sea—they will not go far out—I hef seen the East Coast men coming along here and tekkin the herring from under their very eyes. There is one of the Government boats that they got; and it is not paid for yet; and it is lying half-covered with sand at Achnacross, and no one using it at ahl. Ay, and the curers willing to give elevenpence a piece for ling. Ay, and I wass into Loch Hourn, and I got fifty crans of herring, and I wass curing them myself——"

"But wait a moment," said Mary, to whom this information seemed a little confused. "If you are not tired, won't

you keep on your way to the village, and we will walk
with you? You see, I am anxious to get all the information I can about this place; and the people here don't
seem to be very communicative—although it is altogether
in their own interests that I should like to make inquiries.
But they appear to be afraid of me—or there is some
quarrel, or ill-will, that I don't understand——"

"A quarrel with Miss Stanley?" said the lobster-
fisherman, deprecatiugly—for he was in a mellow and
generous mood, "No, no—he would be a foolish man that
would be saying that."

"Very well," said Mary, as they were all three going on
to the village, "tell me about your own circumstances.
I want to know how I can be of help to the people about
here. I have not come to Lochgarra to raise rents, and
collect money, and take it away and spend it in London.
I want to live here—if the people will let me; but I
don't want to live among continuous enmity and ill-will."

"Aw, yes, yes, to be sure, to be sure now!" said Archie,
in the most amiable way, and Mary was entirely grateful
to him for his sympathy—it was so unexpected.

"Tell me about your own circumstances," she went on.
"Is there anything I can do for you and the other lobster-
fishermen?"

"Aw, Cosh!" he cried (but it was the whisky that
was responsible: Archie himself meant to be most polite).
"Would Miss Stanley be doing this for us, now—would she
be writing a letter for us to the Fishery Board?"

"Oh, certainly," she answered with promptitude, "if
that will be of any service to you. What about?"

And here Big Archie (Gilleasbuig Mòr, as they called
him) in his eagerness to tell his tale, stopped short, and
deposited the lobster-box in the road.

"It's this way now—that there will be many a brokken
head before long if something is not done. For they are
coming from ahl quarters to the lobster-fishing—stranchers
that hef no business here at ahl; and they are building
huts; and where there is a hut there will soon be a house;
and it does not require the wise man of Mull to tell any one
the truth of that. Yes, and they will be saying they hef
the right from the Fishery Board; but as I am thinking

that is nothing but lies; for how can the Fishery Board give stranchers the right to come here and build huts on the crofts above the shore—ay, and going on, and paying no rent, either to Miss Stanley, or the crofter, or to any-one? And Gillie Ciotach and me, ay, and two or three of the young lads, we were saying we would tek sticks and stones, and drive them into the sea—ay, though there might be a bluidy nawse here and there; and others would be saying no, that it was dancherous to do anything against the Fishery Board. And would Miss Stanley be for sending a letter to the Board, to ask if it is lies those people are telling us, and whether they can come and build a hut whenever they like?"

"Certainly I will," said she. "Only, there is to be no fighting and bloodshed, mind. Of course, the space occupied by a hut is a very trifling matter; I suppose what you really object to is those strangers coming to your lobster-ground?"

"Ay, chist that!" said Big Archie, eagerly.

"Very well. It seems to me quite absurd to think that the Fishery Board should have given any one the right to build huts; however, I will inquire; and then, if I get the answer I expect, you must go peaceably and quietly to those people, and tell them they are mistaken, that they have no right from the Fishery Board or from any one else, and that they must leave——"

"Evictions!" said Käthchen, under her breath; she saw trouble coming.

"Quite peaceably and quietly, you understand," Mary continued; "there must be no broken heads or anything of that kind; you must tell the people what the Fishery Board says, and then they will see that they are bound to go."

"Ay, ay, chist whatever Miss Stanley pleases," said Big Archie; and therewith he shouldered the heavy lobster-box again, and resumed his patient trudge, while he proceeded to give Miss Stanley some further information about those marauding fishermen and their evil ways.

But when they were nearing Lochgarra, Mary, who had been rather silent and abstracted for some little time back, said to him—

"I suppose you have a boat, Mr. MacNicol?"

"Aw, ay, and a fine boat too," said Archie. "And if Miss Stanley herself would be wishing for a sail, I would bring the boat round from Camus Bheag."

"That is just what I have been thinking of," Mary said: they were now come in sight of the sea, and she was absently looking out towards the horizon.

"Ay, chist any time that Miss Stanley pleases, and I will not be charging anything," said the good-natured giant with the friendly (and bemused) eyes. "Aw, naw, there would be no charge at ahl—but chist a gless of whisky when we come ashore."

"Oh, I must pay you for your time, of course," said she, briefly. "I suppose you could bring your boat round this evening so that my friend and myself might start pretty early to-morrow morning? We should be ready by ten."

Käthchen turned wondering eyes upon her.

"But where are you going, Mamie?"

"I am going out to Heimra Island," she said.

CHAPTER VII.

THE PIRATE'S LAIR.

IT was a bold undertaking; and Käthchen hardly con cealed her dismay; but Mary Stanley was resolute.

"I must see my enemy face to face," she said. "I want to know what he means. Why should he stir up enmity and malignity against me? If he had any thought for those people who seem to regard him with such devotion, he would be on my side, for I wish to do every-thing I can for them. He ought to welcome me, instead of trying to drive me out of the place. And if he fishes and shoots over the Lochgarra estate simply to spite me, suppose I refuse to be spited? Suppose I present him with the shooting and fishing, on condition that he allows me to be kind to these people? How would that do, Käthchen? Wouldn't that be a fine revenge? I think that ought to make his face burn, if he has anything of gentle blood left in him!"

There was a vibrant chord of indignation in her tone, as there generally was when she spoke of this young man; for she did not think she was being fairly treated. But Käthchen, ignoring the true sources of her dismay, began to urge objections to this proposed visit, on the ground of social observances.

"I do really think, Mamie, it will look strange for two unmarried girls to go away out and pay such a visit—and—to that lonely island. Now if you would only wait until the Free Church Minister comes home, he might go with us, and then it would be all right. Not that the Free Church Minister is certain of a welcome—if the young man is what he is said to be; but at all events he would be a chaperon for us."

But Mary would not hear of waiting; she would challenge her secret antagonist forthwith.

"Very well, then," said Kate Glendinning, more seriously than was her wont, "if we do go, we must have some excuse; and you must tell him you have come to thank him for having got us out of that frightful bog."

Nor did the uninviting look of the next morning cause Miss Stanley to alter her resolve. It was hardly a day for a pleasure sail. The wind, it is true, had abated during the night; and there was not much of a sea on; but the skies were heavy and lowering; and dark and sombre were those long headlands running out into the leaden-hued main. But there was the lobster-boat lying at anchor, in charge of a young lad; and the dinghy was drawn up on the beach; and a message had just come in that Big Archie was waiting below to carry wraps and rugs.

"Käthchen," said Mary, sitting hastily down to her writing-desk, "I have discovered that the Fishery Board sits at Edinburgh; but I can't find out who are the members. Do you think I should begin 'My Lords and Gentlemen,' or only 'Gentlemen'?"

"I don't know," said Käthchen; "I should think 'Gentlemen' would be safer."

So, in happy singleness of purpose, Mary proceeded to write her letter about the alien lobster-fishermen—little thinking to what that innocent action was to lead; then she went and quickly got ready; and by-and-by the two girls were on their way down to the beach, accompanied by the gigantic and massive-shouldered Gilleasbuig Mòr. Big Archie, if the truth must be told, was moodily silent this morning : the fact being that on the previous evening he had wound up the day's promiscuous indulgence by "drinking sore," as they say in those parts ; and now his physical conscience was troubling him. But if his conversation was limited to monosyllables, and if he wore a sad and depressed look, he was, nevertheless, most kind and assiduous in his attentions to the two ladies ; and when he had rowed them out in the dinghy, and got them ensconced in the stern of the bigger boat, he did everything he could for their comfort, considering the rudeness of their surroundings. And presently, when the anchor was got up, Big Archie came aft to the tiller ; the young lad lay prone on the bit of deck forward, to keep a look-out ; and Mary and her companion knew they were now pledged to the enterprise, whatever might come of it.

Indeed the two girls were themselves rather inclined to silence. It was a gloomy sort of morning ; there was even a threatening of rain brooding over the distant headlands ; and the dark sea lapped mournfully around them, with not a single swift-glancing flash of white. But the light breeze was favourable, and they made steady progress, unfamiliar features of the coast-line becoming visible on right hand and on left as they made further and further out to sea.

It seemed a long and weary time—given over to dreamings, and doubtings, and somewhat anxious forecasts. But all of a sudden Mary was startled by the voice of the skipper.

"Will Miss Stanley be for going in to Heimra ?"

And then for the moment her courage failed her.

"What do you say, Käthchen ? Do you think—we should send a message—before calling—— ?"

"Oh, yes, certainly," said Käthchen, with eagerness. "That is certainly what we ought to do."

"Oh, very well, then," said Mary, turning to the steersman (but there was a flush of self-conscious shame on her cheeks), "you need not take us to the house—we will merely have a look at the island—and some other day we will come out, when we have told Mr. Ross before hand."

"Very well, mem," said Big Archie, holding on the same course, which was taking them by the south side of the island.

It was an angry-looking coast—steep and sheer—a long, low, heavy surge breaking monotonously along the black rocks. But when they got round the westward-trending headland, they gradually came in sight of the sheltered waters of the little bay, and of the sweep of silver beach, and the solitary cottage perched on its small plateau. And of course Käthchen's eyes were full of intensest interest, with something, too, of apprehension; for this (according to Mr. Purdie) was the pirate's den; this was the home of the outlaw whose deeds by night and day, by sea and shore, had gained him so dark a renown. But Mary's attention had been attracted elsewhither. She was regarding a white marble slab, placed high on the top of the cliff, facing the western seas.

"Look, Käthchen," she said, in rather a low voice. And then she turned to the silent little bay before her. "Poor woman!" she said. "It was a lonely place to live all those years."

Presently Mary bethought her of the errand that had brought her so far; and she repented of her irresolution.

"Can you take us into the bay, Mr. MacNicol?" said she, without staying to consult Käthchen.

"Aw, yes, mem, zurely."

"For it is a long way to have come—and—and I am anxious to see Mr. Ross."

"Aw, very well, mem," said Archie, at once altering his course.

And then she said, looking all round the bay—

"But where is the yacht?"

"Is it Mr. Ross's yat, mem? It wass lying in Camus Bheag when I wass coming aweh last evening."

"And was Mr. Ross on board?" Käthchen asked, with a quick sense of relief.

"Indeeed I am not zure of that," said Archie. "For mebbe he wass sending the men over to the mainland, and himself staying on the island."

" In any case, Käthchen, that need not matter to you," Mary interposed. " You can remain where you are, and I will go up to the house by myself. Why should you bother about my business affairs ? "

This was a view of the case that was not likely to commend itself to Kate Glendinning, who could nerve herself on occasion. When the lobster-boat had come to anchor, and they had gone ashore in the dinghy, she proceeded to walk up to the house along with her friend just as if nothing unusual was happening to her. She kept watch—furtively ; but her outward air was one of perfect self-possession. As for Mary, she was too deeply engaged in thinking how her complaints and demands were to be framed to heed anything else at this moment.

They knocked at the door, and again knocked ; after a little while the old woman Martha appeared—the surprise in her face being obvious testimony to the rarity of visitors to this remote island.

" Is Mr. Ross at home ? " Mary asked.

It was a second or so before Martha recovered from her amazement—for she had not seen the lobster-boat appear in the bay, nor yet the strangers come ashore.

" Oh, no—he is over on the mainland," said the trimly-dressed old woman. " What a peety—what a peety ! "

Mary was rather taken aback ; however, she said-

" It is not of much consequence, for, if he is on the mainland—or if he is in the neighbourhood—I daresay I shall be able to see him before he returns to Heimra."

And then she was about coming away when Martha interposed, with Highland courtesy.

" But would not the leddies come in and sit down for a little while—and hef some tea, or a little milk, or something of that kind ? Mr. Ross very sorry when he knows —to be sure—and a great peety him not here——"

" Oh, thank you," said Käthchen (whose face had lightened considerably when she heard of Donald Ross being absent), " it is very kind of you ; and I am sure I shall be very glad to have a glass of milk, if you will be so kind."

Käthchen wanted no milk ; but she suddenly saw before her a chance of having her curiosity satisfied without risk :

she would be allowed to see what kind of lair this was in which the savage outlaw lived. And so the unsuspecting Martha led the way; and the two young ladies followed her into the passage, and into the first room leading therefrom, which was a kind of morning-apartment and study combined. They seated themselves, and she left to get them such refreshment as the out-of-the world cottage could afford.

The two girls were silent; but their eyes were busy. The first thing that attracted their notice was a portrait over the mantelpiece—the portrait of a very beautiful woman, pale somewhat and dark, with refined and impressive features, and of a simple yet dignified bearing. A sad face, perhaps; but a face full of character and distinction: the first glance told you this was no common person who looked at you so calmly. Mary said nothing; Käthchen said nothing; but they knew who this was—the likeness was too obvious.

And as for the other contents of the room?—well, there were neither guns, nor rods, nor splash-nets, nor anything else connected with fishing or shooting, legal or illegal; but there was an abundance of books on the shelves that lined three walls of the apartment. Moreover, there was one volume lying on the table before them—beside a wooden pipe. They regarded this for some little time; but it was Käthchen who spoke first.

"Mary, would it be very impertinent if I looked?"

Mary Stanley laughed.

"I don't know," she said. "Most people do pick up things when they are left in a room. But we are in a peculiar position. We are here without the consent of the owner."

"Yes, that is so," said Käthchen, resignedly, and she remained still.

But she continued looking towards the book in a wistful way.

"It's only the title I should like to see," she began again. "What harm can there be in that? If Mr. Ross were here himself, I would take up the book in a minute— yes, I would! What do you say, Mary?"

"Well," said Mary, frankly, "I really should like to

know what kind of literature commends itself to any one living in a strange place such as this. But at the same time we are not his guests—we are intruders—or if we are guests, we are the housekeeper's guests, and it is but fair to her we shouldn't pry into secrets."

Käthchen had risen and gone across to the table: perhaps it would not be breaking the laws of hospitality if she could get a glimpse of the title of the book without actually laying hands on it? But the back of it was away from the light. In these desperate circumstances, Käthchen yielded to temptation; she hastily snatched up the volume, glanced at the title, and as quickly returned to her seat again.

"Good gracious!" said she. "That is fine entertainment for a lonely island—Joshua Williams's 'Real Property'!"

"A law book?" said Mary, with her face becoming suddenly grave. "I hope there is not going to be—any trouble—a lawsuit is such a dreadful thing——"

"Oh, no; I understand what that means," said Käthchen, "I know quite well. That is one of the books my brother had when he was reading up for the bar—I remember it because I spilt some ink over it, and he made me buy him another. I wonder, now, if Mr. Ross is reading up for the bar? Wouldn't that be a blessed dispensation of Providence for you, Mamie—if he were to go away and shut himself up in the Temple, and leave you Lochgarra entirely in your own hands, shooting, and fishing, and everything? Only," she added, "I don't quite understand how such a wild savage as Mr. Purdie described to us would be likely to get on with the Judges. I am afraid there would be scenes in court. What do they call dismissing a barrister?—not cashiering?—unfrocking?——"

Käthchen had suddenly to cease; for here was the elderly Martha, carrying a large tray amply provided with homely and wholesome fare—oatmeal cake, soda scones, marmalade, strawberry jam, fresh butter, and a jug of milk. And Mary did not pause before breaking bread in the house of her enemy; for she saw that the old housekeeper was anxious that her bounties should be appreciated; and besides, oat-cake and marmalade and fresh milk ought to recommend themselves to any healthily-constituted young woman. By and by, when Martha had left the room, Miss Stanley said—

"What shall I give her as we are going away, Käthchen? Half-a-sovereign?"

"Oh, for goodness' sake, Mamie, don't think of such a thing!" Käthchen exclaimed. "At any other time give her anything you like; but you must not pay for food in this house; you cannot imagine how offended she would be. She would take it as an insult offered to her master: she represents Mr. Ross in his absence—it is Mr. Ross who is entertaining us now——"

"Oh, it is Mr. Ross who is entertaining us?—yes of course," said Mary thoughtfully; and—perhaps without noticing the coincidence—she put down the piece of oat-cake she held in her hand, nor did she take it up again.

And furthermore, as they were going down to the boat—having made due acknowledgments to Martha for her hospitality—Mary walked as one in a dream; while Käthchen, rejoiced to have come through this dreaded ordeal with such unexpected ease, was in the gayest of humours. She did not notice her friend's reverie; she was chattering away about their foolhardiness in entering the savage's lair—about her surprise in finding no skulls and bones lying in corners—about the quiet and studious aspect of the place being a pretty cover for all kinds of dark and lawless deeds. Mary did not reply; once or twice she looked up to the white grave on the hill—she was thinking of other things.

But when they had all got into the larger boat again, and set out on their return voyage, Käthchen found a companion more of her own mood. The truth is that while the young ladies were being entertained in the front part of the house, Big Archie had slipped up to the back, had paid his respects to Martha, and had been presented, as is the custom in the west, with his morning dram. This welcome mitigation of his *Katzenjammer* had made a new man of him; and he was now disposed to be as talkative as hitherto he had been morose; so that, as he sate with his arm on the tiller, he was cheerfully telling the young lady all about himself, and his doings, and circumstances. And Käthchen, finding him thus sociable, and friendly, affected much interest, and plied him with appropriate questions.

"Do you keep a cow, Mr. MacNicol?" said she.

"Aw, now," said he, deprecatingly, "the young leddy will be mekkin me ashamed. It's chist Archie they'll be calling me."

"Very well, Archie—do you keep a cow?"

"I starve one," said Archie, with ironical humour.

"And a kitchen garden?"

"Aw, is it a garden? And you will not know that I wass tekken the prize for the garden, ay, more as three or four years? Well, well, now, there is no longer a prize given for the best garden, and it's a peety, too——"

"But tell me," said Käthchen, with some astonishment, "why was the prize stopped? It seems a very reasonable thing, a prize for the best kitchen garden among the crofters and fishermen—I'm quite sure Miss Stanley would give such a prize. Why was it stopped?"

Big Archie hesitated for a second or two; then he said, with a grin of confession—

"Well, now, I will tell you the God's truth, mem; for there's two ways about every story; and there's my way of it, and there's Mr. Purdie's way of it; and mebbe the one is true or the other. And this is my way of it: I wass gettin the prize—oh, yes, I will not deny that—year by year, and very proud I wass, too, of the cabbages, and the scarlet beans, and the like of that, and the thirty shullins of the prize a very good thing for me. And then kem the time the Minard crofters they were for sending an appligation to Mr. Stanley for to have the rents revised, and I put my name to the paper too; but Mr. Stanley he would do nothing at ahl—he said 'Go to Mr. Purdie.' Then Mr. Purdie he sees my name on the paper; and he says, 'Very well, there will be no more prize for the garden, and you can do without your thirty shullins.' It wass a punishment for me, that I wass putting my name on the paper. Now, mem, that is my story about the prize——"

"I think it was very shabby treatment!" Käthchen exclaimed.

"And that is the way I see my side of it," continued Big Archie, honestly; "but I am not denying there may

be another way.   Aw naw, mem, I want to tell you fair ;
and Mr. Purdie he would hef another version for you, if
you were to believe it——"

"Well, then, what is his version ? " said Käthchen—for
the time being rather priding herself on playing Mary
Stanley's part.

"Well, I wass speaking to Mr. Pettigrew, the minister,
and he wass speaking to Mr. Purdie, about getting the
prize back, and Mr. Purdie he says to Mr. Pettigrew, ' No,
I will not give the prize back ; for there was not enough
competition, and Archie MacNicol he wass always tekkin
the prize, and it wass the same as thirty shullins a year off
his rent.   The prize,' he wass saying, ' wass to encourache
ahl the people to attend to their gardens, and not to give
Archie MacNicol thirty shullins a year.'   And that's the
God's truth, mem, and both ways of the story ; but what
I will be thinking to myself is that there wass no talk of
stopping the prize till Mr. Purdie found my name on the
paper.   That's what I would be thinking to myself sometimes."

Käthchen glanced rather timidly at her friend.   But
Mary was still in that curiously abstracted reverie—her
eyes turned wistfully towards the now receding Eilean
Heimra—her thoughts remote.   So Käthchen merely said
in an undertone—

"Very well, Archie, I will put both versions of the
story before Miss Stanley, and I have no doubt she will
do what is right.   For my own part, I don't see why you
should be deprived of the prize simply because you keep a
smarter garden than the other people."

A great event happened this afternoon—nothing less
than the arrival from the South of Mr. Watson, the sheep-
farmer, Miss Stanley's principal tenant.   The two girls had
landed from the boat, walked along the shore, and were
just about turning off towards Lochgarra House, when
they were overtaken by some one riding a stout and ser-
viceable little cob ; and Mary instantly guessed who this
must be—for persons on horseback are rare at Lochgarra.
The stranger lifted his hat, but did not draw rein.

"Mr. Watson," said she—looking towards him with a
plain intimation that she desired to speak with him.

Mr. Watson immediately pulled up, dismounted, and came towards her, leading the cob by the bridle. He was a middle-aged man with a fresh complexion, grizzled hair, short whiskers, and shrewd blue eyes—looking prosperous and well-satisfied with himself, and with some little turn for jocosity about his firmly-set lips.

"I beg your pardon," she said, with a little embarrassment, " but—I wished to speak with you——"

" Miss Stanley ?—I am glad to make your acquaintance," said he, in a marked south-country accent. And he bowed to Miss Stanley's companion.

" Won't you come into the house for a moment or two ? " said Mary, with a vague notion that she ought to be polite to a tenant who paid her £1400 a year : moreover, she had ulterior ends in view. Mr. Watson consented ; Mary went and called a gardener, who took charge of the cob ; and then the two young ladies and the farmer proceeded up the stone steps, and through the hall, and into the wide hexagonal drawing-room in the tower. Then she asked him to be seated, adding some vague suggestion about a glass of wine and a biscuit after his ride.

" No, I thank ye," said Mr. Watson. "I am a teetotaller—not an ordinary thing in these parts. Ay, and a vegetarian. But I practise—I don't preach," he explained, with a complacent smile ; " so I do no harm to other folk. Both things suit me ; but I let other people alone. That's the fair way in the world."

" I wanted to ask you, Mr. Watson," said she, with a certain timidity, " whether you would be disposed to give up the pasturage of Meall-na-Cruagan ? "

In a second the shrewd and humorous blue eyes had become strictly observant and business-like.

" To give it up ? " he said slowly.

" I mean," she interposed, " at a valuation. I know it is yours under the lease ; we cannot disturb you ; nor should I wish to do so, except entirely with your own goodwill."

" Miss Stanley," said he, " I will ask ye a plain question : what for do ye want me to give up the Meall-na-Cruagan ? "

" The crofters——"

"Ay, ay, just that," said he, without much ceremony. "They've been at ye, in the absence of Mr. Purdie. Well, let me tell ye this: I am willing on my part to give up the Meall-na-Cruagan, at a fair valuation; but I warn ye that if ye hand it over to the crofters, they'll be not one penny the better off, and you'll be just so much the worse. Where are they to get the stock to put on it? They've enough grazing for what stock they've got."

"Yes, but it is not wholly that," said Mary. "I want to have them satisfied."

"Ye'll never see them satisfied, though ye gave them the whole Lochgarra estate for nothing," said this very plain-spoken person. "Surely ye are aware that the agents of the Highland Land League have been here, as they have been in every hole and corner of the Highlands; and while some of them have been making reasonable enough demands, others of them have been showing themselves nothing but irresponsible mischief-makers, firing the brains of these poor creatures with revolutionary nonsense, and trying to turn the whole place into another Ireland. Well, well, it's not my business; it's not for me to speak; but I warn ye, Miss Stanley, that giving up Meall-na-Cruagan will not satisfy them. What many of them want—especially what the more ignorant among them want—is for the landlords to quit the country altogether, and leave them the entire stock, lock and barrel of the estates—the land and all that belongs to it."

"I know," said Mary, quietly, "what the Land League have been doing; but if there had not been widespread discontent and distress they could not have done anything at all. And surely there was reason for the discontent; look at the reductions the Crofter's Commission have made—thirty and forty per cent. in some places. However, I am not concerned with the economic question of the Highlands generally; I am concerned merely with Lochgarra; and I want to do what is fair by the tenants; I want to see them satisfied, and as well-to-do and comfortable as the circumstances will allow. But what has been puzzling me since I came here," she continued—for this seemed a frank and well-wishing kind of man, and she was glad to have any sort of help or advice—"is that when I have spoken about lowering the rent, they have had nothing to say in reply. They seem rather to look to the Government for aid. Yet you would imagine that the lowering of the rent would be the first and all-important thing."

Mr. Watson smiled, in a condescending way.

"I think ye might understand why they would not complain to you about the rent."

"Why?" she demanded.

He hesitated—and there was an odd look on his face.

"I do not wish to say anything against friend Purdie," he observed.

"But I want to know the truth," she insisted. "How am I to do anything at all unless I know the exact and literal truth?"

"Well, well, let us put it this way," said Mr. Watson, good-naturedly. "There's some that would call Mr. Purdie a hard man; and there's some that would call him an excellent factor, business-like, thoroughgoing, and skilled in his work. It's not a nice position to be in at the best; it's not possible to please everybody. And there's different ways of dealing with people."

All this sounded very enigmatic. Mary could not in the least understand what he meant.

"I wish you to speak plainly, Mr. Watson," said she "You may be sure it will be in absolute confidence."

He considered for a moment. Then he said—

"It's of little consequence to me. Friend Purdie and I get on very well, considering; and besides I have my lease. But I'll just give ye an instance of what has happened on this estate, and you'll judge for yourself whether it's likely the tenants would come to you for a reduction of rent, or ask ye to interfere in any way whatever. It was about four years ago that one of the crofts over at Cruagan fell vacant. Very well. Then Mr. Purdie would have it that the pasture of that croft should be taken by the other Cruagan crofters, each one paying his share of the rent; while the arable land of the croft should be added to the Glen Sanna farm, which was also vacant just then. The Cruagan crofters objected to that arrangement; Mr. Purdie insisted; and at last the crofters sent a petition to Mr. Stanley, asking to have the arable land of the croft at well, or else to be let alone.   I am not saying anything against your uncle, Miss Stanley."

"But I want to get at the truth of the story, Mr. Watson," said Mary, firmly.   "That is the main point.   What happened?"

"I may explain that your uncle never interfered with Mr. Purdie," the farmer continued, rather apologetically, "and that's no to be wondered at.   Many landlords make it a rule not to interfere with their factor, for of course he's doing the best he can for the estate, and knows about it better than they can know themselves.   Then what happened, do ye say?   What happened was this—at the very next term every crofter that had signed the petition was served with a notice to quit; and that was only withdrawn when they undertook to pay, each man of them, £3 a year additional rent—that is 15s. for their share of the added pasture, and £2 5s. as a fine for having objected to Mr. Purdie's arrangements.   That's just what happened, Miss Stanley."

Mary was silent for a second or so—looking towards Käthchen, her eyes full of indignation.

"Why, it is one of the most abominable pieces of tyranny I ever heard of!" she exclaimed.   And then she turned to Mr. Watson.   "If people are treated like that, can you wonder if the Land League should find it easy to put revolutionary ideas into their head?"

"At all events," said Mr. Watson, with a shrewd and cautious smile, "ye will understand that they are not likely to apply to you for any lowering of rent.   They know the consequences."

"Ah, do they?" said she quickly.   "Well, I must show them that they are mistaken.   I must convince them they have nothing to fear.   They must learn that they can come to me, without dread of Mr. Purdie or anyone else. But," she added, with a bit of a sigh, "I suppose it will take a long time."

After some little further conversation, of no great moment, but marked by much civility on both sides, the farmer rose.

"Any time ye're passing Craiglarig, Miss Stanley, I should be proud if ye'd look in."

"Indeed I will," said she, going with him to the door, "But I must tell you now how deeply I am indebted to you. And of course what you have said shall be kept in the strictest confidence."

"I have told ye the truth," said he, "since ye asked for it. But just mind this, Miss Stanley—good factors are no that common; and friend Purdie understands his business. He drives a hard bargain; but it's on your behalf."

"Yes," said she, "and now I am beginning to see why it is the people hate me."

That same evening the two girls, who had been out for a long walk, were coming down the Minard road towards Lochgarra. The twilight was deepening; the solemn inland hills were growing slowly and slowly darker, and losing their individual features; the softly lilac skies overhead were waiting for the coming night. Silence had fallen over the woods, where the birches showed their spectral arms in the dusk, and where the russet bracken and withered grey grass were now almost indistinguishable. It was a still and tranquil hour; sleep stealing upon the tired world; a little while, and the far, wide, mysteriously-moving sea would be alone with the stars.

But for Mary Stanley there was no sense of soothing quiet, even amidst this all-prevailing repose. On the contrary, her heart was full of turmoil and perplexity; insomuch that at times her courage was like to give way; and she was almost ready to abandon the task she had undertaken, as something beyond her strength. And then again a voice seemed to say to her "Patience—patience—hold on your way—dark as the present hour may be, the day will dawn at last." And in Käthchen she had an excellent counsellor; for Käthchen had an admirable habit of making light of troubles—especially those that did not concern herself; and she was practical, and matter-of-fact, neither over-sanguine nor liable to fits of black despondency. On the present occasion this was what she was saying, in her cool and self-possessed way:

"You see, Mamie, I understand the Highland character better than you do. All that sullenness and ill-will doesn't arise merely from high rent and Mr. Purdie's tyranny—

though that no doubt has something to do with it. There are sentimental influences at work as well. There is the strong attachment towards the old family—very unreasoning, perhaps, but there it is; and there is resentment against those who have displaced them. Then there may be anger about your uncle for having destroyed the ancient landmarks; and injuries of that kind are not easily forgotten or forgiven. But every hour that I am in this place," continued Käthchen, as they were making home through the strangely-silent dusk, "I am more and more convinced that what Mr. Purdie said was perfectly correct—that young Donald Ross of Heimra is just everybody and everything to those people. He is all-powerful with them. Very well. I cannot believe that he has stirred up ill-will against you, or even that he wishes it to continue. He may do everything he can to thwart and madden Mr. Purdie—why not?—I would do that myself, if I were in his place!—but how can he have any wish to injure you? Then what I say is this: if you really mean to go and see him, put entirely out of your mind what you may have heard about his private character, and his poaching and smuggling, and remember only that his influence over those people could make everything quite pleasant to you. Don't go to him as you did this morning, as an enemy to be challenged and reproached: no, what you have to do is just to lower your pride a little, and tell him that you have come to beg for a favour. In fact I am convinced that a word from him would entirely change the situation. Mamie, are you going to ask for it?"

Mary Stanley did not answer: she walked on in silence.

CHAPTER VIII

FACE TO FACE.

SHE was out in the solitude of the woods, and she was alone. It was early morning, clear, and calm, and still; the sun lay warm on the silver lichened boulders that were dappled with velvet-green moss; the wandering air that stirred the pendulous branches of the birches brought with it a resinous odour, from the innumerable millions of opening buds. A profound silence prevailed, save for the hushed continuous murmur of an unseen rivulet, and the occasional distant call of a curlew.

A vague restlessness, and something even akin to despair, had brought her hither. For of course like other young people of the day she had coquetted with the modern doctrine that in times of trouble our great and gentle Mother Nature is the true consoler and comforter; she had read Wordsworth; and she had read Matthew Arnold upon Wordsworth:

> "He too upon a wintry clime
>   Had fallen—on this iron time
>   Of doubts, disputes, distractions, fears.
>   He found us when the age had bound
>   Our souls in its benumbing round—
>   He spoke, and loosed our heart in tears.
>   He laid us as we lay at birth
>   On the cool flowery lap of earth;
>   Smiles broke from us and we had ease.
>   The hills were round us, and the breeze
>   Went o'er the sun-lit fields again;
>   Our foreheads felt the wind and rain.
>   Our youth return'd; for there was shed
>   On spirits that had long been dead,
>   Spirits dried up and closely furl'd,
>   The freshness of the early world."

And now if she wished to forget the untowardness of human nature—if she wished to escape from her bitter disappointment on beholding her large and generous schemes met and checked on every hand by a sullen ingratitude— surely here was a seclusion that should have brought balm to her wounded heart. Moreover the morning light was cheerful; April as it was, a quiet warmth prevailed; she tried to please herself by recollecting that this fairy paradise actually belonged to her. And if human beings were so hard and unapproachable, why, then, she could interest herself in these harmless living creatures that were all so busy around her, under the quickening influences of the spring. From the dusty pathway in the opener glades the yellow-hammers were picking up bits of withered grass for their nest-building; black-caps swung back-downward from the sprays, to wrench the buds off with their bills; she stopped here and there to watch a beautiful beetle—

shining bronze, or opaque green with a touch of scarlet on
its legs ; a tiny grey lizard, with its small eye bright as a
diamond, lay basking on a shelf of rock, and remained
absolutely motionless, hoping to be passed unnoticed.
Then she came upon a little tuft of primroses—so shining
pale—so full of dim suggestions—and of associations with
the poets. Well, she looked at the primroses. They were
very pretty. But somehow she could not keep thinking
of them, nor of the fine things the poets had said of them.
The fact was, in her present straits her heart was craving
for human sympathy ; she wanted to be of some use in the
world : she wished to see eyes brighten when she appeared
at the door, however poor the cottage might be. Primroses
were pretty, no doubt—the firstlings of the year awoke
pleasant and tender memories—but—but why were those
people so obdurate ? No, there was no solace for her ;
the sweet and soothing influences of nature were intruded
upon, were obliterated, by the harsh facts and problems of
human life. With those men and women almost openly
declared her enemies, and with all her grand schemes gone
away, what good could she get from primroses ? And
so, humiliating herself with the conviction that she was
nothing but another Peter Bell, she passed on through the
woods, and eventually got down to the sheltered little bay
where she had first met Anna Chlannach.

And on this occasion also she was destined to make a
new acquaintance. She was idly walking up and down
the lilac and cream-hued beach—and trying to persuade
herself that she had found a refuge from the perplexities
and mortifications that seemed to surround her in the
busier world she had left—when a sound she had distantly
heard from time to time now rose in tone until there could
be no doubt about its nature : it was a human voice, proceeding from the neighbouring bay. She went as close as
she could to the intervening promontory ; then curiosity
led her stealthily to climb the heathery slope ; she made
her way between rocks and under birches ; and at last she
paused and listened. It was a man's voice, of an unnaturally high pitch, and curiously plaintive in its monotonous sing-song. In the perfect silence she distinctly
heard these words—

"Oh, my brethren, I charge you—I charge you by all that you hold dearest—that you keep the little children from the ruby wine!"

What could this mean? She pushed her way a little further through the thick underwood, and peered over. There was a small boat drawn up on the shore. Pacing slowly backwards and forwards on the shingle was a man of about twenty-eight or thirty, with a long and lugubrious face, a shaggy brown beard, and deep-set eyes. Sometimes his head was bent down, as if in deep thought; and then again he would raise it, and extend his arm, as if addressing the opposite side of the bay, or perhaps Eilean Heimra out at sea; while ever and anon the curious feminine falsetto came back to the admonition—"Oh, my brethren, keep the little children from the ruby wine!"

Mary began to guess. Was this the Minister? Had he returned home; and had he seized the first opportunity to come away over to this solitary place, to rehearse his sermon for the following Sabbath, with appropriate intonation and gesture? She listened again:

"'Who hath woe? who hath sorrow? who hath contentions? who hath babbling? who hath wounds without cause? who hath redness of eyes?' Ah, my friends, now that I have addressed each section of the community, each member of the family circle, now we come to the little babes —those tender flowers—those blossoms along the rough roadway of life—smiling upon us like the rainbows of the morning—and bedewing the earth with their consecrated tears. When I behold those gems of purest ray serene," continued the Minister, in his elevated chant, "my soul is filled with misgivings and sad prognostications. I observe in my daily walk the example that is set before them; the fathers in Israel are a stumbling block to their own children; nay, even of the wisest it has been said, 'The priest and the prophet have erred through strong drink, they are swallowed up of wine, they are out of the way through strong drink; they err in vision, they stumble in judgment.' My friends, is it not a terrible thing to think of these blessed babes—these innocent tendrils sprouting up into glorious flowers, even as the Rose of Sharon and the lily of the valley—to think of them babbling with red mouths curses they cannot comprehend? Hold them back, I say! Snatch the fatal goblet from them! Let pleasure wave her ambrosial locks when and where she pleases— let mirth and joy prevail—but when the timbrel sounds and the cymbal is heard in the hall—then, at all events let those innocent ones be restrained from the deadly snare —keep, oh, keep the little children from the ruby wine!"

Unluckily this last appeal was addressed to Mary herself, or at least she thought so in her fright when she found the Minister's eyes turned towards her: instantly she bobbed her head down in the heather, and remained hidden there until the sermon—or perhaps it was a temperance lecture? —was ended. It did not last much longer. After the sonorous sentences had ceased, there was a moment's silence; then a grating on the beach; then a measured sound of oars: she concluded that the Minister, his flowery harangue rehearsed, was now making for home again; and she was free to get up from her concealment and return to Lochgarra House.

"Käthchen," she said, "the Minister has come back. I have seen him—though I—I didn't speak to him. Now don't you think we ought to go along and make his acquaintance at once? He might help us: you say yourself the Free Church Ministers have an enormous influence in the Highlands."

Kate Glendinning did not receive this proposal with any great enthusiasm.

"There is one thing he might do," said she, "as I told you before, Mamie. It would be much easier for us to go and see Mr. Ross, if the Minister would take us under his escort."

"Mr. Ross!" said Mary, impatiently. "It is Mr. Ross, and Mr. Ross, with you from morning till night, Käthchen! You would think he owned the whole place!"

"Yes," said Käthchen, demurely, "that is just what he seems to do."

However, the interview to which both the young ladies had looked forward with so much anxiety came about in the most natural way in the world; and that without any intervention whatever. Mary and Käthchen, being down in the village, had gone into the post-office to buy some packets of sweets—bribes for the children, no doubt; and they were coming out again from the little general store when, in broad and full daylight, they met young Ross of Heimra face to face. There was no escape possible on either side; he was going into the post-office; they were coming out; and here they were, confronted. Well, it must be admitted that at this crisis Mary Stanley's presence of mind entirely forsook her. Ten hundred thousand things seemed to go through her brain at once; she could not speak; confusion burned red in her cheeks and on her forehead. And then he was so pale and calm and collected; for a second he regarded them both—and with no furtive glance; he slightly raised his peaked cap, and would have passed them without more ado. It was Käthchen who made bold to detain him.

"Oh, Mr. Ross," said she, breathlessly, "we have never had an opportunity of thanking you—you left the cottage before we knew—and—and it was so kind of you to send the carriage——"

And here for a moment Käthchen also lost her head, for she had a horrible consciousness that when a man has saved your life it is ridiculous to thank him for sending a carriage. And then those coal-black eyes were so calmly observant; they were not generously sympathetic; they seemed merely to await what she had to say with a respectful attention. But Käthchen bravely began again: "You—you must not think us ungrateful—you see, you had left the cottage before we knew—and when we went out to Heimra, we did not find you at home——"

"I am sorry I was not there," he said.

"And—and of course we knew quite well what a dreadful position we were in—I mean that night when we wandered into the morass," continued Käthchen. "But for you we never should have got out again—we dared not move—and in the darkness what could we have done?"

"It is a dangerous place," he said.

"I—I am going to give Mrs. Mac Vean a cow in place of the one that was lost," Mary now ventured to put in; and here was she—the bold, the dauntless, the proud-spirited one!—here was she standing timidly there, her face still suffused, her eyes downcast. And this little speech of hers was like a plea for merciful consideration! He turned to her.

"The Mac Veans have had a bad time of it since the shepherd died," the young man said, in a distant sort of way—but he was regarding her curiously.

Then all of a sudden it occurred to Mary that she ought not to stand there as a suppliant. Some sense of her wrongs and her recent trials came back to her; and here was the one whom she suspected of being responsible—here was her secret enemy—the antagonist who had hitherto concealed himself in the dark.

"I hope the widow will condescend to accept it, but who can tell?" said she, with greater spirit. "Really, they are the most extraordinary people! They seem to resent your trying to do them a kindness. I have been offering them all sorts of things they stand in need of; I am willing to lower their rents; I am going to arrange for more pasture; I propose to give prizes for the best home-spun materials; and I would pay for getting over some of the Harris people, if instruction were wanted in dyeing or weaving—but they seem to suspect it is all for my own interest. I make them these offers—they will hardly look at them!"

"You may teach a dog to love you by feeding it," said young Donald Ross, coldly; "but the Highlanders are not dogs."

At this she fired up—and there was no more shamefaced girlish blushing in her cheeks. Her eyes were as proud as his own.

"They are human beings, I suppose," said she, "and a human being might at least say 'Thank you.' But I do not know that I blame them," she continued—to Käthchen's great anxiety. "It seems to me there must be secret influences at work about here. It is not natural for people to be so ungrateful. Self-interest would make them a little more—a little more—amenable—if it were not for some evil instigation at work among them. And what can any one gain by stirring up ill-will? What can be the motive? At any rate, whatever the motive, and whoever he is, he might consider this—he might consider the mischief he is doing these poor people in making them blind to their own welfare. It seems a strange thing that in order to gratify envy, or hatred, or revenge, he should sacrifice the interests of a number of poor people who don't know any better."

Käthchen glanced apprehensively from the one to the other; but there was no flash of anger in those dark eyes, nor any tinge of resentment in the pale, olive-tinted face. The young man maintained a perfectly impassive demeanour —respectful enough, but reserved and distant.

"I wish them nothing but good," Mary went on, in the same indignant way, "but how can I do anything if they turn away from me? Why do they not come and tell me what they want?"

"Come and tell you what they want?—when they daren't call their souls their own!" he said.

"Of whom are they afraid, then?" she demanded.

"Of your agent, Miss Stanley," said he (and here indeed Käthchen did notice something strange in his eyes—a gleam of dark fire in spite of all his studied restraint). "What do they care about philanthropic schemes, or how can you expect them to talk about their wants and wishes, when what they actually know is that Purdie has the face of every one of them at the grindstone?" He altered his tone. "I beg your pardon. I have no right to interfere —and no wish to interfere. If you should think of coming out again to Heimra, Miss Stanley, to have a look over the island, I hope I may be at home. Good-morning!"

He again raised his cap—and passed on into the office. Mary stood undecided for a moment; then moved slowly away, accompanied by Käthchen. Before them was the wide sweep of the bay, with Lochgarra House at the point, and its background of larches. The sea was calm; the skies clear; it was a peaceful-looking morning.

Of a sudden Mary Stanley stopped—her eyes full of disappointment and vexation.

"Everything is at sixes and sevens—and worse than before!" she exclaimed to her companion. "What did I say, Käthchen? What did he say? Wasn't he very insolent?—well, not that, exactly—not exactly insolent— but—well, I am not used to being treated with disdain. Why did he break off like that—with everything unsettled?

Wasn't he very insolent?—or, at least, disdainful?—what did I say that he should treat me like that?"

"I know this," said the frivolous Käthchen, "that he has the most splendid eyes I ever saw in a human creature. I call him just distressingly handsome!"

"There is nothing so contemptible as a beauty man," said Mary, impatiently. "What has that got to do with it? I want to know why he treated me like that!"

"I thought he behaved with very great courtesy and self-respect," Käthchen made answer, "considering that you plainly intimated to him that it was he who stirred up all that ill-feeling against you."

"Very well: he had nothing to say for himself!" Mary exclaimed. "He made no defence. And then, you see, I—I wasn't quite prepared—I did not expect to see him—and I forgot about the fishing and shooting, or that might have made him a little ashamed of himself, and a little less arrogant." She turned and looked towards the post-office. "I wonder whether that was a map that he had rolled up in his hand or a chart? If he is going on board his yacht again, he must pass this way. I cannot have things left as they are—worse than ever!"

"I don't see how you are to mend them at present," said Käthchen. "If you had kept on as you began, in that friendly way, it might have been all very well; but then you grew indignant, and almost charged him with being the mischief-maker. And I must say I think he behaved with very great consideration and courtesy."

"Do you really think so?" said Mary, quickly—with her eyes still fixed on the post-office. And then she hesitated. And then she said: "Come, Käthchen, let us go back. I wish to make an apology to him."

"Mary!" her friend protested. "How can you think of such a thing!"

"Oh, but you do not know. It is not about anything that has just happened. It is about the lake and the old castle. I quite forgot. And perhaps it is that that makes him so unforgiving. I must tell him that I am sorry."

But Käthchen shrank back.

"Make an apology for that?" said she. "You don't seem to understand, Mary. It is too serious for an apology.

If you murder a man's father or mother, you can't go to
him and say, 'I am very sorry.'"

"Will you go on to the house, then, Käthchen?" said
Mary, simply. "I must put myself right with him—and
after that he can be as disdainful as he chooses."

Of course Käthchen refused to be released; she went
back with her; and just as they reached the little building,
young Ross of Heimra came out. He had neither chart
nor map in his hand now; whichever it had been, he had
no doubt sent it away by post.

He seemed a little surprised; but was just as attentive
and respectful as before.

"There was something I forgot to say," she began,
with obvious embarrassment, "and—and it is difficult to
say it It was not till I came here that I knew what
my uncle had done—about—about Loch Heimra—and
Castle Heimra. Well, there are some injuries, my friend
here says, that can never be repaired. I suppose that is
so. But at least you will allow me to say that I am sorry
—more deeply sorry than you can imagine perhaps——"

"And there are some things that are best not spoken
of," he said, calmly.

"Yes, I daresay that is so," she made answer, with a
hopeless feeling at her heart that his tone and manner
were alike implacable. "No doubt that is so. And yet—
yet some little consideration might be shown towards any
one who wishes to express regret. It was none of my doing;
it never would have been of my doing. And though you,
of course, would rather hear no apology—would rather
not have the subject mentioned—still, there is another
thing. The people about here—if they have any resentment
against me because of the pulling down of Castle Heimra
—then that is not fair. And any one having influence
with them—well, it would be ill done of him to stir up
anger against me on that account. I had nothing to do
with it—I am very sorry it ever happened."

"Miss Stanley," said he—for he plainly did not wish to
speak of this thing—"I think you are mistaken in supposing that any one is stirring up ill-will against you; and
even the most ignorant of the people must know that you
are not responsible for what happened before you came

here. As regards myself, I do not wish for any apology or expression of regret ; I wish for only one thing—forgetfulness. I think in such a case silence is the only amends."

So they parted for the second time ; and when the two girls had gone some way towards Lochgarra House, Mary said,—

"Yes ; but all the same I told him I was sorry."

And then again she turned and looked. Donald Ross had passed through the village, and was now going up to the Free Church minister's cottage.

"Käthchen," said she, rather absently, "there are a good many of them about here who seem to hate me ; but I know there is not one of them who hates me as he does. And what had I to do with the pulling down of Heimra Castle ?"

And that afternoon, as she stood at one of the windows in the tower, looking away out to sea, she saw the little white-winged yawl making for Heimra Island. She knew who was at the tiller—the man before whom she had abased herself, craving, and craving in vain, for some word of consideration and sympathy.

"Proud and implacable," she said to herself ; and her wounded spirit was sore within her, and perhaps a trifle indignant, too ; but she would make no further utterance. He had asked for silence and forgetfulness ; and he had the right to say what was to be.

Meanwhile the message that Mary had sent to the Fishery Board in Edinburgh had been duly received and considered ; and when, after two or three days' interval, the answer came back to Lochgarra, it was to the effect that the alien lobster fishermen had either been misinformed or were making wilful mis-statements : the Fishery Board had not given them the right to build huts, and, indeed, had no power to confer any such right. At once Mary sent for Hector the head-keeper ; and bade him seek out Archie MacNicol, and convey to him this news.

"And tell him from me," she said, "that all he has to do is to explain to these men that they have no right to come here and build huts and use the fishing-grounds that naturally belong to the crofters in possession ; and that they must go—and go peaceably."

"Would Miss Stanley be for having a sheriff's officer over from Dingwall?" suggested the tall and handsome keeper, in his serious way.

"No, no, not at all!" she said. "The men must go, when they learn they have no right to be here. And if they refuse to go, haven't we got our own policemen?"

"Very well, mem," said Hector, and he left.

It was towards the dusk of evening, and raining heavily; but all the same Hector found Big Archie at work in his little bit of a garden. When Archie heard the news, he struck his spade in the ground, and stood upright.

"Aw, that's the fine news!" he exclaimed, joyfully, in Gaelic. "And we will soon be putting an end to the squatters now, Hector! Was I not saying it myself that they had no right to come here?—but now there is the message from the Fishery Board; and we will soon have the devils away from the lobster-ground. And when there is good news coming, you will be for taking a dram with me, Hector?"

Well, it is said that there was once a Highland keeper who refused a glass of whiskey; but his name and neighbourhood are not known now. Hector followed Big Archie into the cottage, and there a black bottle was produced. Thereafter, the two men, having lit their pipes, set out through the dark and wet again, for Hector was returning to his own home, and Archie was going a certain distance with him in search of the Gillie Ciotach.

The stiff glass of whiskey had warmed Big Archie's heart; and as he strode along, the huge and heavy-shouldered giant grew garrulous.

"The young lady that has come here," said he, in his native tongue, "you know as well as I do, Hector, she means very well, but it is not the place for her at all. I say it is not the place for her at all. What can a young lady know about the price of sheep and the price of lobsters? It is a foolish thing! The place for her, now, Hector, that place is London, at the court of the Queen, among the great ladies, in their fine clothes and jewels. You think I do not know about such things; but I do know; for I myself have relations with London; and it is from London I am hearing every fortnight, from Corstorphine. And the other day, when she was in my boat, I was saying to myself 'There is a fine and beautiful lady to be sitting in a coarse lobster-boat; and it is at the court of the Queen she ought to be; and not going about asking people to put in better chimneys, and the like of that. A woman—a woman has no right to be at the head of an estate; and I am not sure that the law allows it; maybe she is here only through Purdie, and he the master of the estate. Just think of that, Hector—if it is only Purdie that keeps out Young Donald from the estate: would not that be a thing to be considered? Now you know I am not from this place myself; I am from much further south; but I am a Gael; I have no love for any Albannach or Sassunnach coming into this country against the wishes of the people; and if it is only Purdie, aw, God, it's myself that would willingly give Purdie a crack on the head. And think of young Donald of Heimra coming into the estates, would it not be a grand day that, Hector?—ay, and many a gun fired off, and the bagpipes, and flags, and taking the horses out of the carriage. Sure I am the Gillie Ciotach would go mad that day."

The mention of the Gillie Ciotach recalled the keeper to his own immediate affairs.

"If you see Gillie Ciotach, Archie," said he, "perhaps you will give him a word of caution. The other evening I heard a shot up by the Crom-allt; and I did not look. But the next time I hear a shot, I will look; and if I catch Gillie Ciotach, I will break his gun over his head, yes, and I will shoot his thief of a dog, too; for I am not going to get myself into trouble on account of the Gillie Ciotach. This you know, Archie, that when old Mr. Stanley was here, there was not much goodwill; and perhaps some of us may have shut our eyes a little; but things are different now; for here is my sister Barbara telling me again and again that the Baintighearna is the kindest lady she has ever known in the world, and that it is not at all what Purdie wishes to have done that she means to have done. Well, well, that is not my business; but my business is to look after myself; and I am not going to get into trouble on account of Gillie Ciotach."

At this point the two parted; and Big Archie went on

to the inn. But he did not enter by the front door ; he passed round by the stable-yard, and made his way to a small lighted window that was partly open. He peeped in and listened at the same time—with a grin of satisfaction on his face, for he had found what he sought.

There were three men in this little sanded parlour, which was a sort of adjunct to the inn. They were seated round a table on which was an oil-lamp ; and in front of each man stood a small pewter measure and also a glass. Two of the men were middle-aged, and of a sailor-like type ; the third was a young fellow of about four-and-twenty, whose bronzed complexion, regular features, and short-cropped, curly brown hair made him rather good-looking, only that in regarding him one did not notice these things so much as the dare-devil expression of both eye and mouth. He also was dressed in something of a sailor-like attire ; while his broad Balmoral bonnet, pushed far back on his brown curls, revealed the fact that in his earlier youth he must have received a mighty slash along the side of his forehead. This was the Gillie Ciotach ; and the Gillie Ciotach was singing—in high and nasal tones, while his two companions listened solemnly. Yet this was not really a melancholy song, this *Linn an aigh*, for it described the happy state of affairs that existed long ago, when the heather yielded abundance of honey, and the pastures abundance of milk ; when there was no rent to pay, when any one could fish or shoot wherever he pleased, and when there was neither hatred nor fighting, nor thirst of wealth. Indeed, there was perhaps a touch of sarcasm in the verses ; for the refrain informed whosoever might wish to know at what period of the world's history this golden age existed that it was *An uair bha Gàilig aig na h-eòin*— that is to say, *When all the birds in Gaelic sang.* However, whether the song was or was not intended to be merry, the audience received it in precisely the same fashion : when it ended, the one said ' Ay, ay' in a sad tone ; the other sighed deeply ; and then each mechanically proceeded to pour out a glass of whiskey. The Gillie Ciotach did likewise ; by all three the whiskey was drunk in absolute silence ; there was a pause of internal meditation—and at this point Big Archie thought fit to open the door and enter, for he had been long enough out in the rain.

And no sooner had he told his story than the dare-devil leapt to his feet, a wild delight in his eyes.

"Aw, *Dyeea*, this is a fine thing !" he cried, sniffing the battle from afar. "I tell you now we will make short work of it—we will drive the squatters into the Minch, and if the devils can swim across the Minch, let them swim across the Minch, and if they cannot swim across the Minch, they can go to their master below. Come away boys, and make the preparation ; for there will be a gay dance to-morrow !"

The big giant caught him by both shoulders, and threw him back into the chair.

"Did you hear me ?" said he (but there was an ominous mirth in his eyes too). "Peaceably, peaceably ; the Baintighearna says peaceably—they are to go peaceably."

"Aw, is it peaceably ?" the Gillie Ciotach cried, with a loud laugh. "Well, if they will go peaceably, that is very good ; but if they will not go peaceably, then we will make them sing a little song to-morrow—by God, Archie MacNicol, will make them sing 'Farewell to Fiunary,' and maybe it is on the wrong side of their mouth they will be singing the 'Farewell to Fiunary !'"

CHAPTER IX.

THE BATTLE OF RU-MINARD.

ALL that night there was marching and counter-marching, and whipping up of recruits, and drinking of whiskey, and singing of *Gabhaidh sinn an rathad mòr.** Big Archie and his peaceful, or pseudo-peaceful, counsels were no longer heeded ; the movement had been taken up by the younger fellows, headed by the mischievous Gillie Ciotach ; and the belief became general that orders had been received from the Fishery Board in Edinburgh to the effect that the Ru-Minard squatters were forthwith to be driven into the sea. And if the aliens should refuse to be so driven—

---

* "We will take the highway."

should stand up in defence of their little bits of homesteads—what then ?

"It is a lesson they will want," said the Gillie Ciotach,
gaily, to his comrades (they were having a friendly glass
together, in a barn lit up by a solitary candle), "not
to come thieving on other people's lobster-ground, and
building huts wherever they like, and not a penny of rent
to the holder of the croft. It is a lesson they will want;
and it is a lesson they will get—to take back home with
them, and keep the others from coming here. Well, now,
this is my opinion, that the best thing for giving a man
a rap over the head is a tiller—a tiller with a handle to
it—aw, that is a fine convenient thing !"

"I am going to take an oar over my shoulder," said a
brawny young Hercules.

"And the more fool you, then," said the Gillie Ciotach,
who was a blunt-spoken youth. "For I will tell you this,
Feargus : if you strike at a man with an oar, and he steps
aside so that you miss him, then he has you at his mercy—
it does not need a wise man to show you that. Aw, God,
a tiller is a fine thing, when the wood is strong—it is a
tiller that will be my *orra-an-donais* * to-morrow." He
broke into a loud laugh. "We will teach them to be
telling lies about the Fishery Board !—and it is little they
are thinking now that to-morrow they will be singing
Farewell, farewell to Fiunary ! "

In the morning it was found that the rain had ceased ;
but worse than rain was threatening ; for all along the
west the skies were of a heavy and thunderous purple—
a louring dark wall, as it were—while torn shreds of grey
cloud were being blown along in advance, the precursors of
a gale. Mary and Küthchen were both at the window,
looking out at the angry heavens and the livid sea beneath,
when the maid Barbara came quickly into the room.
For the moment Barbara had lost her pretty shyness of
manner ; she was breathless and excited ; her eyes were
full of apprehension.

"Oh, mem," she said, " do you know what is happening ?
They have gone aweh up the road, a great many of the

* *Orra-an-donais*—an amulet for sending one's enemy to perdition.
Donais is Satan.

young lads, and others ; and they have sticks with them ; and they are singing *Gabhaidh sinn an rathad mòr*.   Oh, I am sure there is harm coming of it ! They were saying something of the strange fishermen out at Ru-Minard— and there will be fighting."

A sudden dismay filled Mary's heart—dismay, and a curious sense of helplessness. To whom could she turn for aid in such a crisis—and with every moment a thing of value ?

"Barbara," she said quickly, "I must have some one to go with me.   Is Hector there ?"

"No, mem, he went up the hill this morning."

"Or Hugh ?"

"No, mem, he was going over to Cruagan, to arrange about the heather-burning, so I was hearing him say."

Then Mary turned to her friend.

"Käthchen, who is there ? Shall we ask the Minister ?"

"Of course, he is the very person to ask—if you really mean to go, Mamie.   But do you think you should ?" Käthchen asked, with serious eyes.   "It sounds like an open riot."

"I don't care—I must try what I can do—for I fear I am responsible," Mary said, in a kind of desperation ; and then she turned to the young Highland lass : "Barbara, we shall want the carriage at once—as soon as ever the horses can be put to. Tell Sandy we are going over to find Mr. Pettigrew ; he can come along and meet us. Tell him not to lose a second."

And almost directly afterwards the two girls were out-of-doors, hurrying along to the other side of the village, where was the Minister's cottage. Käthchen was unmistakeably frightened ; but all the same she ventured to say—

"Well, Mamie, your friends in London have almost given up asking when you are going to marry your cousin —you have kept him at arm's length so long. But I think if Mr. Meredyth were here just now, he would have a very good chance."

"Why ?" said Mary, with a certain coldness.

"Because you want a man's assistance and advice," said Käthchen. "Isn't it as clear as daylight ? The moment this news comes, you look round for some man to help you. Is the head-keeper there? No. Or the under-keeper? No. Then you think of the Minister—anybody so long as he is a man. All quite natural, of course. Only I think if Mr. Frank Meredyth were here—and you finding yourself in constant trouble and perplexity—well, I think he would soon take up a very important position. He might even persuade you to let him send in to Inverness for a wedding-ring."

"People don't get married in order to make peace among their tenantry!" said Mary, a little proudly.

"Is he coming here in August?" asked the shrewd Käthchen.

"Fred wants me to ask him," Mary said, briefly; indeed, at such a time she was not thinking of any suitor; she was thinking of what might even now be going forward on the shores of Minard Bay.

The Rev. Mr. Pettigrew received the intelligence of the rising with a calm and gentle compassion.

"Dear me, dear me!" he said, in his high-pitched, un-natural voice, and he thoughtfully stroked his long and straggling beard. "What a sad thing to think of, when brethren might be living together in peace and ahmity! The heart of man is full of dangerous possibeelities—it is a sad thing to think of—at this season of the year, when all nature seems to know that the verdant spring is around us—when all is harmony and peace—to think that angry passions should arise in the heart of man—"

"Yes, but won't you come at once, Mr. Pettigrew?" said Mary, with distress in her eyes. "We may be able to do something to prevent bloodshed. The carriage will meet us—we may be able to overtake them."

But the Minister paused to consider.

"No doubt," said he, reflectively, "to prevent the shedding of blood is an admirable thing, a commendable thing, and praiseworthy. But there are times and seasons when even the wisest counsel is of no avail—when the heart of man is as a fiery steed, untameable, not to be bridled; and in these times and seasons, what is demanded of us is a judeecious sympathy, a constant sympathy, a sympathy that does not take sides, but longs for the return of peace and goodwill. Strange, indeed, that at this time of the year—"

"But won't you come with us at once, Mr. Pettigrew?" Mary said, in her despair. "The carriage will meet us. We must try what we can do. You see, I am in a measure responsible. I told them what the Fishery Board had said—that the stranger fishermen had no right to build huts—and—and I hoped they would go away quietly— but if there is to be fighting, then surely it is the Minister who should come and try to make peace."

"Ah, the carriage?" said Mr. Pettigrew, thoughtfully, as he took down his hat from a peg in the lobby. "That is well considered—well considered. For if in their anger these misguided craytures should take to throwing of stons, the carriage could be closed. Ay, ay, that is very well now ; and if their wrath should be intemperate—for who can gauge the stubbornness of man?—then the carriage can be driven away at any moment. But what a sad thing to think of—sad thing !—when all might be dwelling in peace and ahmity—in peace and ahmity."

However, it was no consideration of personal safety that was uppermost in Mary Stanley's mind at this moment ; indeed, so anxious was she to overtake the rioters that she and her two companions had very nearly got back to Lochgarra House before they met the carriage. Then the horses were turned round ; and on they drove—past the brawling stream—past the larch woods—and up to the height commanding a view of Minard Bay. And here, at the top, they encountered the first human being of whom they could ask the news. It was John the police- man. The plump, roseate, good-natured Iain was calmly seated on a low wall by the roadside ; and he was uncon- cernedly regarding the wide stretch of white sand across which some small black figures were now seen to be in motion.

"What are you doing here, John?" said Mary, in- dignantly.

"I was just looking," said Iain, with an amiable smile— and he glanced in the direction of the people crossing the white sands.

"Yes, but why are you waiting here?" said she. "Don't

you know that there is likely to be fighting? And it is your duty to prevent that!"

"They will be telling me," said Iain, slowly and comfortably, "that the strange fishermen have no right to be in the place. Very well, then. And if they are to be put out of the place, it's not for me to interfere. If they are wrong, let them go aweh; and if they will not go aweh, they will have to be put aweh."

This seemed a sound argument—to John.

"But what did the Lochgarra people say to you as they went by?" Mary demanded. "Didn't you see they were armed with sticks? Don't you know there will be fighting and bloodshed?"

"Aw, there may be a brokken head or two," said John, with a demure smile.

"Well, it is your duty to prevent that! These men have no right to take the law into their own hand. If the strangers will not go peaceably, they must be removed by the law—not by beating them with sticks. And you are standing back here—and letting them do what they like!"

"And if they tek to fighting," said John, "it's not me that can stop them."

This also seemed painfully true.

"But you can do something," she insisted. "You can warn them. You can take their names. You can threaten them with a prosecution. You can tell them that—that —Mr. Pettigrew, who is it that prosecutes here?—the Sheriff at Dingwall?"

"Nay, but I am considering that there is much of reason in what John says," observed the Minister, in his lofty sing-song; "and perhaps we should do well to follow his example, and remain as spectators and witnesses. I perceive that this carriage cannot be closed; and therefore I do not think it would be prudent—rather would it be rashness and culpable rashness—to go forward amid a storm of angry passions. Surely it would be more prudent for us to remain here, with the constituted representative of law and order?"

"But I am not going to remain here. John," she said, peremptorily, to the young policeman, "get up in front. Sandy, drive on quickly; we may get between those people yet, before the mischief has begun."

And so the horses went forward again—rattling away down the stony hill until they reached the soft and sandy road skirting the bay. The little township of Minard was quite deserted, save for the women, who stood in small groups in the fields, or at the cottage-doors, watching what was going forward out there towards the long headland. Not that they could see very much, once the black figures had crossed the white breadth of sand; for the morning was dull and sombre; and the rocks of Ru-Minard, along which the crofters and fishermen were now making their way, were dark. But this much was obvious, that at a certain point the crowd stopped; while two of their number went forward—one of these being of gigantic size.

"This is Big Archie," said Mary, almost to herself, "and I warned him that he must get them to go away peaceably."

And no doubt it was as a deputation carrying peaceful proposals that Big Archie and his companion were now going forward to certain huts scattered just above the rocks, where also a number of dark figures could be dimly descried. Peaceful or not peaceful, the negotiations at all events involved delay; and this delay enabled the party in the carriage to drive along the road as far as was practicable; then the horses were stopped, and Mary got down to follow the rioters on foot. It was in vain that the Minister sought to dissuade her with plaintive remonstrances; she intimated to him that he could remain in the carriage if he chose. Käthchen, on the other hand, though she was thoroughly frightened, had but the one and sole idea—to remain by Mary Stanley's side, whithersoever she went. As for the easy-going Iain, he was distinctly inclined to hang back.

"What can I do?" said he, with occult amusement in his eyes. "If they will brek one another's heads, how can I prevent it? If it is right that these men should go aweh, and if they will not go aweh, they cannot complain if they get their heads brokken for not going aweh."

But Iain's humorous indifference did not last very long. Mary, hurrying forward, and with eyes anxiously straining, could make out that the two men were now returning to their friends; presently the blustering wind blowing in from the sea brought a sound of confused and prolonged cheering; and she now perceived that the scattered assemblage was moving on. At the same moment there was the sharp report of a gun; and then it was that the policeman's face grew grave.

"Is there going to be murder?" said he.

She did not answer him; she was running now—and Käthchen by her side.

"We must—go right into the middle of it," she said, panting for breath, "and then—perhaps they will stop."

At first the Lochgarra and Minard fishermen advanced but slowly and cautiously upon the huts, not knowing where the enemy might mass himself. The fact is the aliens had been taken unawares; for while they were as determined as men could be to defend their homesteads, they had no time to seek for arms, supposing they could have obtained any, while up here on the rocky knolls there were no stones. They were running hither and thither about the huts, picking up any bit of wood or any broken oar they could find; but when they made a sort of group of themselves, to await the onset of their antagonists, it was clear that timber had failed them, and other weapons they seemed to have none. But there they stood, dauntless, sullen, silent—the sea behind them—their outnumbering foes in front.

And now the invaders knew what was expected of them. It was a shrill cry from the Gillie Ciotach that led the great hoarse volume of their cheers; and then, with all kinds of minatory exclamations, they rushed forward on the devoted band. Who could resist this whirling, tempestuous, compacted shock? For two or three wild seconds there was inextricable confusion; and snap here, snap there, cudgel met cudgel, or descended on solid crown; but it was all over directly; and the next phase of the battle was that the aliens, as if by one common impulse, had turned and fled—fled pell-mell down the rocks and towards the shore, their foes pursuing with fierce and joyous cries. And here it was that Mary Stanley made her appearance—breathless, dishevelled—trying to throw herself in the way of Big Archie, who was leading the pursuit "Archie!" she called to him. "How dare you! Let those men alone! I command you!"

But very little indeed did Big Archie care for her commands; it was another consideration altogether that at this moment caused himself and his companions to pause. For the fugitives, as soon as they gained the beach, had taken refuge behind two boats drawn up there; and as the boats, with their spars and sails astern, and their lobster-creels and barrels at the bow, offered excellent shelter, while the beach afforded unlimited ammunition, the battle was not yet over. In truth, the stones that were now flying through the air decidedly checked the ardour of the pursuers; and it was at this moment that Mary again got up to Gilleasbuig Mòr.

"Archie!" she said, indignantly.

An accidental stone struck her on the shoulder. She did not mind. But another and a sharper one struck her on the wrist; and inadvertently she drew up her hand with a piteous little cry. She had been cut over the bone; blood was flowing profusely; and at sight of that, Big Archie—his eyes blazing with wrath—seemed to go mad altogether.

"Aw, *Dyeea!*" he cried; and he ran forward and leapt into the boat, on to the middle thwart; he sprang out on the other side; and began to lay about him with his cudgel as with the hammer of Thor, smiting and scattering his enemies in all directions. But she was after him in a moment—nimbly getting round the stern of the boat—and before he had wholly wreaked his vengeance, she had him by the arm. And here her interposition did save bloodshed; for the men, finding her between Big Archie and themselves, refused to throw the stones they had hastily picked up; quietude was secured at least in this corner of the battlefield.

But indeed the general interest had already been attracted elsewhere. When Mary turned to see what was going on landwards, she happened to notice certain small wavering shreds of pink. It was a very pale pink; on a clear day, it would hardly have been visible; but against the lurid sky it was distinct enough.

"What is that?" she said, with a sudden, conscious fear, to Big Archie.

The huge, heavy-shouldered fisherman (who was keeping an eye on his discomfited foes as he led the way round the stern of the boats) glanced towards the rocky knolls that had been the scene of the first onslaught, and said grimly —

"It wass the Gillie Ciotach he wass bringing a can of petroleum with him this morning, and lobster-creels will be easy to set on fire."

"Do you mean to say they are burning down those poor men's huts?" she demanded, in a perfect agony of helplessness. "Archie, what is to be done? Why does not the policeman interfere?"

"Aw, it is no use now," said Big Archie, with much composure. "They are ahl on fire already—and a good job too!—for we won the fight, and that is a proper end to it."

"And this is how you have kept your promise to me!" Mary said, in accents of bitter reproach.

"As sure as death, mem," said the big good-natured giant, "I wass doing everything Miss Stanley said—peaceably, peaceably. When I went to them this morning, I wass saying to them 'You hef no right here.' They said, 'We hef the right here.' I said 'It's no use telling lies; for Miss Stanley she has written to the Fishery Board; and they hef given you no right whatever.' And then I says 'It is a fine thing for you to come here and tek what piece of land you want, and build your houses on it, and you not paying a penny of rent to the man that has the croft.' Then they said 'The land is not worth anything; it is only rock' Then I says 'That is not your business, as you know very well; and other people have to pay rent for it, whether it is rock or good land; and it is impudent men you are to come and tek things for nothing. I am from Tarbert on Loch Fyne,' says I, 'and it's stealing they would be calling that down there.' Well, mem, they were not liking that—"

"I should think not!" said Mary. "Is that what you call asking them to go away civilly and quietly?"

"But they would not go aweh at ahl, mem!" Archie protested, still looking towards those pink shreds of flame (and alas! for the poor discomfited aliens—they had

K

emerged from their shelter, and gone a few yards up the beach, and were also regarding, hopelessly enough, the distant crowd and the work of destruction). "They were growing more and more impudent, mem; and they said they would not go aweh; and I said we would drive them aweh; and they said we could not do it. And then says I to them 'Do you see the carriage yonder?—for if you can mek out the people, it is the proprietor herself, and the Minister, and the policeman, and they are come down to see that you go aweh from this place altogether, and, by God, if you do not go aweh, we will drive you into the sea, and set fire to your houses.' 'You cannot do it,' says they—"

"But how dared you tell them that we had come down for any such purpose," said Mary, indignantly, "when we only came to prevent violence?"

"And how wass I knowing that, mem?" said he cunningly. "But I am sure there wass only the one end to it in any case, when they began to pick up the sticks. And we were not going to hef the land stolen, and the lobster-ground tekken up, and be beaten as well; for a man cannot stand everything, and we had sticks as well as they had sticks—"

"And so you began to fight in spite of all I told you!" she said. "And I do not know what harm has been done or how many have been hurt. You yourself, you would have been murdered if I had not come round by the boats and dragged you away."

"Is it murdering, mem?" said Big Archie,. with a grin. "Aw, Cosh, there would hef been some murdering going before they murdered me!"

And now they came upon Käthchen, who was standing as one paralyzed, gazing upon the excited crowd who were collected round the burning huts, and listening to their shouts and laughter. The moment she turned, she caught sight of Mary's hand, and uttered a quick cry of alarm.

"It is nothing, Käthchen," her friend said, "only I wish you'd tie this handkerchief round my wrist—and pull it tight; it will hurt less then."

"What made you go away down there, Mamie?" said Käthchen, in her distress. "I—wanted to stay by your side—but—but I could not face the stones. It was madness—"

"They did not intend to strike me," said Mary (whose shoulder was aching cruelly, as well as her wrist). "These poor men, they have nothing left now but their boats." And then she demanded: "But where was that booby of a policeman?—why did he not prevent them setting fire to the huts? And where is the Minister?"

Käthchen did not know; nor did she care much; all her interests were engrossed by the strange scene being enacted up there among the rocky knolls. For, despite the petroleum, and the heaping-on of lobster-creels and float-barrels, the huts did not burn well; the rain of the previous night had soddened the thatch, and perhaps the interiors were none too dry at the best of times; so that the incendiaries had to keep opening up draught-holes, or flinging on more petroleum, in order to encourage the flames. And then again that proved too slow work for their impatience. They got poles and broken oars to use as battering-rams; they charged the ineffectual doors, and tore down the smouldering roofs; and when the demolition of this or that rude dwelling was complete, there were loud and triumphant cheers. Mary did not seek to interpose. It was too late now. She looked on sadly, wondering what the poor wretches down by the boats were thinking, and not without some half-terrified consciousness that she was answerable for all this wreck and ruin.

"It is shameful!—it is shameful!" she said—almost to herself.

"Well, mem," said Big Archie, who still remained with the two young ladies, "I will ask you this—when you will find a wasps' nest in your garden, what will you do? You will not be for going forward and telling them they were right in tekkin' up the place, and that you will not disturb them; aw, no!—I think it is a bunch of straw you will be carrying to the place, and setting a light to it, and putting the nest on fire. Aw, Cosh, that is the sure weh to get rid of them—"

"But these were not wasps—these were men like yourselves," said she, sharply. "They have as much right to live as you—"

"Ay," said Big Archie, scratching his head in assumed

perplexity, "mebbe they hef as much right to live as wè hef—but *not there.* For it wass Miss Stanley herself thnt would be saying that."

Mary's face flushed.

"I told you they were wrong in thinking they had any right to be there; but I did not tell you to go and break out into lawlessness and set houses on fire with petroleum. Do you think that can be allowed? Do you think there is no government in this country? Do you think you can do just as you please? I tell you, the Sheriff from Dingwall will have to inquire into this matter."

Gilleasbuig Mòr did not like the mention of Dingwall.

"If it was brekkin the law," said he, rather gloomily, "it wass not us that wass brekkin it first. It was them fishermen. And now they can go aweh hom; and if they ever think of coming back here, they will remember the day they sah their houses on fire at Ru-Minard."

The work of demolition was now complete. Smouldering thatch and blackened rafters strewed the ground; nothing remained erect but the rude stone walls; the alien colony had lost its habitation. And then the invaders formed once more into a sort of irregular procession; they shouldered their staves and clubs; three ringing cheers were given—as a significant message to their vanquished opponents, who still remained down by the boats; and then the victors set out on their homeward march, the Gillie Ciotach's shrill voice leading off with "*Gabhaidh sinn an rathad mòr,*" * while a rough and ready chorus was volunteered by the straggling ranks. Mary Stanley and Käthchen, accompanied by Big Archie, slowly followed, some distance intervening. In truth, Mary's heart was as lead: all things seemed to be going so ill—in spite of her most patient and unselfish endeavours.

* The chorus of this gay ditty has been thus Englished:

   ' We will take the good old way,
    We will take the good old way,
    We will take the good old way,
    The way that lies before us,
    Climbing stiff the heathery ben,
    Winding swiftly down the glen,
    Should we meet with strangers then,
      Their gear will serve to store us."

And now they came upon Iain the policeman—bland, benign, complacent as usual. Iain had remained some little way apart, to let the rioters go by ; his share in the day's proceedings had been limited to a discreet and not unamiable observation.

"What are you doing here ? " said Mary. " Why did you not interfere before they had set the huts on fire ? Don't you see the mischief that has been done ? "

There was a whimsical, demure smile in Iain's eyes.

" I could not be tekkin up all them men, ' said he.

" Then what are you put here for at all ? " she demanded. " Why did they send you to Lochgarra if you have no authority ? What use are you in the place ? "

Iain was far too smooth-tempered to take any umbrage. He did not even claim to be of any use.

" Aw, well," said he—and he lifted up a bit of dry seaweed and slowly pulled it to pieces, " the people about Lochgarra, there is not much harm in them."

" Do you call that no harm—setting fire to houses ? "

Iain hesitated—for he wished to be very respectful.

" But if the fishermen had no right to build the houses ? " he ventured to say, with downcast eyes, and in the most propitiating tones. " And it was Miss Stanley herself who was telling them that."

" Did I tell them to set the houses on fire ? Did I tell them to go and fight with sticks and stones ? I told them to go and try to get those people away peaceably ; and instead of that, here they break out into open riot, and work all the mischief they can, and you stand by and look on ! "

" Aw, well," said Iain, pulling away at the seaweed, " there is not much harm done. There is not more than one or two has got a knock."

The hoarse, triumphant chorus—

> " *Gabhaidh sinn an rathad mòr*
> *Gabhaidh sinn an rathad mòr*
> *Gabhaidh sinn an rathad mòr*
> *Olc air mhath le càch e !* "

was growing more distant now ; the men were ascending the hill, towards their own homes—or still more likely they were going on to the village, to have a good, solid dram after this great exploit. And here was the wag-gonette, and Mr. Pettigrew therein, apparently confining his attention to certain slips of paper. When the two young ladies appeared and got into the carriage, the Minister put away his MS.; and when the horses had started for home, he lifted up his high and feminine voice, and said—

"It is a sad sight we have seen to-day—a sad sight—angry passions surmounting what should be the calm of the Christian soul—and among those who might well be living in peace and ahmity. And it is well for us who can keep apart, and view these things as a passing vision, and comfort ourselves with pious thoats. 'For they that sleep sleep in the night; and they that be drunken are drunken in the night. But let us, who are of the day, be sober, putting on the breastplate of faith and love; and for an helmet, the hope of salvation.' As for those poor men out at Ru-Minard, I fear they will be as the beasts of the field and the birds of the air in the matter of habitation; but they must seek for higher things; they must say to themselves 'For here have we no continuing city, but we seek one to come'!"

"You might have gone and tried to save their houses for them!" Mary exclaimed, bitterly.

But she would say no more. Indeed, she was silent all the way home. A sense of helplessness, of failure, of despair weighed upon her; all her fine courage and heroic spirit seemed to have fled. When they got to the top of the hill at Minard, she turned and looked towards the long promontory beyond the bay; and there was still a little smoke showing here and there amongst the smouldering ruins. In spite of herself tears rose to her eyes. This was the climax of all her splendid schemes. This was what she had been able to do for the neighbourhood that had been entrusted to her. Might it not be said of her—

> "The children born of thee are sword and fire,
>   Red ruin, and the breaking up of laws?"

How long was it since she had come to Lochgarra?—and this was the end.

But as they drove on, they came in sight of Lochgarra

Bay ; and out there was Eilean Heimra. And no sooner
had Mary Stanley's eyes lit on the distant island than
something seemed to stir her heart with a proud indignation ; and if she had spoken, as she dared not speak,
she would have said—

"Ah, it is you, it is you out there who are responsible.
It is not I. It is you alone who have control over these
people ; and yet you go and shut yourself up in selfish
isolation ; and leave me, a woman, to contend, and strive,
—and break down !"

CHAPTER X.

A VISITOR.

BLACK night lay over sea and land ; there was a low continuous murmur round the rocks and shores ; and out
here, at the end of the little wooden quay, two men were
slowly pacing up and down in the dark. They were the
serious-visaged Coinneach Breac and his taller and younger
companion Calum-a-Bhata. The whereabouts of the village,
across the bay, was revealed by a solitary light in one of
the windows : no doubt the man who looked after the pier
was enjoying the comfort of his own home as long as was
possible, before coming down to make ready for the expected steamer.

The influence of the hour was upon Coinneach.

"I will tell you this, Calum," he was saying, in his
native tongue—and speaking in rather a low tone, as if he
did not wish to be overheard—"that there are many
strange things happen to them that have to watch through
the night ; and they are never mentioned ; for it is not
safe to mention them. You do not know who may hear—
perhaps some one at the back of your shoulder. And the
speaking of such things is harmful. When I was telling
you, Calum, about the Woman and her overtaking me as I
was on the way home from Ru Gobhar, well, it all came
over me again, and it was as if someone had me by the
throat again, and I could not move, no, nor say some good
words to get free from her and escape. But I will tell
you of another strange thing now, that did not happen

to me, so that I can talk of it, and without danger to anyone. It happened to my uncle, Angus Roy, that used to be out at Ardavore Lighthouse. Ah, well, now, if they would only speak, it is the lighthouse-men that could be telling you of strange things—ay, like the ringing of the fogbell on clear nights, and the men looking at each other. Well, now, about my uncle, Calum; you know the men at the lighthouse have little occupation or amusement when they are not attending to the lamps; and sometimes, when it was getting dark, my uncle would go away down the iron ladder on to the rocks, and he would have a rod and a stout line and a big white fly, and he would go to where the water was deep, and maybe he would get a lythe or two for his supper. Well, one night, he came up the ladder, and when he came in he was nearly falling down on the floor, and he was all trembling, and his face was white. 'Duncan,' says he, 'I have been bitten by a dog.' 'You are dreaming, Angus,' said the other, 'for how could there be a dog on the Ardavore rocks?' 'See that,' says my uncle, and he was holding out his hand. And there, sure enough, was the mark of the dog's teeth. 'It was trying to pull me into the water,' says he, 'and when I escaped from it, it followed me, and when I got up the ladder, I looked down, and there it was, with its fore-paws on the first rung, and its eyes glaring on me. God help us all this night, Duncan,'—that is what my uncle was saying, 'if there is a dog on the island.' Now you know, Calum, there is no whiskey or brandy allowed in the lighthouses, except for medicine; and Duncan MacEachran, he was the captain of the lighthouse, and he went to the chest and got a glass of brandy for my uncle, and says he, 'Drink that, Angus, and do not think any more of the dog, and in the morning we will search for the dog'—and so that was all for that night. Then the next day they searched and searched, and there was not any sign of a dog; for how could a dog get out to Ardavore, that is fourteen miles from the mainland? And another thing I must tell you, Calum, is that the marks of the dog's teeth on my uncle's hand they were almost away the next morning, and white. Very well. Duncan would think no more of it; and my uncle would think no more of it; and the marks would go away altogether. But now I will tell you what happened, and you will see whether it would not make a strong man afraid. As the evening came on, my uncle he was getting more and more uneasy; and he was looking at his hand; and the marks were becoming red now, instead of white. My uncle he could not sit still; and he could not do his work; what he said was, 'Duncan, it is the dog coming for me, to drag me into the water.' Then says Duncan, 'How can he come for you? How can he climb up the ladder? But when it is the same hour that you were down on the rocks last night, then I will look out and see what I can see.' And he did that. He opened the door, and looked down; and there was the dog, with its fore-paws on the first rung of the ladder, and its eyes glaring up. I can tell you, Calum, he did not wait long; he was himself like to fall down with fright; and when he got the door closed again, he put in all the iron stanchions as quickly as he could. And then he went and sate down. My uncle he was a little better by this time. 'The dog has gone away now,' says he. 'I know it. But to-morrow night it will be back—and the next night—and the next night—until it drags me into the water. What is the use of fighting against it, Duncan? I might as well go down, and be drowned now; for the dog is coming back for me.' But Duncan would not say that. He said 'I will contrive something. Perhaps it is not only drowning that is meant. And a man must not give up his life.' And Duncan MacEachran was right there, Calum," continued Coinneach, in an absent kind of way, "for you know what the pro-verb says—'*There may be hopes of a person at sea, but none of one in the grave.*' Very well, then, the next day he went into the store-room and he searched about until he found a trap they had brought out to see if they could get an otter; and during the afternoon he took down the trap to the rocks, and he was placing it at the foot of the ladder, and concealing the most of it with seaweed. But do you know what he put into the trap, Calum? No, you do not know; and if you were guessing for a hundred years, you would not guess. He put a New Testament— ay, that is what he was putting into the trap—a New

Testament with a dark cover, in among the seaweed 'Because,' says he, 'if he sets his foot in the trap, then he will be caught, and we will see what kind of a dog he is ; but if he is a kind of dog that cannot be caught in a trap, then the New Testament will burn his foot for him, and we will hear of him no more.' That is what he was saying to my uncle. Then the evening came, and my uncle he got worse. He could not sit still ; and he could not do his work. The marks on his hand were red again ; and he knew that the dog was coming. Duncan MacEachran, perhaps he was frightened ; but he would not say he was frightened ; all that day, my uncle was telling me, Duncan was hardly speaking a word. My uncle he was sitting in the chair, and looking at his hand, and moaning ; and the redder and redder grew the marks ; and at last he got up, and says he, 'Duncan,' says he, 'something has come over me ; something is drawing me ; will you open the door, for I have no strength to open the door ?' His teeth were chattering, as he was telling me long after, and himself shaking, and sweat on his forehead. 'No, by God, Angus,' says Duncan, 'I will not open the door this night —nor you either—and if you come near the door, it will be a fight between you and me.' 'I am not wishing for any fight,' says my uncle, 'but there is something in my head—and I would like to look down the ladder—to see what is at the foot of the ladder.' 'Be still, for a foolish man !' says Duncan. 'Would you fall and smash yourself on the rocks ?' Well, the time was come. My uncle's teeth were chattering ; but he did not speak now ; he was sitting and moaning, for he knew the beast had put something over him, and was coming now to claim him. And then they were listening ; and as they were listening there was a terrible clap of thunder, and another, and another—three there were—and then silence. My uncle was telling me he did not speak ; and Duncan looked at him. They waited a while. And then my uncle rose, and says he, 'Duncan, the beast has gone away. Do you see the marks ?—they are white now.' And perhaps, Calum, you would have opened the door and gone down the iron ladder to see what had happened at the foot of the ladder —although it was dark—and the dog might still be there ;

but let me tell you this, that if you had been living in a lighthouse, you would not have gone down; for the men who live in the lighthouses they think of many things. It was not till the next morning that they went down the ladder; and do you know what was there ?—the otter-trap was closed together, and yet there was nothing in it. Do you see that, now—that the trap had closed together and caught nothing; but I am thinking that the beast, whatever kind of beast it was, had got a fine burn on his foot when he touched the New Testament. I am thinking that. And the marks on my uncle's hand, they went away almost directly; and the dog was never heard of again : I tell you, Calum, I tell you it was a clever thing of Duncan MacEachran to put the otter-trap and the New Testament at the foot of the ladder. But those men at the lighthouses, they come upon strange things, and they will not always speak of them, because it is safer not to speak of them."

"I am glad I am not at a lighthouse," said Calum, slowly ; and thereafter for some little time the two men walked up and down in silence.

The dim red light in the distant cottage went out; and presently another and stronger appeared — moving along by the side of the shore. They watched its course as it drew nearer and nearer; then in the silence of the night they could make out footsteps; finally, with a slow tramp along the wooden structure, the pier-keeper came up —and greatly surprised was he to find the two men there.

"Well, it was this weh, Thomas," said Coinneach, in English, "Calum and me we were thinking it was as easy waiting here for the steamer as on board the yat, and less trouble in pulling ashore in a hurry. And the steamer, will she be late now, do you think ?"

"Oh, yes, indeed," said the pier-keeper, as he proceeded to sling up the big lantern he carried, "for there has been heavy weather in the south. And you might have been sleeping in your beds for some while to come."

Coinneach did not like this reproach.

"Then perhaps you are not knowing what it is to have a good master," said he, " or perhaps you are your own master, which is better. But listen to what I am telling you now :

if my master wishes to have things put on board, or brought ashore from the steamer, then it's me that is willing to wait up half the night, or ahl the night, to be sure to catch the steamer; for I know he will seh when I go out to the yat again, 'Coi.neach, go below now, and have a sleep.' That is when you have a good master; but if you had a bad master, would you be for walking up and down a dark pier through the night? It's me that would see him going to the tuffle first!"

"Can you give me a fill of a pipe, Coinneach?" asked the pier-keeper; and then he added facetiously: "for they say there's always plenty of tobacco at Eilean Heimra."

"Ay, are they sehing that?" answered Coinneach, as he drew out a piece of tobacco from his waistcoat pocket. "And mebbe they'd better not be sehing that to me, or they'll have to swallow their words—*and the bulk of my fist as well!*"

The three men sate and talked together, and smoked; and as the time went by, a faint, half-bluish light began to appear over the low-lying hills in the east; the cottages across the water became visible; there were gulls flying about. The dawn broadened up and declared itself; something of a warmer hue prevailed; a solitary thin thread of smoke began to ascend from one of the chimneys. The pier-master lowered his lantern and extinguished it. And yet there was no sign of the coming steamer—no far-off hoarse signal startling the silence of the newborn day.

Then, as the morning wore on, and the sleeping village awoke to life, Coinneach said:—

"I think we will pull out to the yat, Calum, to see if the master will be for coming ashore; and if we should hear the steamer we can turn back."

"Very well, then, Coinneach," said the younger man, "for sure I am the master will be wanting to come ashore to meet the steamer."

And away they went to the boat. But indeed all Lochgarra was astir this morning; for it was not often the villagers had a chance of seeing the steamer come in by daylight; and in any case it was a rare visitor—once in three weeks at this time of the year. So that the long-protracted booming of the steam-pipe brought even the old women out to the doors; and by the time the two red funnels were sighted coming round the distant headland, quite a small crowd of people had come down to the quay.

And here were the two ladies from Lochgarra House, hastening along to be in time: why should they not also join in the general excitement? But just as they arrived at the pier Mary Stanley suddenly stopped short: the very first person she had caught sight of—among that straggling assemblage—was the young laird of Heimra Island.

"Mary, you are not afraid of him!" said Käthchen.

It was but a momentary irresolution, of which she was instantly ashamed; she continued on her way; nay, she went boldly up to him, and past him, and said "Good morning!" as she went by.

"Good morning!" said he—and he raised his cap; that was all.

Then, after a second of vacillation and embarrassment, Mary turned—he was barely a couple of yards distant.

"Mr. Ross," said she, "I suppose you—you heard of what happened at Ru-Minard."

"Yes, I am sorry you should have been troubled," he said, in a formal kind of way.

"But they have built up the huts again!" she exclaimed. "And I suppose the people here will go back and burn them down, and there will be riot after riot —never ending!"

He did not answer her: indeed, there was no question to answer. And Käthchen, standing a little bit apart, was watching these two with the keenest interest, and she was saying to herself—"Well, she has met her match at last. She has been all-conquering hitherto; every man who has come near her has been all complaisance and humility and gratitude for a smile or a friendly look; but this one—this one is as proud as herself! And what will she do?—become angry and indignant, and astonish my young Lord Arrogance? Or become humbly submissive, and beg for a little favour and consideration?—and Mary Stanley, of all people!"

Mary regarded the young man, and seeing that he did not speak, she said—

"A never-ending series of riots, is that what it is coming to? And if not, what is to be done? What am I to do?"

He answered her very respectfully—and very coldly:

"I think you should hardly ask me, Miss Stanley. If you consider, you will see that I could not well interfere—even so far as to offer advice. You will find Mr. Purdie will know how to deal with such a case."

"Mr. Purdie!" she said. "I cannot have Mr. Purdie here the whole year round. Surely I can do something myself? Cannot you tell me what to do?"

He hesitated. But here was a very beautiful young woman, appealing to him, and apparently in distress.

"Well," said he, at length, "I am not quite sure, but I fancy if you wish to have those men removed, you would have to take proceedings under the Vagrant Act. I am not quite sure; I fancy that is so. But then, if you do that, you will be denounced by the Highland Land League, and by plenty of the newspapers—natural enough on the part of the newspapers, for they would know nothing of the circumstances."

Käthchen thought that the outlaw and savage (as he had been described to her), talked very reasonably and intelligently; but Mary Stanley was quite as much perplexed as before.

"I don't want to bring the law to bear on anybody," she said. "I don't want to injure anybody. Surely there are other ways. If I go to those men, and show them they have no right to be there, and pay them for the lobster-traps that were burned, and give them each a sum of money, surely they would go away home to their own island?" And then she added (for she wasn't a fool), "Or might not that merely induce a lot more to come in their place?"

"I am afraid it would," said he.

But by this time the big steamer was slowing in to the pier.

"Miss Stanley," said young Ross, "would you mind coming this way a little—to be out of the reach of the rope?"

She politely thanked him, and moved her position; then he left her, making his way through the people; and the next she saw of him was that he was on the bridge, talking to the captain.

There was a good deal of cargo—barrels, bales, and what not—to be landed; but only one passenger came ashore, a white-haired little woman, whose luggage consisted of an American-looking trunk and also the head and enormous horns of a Wapiti deer, the head swathed in canvas. The little dame was of a most pleasant appearance, with her silvery hair, her bright eyes, and a complexion unusually fresh and clear for one of her age; and she was smartly and neatly dressed, too; but when once she had come along the gangway, and passed through the crowd, hardly any further notice was taken of her, all attention being concentrated on what was going forward on board the steamer. The poor old woman seemed bewildered—and agitated; her hands were trembling; she was staring back in a curious way at the vessel she had just left. Mary (of course) went up to her.

"Can I be of any assistance to you?" she said, in her gentle way.

And then perhaps she would rather have drawn back; for she found that the old dame's eyes were overflowing with tears.

"That—is the young master?" the old woman asked, in tones of eager and yet subdued excitement—and she was still staring at the two figures on the bridge.

"That is Mr. Ross of Heimra," Mary said, "who is talking to the captain."

The silver-haired old dame clasped her trembling hands together.

"Dear, dear me!" she said—and there were tears trickling down her face—"the fine gentleman he has grown! And we were all saying that long ago—we were all saying that—but who could have told?—so fine and handsome he has grown up as a man!—Ay, ay, I made sure it was young Donald himself, when he came on board, but he was not looking my way——"

"Would you like to speak to Mr. Ross?" said Mary, in the same gentle fashion.

Then the little white-haired old woman turned to this tall and beautiful young creature who was addressing her and a curious, wondering, and glad light shone through her tears.

"You, mem," said she, timidly—"perhaps you are his good lady, mem?"

Mary's face flushed.

"I hardly know Mr. Ross," said she coldly. "But if you wish to see him, I will fetch him—or send for him—"

"Mem," said the old dame, piteously, and the tears were now running freely down her face, "I have come all the way from Canada, just—just to have one look at young Donald—that—that was the lamb of my heart! My two boys, mem, they were thinking I should go and pay a visit to their uncle, who is in Sacramento; and they are very good boys; one of them—one of them would have gone as far with me as Detroit, and put me safe there on the line; but—but I said to them, if there is so much money to be spent, and if your old mother can go travelling anywhere, well, then, it is just away back to Lochgarra I am going, to see the young master once again before I die. But no, mem," she said, somewhat anxiously, "I do not wish to speak to him, in case he is not remembering me. I will wait a little. Maybe he will be remembering me, and maybe not—it is sixteen years since I left this place—and he was just ten, then—but such a young gentleman as you never saw, mem!—and the love of every one! And I will just wait and see, mem—perhaps he is not remembering me at all—but that is no matter—I will go back to my boys and tell them I saw the young master, and him grown to be such a fine gentleman—it is all I was coming here for—ay, and I knew it was young Donald the moment I saw him—but—but maybe he is not remembering me——"

"Oh, but indeed you must speak to him!" said Mary. "I will go and fetch him myself."

For at this moment the steamer was making preparations to be off again—there being little traffic at Lochgarra. The bell was rung, but merely as a matter of form; there was no passenger going on board. Donald Ross bade good-bye to the captain, and stepped ashore. The gangway was withdrawn. Then the captain signalled down to the engine-room; the blades of the screw began to churn up the clear green water into seething foam ; and the great steamer was slowly moving out to sea again.

"Mr. Ross," said Mary (and he turned round in quick surprise) "there is someone here who wishes to speak to you."

He looked towards the old dame who was standing there in piteous expectancy—went up to her—and, after a moment of scrutiny and hesitation, said—

"Why, surely you are Ann !"

The sudden shock of joy was almost too much for her ; she could not speak ; she clung to the hand he had frankly offered her, and held it between her trembling palms ; she was laughing and crying at the same time—great tears rolling down her cheeks.

"Well, well," said he, with a very friendly and pleasant smile lighting up his face, "you have come a long way. And are you going to live in the old place now—and leave the farm to your sons ? They must be great big fellows by this time, I suppose.   And that—what is that you have brought with you ? You don't have beasts like that coming about the house at night, do you ? "

She tried to speak ; but it was only in detached and incoherent sentences—and there was a bewilderment of gladness in the shining eyes with which she gazed on him.

"I was feared, sir, you might not be remembering me—and—and you have not forgotten Ann, after all these years —oh, yes, yes, a long way—and every night I was saying 'Will the young master be remembering Ann ?' And the deer's head, sir ?—oh, no, there are no deer at all in our part of the country—but—but it was my boy Andrew, he had to go down to Toronto, and he saw the head, and he brought it back, and says he 'Mother, if you are going away back to Lochgarra, take this head with you, and tell the young master it is a present from the whole of us, and maybe he will hang it up in the hall.'"

"We have no hall to hang it up in now," said he, but quite good-naturedly—for Mary Stanley was standing by, not unnaturally interested. "However, you must come out and see where I am living now—at Heimra Island. You remember Martha ? "

"Oh, yes, yes," said the old dame, who had dried her

tears now, and was looking most delighted and proud and happy.

"But you have not told me yet what has brought you all the way back to Lochgarra," said he.

She seemed astonished—and even disappointed.

"You cannot tell that, sir? Well, it was just to see yourself—nothing else but that—it was just to see young Donald, that I used to call the lamb of my heart. But that was when you were very young, sir."

Donald Ross laughed.

"Come away, Ann," said he, and he put his hand affectionately on the old dame's shoulder. "You must come out to Heimra Island, and Martha will look after you, after all your travelling. Now let me see; we shan't be getting up anchor for an hour or an hour and a half; but I shall have your things put on board, and in the meanwhile you can go round to the inn and wait for me there. Tell them to give you a room with a good fire in it.   And, by the way, you don't want me to call you by your married name, do you?—for to tell you the truth, I don't remember it!"

"Oh, no, no, no, sir!" said the trim little old lady, who could not take her glad, and wondering, and admiring eyes off 'the young master.' "I'm just Ann, if you please, sir—just Ann, as I used to be."

Young Ross turned to call up Coinneach and Calum, who were waiting at the end of the quay, in order to give them instructions about the luggage; and it was at this moment that Mary stepped up to the stranger.

"Instead of going to wait at the inn," said she, "wouldn't you rather come with me? Lochgarra House is quite as near—and you would not be sitting alone."

It was a gentle face that was regarding her, and a gentle voice that spoke.

"Oh, yes, mem, if you will be so kind," was the answer.

"Then tell Mr. Ross you have gone on with me; and he can send one of the men for you when he is ready," Mary said; and by this little arrangement she was saved the necessity of having any further conversation with young Ross of Heimra, if such was her intention.

They moved away.

"Do you think you will know many of the people about here, after so long a time?" asked Mary of her new acquaintance, as they left the quay—the silent, but not unobservant, nor yet unamused, Käthchen accompanying.

"Oh, no, mem," was the answer (but, as she talked, the old woman turned from time to time to see if she could not get some brief further glimpse of her heart's idol) "my people they were all about Dingwall; and it was from Dingwall I came over here to serve with Mrs. Ross. Ah, she was the noble lady, that!" continued the faithful Ann, looking back over many years. "When we heard of her death, it was then, more than ever, that I thought I must go away to Lochgarra, to see the young master. For she was so careful of his upbringing; and they were just constant companions; and he was always the little gentleman, and polite to every one—except when Mrs. Ross had a headache—and then he would come downstairs, ay, into the servants' hall, or even to the door of the kitchen—and proud and fierce, as if he would kill some one, and he would say 'What is this noise? I order you to be quiet, when my mamma is asleep!' And you would have heard a pin drop after that, mem. Rather too fond of books he was," continued the silver-haired old dame, whose newly-found happiness had made her excitedly talkative, "and rather delicate in health; and then Mrs. Ross would be talking to him in different languages, neither the Gaelic nor the English, and he would be answering her as well as he could—the little gentleman!—when they were sitting at the table. Indeed, now, that was making the old Admiral —that was Mrs. Ross's uncle, very angry; and he was swearing, and saying there was no use for any language but the English language; and many's and many's the time he was taking young Donald away with him in his yacht, and saying he would make a sailor and a man of him. Well, well, now, who would think the young master had ever been delicate like that, and fond of books—so fine and handsome he has grown—and the laugh he has—ay, a laugh that carries a good story of health and happiness with it!"

"No, he does not look as if he had ever been very delicate," said Mary, absently. "Perhaps the rough life out there on that island was the very best thing for him."

When they got to the house, Mary escorted her guest up to the drawing-room in the tower, and was most assiduous in her pretty little attentions, and had wine and biscuits brought in, for Mrs. Armour (as the old woman's name turned out to be) had breakfasted early on board the steamer. And Mrs. Armour repaid these kindnesses by eagerly talking about young Donald and nothing else; she seemed to think that the two young ladies were as interested as herself in that wonderful subject; and here was the very house in which she had lived, to suggest innumerable reminiscences. She did not say anything about Miss Stanley's occupation of the house; nor did she ask how it came about that Donald Ross was now living on the island they could see from this room: no doubt she had heard something, in her remote Canadian home, of the misfortunes that had befallen the old family. But even while she talked her eyes would go wandering to the window that commanded a view of the village; it was like a girl of eighteen watching for her first sweetheart: she was talking to these very kind ladies—but it was young Donald of Heimra that her heart was thinking of all the time.

Then the welcome summons came, and away she went with Coinneach Breac. The two girls watched them go along to the boat in which "the young master" was waiting; then the men took to the oars, and made for the yacht. The mainsail and jib of the *Sirène* had already been hoisted; very soon the anchor was got up; and with a light southerly breeze favouring them they had set out for the solitary island that was now Donald Ross's home.

"Well, Mamie," said Käthchen, who was still standing at the window and looking at the gradually receding yacht, "that is a very strange young man. I have been a spectator this morning; and I have been interested. I have seen a young man approached by a beautiful young woman—a damsel in distress, you might almost say—who condescends to appeal to him; and in return he is barely civil—oh, yes, let us say civil—and even polite, but in a curiously stand-off manner. And then an old Highland

servant appears; and behold! his face lights up with
pleasure; and he is as kind as kind can be, and affec-
tionate; he puts his hand on her shoulder as if she were
some old schoolmate, and nothing will do but that she
must go away out to see his home. To tell you the truth,
I did not think he had so much human nature in him. I
thought living in that lonely island would have made him
a misanthrope. But I shall never forget the expression of
his face when he recognised the old woman that had been
his mother's servant."

Mary Stanley was silent for a little while; then she
said—

"It is a wonderful thing, the affection and devotion
that could bring an old woman like that all the way
across the Atlantic for a glimpse of one she had known
only as a child. And it seems to be a thing you cannot
purchase with money, nor yet with good intentions, nor by
anything you can do, however hard you may try." She
turned away from the window. "But—but I haven't
given up yet, Käthchen."

"You never will give up, Mamie," said her friend; and
then she added complacently: "For you don't know how."

CHAPTER XI.

A DEFORCEMENT.

BUT wonders will never cease. It was a couple of days
after these occurrences, and Mary Stanley and Kate Glendinning were just about to sit down to lunch, when the
Highland maid Barbara came into the room, with a curious
expression on her face. And it was in almost awe-stricken
tones that she spoke:

"It's Mr. Ross, mem," said she—her pretty, soft, shy
eyes now full of a vague astonishment.

"Mr. Ross?—Mr. Ross of Heimra? Well, what about
him?" Mary demanded, little guessing at the true state
of affairs.

"He's in the hall, mem," said the startled Barbara.
"He says would Miss Stanley speak with him for a moment,
and he would not keep you more than a moment, mem."

The blood rushed to Mary's forehead, and for a second she was embarrassed and speechless; then, with a certain impatience of her own confusion, she said—

"Well, ask Mr. Ross to go into the drawing-room, Barbara—and tell him I will be there directly."

She turned quickly to her friend. "Käthchen, would you mind going and speaking to him ?—I shall be down in a minute."

Possibly Käthchen did not quite like this commission; but then she was in the habit of reflecting that as a salaried companion she had duties to perform; and so with much good nature she went away into the drawing-room, to receive this unexpected visitor. It was some minutes before Mary reappeared. The male eye could not have detected any difference between the Mary Stanley of the dining-room and the Mary Stanley of the drawing-room; but Käthchen instantly perceived the minute alterations. Mary had whipped off to her room to exchange the stiff linen collar that she wore for a piece of soft frilling—a more feminine adornment. Moreover, she came into the room, not radiant in her beauty and self-possessed as was her wont, but with a kind of timid, modest, almost shamefaced gratitude for this act of neighbourliness, and in her clear eyes a manifest pleasure shone. Käthchen, now relieved of her duties, and become a mere onlooker, said to herself: "I don't know what Mamie means; but that young man had better take care."

He, on his side, certainly showed no lack of self-possession—though he still remained standing, his yachting cap in his hand.

"I hope I am not inconveniencing you," said he to Miss Stanley. "The fact is, we got becalmed just outside the bay——"

"But won't you be seated ?" said she, and she herself took a chair. Käthchen retired to one of the windows—not to look out, however.

"First of all, I wish to thank you for your kindness to Mrs. Armour," said he. "She is very grateful to you; for of course it was pleasant to the old dame to have a friendly hand held out to her, when she was rather frightened she might be coming back among strangers."

"Oh, that is nothing," said Mary; and then she was emboldened to add, "The wonderful thing was to find any one connected with this place who would accept of any civility. But then she has been away a long time."

If this was a taunt, unintentional or otherwise, he took no heed of it.

"What I really wished to see you about, however, was this," he went on. "It was only last night that I heard of the sheriff's judgment in the case of James Macdonald—James Macdonald, the crofter, at Cruagan——"

"I know him," said Mary. "But what case? I never heard of it!"

"An action brought by Mr. Purdie on your behalf," he answered briefly.

"Why was I not told of this?" she said.

"The proceedings began some little time ago," he said. "And indeed, Miss Stanley, I must apologise to you for seeming to interfere. I do not wish to interfere in any way whatever; it would be most impertinent on my part; and besides—besides, I have no desire to interfere. But in this particular case I think you should know what is going on, for Macdonald is a determined man; and if the sheriff's officer and his concurrents come out this afternoon by the mail-car, as they are likely to do, I'm afraid there will be trouble. The sheriff has granted a decree of removal; but I don't think Macdonald will go; while it is just possible the other crofters may back him up. I thought if you would go along and ask the sheriff's officer to stay proceedings until Macdonald could be talked to by his own friends——"

"Well, of course I will!" said she, instantly. "But I want to know what this action is all about? It seems to me that I ought to be consulted before Mr. Purdie takes to evicting any of the tenants."

There was a curious, covert gleam of satisfaction in the young lustrous black eyes; but he went on to say very quietly—

"I am afraid Macdonald has put himself entirely in the wrong. For one thing, he is over two years in arrear with his rent; and that of itself, according to the Crofters Holding Act, forfeits his tenancy. And then, again, he refuses to pay because of reasons that won't hold water He claims compensation for improvements——"

"Why not?" said she—promptly taking the side of the tenant, and talking to young Ross as if he were advocating the landlord's interest.

"Well," said Young Donald, "he has cut a few drains and covered them in; but the sheriff found that this was counterbalanced by his neglect of other parts of the croft, and that there was no just claim. His other reason for refusal was that he wanted an allowance made to him for Mr. Watson's sheep being permitted to graze over the Cruagan crofts after the crops were reaped."

"And why not?" said Mary again. "Why should Mr. Watson's sheep graze over the crofts? That seems to me a great injustice—unless compensation is given."

"Well, it is a practice of long standing," said the young man (and Käthchen, who cared very little about rents and holdings and drains, nevertheless thought he had so agreeable a voice that it was quite a pleasure to listen to him). "The crofters took the crofts knowing of this condition, and the rents were fixed accordingly. However, this is the present state of affairs, that the sheriff-substitute has decided against Macdonald—as he was bound to do, I admit. He has found him liable for arrears of rent, with interest and costs; and he has granted a warrant to turn him out. Now Macdonald is a stiff-necked man, a difficult man to deal with; and he doesn't know much English; it will be no use for the sheriff's officer to argue, and say he is only doing his duty——"

"I disapprove of the whole proceedings," said Mary, with decision. "Mr. Purdie had no right to go to such extremes without consulting me—and I will take care that it does not happen again. By the mail-car, did you say? Well, that won't be coming by Cruagan before half-past two; and I can be there by then. The sheriff's officer and his—his what did you call them?"

"His concurrents—assistants."

"They must wait for further instructions; and I will inquire into the matter myself."

He rose.

"I hope you will forgive me, Miss Stanley," said he, as

he had said before, "for seeming to interfere. I have no wish to do anything of the kind. But I thought you ought to know in case there might be any trouble—which you could prevent."

"Mr. Ross," said she, "I am very much obliged to you. I—I don't get very much help—and—and I want to do what little I can for the people."

"Good morning!" said he; and he bowed to Kate Glendinning: he was going away without so much as shaking hands with either of them, so distant and respectful was his manner. But Mary, in a confused kind of fashion, did not seem to think this was right. She accompanied him to the door; and that she left open; then she went out with him into the hall.

"I cannot believe that James Macdonald should have any serious grudge against me," she said, "for I told Mr. Purdie to tell him that the tax for the dyke was abolished, and also that fifteen years' of it was to be given back. And, besides that, I said to Macdonald myself that thirty shillings an acre was too much for that land; and I propose to have it reduced to a pound an acre when I have all the rents of the estate looked into."

"Do you think Purdie did tell him?" young Donald Ross asked coldly.

"If he has not!" said Mary. . . . "But I am almost sure he did—I spoke to Macdonald myself almost immediately afterwards. And—and I wished to tell you, Mr. Ross," she continued (as if she were rather pleading for favour, or at least expecting approval), "that I have been down to the stranger fishermen at Ru-Minard, and I think it is all settled, and that they are going away peaceably. I am paying them for the lobster-traps that were burned —and perhaps a little more; and they understand that the Vagrant Act can be brought to bear on any others who may think of coming."

"Oh, they are going away?" said he.

"Yes."

"Mr. Purdie will be sorry for that."

"Why?"

"He could have had them removed, if he had wanted;

but so long as they were an annoyance and vexation to the people here, he allowed them to remain—naturally."

These accents of contemptuous scorn : she was sorry to hear them somehow : and yet perhaps they were justified —she did not know.

"Good-bye," said she, at the hall door, and she held out her hand. "I am so much obliged to you."

And then of course he did shake hands with her in bidding her farewell—and raised his cap—and was gone.

Mary returned to the dining-room.

"Well Mamie," said Käthchen, with a demure smile, "that is about the most extraordinary interview I ever heard of. A most handsome young gentleman calls upon a young lady—his first visit—and there is nothing talked of on either side but sheriff officers and summonses, rent, compensation, drains, crofts, grazing, and Acts of Parliament. Of course he was quite as bad as you ; but all the same, you might at least have asked the poor man to stay to lunch."

"Oh, Käthchen !" Mary exclaimed, starting to her feet, her face on fire. "Shall I send Barbara after him ? I never thought of it ! How frightfully rude of me—and he has come all the way over from Heimra to tell me about this eviction. What shall I do ? Shall I send after him ?"

"I don't think you can," said Käthchen ; "it would make the little oversight all the more marked. You'd better ask him the next time you see him—if you have forgotten certain warnings."

"What warnings ?"

"Why, about his general character and his occupations," said Kate Glendinning, regarding her friend.

Mary was silent for a moment or two ; then she said—

"We need not believe the worst of any one ; and when you think of that old woman coming all the way from Canada to see him, that of itself is a testimonial to character that not many could bring forward—"

"But you must remember," said Käthchen, "the young master was a little boy of ten when Mrs. Armour left ; and little boys of ten haven't had time to develop into dangerous criminals."

"Dangerous criminal?" said Mary, rather sharply; "that is hardly the—the proper phrase to use—with regard to—to a stranger. However, it is not of much consequence. Käthchen, are you going to drive with me to Cruagan to get that sheriff's officer and his men sent back?"

"Yes, certainly," said Käthchen, in her usual business-like fashion, "as soon as we have had lunch. And remember, Mamie, it wasn't *I* who forgot to ask him to stay."

Luncheon did not detain them long, and immediately thereafter they got into the waggonette that was waiting for them, and drove off. But it was not of the eviction and the possibility of another riot that Mary was mostly thinking; something very different was weighing, and weighing heavily, on her mind. They drove through the village in silence; they crossed the bridge; and they had begun the ascent of the steep hill before she spoke.

"The more I consider it," she said, "the more ashamed I am."

"Consider what?" said Käthchen.

"Why, neglecting to ask him to stay to lunch," she made answer—for this was what she had been brooding over.

"Why should you worry about such a trifle!" Käthchen protested.

"It isn't a trifle—in a Highlander's estimation, as you know well enough. They pride themselves on their hospitality; and they judge others by their own standards; so that I cannot but keep wondering what he must be thinking of me at this moment. Remember, Käthchen, when we went over to Heimra, even the old housekeeper entertained us, and did her best for us, in that out-of-the-world place; and here he comes to Lochgarra House— his first visit—he comes to do me a kindness—he comes to prevent mischief—and comes into the house that once was his own—and I don't offer him even a biscuit and a glass of sherry——"

"Really, Mary, you needn't worry about such a mere trifle!" Käthchen protested again.

"But I do worry!" she said. "I can imagine what

he thought of me as he went away. For you must not forget this, Käthchen : it was a very awkward position he put himself into in order to do me a good turn. Think of his coming to the house, that ought to be his own— asking the servants if he might be admitted—sending up his name as a stranger—then he remains standing in the drawing-room—and he is for going away without shaking hands—as if he were hardly to be considered one's fellow-creature." She was silent for a second or two; then she said, with a sudden touch of asperity : " At the same time there is this to be remembered, that the pride that apes humility is the very worst kind of pride. Often it simply means that the person is inordinately vain."

" Poor young man ! " said Käthchen, with a sigh. " He is always in the wrong. But I'm sure I did not object to his manner when he showed us the way out of the Meall-na-Fearn bog."

About a couple of hundred yards on the Lochgarra side of Cruagan they met the mail-car ; and when, a minute or two thereafter they came in sight of the scattered crofts, it was obvious from the prevailing commotion that the sheriff's officer and his assistants had arrived. Indeed, when Mary and Käthchen descended from the waggonette and walked up to James Macdonald's cottage, the business of getting out the few poor sticks of furniture had already begun—the only on-looker being an old white-haired man, Macdonald's father, who was standing there dazed and bewildered, as if he did not understand what was going forward. Just as Mary got up, one of the con-currents brought out a spinning-wheel and put it on the ground.

" Here—what are you doing ? " she said, angrily, to the man who appeared to be the chief officer. " Leave that spinning-wheel alone ; that is the very thing I want to see in every cottage ! "

" I've got the sheriff's warrant, ma'am," said the man, civilly enough. " And we must get everything out and take possession."

" Oh, no, you mustn't ! " she said. " This man Macdonald claims compensation—the case must be inquired into."

"I have nothing to do wi' that, ma'am," said the officer, who seemed a respectable, quiet-spoken, quiet-mannered kind of a person. "I'm bound to carry out the warrant—that's all I've to heed."

"But surely I can say whether I want the man turned out or not?" she protested. "He is my tenant. It is to me he owes the money. Surely, if I am satisfied, you can leave the man alone. But where is he? Where is Macdonald?"

"As for that, ma'am," said the officer, "he is away down the road, and he says he is going to fetch a gun. Very well. If he presents a gun at either me or my concurrents I will declare myself deforced, and he will have to answer for it before the sheriff."

"A gun?" said Mary, rather faintly. "Do you mean to drive the poor man to desperation?"

But there was a more immediate danger to be considered. As the two girls had driven up they had heard a good deal of shrill calling from croft to croft and from house to house; and now there had assembled a crowd of women—a crowd hostile and menacing—that came swarming up, uttering all sorts of angry and reproachful cries. Each time that the sheriff's officer's assistants appeared at the door of the cottage there was another outburst of hooting and groaning; while here and there a bare-armed virago had furnished herself with an apron-full of rubbish — potato-peelings, cabbage-stalks, stale fish, and the like—and these unsavoury missiles began to hurtle through the air, though for the most part they were badly aimed. The sheriff's officer affected to pay no heed. He calmly watched the proceedings of his men; the rubbish flew past him unregarded; and the women had not yet taken to stones.

But Käthchen beheld this advancing crowd with undisguised alarm.

"Mary," she said, hurriedly, "don't you think we should go back to the waggonette? Those people think it is you who are setting the sheriff's officers on—they are hooting at us as well."

There could be no doubt of the fact; and the infuriated women were drawing nearer and nearer; while, if their taunts and epithets were to her unintelligible, their

wrathful glances and threatening gestures were unmistake-
able. Mary Stanley found herself helpless. She could not
explain to them. She had not the self-possession with which
to address this exasperated mob, even if she knew the
language in which alone it was possible to appeal to them.
Nor dared she retreat, for would not that be simply inviting a general attack? So she was standing, irresolute
and bewildered, when there was a new diversion of interest :
the man Macdonald made his appearance. She looked at
him ; she hardly recognised him—so ashen-grey had his
cheeks become with excitement and wrath. One trembling
hand held a gun ; the other he clenched and shook in the
face of the officer as he went up to him.

"I—not owing any money !" said the Russian-looking
crofter, and his features were working with passion, and
his eyes were filled with a baleful light under his shaggy
eyebrows. "No—no—God's curse to me if I pay money
when I not owing any money ! Go away, now—go away
back to Dingwall—or it is murder there will be !"

Mary was very pale ; but she went forward to him all
the same.

"Put away that gun," she said, and she spoke with firmness, though her lips had lost their natural colour. "Put
away that gun ! These men are doing their duty—you
have brought it on yourself."

He turned upon her savagely.

"You—it's not you—my laird—Ross of Heimra, he my
laird—you come here, ay, to steal the land—and—and put
me from my croft—ay—will you be putting me from my
croft ?"

In his fury he could find no more English ; but he
advanced towards her, his clenched fist raised ; and here
it was that Käthchen (though her heart was beating wildly)
thrust herself forward between them.

"How dare you !" she said, indignantly. "Stand back !
How dare you !"

For an instant the man's eyes glared at her—as if in
his indescribable rage he knew neither what to do or say ;
but just at this moment his attention was drawn elsewhither ; a volley of groans and yells from the crowd had
greeted the reappearance of the assistants. At sight of

these enemies bringing out his poor bits of things, Macdonald's wrath was turned in a new direction; he made a dash for the cottage—managed to get inside—and the next second the two men were flung headlong out, while the door was instantly slammed to behind them. A great shout of triumph and laughter arose from the crowd, while the discomfited officers picked themselves up and gazed blankly at the barred way.

"I call you to witness," said their chief to Miss Stanley —and he spoke in the calmest manner, as if this were quite an every-day occurrence—"that I have been deforced in the execution of my duty. This man will have to answer for it at Dingwall."

But his assistants were not so imperturbable. Smarting under the jeers of the crowd, they proceeded to cast about for some implement with which to effect an entrance; and presently they found an axe. With this one of them set to work: and crash! crash! went the weight of iron on to the trembling door. The wood began to yield. Splinters showed—then a narrow breach was made—the hole grew wider—and just as it became evident that the demolition of the door was but a matter of a few minutes, a heavier stroke than usual snapped the shaft of the axe in twain, the iron head falling inside the cottage. By this time the attitude of the crowd had again altered—from derision to fierce resentment; there were groans renewed again and again; missiles flew freely. And then again, and quite suddenly, an apparently trivial incident entirely changed the aspect of affairs. At that ragged opening that had been made in the door there appeared two small black circles, close together; and these were pushed outward a few inches. The concurrents fell back—and the crowd was silent; well they perceived what this was; those two small circles were the muzzle of a gun; at any moment, a violent death—a shattered corpse—might be the next feature of the scene.

"What does that madman mean to do?" Mary exclaimed, in a paralysis of terror—for it appeared to her that she was responsible for all that was happening or might happen.

"Mary," said Käthchen, under her breath—and she

was all trembling with excitement, "you must come away at once—now—while they are watching the gun. Perhaps they won't interfere with us—we may get down to the waggonette—we may have to run for it, too, if those women should turn on us."

"I cannot go and leave these poor men here," Mary said, in her desperation. "They will be murdered. That man in there is a madman—a downright madman."

Käthchen lowered her voice still further.

"There is Mr. Ross coming—and oh! I wish he would be quick!"

Indeed it was no other than Donald Ross, who, immediately after leaving Lochgarra House, had struck off across the hills, hoping by a short cut to reach Cruagan not long after Miss Stanley's arrival. And now that he appeared, all eyes were turned towards him; there was no further groaning, or hooting, or hurling of missiles. He seemed to take in the situation at a glance. He asked a question of the sheriff's officer.

"I'll just have to come back, sir," said the man, "with an inspector and a dozen police; but in the meantime I declare that I have been deforced, and this man Macdonald must answer for it. I hope ye'll give evidence, sir, if the leddies would rather not come over to Dingwall. You were not here when my assistants were thrown out of the house; but at least you can see a gun pointed at us— there it is—through that door."

Young Ross did not go directly forward to the muzzle of the gun—which would have been the act of a lunatic, for the man inside the cottage might make a mistake; but he went towards the front of the house, then approached the door, and struck up the gun with his fist. One barrel went off—harmlessly enough.

"Hamish!"

He called again; and added something in Gaelic. The door was opened. There was some further speech in the same tongue; the shaggy-browed crofter laid aside the gun, and came out into the open air, looking about him like a wild-beast at bay, but following the young master submissively enough. Donald Ross went up to Miss Stanley.

"I was afraid there might be a little trouble," said he.

"Well, I can answer for this man—if you will get the sheriff's officer and his assistants to go away."

"I want them to go away!" she said. "I have no wish at all to put James Macdonald out of his croft—not in the least—and I will give him time to pay up arrears, especially as there is to be a re-valuation. I wish you would tell him that. I wish you would tell him that I had nothing to do with these proceedings. Tell him I want to deal fairly with everybody. You can talk to him—I cannot— I cannot explain to him."

But Macdonald had been listening all the same.

"That woman," said he, sullenly, "she—no business here. The land—Ross of Heimra's——"

Young Ross turned to him with a muttered exclamation in Gaelic, and with a flash of flame in the coal-black eyes that did not escape Käthchen's notice. The stubborn crofter was silent after that—standing aside in sombre indifference.

"The officer can bring his action for deforcement, if he likes," Ross said, "and I suppose Macdonald will be fined forty shillings. But no one has been hurt; and it seems a pity there should be any further proceedings, if, as you say, you are going to have a re-valuation of the crofts"— and then he suddenly checked himself. "I hope you will forgive me for interfering," he said, quite humbly; "I did not intend to say anything; it is Mr. Purdie's business— and I do not wish even to offer you advice."

"I wish I could tell you how much I am obliged to you," she said, warmly. "If you had not let me know about those men coming, and if you had not appeared yourself, I believe there would have been murder done here this day. And now, Mr. Ross, would you get them to go on at once to Lochgarra, so as to be out of harm's way—and to-morrow they can go back by the mail-car? I will write to Mr. Purdie. There must be no further proceedings; and James Macdonald will not be put out of his croft—not if I have any say in the matter."

So the three officials were started off for the village; the morose crofter proceeded to pick up his bits of furniture and get them into the house again; and the crowd of women began to disperse—not silently, however, but with much shrill and eager decision—towards their own homes.

Young Ross of Heimra went down with the two young
ladies to the waggonette, which was waiting for them
below in the road.

He saw them into the carriage.

"But won't you drive back with us?" said Mary.

" Oh, thank you—if I may," he said, rather diffidently;
and therewith he went forward to get up beside the coachman, just as Mr. Purdie would have done.

The colour rushed to Mary's forehead.

" Mr. Ross," she said, " not there ! "—and she herself
opened the door of the waggonette for him, so that perforce
he had to take his place beside them. And was this again
(she may have asked herself) the pride that apes humility;
or was it only part of his apparent desire to keep a
marked distance between himself and her? She was vexed
with him for causing her this embarrassment. He had no
right to do such things. He might be a little more friendly.
She, on her part, had been frank enough in expressing her
obligations to him; nay, she had gone out of her way to
ask, in a kind of fashion, for his approval. Were all the
advances to come from her side?

But Kate Glendinning noticed this—that as they drew
near to the dried-up waste that had once been Loch Heimra,
and as they were passing the tumbled-down ruins of the
ancient stronghold, he pretended that he did not see
anything. He rather turned away his face. He talked of
indifferent matters. Mary had forgotten that they would
have to pass by Loch and Castle Heimra, or perhaps she
might have thought twice about inviting him to drive with
them. But quite simply and resolutely he turned away
from those things that all too eloquently spoke of the
irreparable wrong that had been done to him and his, and
affected not to see them or remember them ; and Käthchen
—a not uninterested observer—said proudly to herself:
" If that is not Highland courtesy, I do not know what is."

Wonders will never cease, truly. That evening the
astounding rumour had found its way through the length
and breadth of the township : there were eye-witnesses
who could testify : Young Donald of Heimra had been
seen in the same carriage with the two ladies from Lochgarra House.

CHAPTER XII.

A CROFTERS' COMMISSION.

ONE morning Mary Stanley and her companion had been away on some distant errand, and when on their return they came to the summit of the hill overlooking the bay, Mary paused for a moment to take in the prospect—the wide, grey, wind-swept plain of the sea, the long headlands, and the lonely Heimra Island out in the west. But Käthchen did not cease her discourse—in which she was endeavouring to account for the comparative failure, so far, of her friend's fine philanthropic schemes.

"The truth is, Mamie," said she, "what has disappointed you here has been the prevalence of hard facts—very hard facts—facts as hard as the rocks on which the poor people try to live. You wanted to play the part of Lady Bountiful; and you yourself are just full of enthusiasm, and generous emotion, and ideals of duty and self sacrifice, and —and—romanticism generally, if I may say so. And for all these qualities you find no exercise, no outlet. I can imagine you in very different circumstances—in London, perhaps, or in some English village : I can imagine your going into a squalid room where there is a poor widow by the bedside of her dying boy; and the Lady Bountiful brings little comforts for the sick child, and words of kindness and consolation for the mother ; and the poor woman looks on you as an angel, and would kiss the hem of your gown ; and it's all very pretty and touching. But, you see," continued the practical Käthchen, "how you are baffled and thwarted in this obdurate place ; for there isn't a single case of illness in the whole district—not one— which is no doubt owing to the valuable antiseptic properties of peat smoke ! "

"Oh, well," said Mary, cheerfully, as they went on again, "I can put up with being disappointed on that score— and the longer the better. But, Käthchen, when you said there was nothing but hard facts about here—no pretty sentiment and sympathy—you weren't keeping your eyes open. Look down there at the bridge ; what is that if not pretty sentiment?—two lovers talking—why, it is quite a charming picture?—and isn't there some rustic custom of pledging troth over a running stream?"

Her face suddenly grew grave; and Käthchen, also regarding those two figures, was struck by the same surmise.

"It is Mr. Ross, Mamie!" she exclaimed, in an undertone—though they were still a long way off.

Mary said nothing. She walked on calmly and indifferently, sometimes looking up to the hills, sometimes looking out to Heimra Island and the sea. It was Käthchen, keeping her eyes covertly on those two figures by the bridge, who observed that the girl suddenly separated herself from her companion, and disappeared into the woods by the side of the Garra. As for Donald Ross, he made no sign of going away: on the contrary, he remained idling by the rude stone parapet, occasionally looking into the water underneath. And he must have known that he was intercepting the two ladies from Lochgarra House—there was no escape for them.

Mary maintained a perfect self-possession; and when they came up to him she was for passing with a little bow of recognition; but he spoke.

"I have a small petition to put before you," said he, with a smile (Käthchen thought that, though he looked extremely handsome, this pleasant and familiar smile was in the circumstances something of an impertinence).

"Indeed," said Mary—and she waited.

"From a very humble petitioner," he continued (and Käthchen began to consider him a most unabashed young man—so easily and lightly he spoke), "one who has no English, and she has asked me to interfere and tell you all about her case. She was talking to me just now; but when she caught sight of you she fled off into the woods, like a hare."

"Why?" said Mary, coldly.

"Because she is afraid of you," said he. "She thinks you are a friend of the *Troich Bheag Dhearg*—the Little Red Dwarf—as they call Mr. Purdie about here. And that is quite enough to frighten Anna——"

"Anna?" said Mary. "Do you mean Anna Chlannach

—the half-witted girl ?"—and as she guessed the simple and harmless truth an indescribable confusion appeared on her forehead and in the self-consciousness of her eyes.

"Yes," said he, apparently not noticing. "Anna says that you spoke to her once; but she has no English, and could not tell you anything; and she saw Purdie with you, and ran away. 'So much I made out, though she talks rather wildly, and mysteriously as well."

"Oh, but Mr. Ross," said Mary, with some eagerness, "I wish you would tell Anna Chlannach that she has no reason to be afraid of me—surely not! Why, she was the first creature in the place who seemed a little friendly. Will you tell her I will do everything for her I can; and that she must come and see me; and there will be no fear of her meeting Mr. Purdie; and Barbara can be the interpreter between us ? Will you tell her that ? Could you find her now ?"

"There's no one in this neighbourhood who could find Anna Chlannach if she wants to be hidden," he said, with a bit of a laugh that showed beautiful teeth—as Käthchen remarked. "But I shall come across her some other time, and of course, if you grant her petition, she must go to you and thank you."

"What is her petition ?" said Mary, who had recovered from her momentary confusion, and was now prepared to be entirely bland and magnanimous—which, indeed, was her natural mood.

"Well," said he, "Purdie — Mr. Purdie — has been threatening to have her shut up in some asylum for imbeciles—so they say—and Anna is in a great state about the possibility of her being taken away from among the people she knows. I don't think it is true, myself; indeed I doubt whether he could do anything of the kind, without the consent of her relatives, and she has got none now; but I am not quite sure what the law is; anyhow, what I imagine to be the case is simply that Mr. Purdie has been making use of these threats to spite the people with whom Anna Chlannach is a favourite. For she is a general favourite—there is no harm in the girl——"

"Why, so Barbara said !" Mary exclaimed.

"It is quite true that she is rather useless about the

place," Donald Ross went on. "Sometimes they have tried her with a bit of herding; but then, if she saw a boat out at sea, she would imagine her mother was coming back, and she would go away down to the shore to meet her, and spend her time in gathering white shells, that she thinks is money, to give to her mother. Well, you see, that is awkward. You couldn't leave sheep or cows under Anna's care without asking somebody to keep an eye on Anna herself. The truth is, she is useless. But there's no harm in the lass; and the people are fond of her; there's always a bit of food, or a corner for her to sleep in; so that she's not a cost to anyone except to those that are willing to pay it—a mere trifle—and in any case it does not come out of Mr. Purdie's pocket——"

"She shall not be shut up in any asylum, if I have any say in the matter!" Mary interposed, with a touch of indignation.

"I asked her to stay and appeal to yourself," he continued. "But she was frightened of you——"

"Yes," said Mary, "everyone is frightened of me—or set against me—in this place!"

"There is another thing I should mention," he proceeded—ignoring this taunt, if it was meant as a taunt; "the young girls and lads about here are not very considerate if there's any fun going on; and they've heard of this proposal of Purdie's; and so they amuse themselves by telling Anna Chlannach that she is going to be taken away and shut up in an asylum, and the poor girl is dreadfully frightened. But if you can assure her that you will not allow Purdie to do any such thing——"

"Well, of course I will, if you will only bring her to me!" said Mary, impetuously. "Why haven't you brought her to me before?"

He hesitated. Then he said—

"I am very much obliged to you. I will tell Anna Chlannach the first time I see her. Good morning, Miss Stanley!"

But Mary would not have that; she said boldly—

"Are you not going down to the village?—won't you walk with us?"

He could hardly refuse the invitation; and as they went

on towards the little township, what she was saying in her heart was this—"Here, you people, all of you, if you are at your cottage doors or working on your crofts, don't you see this now, that Mr. Ross of Heimra is walking with me, with all the world to witness? Do you understand what that means? It is true my uncle drained Loch Heimra and tore down Castle Heimra into a heap of ruins; and the Rosses of Heimra, and you also, may have had reason to hate the name of Stanley; But look at this—look at Young Donald walking with me—in a kind of a way proclaiming himself my friend—and consider what that means. A feud? There is no feud if he and I say there shall be none. I cannot restore Castle Heimra, but it is within his power to forgive and to forget."

That is what she was somewhat proudly saying to herself as they walked into the village—past the smithy—past the weaver's cottage—past the school-house—past the post-office—past the inn and its dependencies; and she hoped that every one would see, and reflect. But of course she could not speak in that fashion to Donald Ross.

"You might have told me about Anna Chlannach before," she said.

"I did not like to interfere," he made answer.

"You seem very sensitive on that point!" she retorted.

"Well, it is natural," he said, with something of reserve; and instinctively she felt that she could go no further in that direction.

"Are you remaining long on the mainland at present?" she asked, in an ordinary kind of way.

"Until this afternoon only: I shall go back to Heimra after the mail-cart has come in."

"It must be very lonely out there," she said—glancing towards the remote island among the grey and driven seas.

"It is lonely—now," he said.

And then she hesitated. For he had never spoken to her of his circumstances in any way whatever; he had always been so distant and respectful; and she hardly knew whether she might venture to betray any interest. But at length she said—

"I can very well understand that there must be a charm in living all by one's self in a lonely island like that—for a

time, at least—and yet—yet—it does seem like throwing
away one's opportunities. I think I should want some
definite occupation—among my fellow creatures."

"Oh, yes, no doubt," said he, in no wise taking her
timorous suggestion as a reproach. "In my own case, I
could not leave the island so long as my mother was alive;
I never even thought of such a thing; so that being shut
up in Eilean Heimra was not in the least irksome to me.
Not in the least. She and I were sufficient companions
for each other anywhere. But now it is different. Now
I am free to look about. And I am reading up for the
Bar as a preliminary step."

"Oh, indeed?" said she. "Do you mean to practise
as a lawyer?"

"No, I think not," he made reply; and now Käthchen
was indeed listening with interest—more interest than
she usually displayed over rents and drains and sheriff's
decrees. "But being a barrister is a necessary qualifica-
tion for a good many appointments; and if I were once
called to the Bar I might perhaps get some sort of post
in one of the colonies."

"In one of the colonies?" Mary repeated; "and leave
Eilean Heimra for ever?"

"Well, I don't know about that," said he, absently.
"At all events, I should not like to part with the island
—I mean, I should not like to sell it. It is the last little
bit of a foothold; and the name has been in our family for
a long while; and—and there are other associations. No;
rather than sell the bit of an island, I think I should be
content to remain a prisoner there for the rest of my life.
However, all that is in the air at present," he continued
more lightly. "The main thing is that I am not quite so
lonely out at Eilean Heimra as you might imagine—I
have my books for companions any way."

"Then you are very busy?" she said, thoughtfully. "I must
not say I am sorry; and yet I was going to ask you——"

"I should be very busy indeed," said he, "if I could
not find time to do anything for you that you wished me
to do." (And here Käthchen said proudly to herself:
'Well, Mamie, and what do you think of that as a speech
for a Highlander?')

"Ah, but this is something rather serious," said she. "The fact is, I want to form a little private commission—a commission among ourselves—for the resettlement of the whole estate. I want every crofter's case fully investigated ; every grievance, if he has any, inquired into ; all the rents overhauled and reduced to what is quite easy and practicable and just ; and a percentage of the arrears—perhaps all the arrears—cut off, if it is found desirable. I want to be able to say : 'There, now, I have done what is fair on my side : are you going to do what is fair on yours ?' And I have got Mr. Watson to consent to give up the pasturage of Meall-na-Cruagan ; and that must be valued and taken off his rent ; and then when the pasturage is divided among the Cruagan crofters—oh, well, perhaps I shan't ask them for anything !"

"You seem to wish to act very generously by them," said he with a grave simplicity.

"Oh, I tell you I have plenty of schemes !" she said, half laughing at her own enthusiasm. "But I get no sympathy—no encouragement. There is Miss Glendinning, who simply sits and mocks——"

"Mamie, how can you say such things !" Käthchen protested—for what would this handsome young gentleman from Heimra think of her ?

"I have two new hand-looms coming next week," Mary continued ; "and I am going to send to the Inverness Exhibition, and to Dudley House, if there is another bazaar held there ; and I am going to give local prizes, too ; and I may get over some of the Harris people to show them the best dyes, and so forth. But all that will take time ; and in the meanwhile I am chiefly anxious to put myself right with the tenants by means of this commission and a complete revision of the rents. A commission they can trust—formed of people they know——"

"They will be ill to please if they don't meet you half way—and gladly," said young Ross.

Mary Stanley's eyes shone with pleasure at these hopeful words : she had not met with much encouragement hitherto.

"Does Mr. Watson know Gaelic ?" was her next question.

"In a kind of a way, I should imagine," he said. "He

is a south countryman; but I should think he knew as much Gaelic as was necessary for his business."

"And to talk to the people about general things—about their crops—and their rents?" she asked again.

"In a kind of a way he might."

"But you—you know Gaelic very well?" she said.

"I think I may fairly say that I do," he confessed frankly enough.

"Then," said she, "if you could find the time, would not that be sufficient to form a commission—Mr. Watson, and you, and I? There would be no kind of conflicting interests; and we should all want to do what was equitable and right by the people."

"Oh," said he, in a wondering sort of way, "there would be only these three—Mr. Watson, yourself, and I?"

"Mr. Purdie," said she, "would simply be a kind of clerk——"

And instantly his face changed.

"Mr. Purdie," said he, "is he coming to take part in it?"

"Only as a kind of clerk," she said quickly. "He would merely register our decisions. And of course he knows the people and all the circumstances; he could give us what information we wanted, and we could form our own judgment."

But there was no return to his face of that sympathetic interest that she had read there for a brief moment or two. His manner had entirely altered; and as they were now close to Lochgarra House, he had to take his leave.

"As far as I am concerned, Miss Stanley," said he, "I would rather leave this resettlement in Mr. Purdie's hands. Intermeddlers only make mischief, and get little thanks for their pains."

She was disappointed and hurt; and yet too proud to appeal further. He bade them good-bye—a little coldly, as Käthchen thought—and left; and Mary Stanley and her friend went into the house. All that Mary said was—

"Well, we must do the best we can, Mr. Watson, Mr. Purdie, and myself. I don't suppose Mr. Watson has any reason to be stiff-necked, and malevolent, and revengeful."

A couple of days thereafter Mr. Purdie arrived; and

the Little Red Dwarf appeared to bear with much equanimity the rating that Miss Stanley administered to him over his action in the James Macdonald case.

"Oh, ay," said he, "Macdonald will find out now who is master—the law, or himself. He is the most ill-condeetioned man in the whole district—an ill-condeetioned, thrawn, contentious rascal, and the worst example possible for his neighbours; but he'll find out now; he'll find out that the law is not to be defied with impunity——"

"What do you mean?" said she. "I told you to stop all proceedings."

"I cannot stop the Procurator-Fiscal," said the Troich Bheag Dhearg, grimly, "when he institutes a prosecution for deforcement of the sheriff's officer."

"But I got the sheriff's officer to go away peaceably," said she; "and I told him that the case would be inquired into."

"Just that," replied Mr. Purdie, with a certain self-assurance. "But it was not the business of the sheriff's officer to inquire into the case at all. He had merely to execute the sheriff's warrant; and in doing that, as he now declares, he was deforced. Macdonald will find out whether he can set the law at defiance—even with that mischief-making ne'er-do-weel Donald Ross at his elbow egging him on."

"Mr. Ross did not egg him on!" said Mary Stanley indignantly; "for I was there, and saw the whole transaction. Mr. Ross interfered for the sake of peace, or there would have been murder done."

"Ay? and I wonder what right has Mr. Ross to interfere wi' the Lochgarra tenants!" said Mr. Purdie, rather scornfully—but with an angry light twinkling in his small blue eyes.

"Because I asked him," said Mary, drawing herself up. "And I will ask him again, when it suits me."

Mr. Purdie said nothing. His heavily down-drawn mouth was more than usually dogged in expression; and it was with difficulty Mary extracted from him the information that the punishment the sheriff would most likely inflict on Macdonald was a fine of forty shillings, with the alternative of three weeks' imprisonment.

"I will pay the fine," said she, promptly. "I did not authorise you to have that man turned out of his croft; and I won't have any one turned out until I have a thorough investigation made, and the rents revised, and the arrears cancelled."

But when she proceeded to place before him the comprehensive project she had formed—to carry out which he had been summoned from Inverness—the factor abandoned his obstinate attitude, and became almost plaintive.

"Ye'll ruin the estate, Miss Stanley; and ye'll not make these people one whit more contented. Have I not had experience of them, years and years before you ever came to the place? And now that the Land League is their god, nothing will satisfy them but getting crofts and farms, arable land and pasture, all rent free, and the landlords taking the first train for the South. The poor, deluded craytures—if it was not for their spite and ill-will one could almost peety them; for what would be the advantage to them of a lot of useless land, with no stock to put on it? But maybe they expect to have the stock bought and given to them as well? I would not wonder? There's they scoundrels in the newspapers, that do not know the difference between a barn-door and a peat-stack, they've filled the heads o' the ignorant craytures with all kinds of nonsense, and they would have the deer-forests divided up —the deer-forests!—they might as well try to plough, sow, and reap the Atlantic—"

"All that does not concern me," she said, interrupting him without scruple. "What does concern me is to have myself put right, in the first place. That is to say, I wish to have rents fixed that the people can pay without getting into arrears—just rents, so that they can have no right to complain."

"Ay, and ye'll go on remitting this and remitting that," said the factor; "and if ye remitted everything they would still grumble! I tell ye, Miss Stanley, I've had experience! and it's not the way to treat these people. The more ye give them, the more they'll ask. What you consider justice, they will consider weakness; they will expect more and more; and complain if they do not get it. I'm telling ye the truth, Miss Stanley, about these idle, and ill-willed, and ill-thrawn craytures : what you propose is no the way to deal wi' them at all——"

"But I propose to take that way none the less," said Mary. And Käthchen, sitting there, and listening, and regarding the Troich Bheag Dhearg, said to herself : 'My good friend, you have tremendous shoulders and a powerful mouth, and suspicious and vindictive eyes ; but you don't in the least know with whom you have to do. Your obstinacy won't answer ; and if you are discreet you will allow it to subside.'

"I have done my best for the estate," he said, with some stiffness.

"Yes," said Mary, "no doubt. But then the result that has been arrived at is not quite satisfactory—according to modern notions. Perhaps the old way was the best ; but I am going to try the new—and I suppose I can do what I like with my own, as the saying is. And so, Mr. Purdie, I wish you to go out to-morrow morning and call on Mr. Watson, and give him my compliments—oh, no," she said, interrupting herself : " on second thoughts, I will drive out to Craiglarig myself—for it is a great favour I have to ask. Will you dine with us this evening, Mr. Purdie ?"

"I thank ye, but I hope ye'll excuse me," said the factor. "I have some various things to look into, and I'll just give the evening to them at the inn."

"Then we shall see you in the morning"—and therewithal the Little Red Dwarf took his departure.

Now to tell the truth, when the sheep-farmer of Craiglarig was asked to assist in this scheme, he did not express himself very hopefully as to the issue ; but he was a good-natured man ; and he said he would place as much of his time at Miss Stanley's disposal as he reasonably could. And so they set to work to revalue the crofts. No doubt the composition of this amateur court might have been impugned, for it consisted of the owner of the estate, her factor, and her chief tenant ; but then again Mary constituted herself, from the very outset, the champion of the occupants of the smaller holdings, Mr. Purdie took the side of the landlords, while Mr. Watson, apart from his services as interpreter, maintained a benevolent neutrality. It was slow and not inspiriting work ; for the crofters did not seem to believe that any amelioration of their condition was really meant; they were too afraid to speak, or too sullen to speak; and when they did speak, in many cases their demands were preposterous. But Mary stuck to her task.

"I must put myself right, to begin with," she said, as she had said all along. "Thereafter we will see."

And sometimes she would look out towards Heimra Island; and there was a kind of reproach in her heart. How much easier would all this have been for them, if only young Ross had consented to put aside for the moment that fierce internecine feud between him and the factor! Was Mr. Purdie, she asked herself, the sort of man that Donald Ross of Heimra should raise to the rank of being his enemy? However, the days passed, and there was no sign—no glimmer of the white sails of the *Sirène* coming away from the distant shores—no mention of the young master having been seen anywhere on the mainland.

"I warrant," said Mr. Purdie, when some remark chanced to be made, "I warrant I can tell where that cheat-the-gallows is off to—away to France for more o' that smuggled brandy so that he can spend his days and nights in drunkenness and debauchery?"

"You forget, Mr. Purdie," said Käthchen, with something very nearly approaching disdain, "that we have made the acquaintance of Mr. Ross, and know something of himself and his habits."

"Do ye?" he said, turning upon her. "I tell ye, ye do not! And a good thing ye do not! A smooth-tongued hypocrite—specious—sly—it is well for ye that ye are ignorant of what that poaching, mischief-making dare-devil really is; but ye'll find out in time—ye'll find out in time."

And indeed it was not until the self-appointed commission had done its work, and Mr. Purdie had gone away to the south again, that young Ross of Heimra reappeared, he said he had heard of what had been arranged; and he thought Miss Stanley had been most generous. This casual encounter took place just as Mary and Kate Glendinning were nearing Lochgarra House; and when they had gone inside, Käthchen said—

"Well, I don't know what has come over you, Mamie. You used always to be so self-possessed—to seem as if you were conferring a favour by merely looking at any one. And now, when you stand for a few minutes talking to Mr. Ross, you are quite nervous and shamefaced—and apparently anxious for the smallest sign of approval——"

"You have far too much imagination, Käthchen," said Mary, as she went off to her own room.

And then again, that same night, Käthchen was at one of the windows, looking out. She could not distinguish anything, for it was quite dark; she could only hear the wind howling in from the sea.

"Do you know where you should be at this moment, Mamie ?" she said. "You ought to be going up the grand staircase of some great opera-house—your cloak of crimson velvet, white-furred—the diamonds in your hair shining through your lace hood—and you should have at least three gentlemen to escort you to your box, carrying opera-glasses, and flowers. That's more like you. And yet here you banish yourself away to this out-of-the-world place—you seek for no amusement—you busy yourself all day about peats, and drains, and seed-potatoes—and the highest reward you set before yourself is to get a half-hearted 'Thank you' from a sulky crofter——"

"Käthchen," said Mary, "I would advise you to read the third chapter of the General Epistle of James."

"Ah, well," said Käthchen—and she was not deeply offended by that hint about the bridling of the tongue—"wait till your brother and Mr. Frank Meredyth come up—and you'll find them saying the same thing. Philanthropy is all very well; but you need not make yourself a white slave." And then she turned to the black window again, and to her visions. "There's one thing, Mamie : I wish Mr. Ross could see you going up that grand stair-case."

CHAPTER XIII.

HER GUEST.

"It will be all different now," said Käthchen, one evening, when they were come to within a week of the arrival of Mary's brother and his friend Frank Meredyth. "And you deserve some little rest, Mamie, and some little amusement, after all your hard work. And I want you to be considerate—towards Mr. Meredyth, I mean. It isn't merely grouse and grilse that are bringing him here. You know what your brother says—that there is no one in such request for shooting parties; he could just have his pick of invitations, all over Scotland, every autumn; so you may be sure it isn't merely for the grouse and the salmon-fishing he is coming to a little place like Lochgarra. Oh, you need not pretend to deny it, Mamie! And all I want is that you should be a little considerate. He may be very anxious to have you, and yet not quite so anxious to take over your hobby as well. He may not even be interested in the price of home-knitted stockings."

Mary Stanley did not answer just at once. The two girls were slowly walking up and down the stone terrace outside the house. It was ten o'clock at night; but it was not yet dark, nor anything approaching to dark. All the world was of a pale, clear, wan lilac colour; and in this coldly luminous twilight any white object—the front of a cottage, for example, or the little Free Church building across the bay—appeared startlingly distinct. There was an absolute silence; the sea was still; two hours ago the sun had gone down behind what seemed a vast and motionless lake of molten copper; and now there was a far-reaching expanse of pearly grey, with the long headlands and Eilean Heimra gathering shadows around them. The heavens were cloudless and serene; over the sombre hills in the east a star throbbed here and there, but it had to be sought for. There appeared to be neither lamp nor candle down in the village—there was no need of them on these magical summer nights.

"I do not see that it will be so different," said Mary, presently. "Fred will have to look after Mr. Meredyth. No doubt there will be something of a commotion in so quiet a place—the dogs, and keepers, and ponies; by the way, there will be gillies wanted for the fishing as well as for the shooting later on——"

Käthchen began to snigger a little.

"I do believe, Mamie," she said, "that that is all the interest you have in the shooting—it will provide so much more employment for your beloved crofters."

"Oh, yes, I suppose the place will be a little more brisk and lively," Mary continued, "though that won't improve it much in my estimation. I wonder what made Fred hire that wretched little steam-launch." She looked towards the tiny vessel that was lying close to the quay : the small white funnel and the decks forward were visible in the mystic twilight ; the hull was less clearly defined. "Fancy that thing coming sputtering and crackling into the bay on a beautiful night like this !"

"It would be very handy to take a message out to Heimra Island," said Käthchen, demurely.

Mary glanced at her, and laughed.

"My dear Käthchen, curiosity is a humiliating weakness ; but I will tell you what is in the letter that is lying on the hall table—and that is likely to lie there, unless a wind springs up from some quarter to-morrow. It is an invitation to Mr. Ross to come and dine with us on Monday next."

"Monday ?" said Kate Glendinning, looking surprised. "The very day your brother and Mr. Meredyth come here ?"

"For that very reason," said Mary. "I wish Mr. Ross to understand why we have never asked him to dine with us—well, of course he would understand for himself—two girls, living by themselves—and—and knowing him only for so short a time. But now, you see, I ask him for the very first evening that my brother is in the house—and that's all right and correct—if there's any Mrs. Grundy in Lochgarra."

"The Free Church Minister !" said Käthchen, spitefully —for she had never forgiven the good man for his having kept aloof from the fray at Ru-Minard.

"Mr. Ross has been very kind to me—in his reserved and distant way," Mary said, "and I should not like him to think me ungrateful——"

"He cannot do that," said Käthchen, "if he hasn't been blind to what your eyes have said to him again and again."

"What do you mean, Käthchen ?" Mary demanded—at once alarmed and resentful.

Käthchen retreated quickly : it had been a careless remark.

"Oh, I don't mean anything. I mean your eyes have said 'Thank you,' again and again ; and it is but right they should. He has indeed been very thoughtful and kind—and always so respectful—keeping himself in the background. Oh, you need not be afraid, Mamie : you won't find me suggesting that you shouldn't have the most frank and friendly relations with Mr. Ross. At the same time——"

"Yes, at the same time ?"

"I was wondering," said Käthchen, with a little hesitation, "how he might get on with your brother and Mr. Meredyth—or rather, how they might get on with him——"

"My brother and Mr. Meredyth," said Mary, a little proudly, "will remember that Mr. Ross is my guest : that will be enough."

But Kate Glendinning's uneasy forecast was not without some justification—as Mary was soon to discover. The two visitors from the South arrived on the Monday afternoon, and there were many curious eyes covertly following the waggonette as it drove through the village. Of the two strangers, the taller, who was Mary Stanley's brother, was a young fellow of about four or five-and-twenty, good looking rather, of the fair English type, with an aquiline nose, a pretty little yellow-white moustache, and calm grey eyes. His companion, some eight or ten years older, was of middle height, or perhaps a trifle under, active and wiry-looking, with a sun-tanned face, a firm mouth, and shrewd eyes, that on the whole were also good-natured. Both of the travellers were in high spirits—and no wonder : they had heard good accounts of the grouse; they had just caught a glimpse of the Garra, which had plenty of water after the recent rains ; over there was the little steam launch that could amuse them now and again for an idle hour ; and beyond the bay, the big, odd-looking house, against its background of fir and larch, seemed to offer them a hospitable welcome.

Mary was at the top of the semicircular flight of stairs to greet them ; but even as she accompanied them into the great oak hall she instinctively felt that there was something unusual in her brother's manner towards her. And when, presently, Mr. Meredyth had been taken away to be shown his own room, Fred Stanley remained behind ; Käthchen had not yet put in an appearance, for some reason or another.

"Well, what's the matter, Fred?" Mary said at once.

He had been kicking about the drawing-room in a discontented fashion, staring out of the windows or glancing at the engravings while his friend was there ; but now these two were alone.

"The matter?" said he. "Plenty the matter! I don't like to find that you have been making a fool of yourself, and that you are still bent on making a fool of yourself."

"But we can't help it if we are born that way," she said, sweetly.

"Oh, you know quite well what I mean," said this tall young gentleman with the boyish moustache. "I had heard something of it before ; but I thought we might as well stop the night at Inverness on the way north ; and I saw Mr. Purdie. Now, mind you, Mamie, don't you take it into your head that Purdie said anything against you —he did not. He's a shrewd-headed fellow, and knows which side his bread is buttered. But he answered my questions. And I find you have just been ruining this place—turning the whole neighbourhood into a pauper asylum—and—and flinging the thing away, as you might call it."

"But it wasn't left to you, Fred," she reminded him, gently. "And I have been doing my best—after inquiry."

"Oh, I know," he said impatiently ; "you've been got at by a lot of sentimentalists in London—faddists— slummers—popularity hunters ; and now, here in the Highlands, you have been working into the hands of those agitator fellows who are trying to stir up anarchy and rebellion everywhere ; and you let yourself be imposed upon by a parcel of scheming and cunning crofters, who don't thank you, to begin with, and who would pull down this house to the ground and burn it the moment your back was turned if they dared."

"You haven't been very long in Lochgarra," said she, with much good humour, "but you seem to have used your time industriously. You know all about it——"

"Oh, it isn't only this place!" he said. "Every one who reads the papers—who knows anything of the Highlands—is aware of what is going on. And you have allowed yourself to be taken in! For the credit of the family—for the sake of your own common sense—you might have waited a little. Here was Mr. Purdie, who knew the place, who knew the people; but you must needs take the whole matter in your own hands, and begin to throw away your money right and left, as if you had come into a dukedom? What do you suppose is the rental now —after all your abatements?"

"Well, I don't exactly know," said she. "But isn't it better to take what the people can really give you than nothing at all? You can't live on arrears? And, my dear Fred, what cause have you to grumble? The amount of rent affects me only; whereas I offer you the shooting and fishing, which has nothing to do with these matters. Why can't you amuse yourself and let me alone? What I have done I have considered. I have inquired into the condition of these people. To make rents practicable is not to throw away money. Indeed—but I am not going to discuss the question with you at all. Go away and get out your flybook, and take Mr. Meredyth down to the Garra, and see if you can pick up a grilse before dinner."

But he was not to be put off by her bland amiability.

"Of course," said he, "it is very kind of you to offer me the fishing and the shooting; but I should have been better pleased to have had them without encumbrances."

"What do you mean?" said she.

"Why, who has the fishing and shooting here?" said he. "This poaching scoundrel, Ross. I am told the whole place is in league with him. He can do what he likes."

"And what further information did you gather at Inverness?" she asked, rather comtemptuously.

"Well, but look here, Mamie," he remonstrated, with a sense of his wrongs gaining upon him. "Consider the position you have put me in. You know how Frank is in request at this time of the year—a thundering good shot —and used to managing things about country-houses——"

"As well as leading cotillons in London," she interposed, with smiling eyes.

"And why not?" said he, boldly. "Oh, I suppose you consider that effeminate: you would rather have him living among rocks and caves, like this smuggling fellow, and shooting seagulls for his dinner? However, look at my position. I ask him to come down with me, at your suggestion. I tell him it isn't a grand shooting—and that he'll get more sea-trout than salmon in the river—but he comes all the same; and then we discover that the whole place is at the mercy of this idling blackguard of a fellow —if we get a few birds or find a pool undisturbed, it is with his sufferance——"

"So you have acquired all this information at Inverness?" said she. "But I wouldn't entirely trust it if I were you. I am afraid Mr. Purdie is rather prejudiced. He may have been exaggerating. However, if there is any truth in what he says, I'll tell you what you ought to do: ask Mr. Ross to join your shooting and fishing parties. You'll meet him to-night at dinner."

"Here—in this house?" he exclaimed, jumping to his feet. "Mamie, are you mad?"

"I hope not," she said quietly. "But Mr. Ross has been very kind to me of late, in helping me in various little ways; and as I couldn't well ask him to dinner when only Kate and I were in the house, I took the first opportunity after your arrival——"

"And so Frank and I, after being warned that the great annoyance and vexation we should find in the place is this fellow Ross, are coolly informed that we are to meet him at dinner, and I suppose we are expected to be civil to him!"

"I certainly do expect you to be civil to him," said Mary.

"Oh, but it's too bad!" he said, impatiently, and he went to the window and turned his back on her. And then he faced round again. "I wonder what Frank will think! I was almost ashamed to ask him to come here, even as it was—a small shooting, not much fishing, and the stalking merely a chance; but, all the same, he accepts; then the first thing we hear of on reaching Inverness is all about this vexation and underhand going on; and the next thing is that we are asked to meet at dinner the very

person who causes all the trouble !   Now, Mamie, I appeal
to yourself, don't you think it is a little too hard ?"

She hesitated.   She began to fear she had been thought
less—indiscreet—too much taken up with her own plans
and projects.

"At all events, Fred," she pleaded, "your meeting Mr.
Ross at dinner can't matter one way or the other—and
you will be able to judge for yourself.   To me he does not
seem the kind of young man you would suspect of spending
his time in poaching; in fact, as I understand it, he is
looking forward to being called to the Bar, and I should
think he was busier with books than with cartridges or
salmon flies."

"You are sure he said he would come to-night ?" asked
this young Fred Stanley, looking at his sister.

"Yes."

"Definitely promised ?"

"Yes."

"Well, I don't think he will."

"Why ?"

"Because," said the young man, as he went leisurely
towards the door, "there might be a question of evening
dress.   You haven't a Court tailor at Lochgarra, have
you ?"

Mary flushed slightly.

"I don't care whether he appears in evening dress or
not," said she.   "Most likely he will come along from his
yacht ; and a yachting suit is as good as any—in my
eyes."

That evening, when the young hostess came downstairs,
the large drawing-room was all suffused with a soft warmth
of colour, for the sun was just sinking behind the violet-
grey Atlantic, and the glory of the western skies streamed
in through the several windows.   Käthchen was here ; and
Käthchen's eyes lighted up with pleasure when she saw
how Mary was attired.   And yet could any costume have
been simpler than this dress of cream-coloured China silk,
its only ornamentation being a bunch of deep crimson
fuchsias at the opening of the bodice, with another cluster
of the same flowers at her belt ?   She wore no jewellery of
any kind whatsoever.

"That is more like you, Mamie," said Käthchen, coming forward with a proud and admiring scrutiny. "I want Mr. Ross to see you in something different from your ordinary workaday things. And you look taller, too, somehow. And fairer—or is that the light from the windows?"

At this very moment the door was opened, and Mr. Ross was announced. Mary turned—with some little self-conscious expectation. And here was Young Donald of Heimra, in faultless evening dress; and there was a quiet look of friendliness in his eyes as he came forward and took the hand that was offered him. Käthchen said to herself: "Why is it that the full shirt-front and white tie suit dark men so well? And why doesn't he dress like that every evening?" For Käthchen did not know that that was precisely what Donald Ross had been in the habit of doing all the years that his mother and he had lived out in that remote island; it was a little compliment he paid her; and she liked that bit of make-believe of ceremony in the monotony of their isolated life.

The new-comers who had arrived that afternoon were somewhat late; for they had gone down to the river to have a cast or two—a futile proceeding in the blazing sunlight; but presently they made their appearance, and were in due course introduced to Donald Ross. Käthchen, who was as usual a keen and interested observer, and who had heard of Fred Stanley's indignant protest, could not but admire the perfect good breeding he displayed on being thus brought face to face with his enemy. But indeed the ordinary every-day manner of a well-educated young Englishman—its curious impassivity, its lack of self-assertion—is a standing puzzle for foreigners and for Americans. What is the origin of it? Blank stupidity? Or a serene contempt for the opinion of others? Or a determination not to commit one's self? Or an affectation of having already seen and done everything worth seeing and doing? Anyhow, Fred Stanley's demeanour towards this stranger and intruder was perfect in its negative way; and so was that of his friend, though Frank Meredyth, by virtue of his superior years, allowed himself to be a little more careless and off-hand. However, there was not much time for forming surmises or jumping to conclusions; for presently dinner was announced.

"Mr. Meredyth, will you take in Miss Glendinning?" Mary said. "Fred, I'm sorry we've nobody for you." And therewithal she turned to Donald Ross, and took his arm, and these two followed the first couple into the dining-room. Young Ross sate at her right hand, of course; he was her chief guest; the others belonged to the house.

It was rather an animated little party; for if the Twelfth was as yet some way off, there were plenty of speculations as to what the Garra was likely to yield in the way of grilse and sea-trout. Käthchen noticed that Donald Ross spoke but little, and that they seldom appealed to him; indeed, Mr. Meredyth, professing to have met with un-varying ill-luck on every stream he had ever fished, was devising an ideal salmon-river on which the sportsman would not be continually exposed to the evil strokes of fate.

"What you want first of all," said he, "is to regulate the water-supply. At present when I go to a salmon-river, one of two things is certain to happen: either it's in roaring flood, and quite unfishable, or else—and this is the more common—it has dwindled away all to nothing, and you might as well begin and throw a fly over a pavement in Piccadilly. Very well; what you want is to turn the mountain-lochs into reservoirs; you bank up the surplus water in the hills; and then, in times of drought, when the river has got low, and would be otherwise unfishable, you send up the keepers to the sluices, turn on a supply, and freshen the pools, so that the fish wake up, and wonder what's going to happen. That is one thing. Then there's another. You know that even when the water is in capital order, you may go down day by day, and find it impossible to get a single cast because of the blazing sunlight. That is a terrible misfortune: for you are all the time aware, as you sit on the bank, and hopelessly watch for clouds, that the fine weather is drying up the hills, and that very soon the stream will have dwindled away again. Very well; what you want for that is an enormous awning, that can be moved from pool to pool, and high enough not to inter-fere with the casting. By that means, you see, you could transfer any portion of a Highland stream into the land where it is always afternoon; and the fish, thinking the cool of the evening had already come, would begin to disport themselves and play with the pretty little coloured things that the current brought down. Look at the saving of time! Generally, in the middle of the day, there is a horrible long interval when nothing will move in a river. Whether it is the heat, or the sunlight, or the general drowsiness of nature, there's hardly ever anything stirring between twelve o'clock and four; and you lie on the bank, and consume a frightful amount of tobacco; and you may even fall asleep, if you have been doing a good deal of night-work in London. But if you have this great canvas screen, that can be stretched from the trees on one side to the poles on the other—very gradually and slowly, like the coming over of the evening—then the little fishes will begin to say to themselves, 'Here, boys, it's time to go out and have some fun,' and you can have fine sport, in spite of all the sunlight that ever blazed. However, I'm afraid you'd want the revenue of some half-a-dozen dukes before you could secure the ideal salmon-river."

"They're doing so many things with electricity now: couldn't you bring that in?" said Käthchen. "Couldn't you have an electric shock running out from the butt of the rod the moment the salmon touched the fly?"

But this was sheer frivolity. Frank Meredyth suddenly turned to young Ross and said—

"Oh, you can tell me, Mr. Ross—is the Garra a difficult river to fish?"

Now this was a perfectly innocent question—not meant as a trap at all; but Fred Stanley, whose mind had been brooding over the fact that the poacher was actually sitting at table with them, looked startled, and even frightened. Young Ross, on the other hand, appeared in no wise disconcerted.

"Really, I can hardly tell you," he said, "I am not much of a fisherman myself—there is no fishing at all on Heimra Island. But I should say it was not a very difficult river. Perhaps some of the pools under the woods —just above the bridge, I mean, where the banks are steep—might be a little awkward; but further up it is

much opener; and further up still you come to long
stretches where there isn't a bush on either side."

"Then, perhaps, you can't tell me what are the best sea-
trout flies for this water?" was the next question—with
no evil intent in it.

"I'm afraid you would find me an untrustworthy guide,"
said Donald Ross. "If I were you I would take Hector's
advice."

So there was an end of this matter—and Fred Stanley
was much relieved. What he said to himself was this:
"If that Spaniard-looking fellow is lying, he has a splendid
nerve and can do it well. A magnificent piece of cheek—
if it is so!"

On the whole, at this unpretentious little banquet,
Frank Meredyth did most of the talking; and naturally
it was addressed in the first place to Miss Stanley as being
at the head of the table. He had had a considerable
experience of country houses; he was gifted with a certain
sense of humour; and he told his stories fairly well—
Käthchen rewarding him now and again with a covert
little giggle. As for Donald Ross, he sate silent, and
reserved, and attentive. He was distinctly the stranger.
Not that he betrayed any embarrassment, or was ill at
ease; but he seemed to prefer to listen, especially when
Mary Stanley happened to be speaking. For, indeed, more
than once she let the others go their own way, and turned
to him, and engaged him in conversation with herself
alone. She found herself timid in doing so. If his manner
was always most respectful—and even submissive—his eyes
looked uncompromisingly straight at her, and they had a
strange, subdued fire in them. When she happened to
find his gaze thus fixed on her, she would suddenly grow
nervous—stammer—perhaps even forget what she had been
saying; while the joyous chatter of the other three at table
went gaily on, fortunately for her. Sometimes she would
think it was hardly fair of those others to leave her alone
in this way: then again she would remind herself that it
was she who was responsible for her guest. It was not
that he confused her by an awkward or obstinate silence;
on the contrary, he answered her freely enough, in a
gravely courteous way; but he seemed to attach too

much importance to what she said—he seemed to be too grateful for this special attention she was bestowing upon him. And then again she dared hardly look up; for those black eyes burned so—in a timid, startled way—regarding her as if they would read something behind the mere prettiness of her face and complexion and hair, and apparently quite unconscious of their own power.

At last the ladies rose from the table; and Mary said—

"I suppose you gentlemen will be going out on the terrace to smoke? I wish you would let us come with you. I have not smelt a cigar for months—and it is so delicious in the evening air."

There was not very much objection. Chairs were brought out from the hall; Frank Meredyth perched himself on the stone parapet; the evening air became odorous, for there was hardly a breath of wind coming up from the bay. And as they sate and looked at the wide expanse of water —with only a chance remark breaking the silence from time to time—it may have occurred to one or other of them that the summer twilight that lay over land and sea was growing somewhat warmer in tone. It was Mary who discovered the cause : the golden moon was behind them —just over the low, birch-crowned hill; and the pale radiance lay on the still water in front of them, and on the long spur of land on the other side of the bay, where there were one or two crofters' cottages and fishermen's huts just above the shore. And while they were thus looking abroad over the mystic and sleeping world, a still stranger thing appeared—a more unusual thing for Lochgarra, that is to say—certain moving lights out beyond the point of the headland.

"Look, Mary!" Käthchen cried. "But that can't be the steamer—she is not due till next Thursday!"

Whatever the vessel was, she was obviously making in for the harbour; for presently they could see both port and starboard lights—a red star and a green star, coming slowly into the still, moonlit bay.

"It is the *Consuelo*," Donald Ross said to Mary. "It is Lord Mount-Grattan's yacht : she has come down from Loch Laxford."

They watched her slow progress—this big dark thing

stealing almost noiselessly into the spectral grey world; they saw her gradually rounding; the green light disappeared; there was a sudden noise of the reversal of the screw; then a space of quiet again; and at last the roar of the anchor. The rare visitor had chosen her position for the night.

Almost directly thereafter young Ross of Heimra rose and took leave of his hostess—saying a few words of thanks for so pleasant an evening. The others did not go indoors, however; the still, balmy, moonlight night was too great a temptation. They remained on the terrace, looking at the big black steam-yacht that now lay motionless on the silver-grey water, and listening for the occasional distant sounds that came from it.

But presently they saw a small boat put off from the shore, rowed by two men, with a third figure in the stern.

"That is Mr. Ross!" Käthchen exclaimed. "I know it is—that is his light overcoat."

"Can he be going away in the yacht?" Mary said suddenly.

"Not likely!" her brother struck in. "When you start off on a yachting cruise you don't go on board in evening dress." And then the young man turned to his male companion. "I say, Frank, don't you think that fellow was lying when he pretended not to know anything about the fishing in the Garra?"

It was an idle and careless question—perhaps not even meant to be impertinent; but Mary Stanley flamed up instantly—into white heat.

"Mr. Ross is—is a gentleman," she said, quite breathlessly. "And—he was my guest this evening—though you—you did not seem to treat him as such!"

Käthchen put her hand gently on her friend's arm.

"Mamie!" she said.

And Frank Meredyth never answered the question: this little incident—and a swift and covert glance he had directed towards the young lady herself—had given him something to think about

CHAPTER XIV.

ON GARRA'S BANKS.

IT soon became sufficiently evident that it was not solely
for fishing and shooting that Mr. Frank Meredyth had
come to Lochgarra; keepers, gillies, dogs, guns, fly-books
occupied but little of his attention, while Mary Stanley
occupied much; moreover, the zeal with which he pro-
secuted his suit was favoured by an abundance of opportunities. Indeed it must often. have occurred to our
country cousins—to those of them, at least, who have
ventured to speculate on such dark mysteries—that court-
ship in a big and busy town like London must be a very
difficult thing, demanding all kinds of subterfuges, plans,
and lyings-in-wait. Or is it possible at all? they may ask,
looking around at their own happy chances. The after-
service stroll home on a Sunday morning, along a honey-
suckle lane—the little groups of twos and threes getting
widely scattered—is a much more secret and subtle thing
than the crowded church-parade of Hyde Park, where every
young maiden's features are being watched by a thousand
amateur detectives. To sit out a dance is all very well—
to take up a position on the staircase and affect to ignore
the never-ending procession of ascending and descending
guests; but it is surely inferior to the idle exploration of
an old-fashioned rustic garden, with its red-brick walls and
courts, its unintentional mazes, its leafy screens—while the
tennis-lawn and the shade of trees, and ices and strawberries, hold the dowagers remote. And if these be the
opportunities of the country, look at those of a distant
sea-side solitude—the lonely little bays, the intervening
headlands, the moonlight wanderings along the magic
shores. Even in the day-time, when all this small world
of Lochgarra was busy, there were many chances of companionship, of which he was not slow to avail himself. The
Twelfth was not yet; the water in the Garra was far too
low for fishing; what better could this young man do than
go about with Mary Stanley, admiring her bland, good-
natured ways, sympathising in her beneficent labour, and

participating in it by the only method known to him—that is to say, by the simple process of purchase? One consequence of all which was that he gradually became the owner of a vast and quite useless collection of home-shapen sticks, home-knitted stockings, homespun plaids, and what not; although, being only the younger son of a not very wealthy Welsh baronet, Frank Meredyth was not usually supposed to be overburdened with cash. But he said he would have a sale of these articles when he went south; and if there were any profit he would return it to Miss Stanley, to be expended as she might think fit.

The truth is, however, that Mary was far from encouraging him to accompany her on her expeditions; and would rather have had him go and talk to the keepers about the dogs. For one thing, she did not wish him to know how remote this little community still was from the Golden Age which she hoped in time to establish. For another, she was half afraid that those people whose obduracy she was patiently trying to overcome might suddenly say among themselves, " Oh, here are more strangers come to spy and inquire. And these are the fine gentlemen who have taken away the shooting and the fishing that by rights should belong to Young Donald. We do not want them here; no, nor the *Baintighearna* either; let her keep to her own friends. We do not wish to be interfered with; we are not slaves; when her uncle bought Lochgarra, he did not buy us." And thus it was that she did not at all approve of those two young men coming with her to the door of this or that cottage, standing about smoking cigarettes, and scanning everything with a cold and critical Saxon eye: she wished that the Twelfth were here, and that she could have them packed off up the hill out of everybody's way.

Meanwhile, what had become of Donald Ross of Heimra? Nothing had been heard or seen of him since the moonlight night on which they had watched him go out to the *Consuelo;* and next day the big steam-yacht left the harbour. Mary, though not saying much, became more and more concerned; his silence and absence made her think over things; sometimes Käthchen caught her friend looking out towards Heimra Island, in a curiously wistful

way. And at last there came confession—one evening
that Fred Stanley and Frank Meredyth had gone off on
a stenlock-fishing expedition.

"I hope I am not distressing myself about nothing,
Käthchen," Mary said, "but the more I think of it the
more I fear——"

"What?"

"That something happened to offend Mr. Ross the evening he dined here. Oh, I don't mean anything very serious
—any actual insult——"

"I should think not!" said Käthchen. "I thought
he was treated with the greatest consideration. He took
you in to dinner, to begin with. Then you simply devoted
yourself to him all the evening——"

"But don't you think, Käthchen," Mary said—and she
rose and went to the window, evidently in considerable
trouble—"don't you think that Fred and Mr. Meredyth—
yes, and you, too—that you kept yourselves just a little
too openly to yourselves—it was hardly fair, was it?"

"Hardly fair!" Käthchen exclaimed. "To leave you
entirely to him? I wonder what young man would complain of that! I think he ought to be very grateful to
us. If he had wished, he could have listened to Mr.
Meredyth—who was most amusing, really; but as you
two seemed to have plenty to say to each other—we
could not dream of interfering——"

"But you never know how any little arrangement of that
kind may be taken," Mary said, absently. "The intention
may entirely be misunderstood. And then, brooding over
some such thing in that lonely island may make it serious.
I would not for worlds have him imagine that—that—he
had not been well-treated. If you consider the peculiar
circumstances—asked to a house that used to be his own—
knowing he was to meet a nephew of my uncle—indeed
I was not at all sure that he would come."

"Neither was I!" said Käthchen, with a bit of a laugh.
"It was very generous of him, in my opinion: he must
have had to make up his mind."

"Well, I will admit this," said Mary, with some colour
mounting to her face, "that I put the invitation so that
it would have been rather difficult for him to refuse—I—

I asked him to come as a favour to myself. But that makes it all the worse if he has gone away with any consciousness of affront—and—and, as I say, brooding over it in that island would only deepen his sense of injury." She hesitated for a second or two, and then went on again, in a desperate kind of a way : "Why, for myself, the thinking over the mere possibility of such a thing has made me perfectly miserable. I don't know what to do, Käthchen, and that is the truth. If Fred and his friend weren't here I would go away out to Heimra—I mean you and I could go—so that I might see for myself why he has never sent me a line, or called. There must be something the matter. And as you say, it was a great concession to me—his coming to the house ; and I can't bear the idea of anything having happened to give him offence."

"If you want to know," said the practical Käthchen, "why don't you get Fred to write and ask him over for a day's shooting ? "

Mary was walking up and down : she stopped.

"Yes," she said, thoughtfully. "That might do—if Fred were a little reasonable. It would show Mr. Ross, at all events, that there was no wish to make a stranger of him."

Her two guests came home late ; they had got into a good shoal of stenlock, and had been loth to give up. When they made their appearance they found supper awaiting them ; and not only that, but the young ladies had let their dinner go by in order to give them their company ; so they ought to have been in an amiable mood.

"Where did you go, Fred ? " Mary asked, as they took their places at table.

"Oh, a long way," said he. "We got Big Archie's boat, and then we had her towed by the steam-launch : we made first of all for the headlands south of Minard Bay."

"Then you would be in sight of Eilean Heimra most of the time ? " she said, timidly.

"Oh, yes."

"You did not see any one coming or going from the island ? " she continued, with eyes cast down.

"No ; but we were not paying much heed. I can tell you, those big stenlock gave us plenty of occupation."

"It is rather odd we should have heard nothing of Mr. Ross," she ventured to say.

"He may have gone up to London," Mr. Meredyth put in, in a casual kind of fashion. "Didn't you say he is studying for the Bar? Then he must go up from time to time to keep his terms and eat his dinners."

"No, no—not just now," Fred Stanley interposed, and he spoke as one having authority, for he was himself looking forward to being called. "There's nothing of that sort going on at this time of year: the next term is Michaelmas—in November. My dear Frank, do you imagine that that fellow Ross would go away from Lochgarra at the beginning of August?—why, it's the very cream of the shooting!—a few days in advance of the legal time—the very pick of the year!—especially if you have a convenient little arrangement with a game dealer in Inverness." Then he corrected himself. "No, I don't suppose he carries on this kind of thing for money; I will do him that justice; he doesn't look that kind of a chap. More likely malice: revenge for my uncle having come in and robbed him of what he had been brought up to consider his own: perhaps, too, the natural instinct of the chase, which is strong in some people, even when the law frowns on them."

"I will confess this," Frank Meredyth struck in (for he noticed that Mary was looking deeply vexed, and yet was too proud to speak), "that if I had been born the son of a horny-handed peasant—or more particularly still, the son of the village publican—I should have been an inveterate poacher. I can't imagine anything more exciting and interesting; the skill and cunning you have to exercise; the spice of danger that comes in; the local fame you acquire, when late hours and deep draughts lead to a little bragging. A poacher?—of course I should have been a poacher!—it is the only thing for one who has the instincts of a gentleman, and no money. And in the case of that young Ross, what could be more natural, with all the people round about recognising that that is the inalienable part of your inheritance? The land may have gone, and crops and sheep, and what not: but the wild animals —the game—the birds of the air—the salmon in the stream—they still belong to the old family—they were never sold."

"I beg your pardon—they were sold," said Fred Stanley, bluntly, "and whoever takes them in defiance of the law, steals : that's all about it."

"I dare say the lawyers could say something on behalf of that form of stealing," Frank Meredyth answered, good-naturedly, "only that they're all busy justifying the big stealings—the stealings of emperors, and statesmen, and financial magnates. However, I will admit this is also : it is uncommonly awkward when you have poaching going on. It is an annoyance that worries. And you suspect everybody ; and go on suspecting, until you can trust nobody ; and you get disgusted with the whole place. Your abstract sympathy with the life of a poacher won't comfort you when you imagine that the moor has been shot over before you are out in the morning, and when you suspect the keepers of connivance. It isn't pleasant, I must say ; indeed, it is a condition of affairs that can but rarely exist anywhere, for naturally the keepers are risking a good deal—risking their place in fact——"

"I quite agree with you, Mr. Meredyth," Mary said at this point, with some emphasis. "Indeed, it is a condition of affairs that looks to me absurdly improbable. I should like to have some sort of definite proof of it before believing it. No doubt, there may be some such feeling as you suggest among the people—that Mr. Ross should still have the fishing and shooting : it is easy enough to believe that, when you find you cannot convince them that the land does not belong to him too ; but it is quite another thing to assume that he takes advantage of this prevailing sentiment. However, in any case, isn't the remedy quite simple ? Why shouldn't Fred ask him to go shooting with you ? Surely there is room for three guns ?"

"Oh," said Fred Stanley, with some stiffness, "if you wish to invite him to shoot on the Twelfth, very well. It is your shooting ; it is for you to say. Of course, I did not understand when I left London that there was any stranger going to join the party, or I should have explained as much to Frank——"

"I am sure I shall be only too delighted, Miss Stanley,"

Frank Meredyth put in, quickly, "if any friend of yours should join us—quite delighted—naturally—another gun will be all the better. And when I spoke of the joys of poaching, I assure you it was without any particular reference to anybody; I was telling you what would be my own ambition in other circumstances. Fred will write to Mr. Ross——"

"I beg your pardon," said the young gentleman, with something of coldness. "Mamie, you'd better write yourself."

"Not if there is going to be any disinclination on your part," she said.

"Disinclination?" he repeated. "Well, the way I look at it is simply this: you suspect that poaching is going on, and you ask the poacher to go shooting—why? Because you are afraid of him. It is a confession of weakness. What I would do, if the place were mine, is this: I'd send the keepers packing—and every man-jack of the gillies, too—until I knew I was master. It is perfectly preposterous that your own servants should connive at your being cheated——"

"Doesn't that sometimes happen in other spheres of life?" Frank Meredyth asked—he was evidently bent on being pacificator.

"I don't know—I don't care," said young Stanley, stubbornly. "What I do know is, that if Ross is to come shooting with us on the Twelfth, well, then, Mamie had better send him the invitation: I'm not hypocrite enough to do it."

So matters remained there for the present; but the very next evening a singular incident occurred which caused a renewal of this discussion—with its conflict of prejudices and prepossessions. All night there had been heavy and steady rain; in the morning the Garra had risen considerably; towards the afternoon it was discovered that the river was fining down again; whereupon Fred Stanley proposed to his friend and companion that they should go along as soon as the sun was likely to be off the water, and try for a grilse or a sea-trout in the cool of the twilight. They did not propose to take either gillie or keeper with them; they had found out which were the proper flies;

and they would have greater freedom without professional supervision. So Frank Meredyth shouldered a grilse-rod of moderate length and weight; his companion took with him both landing-net and gaff; and together they walked along to the banks of the stream, passing through the village on their way.

They were rather too early; the sun was still on the pools; but they had the rod to put together, the casting-line to soak, the flies to choose. Then they sate down on the breckan, and cigarettes were produced.

"Don't you think my sister puts me into a very awkward position?" said the younger man, discontentedly.

"Why?" asked his companion—being discreet.

"Keeping up those friendly relations, or apparently friendly relations, with this fellow Ross," Fred Stanley said. "Wouldn't it be very much better, much honester, if we were declared enemies—as the people about here think we are? Then we could give fair notice to the keepers that they must either have him watched or they themselves must go. You see, my sister doesn't care what happens to the fishing or the shooting; but it is a shame she should be imposed upon; and a still greater shame that this fellow should come to the house, and pretend to be on friendly terms with her. You know, Frank, he must be a thundering hypocrite. Do you mean to tell me he has forgiven any one of our family for what my uncle did— you know what Mamie told you—draining the loch and pulling down the old castle? Of course he hasn't! And perhaps I don't blame him: it was too bad; and that's a fact. But what I do blame him for is pretending to be on good terms; coming to the house; and so taking it out of our power to treat him as he ought to be treated—that is, as a person who is defying the law, whom we ought to try to catch. You see, Mamie is so soft; she hasn't that dimple in her cheek for nothing; she's far too good-natured; and this stuck-up Spaniard, or Portuguese, or whatever he is, seems to have impressed her because he looks mysterious and says nothing. Or perhaps she thinks that we have ill-treated him—that my uncle has, I mean. Or perhaps she hopes that through him she will get at those ill-con-ditioned brutes about here—you heard what Purdie said.

I don't know; I can't make out women; they're not sufficiently above-board for the humble likes of me; but this I do know, that I should like to catch that fellow Ross red-handed, carrying a salmon or a brace of grouse, and then we should have it out!"

Frank Meredyth did not reply to this resentful little oration: he had been watching the westering sun, that was now slowly sinking behind the topmost trees of the steep bank on the other side of the river. And at length, when there was no longer a golden flash on the tea-brown ripples that came dancing over the shingle, he went down to the edge of the stream and began to cast, throwing a very fair line. But he was not very serious about it; in this rapid run there was little chance of anything beyond a sea-trout; he had his eye on a deeper and smoother, and likelier pool lower down, where perchance there might be a lively young grilse lying, up that morning from the sea.

Then he called out—

"Come along, Fred, and take the next pool: it amuses me quite as much to look on."

"It amuses me more," the younger man said, taking out another cigarette. "You're throwing a beautiful line —go ahead—you'll come upon something down there."

And indeed Frank Meredyth now began to cast with more caution as he approached this smoother and deeper pool—sending his fly well over to the other side, letting it come gradually round with almost imperceptible jerks, and nursing it in the water before recovery. It was one of the best stretches of the river—they. had been told that; and there was a fair chance after the rain. But all of a sudden, as he was carefully watching his fly being carried slowly round by the current, there was a terrific splash right in the midst of the stream : a large stone had been hurled from among the trees on the opposite bank : the pool was ruined. The fisherman, without a word, let his fly drift helplessly, and turned and looked at his com panion. The same instant Fred Stanley had thrown away his cigarette, ran down the bank, and sprang into the water—careless of everything but getting across in time to capture their cowardly assailant. He had no waders on; but he did not heed that; all his endeavour was to force his way across the current before their unseen enemy could have escaped from among those birches. Meredyth could do nothing but look on. The point at which his companion had entered the stream was rather above the pool, and shallower; but none the less there was a certain body of water to contend with; and out in the middle young Stanley, despite his arduous efforts, made but slow progress. Then there was the catching at the bushes on the opposite bank—a hurried scrambling up—the next second he had disappeared among the birch trees. Frank Meredyth laid down his rod, and quietly took out a cigarette: fishing in this kind of a neighbourhood did not seem to attract him any more.

It was some time before Fred Stanley came back: of course his quest had been unsuccessful—his hampered progress through the water had allowed his foe to get clear away.

"You see you were wrong, Frank," he said, with affected indifference, when he had waded across the stream again. "Our friendly neighbour hasn't gone south to keep the last of his terms, or for any other reason. A pretty trick, wasn't it? I knew there was a dog-in-the-manger look about the fellow; well, I don't care: Mamie can choose her own friends. As for you and me, we are off by the mail-car that leaves to-morrow morning."

He was simply wild with rage, despite all his outward calmness Frank Meredyth looked very grave indeed.

"We can't do that, Fred," said he. "It would be an affront to your sister——"

"Well, then, and she allows my friend—her guest—to be insulted!" he exclaimed. "And all because no one dare speak out! But I've had enough of it. This last is too much—this shows you what the neighbourhood is like; and it is all to be winked at! As I say, I've had enough. I'm off. You can stay if you choose——"

"You know I can't stay here if you go," said Meredyth, in the same grave way: indeed, he did not at all like this position in which he found himself. And then he said: "Come, Fred, don't make too much of a trifle——"

"Do you call that a trifle?" the other demanded. "It is an indication of the spirit of the whole place; and more than that, it shows you the miserable, underhand enmity of this very fellow who has been pretending to make friends with my sister. It is not on my account—it is on your account—that I am indignant. I asked you to come here. This is pretty treatment, is it not?—and a pleasant intimation of what we may expect all the way through, if we stay on——"

"Of course we must stay on," said Meredyth. "I would not for anything have your sister vexed. I would not even tell her of what has just happened. Why should you? Neither you nor I care so much for the fishing——"

"That is not the point, Frank," said young Stanley. "Reel up—and we will go back to the house. I want Mamie to understand what all her pampering of this place has resulted in—nothing but miserable, underhand spite and enmity. And if we do stop on, do you think I'd be frightened away from the fishing? Not if I had to get water-bailiffs up from Inverness, and give them each a double-barrelled breech-loader and a hiding-place in the woods. Pitching stones into salmon pools and then running away is a very pretty amusement; but that skulking and poaching thief would sing another tune if he were brought down by a charge of No. 6 shot!"

And he was in the same indignant mood when they got back to Lochgarra House. He went straight to his sister. He told her the story—and in silence awaited her answer. What was it to be?—an excuse?—an apology? a promise of inquiry and stricter government?

But for a second or two Mary Stanley was thoroughly alarmed. She recalled with a startling distinctness her own experience—her wandering up the side of the river— her coming upon the almost invisible poacher in the mysterious dusk of the twilight—the strange and vivid circles of blue-white fire on the dark surface of the stream whenever he moved—then his noiseless escape into the opposite woods; and she recalled, too, her own sudden suspicions as to who that ghostly fisherman was. Since then she had seen a good deal of Donald Ross, and she had gradually ceased to connect him in any way with that illegal haunting of the salmon-stream; but this new incident—following upon her brother's protests and remonstrances—frightened her, for one breathless moment. Then she strove to reassure herself. The young man who had sate by her side at dinner a few evenings ago—proud, reserved, and self-possessed, and yet timidly respectful towards herself and grateful for the attention she paid him—was not the kind of person to go spitefully throwing stones into a salmon-pool in order to destroy a stranger's fishing. It was absurd to think so!

"I am very sorry, Mr. Meredyth," said she, "that such a thing should have happened. It is a vexatious annoyance——"

"Oh, don't consider me, Miss Stanley!" said he, at once. "I assure you I don't mind in the least. I did not even wish to have it mentioned."

"It is annoying, though—very," she said. "It seems a pity that any one should have such ill-will——"

"But what are you going to do?" her brother demanded. "Sit tamely down and submit to this tyranny? And what will be the next thing?—trampling the nests in the spring, I suppose, so that there won't be a single grouse left on the whole moor. Then why shouldn't they help themselves to a sheep or two, when they want mutton for dinner, or go into the Glen Orme forest for a stag, if they prefer venison?"

Mary rang the bell; Barbara came.

"Barbara," said she, "send a message to Hector that I want to see him."

When the tall and bronze-complexioned keeper made his appearance—looking somewhat concerned at this unusual summons —she briefly related to him what had occurred; and her tone implied that he was responsible for this petty outrage.

"I was offering," said Hector, in his serious and guarded way, "to go down to the ruvver with the chentlemen——"

"Yes, that is true enough," Fred Stanley broke in. "Hector did offer to go down with us. But surely it is a monstrous thing that we shouldn't be able to stroll along to a pool and have a cast by ourselves without being interfered with in this way. Come now, Hector, you must know who was likely to do a thing like that."

Hector paused for a moment, and then answered—

"Indeed, sir, I could not seh."

"Who is it who thinks the fishing in the Garra belongs to him, and is determined no one else shall have it? Isn't there anyone about with that idea in his head?" The question was put pointedly; it was clear what Fred Stanley meant; but there was no definite reply.

"There's some of the young lads they are fond of mischief," Hector said ambiguously. "And there's others nowadays that will be saying everyone has the right to fish."

"And perhaps that is your opinion, too," said Fred Stanley, regarding him.

"Oh, no, sir, not that at ahl," the keeper answered, simply enough. "But such things get into their heads, and sometimes they will be reading it from a newspaper, and the one talking to the other about what the Land League was saying at the meetings. The young lads they speak about new things nowadays amongst themselves."

"And I suppose they want to have the shooting, too?" Fred Stanley continued; "and if we don't give them the shooting they will go up the hill in the spring and trample the eggs?"

"Oh, no, sir, the shepherds are friendly with us," said Hector.

Mary interposed; for this badgering seemed to lead to nothing.

"Couldn't you get some old man to act as water-bailiff, Hector?—some old man to whom a small weekly wage would be a consideration."

"Oh, yes, mem, I could do that," said the keeper.

"And if there are any of those mischievous lads about, why, if he were to catch one of them, a little trip across to Dingwall might frighten the others, wouldn't it?"

"Just that, mem."

"There is old John at the inn—he seems to do nothing—does he know anything about the river?"

"Oh, yes, indeed—he was many a day a gillie," Hector made answer.

"Very well; see what wages he wants; and tell him that when he suspects there's any poaching going on, or any mischief of any kind, you and Hugh will give him a hand in the watching."

" Very well, mem."

And so the tall, bushy-bearded Hector was going away ; but Fred Stanley stopped him. The young man's sombre suspicions had not been dissipated by those vague references to mischievous lads.

" Hector," said he, " is Mr. Ross of Heimra a keen fisherman ? "

" I could not seh, sir," was Hector's grave and careful answer.

" Does he know the Garra well ? "

" I could not seh, sir," Hector repeated.

" You don't happen to have seen or heard anything of him of late ? "

" No, sir," said Hector ; and then he added, " but I was noticing the yat coming over from Heimra this morning."

. " Oh, really, " exclaimed the young man, with a swift glance towards Frank Meredyth. " The yacht came over this morning ? So Mr. Ross is in the neighbourhood ? "

" Maybe, sir ; but I have not seen him whatever."

That seemed to be enough for the cross-examiner.

" All right, Hector—thank you. Good evening ! "

The head-keeper withdrew ; and Fred Stanley turned to his sister.

" I thought as much," said he. " I had a notion that Robinson Crusoe had come ashore from his desolate island. And no doubt he was very much surprised and disgusted to find two strangers intruding upon his favourite salmon pools—on the very first evening there has been a chance of a cast for some time. But he should not have allowed his anger to get the better of him ; it was a childish trick, that flinging a stone into the water ; a poor piece of spite—for one who claims to represent an old Highland family. Don't you think so, Mamie ? "

Well, this at least was certain—that the *Sirène* had come across from Heimra, and was now lying in the Camus Bheag, or Little Bay. And the very next afternoon, as Mary Stanley and her friend Käthchen were seated at a table in the drawing-room busily engaged in comparing samples of dyed wool, the door was opened, and Barbara appeared.

" Mr. Ross, mem ! " said Barbara.

CHAPTER XV.

A THREATENED INVASION.

MARY rose quickly, her clear eyes showing such obvious pleasure that Käthchen was inclined to be indignant. ' Mamie, have you no pride ! ' Käthchen said in her heart. ' It is not becoming in a young woman to be so grateful —for an ordinary piece of civility. And Mary Stanley of all people ! ' Well, Mary Stanley did not seem to be governed by any such considerations ; she went forward to receive her visitor with the frankest smile of welcome lighting up her face ; the magic-working dimple did its part.

"I am so glad you have called," said she, "for I was thinking of writing to you, and I was not sure whether you were at Heimra. We have not seen the yacht coming and going of late."

"No," said he, as he took the chair nearest her (and Käthchen remarked that his eyes, too, showed pleasure, if less openly declared), "I went down as far as Portree in the *Consuelo*—or I would have called before now. Did you want to see me about —about anything ? "

And this question he asked with a curious simplicity and directness of manner. There was none of the self-consciousness of a young man addressing a remarkably pretty young woman. It was rather like an offer of neighbourly help : what trouble was she in now ?

"I was wondering," she made answer, with a little timidity, whether you would care to go out on the Twelfth with my brother and Mr. Meredyth. It is not a very grand shooting, as you know ; but you would get some little amusement, I suppose ; and Miss Glendinning and I would come and have lunch with you—if we were not in the way."

This ought to have been a sufficiently attractive invitation ; but the observant Käthchen noticed that the young man hesitated.

"Thank you very much," said he ; "it is most kind of you to have thought of me ; but the fact is I'm not much of a shot, and I shouldn't like to spoil the bag. Of course, your brother will want to see what the moor can yield; and with fair shooting two guns should give a very good account of Lochgarra; so that it would be really a pity to spoil the Twelfth by bringing in a useless gun. Thank you all the same for thinking of me——"

"Oh, perhaps you don't care about shooting?" said Mary. "Perhaps you are fonder of fishing?"

And hardly were the words out of her mouth when some sudden recollection of that phantom poacher rushed in upon her mind; a hideous dread possessed her; how could she have been so unutterably indiscreet? Not only that, but there was yesterday's incident of the hurling of the stone into the salmon-pool: would he imagine that she suspected him—that she was probing into a guilty knowledge? She was bewildered by what she had done; and yet determined to betray no consciousness of her blunder. A ghastly and protracted silence seemed to follow her question; but that was merely imagination on her part; he answered her at once—and that in the most natural manner, without a trace of embarrassment.

"I am a poor enough shot," said he, with a smile, "but I am even a worse fisherman. You see, there is hardly any shooting on Heimra Island, but there is still less fishing—none at all, practically. As for the shooting, there are some rabbits among the rocks, and occasionally I have seen a covey of grouse come flying across from the mainland; but the truth is, when you get used to the charm of quiet in a place like that, you don't want to have it broken by the banging of a gun——"

"Oh, no, of course not," said Mary, with a certain eagerness of assent—for she was overjoyed to find that nothing had come of her fancied indiscretion. "Of course not. I can quite imagine there must be a singular fascination in the solitariness of such an island, and the—the —silence. A fascination and a charm; and yet when Miss Glendinning and I have been up among the hills here, sometimes it has seemed too awful—too lifeless—it became terrible. Then out at Heimra—the sea being all round you in the night—and the bit of land so small—that must be a strange sensation; but perhaps you don't notice 't as a stranger might; you must have got used to it——"

"Yes," said he, "it is very solitary and very silent. All the same," he added, rather absently, "I dare say I shall miss that very solitariness and silence when I go away from Heimra, as I hope to do ere long. I should not wonder if I looked back with some regret."

"Oh, you are going away from Heimra—and before long?" Mary repeated—and Käthchen glanced quickly at her.

"I hope so," he said. "Well, I would not trouble you with my schemes and plans, but for the fact that they indirectly concern you." She looked startled for a second; but he proceeded with a certain easy cheerfulness of manner which Käthchen thought became him; and he spoke in a confidential and friendly way, more than was his wont: "Yes; if what I am aiming at succeeds it will make your position here a good deal easier. I know the difficulties you have to contend with on an estate like this— the poverty of the soil—families growing up and marrying, and still clinging to the small homesteads—the distance from markets—the climate—and all that. And indeed my first scheme—my ideal scheme," he went on, in this frank kind of fashion, "was comprehensive enough : I wanted nothing less than to take away the whole of the population with me—not the surplus population merely, but the whole of the people bodily, leaving the sheep and the game in undisturbed possession. That would have made matters easy for you—and for Mr. Purdie. I thought I could carry them away with me to one of the colonies ; and get a grant of Crown Lands from the Government ; and be appointed to look after the settlement, so that I could live and die among those I have known from my childhood. There was only one point of the scheme that I was absolutely sure about, and that was that the people would go if I asked them—yes, to the very oldest. 'If I have to be carried on board the ship,' one of them said to me——"

"Have you considered—the terrible responsibility?" she said, in rather a breathless way.

"Yes, indeed," said he, gravely. "And that comprehensive project was not practicable : it was too big—too visionary. But for some time back I have been making inquiries : indeed I went down to Portree chiefly to see one of the Committee who manage the Emigrants' Information Office—he is taking his holiday in Skye at present. And if in a more modest and reasonable way I could take a number of the people away with me, and found a little colony out in Queensland or in Canada, that would give you some relief, and make it easier for those remaining behind—would it not? North-Western Canada and Queensland—perhaps you know—are the only colonies that offer the immigrant a free homestead of 160 acres; and Canada is especially hospitable, for at all the ports there are Government agents, for the purpose of giving the immigrants every information and procuring them work. Oh, I am very well aware," he continued—seeing that she was silent and absorbed—"that emigration is not a certain panacea. There is no assurance that the emigrant is going to leave all his ills and troubles behind him. Very often the first generation have to suffer sore hardship; then the next reap the reward of their toil and perseverance. A home-sickness—well, plenty of them never get over that; and naturally, if they are home-sick, they exaggerate their sufferings and misfortunes." He sought in his pockets and brought out a letter. "Perhaps you would care to read that—I found it awaiting me when I came home this time."

She took the letter, and looked at it in rather a perfunctory way. It was clear that her mind was fixed on something quite different. Perhaps she was thinking of that distant settlement—out among the pines and snows of the North-West—or far away under the Southern Cross: the drafted people working with a right goodwill, and concealing their home-sickness, and making light of their hardships, so long as Young Donald was with them. Perhaps she was thinking of the denuded Lochgarra, and of the empty Eilean Heimra. After all, it was something to have a neighbour, even if he lived in that lonely island. And if she were doing her best with the people who remained—fostering industries, spreading education, bettering their condition in every way—well, there would be no one to whom she could show what she had done. What did her brother care for such things?—her brother was thinking only of grouse, and black-game, and grilse. Frank Meredyth?—she more than suspected that his affectation of interest was only a sort of compliment paid to herself. And then there was another thing, more difficult to formulate; but away deep down in her heart somewhere there had sprung up a vague desire that some day or other she might be able to show Donald Ross how sorry she was for the injuries he had suffered at the hands of her family. When once a close and firm friendship had been established between them, he might be induced to forgive. But if he were going away, while as yet he and she were almost strangers? And she knew that the people who might remain with her at Lochgarra would say to themselves that she was the one who had driven Young Donald across the seas.

She forced herself to read the letter—

"Armadale, Minnesona, Canada.

"Mr. Ross of Heimra.—Sir,—Peter Macleod was showing me the letter you was writing to him, and asking about me, and he said it my duty to answer and give Mr. Ross the news. We have not much comfort here; I think the Lord was not pleased with us that we left our own country and come to America. My wife is very seeck; and while she has the seeckness on her I cannot go away and get railway work; and there are the five children, the oldest of them twelve, and not able to do mich. I have a cow that is giving mulk. I have a yoke of oxen. There is not a well; but I will begin at it soon. I have found a Lochgarra man, wan Neil Campbell, about five miles from here; it is a pleasure to me that I have the jance of speaking my own langwich. I have twelve tons of hay. The soil is good; but the weather verra bad; ay, until the end of May there was frost every night, and many's the time hail stones that would spoil the crop in half an hour. I bought ten bolls of meal forbye* the Government's supply; and if I had not had a little money I do not know what I would have done; and now the money is gone, and I cannot go away to work and leave my wife with the

* *Forbye*—besides.

seeckness on her; and maybe if I did go away I would not get any work whatever. What to do now it is beyond me to say, and we are far away from any friends, my wife and me. When I went to Kavanagh to bring the doctor to my wife I was hearing the news from home that they believed I had brokken my leg. But it is not my legs that are brokken—it is my heart that is brokken. There has been no happiness within me since the day I left Loch Torridon and went away to Greenock to the steamer. That was a bad day for me and my family; we have had no peace or comfort since; it's glad I would be to see Ru-na-uag once more—ay, if they would give me a job at brekkin stones. This is all the news I am thinking of; and wishing Mr. Ross a long life and happiness, I am your respectful servant,

"ANGUS MACKAY."

"Poor man!" said Mary. And then she looked up as she handed back the letter. "I should have thought," she continued addressing Donald Ross, "that a report like that would have caused you to hesitate before recommending any more emigration. Was it you who sent that poor man out?"

"Oh, no," he answered at once; "that Angus Mackay lived at Loch Torridon—a long way south from here. I only got to know something of him accidentally. But mind you, Miss Stanley, I would not assume that even in his case emigration has been a failure. That letter is simply saturated with home-sickness. I should not be at all surprised to hear in a year or two that Angus was doing very well with his farm; and it is almost a certainty that when his family have grown up they will find themselves in excellent circumstances. Of course it is hard on him that his wife should be ill, especially with those young children—but these are misfortunes that happen everywhere."

"Emigration?" she repeated (and Käthchen could tell by her tone that this scheme of his found no favour in her sight). "So that is your cure for the poverty and discontent in the Highlands? But don't you think it is rather a confession of failure? Don't you think if the

landlords were doing their duty there would be no need to
drive these poor people away from their homes? No
doubt, as you say, families grow up and marry, while the
land does not increase; but look at the thousands upon
thousands of acres that at present don't support a single
human being——"

"You mean the deer-forests?" he said quite coolly (for
the owner of the little island of Heimra had not much
personal and immediate interest in the rights and duties of
proprietors). "Yes; they say that is the alternative.
They say either emigration or throwing open the deer-
forests to small tenants and crofters—banishing the deer
altogether, limiting the sheep-farms, planting homesteads.
It sounds very well in the House of Commons, but I'm
afraid it wouldn't work in practice. Such deer-forests as
I happen to know are quite useless for any such purpose;
the great bulk of the soil is impossible—rocks and peat
simply; and then the small patches of land that might be
cultivated—less than two acres in every thousand, they
say—are scattered, and remote, and inaccessible. Who is
to make roads, to begin with—even if the crofters were
mad enough to imagine that they could send their handful
of produce away to the distant markets with any chance
of competition?"

But she was not convinced: a curious obstinacy seemed
to have got hold of her.

"I can't help thinking," she repeated, " that emigration
is a kind of cowardly remedy. Isn't it rather like admitting that you have failed? Surely there must be some
other means? Why, before I came to Lochgarra I made
up my mind that I would try to find out about the crofters
who had gone away or been sent away, and I would invite
them to come back and take up their old holdings."

"It would be a cruel kindness," said he. "And I
doubt whether they would thank you for the offer. Yes,
I dare say some would; and on their way back to their
old home they would be filled with joy. When they came
in sight of Ru-Minard I dare say they would be crying
with delight; and when they landed at Lochgarra they
would be for falling on their knees to kiss the beloved
shore. But that wouldn't last long. When they came to

look at the sour and marshy soil, the peat-hags, and the rocks, they would begin to alter their mind——"

"In any case," said she, "I have abandoned the idea for the present; I find I have already plenty on my hands. And I don't confess that I have failed yet. I am doing what I can. It is a very slow process; for they seem to imagine that whatever I suggest is for my own interest; at the same time, I don't see that I have failed yet. And as for emigration——"

"But, Miss Stanley," said he seriously, "you don't suppose I would take away any number of the people without your consent?"

At this she brightened up a little.

"Oh, it is only if there is a necessity? Only as a necessity, you mean?"

"Perhaps there is something of selfishness in it, too," he admitted. "Of course, I don't like the idea of living in Eilean Heimra all my life—not now: I am free from any duty; and—and perhaps there are associations that one ought to leave behind one. And if I could get some post from the Government in connection with this emigration scheme—if I could become the overseer of the little settlement—I should still be among my own people: no doubt that has had something to do with my forecasts——"

"But at all events," she interposed, quickly, "you won't be too precipitate? It is a dreadful responsibility. Even if they exaggerate their hardships through home-sickness, that is not altogether imaginary: it is real enough to them at the time. And if actual suffering were to take place——"

"I know the responsibility," he said. "I am quite aware of it. All that I could do would be to obtain the fullest and most accurate information; and then explain to the people the gravity of the step they were about to take. Then it is not a new thing; there are quite trustworthy accounts of the various colonial settlements; and this evidence they would have to estimate dispassionately for themselves."

"Mr. Ross!" she remonstrated. "How can you say such a thing? You told me just now that the whole of those people would follow you away to Canada or Australia if you but said the word. Is that a fair judgment of evidence? I don't think you could get rid of your responsibility by putting a lot of Blue-books before them——"

"I see you are against emigration," he said.

"It may be necessary in some places—I don't know yet that it is here," she answered him. "I would rather be allowed to try." And then she said—looking at him rather timidly—"If you think I have not given them enough, I will give them more. There is no forest land, as you know ; but—but there is some more pasture that perhaps Mr. Watson might be induced to give up. I have given them Meall-na-Cruagan; if you wish it, I will give them Meall-na-Fearn. Mr. Watson was most good-natured about Meall-na-Cruagan ; and I dare say there would be no difficulty in settling what should be taken off his rent if he were to give up Meall-na-Fearn and Corrie Bhreag. And—and there's more than that I would try before having people banished."

Kate Glendinning observed that this young man changed colour. It was an odd thing—and interesting to the onlooker. For usually he was so calm, and self-possessed, and reserved : submissive, too, so that it was only at times that he raised his keen black eyes to the young lady who was addressing him : he seemed to wish to keep a certain distance between them. But these last words of hers appeared to have touched him. The pale, dark face showed a sense of shame—or deprecation.

"You must not imagine, Miss Stanley," said he, "that I came to ask for anything. You have already been most generous—too generous, most people would say. It would be imposing on you to ask for more ; it would be unfair ; if I were in your position, I would refuse. But I thought my scheme might afford you some relief——"

"And if you went away with them, what would you do with Heimra Island?" she said, abruptly—and regarding him with her clear, honest eyes.

"That I don't know," said he, "except that I should be sorry to sell it. And it would not be easy to let it, even as a summer holiday place. There is no fishing or shooting to speak of ; and it is a long way to come. For a yachtsman it might make convenient headquarters——"

" But you would not sell the island ?' she asked again.

" Not unless I was compelled," he made answer. " I might go away and leave it for a time—the letting of the pasture would just about cover the housekeeper's wages and the keeping up of the place ; and then, years hence, when my little community in Australia or Canada was all safely established—when the heat of the day was over, as they say in the Gaelic—I might come back there, and spend the end of my life in peace and quiet. For old people do not need many friends around them : their recollections are in the past."

And then he rose.

" I beg your pardon for troubling you about my poor affairs."

" But they concern me," she said, as she rose also, " and very immediately. Besides that, we are neighbours. And so I am to understand that you won't do anything further with your emigration scheme—not at present ? "

" Nothing until you consent—nor until you are quite satisfied that it is a wise thing to embark on. And indeed there is no great hurry : I can't keep my last term until November next. But by then I hope to have learnt everything there is to be learned about the various emigration-fields."

She rang the bell ; but she herself accompanied him to the door, and out into the hall.

" By the way," said she, " what has become of Anna Chlannach ?—I thought you were to tell her to come to me, so that I could assure her she shouldn't be locked up in any asylum ? "

" I'm afraid Anna has not got over her fear of you," said he, with a smile. " She seems to think you tried to entrap her into the garden, where Mr. Purdie was. And it isn't easy to reason with Anna Chlannach."

" Oh, then, you see her sometimes ? " she asked.

" Sometimes—yes. If Anna catches sight of the *Sirène* coming across, she generally runs down to Camus Bheag, and waits for us, to ask for news from the island."

" Will you tell her that I am very angry with her for not coming to see me—when Barbara could quite easily be the interpreter between us ? "

“ I will.   Good-bye ! ”

“ Good-bye ! ” said she, as he left.

But she did not immediately go back to the drawing-room, and to Käthchen, and the dyed wools.   She remained in the great, empty oak hall, slowly walking up and down—with visions before her eyes.   She saw a name, too: it was *New Heimra*.   And the actual Heimra out there—the actual Heimra would then be deserted, save, perhaps, for some old housekeeper, who would sit out in the summer evenings, and wonder whether Young Donald was ever coming back to his home.   Or perhaps an English family would be in possession of that bungalow retreat: the children scampering about with their noisy games : would they be silent a little, when chance brought them to the lonely white grave, up there on the crest of the hill ?

She was startled from her reverie by some sound on the steps outside, and, turning, found her brother and Frank Meredyth at the door.

“ Now, Mamie, see what comes of all your coddling ! ” Fred Stanley exclaimed as he came forward, and he held a piece of paper in his hand.   “ This is a pretty state of affairs !   But can you wonder ?   They easily find out where the place is ripe for them—where the people have been nursed into insolence and discontent—and on the Twelfth, too—oh, yes, the Twelfth !—when they expect the keepers to be up on the hill, so they’ll be able to break a few of the drawing-room windows on their way by——”

“ What are you talking about ? ” she said, in answer to this incoherent harangue ; and she took the paper from him.   It was a handbill, rather shabbily printed ; and these were the contents :—

THE HEATHER ON FIRE !

THE HEATHER ON FIRE !

The Land for the People !—Away with Sheep, Deer, and Landlords !— The Landlords must go !—Compulsory Emigration for Landlords ! — Men of the Highlands, stand up for your rights !—Down with Southren Rack-Renters !

To the

Tenants, Crofters, and Cottars of

Lochgarra and Neighbourhood:

A PUBLIC MEETING

Will be held in Lochgarra Free Church, on Monday the 12th of August, at one o'clock.   Addresses by Mr. Josiah Ogden, M.P., Miss Ernestine Simon, of Paris, and Mrs. Elizabeth Jackson Noyes, of the Connecticut Council of Liberty.   Mr. John Fraser, Vice-President of the Stratherrick Branch of the Highland Land League, will preside.

Admission Free.

Men of Lochgarra!—attend in your hundreds:

" Who would be free themselves must strike the blow!"

Well, Mary was not the least bit frightened.

"I don't see why they shouldn't hold a public meeting," said she, as she handed him back the bill.

"Why, there will be a public riot?" he said. "You haven't seen the great placards they have pasted up on the walls—done with a big brush—I suppose they were afraid to print them ; but if you go down through the village you will see what they're after.   '*Sweep the sheep off Meall-na-Fearn*'—'*Take back the land*'—'*A general march into Glen Orme.*'"

"Glen Orme deer-forest has nothing to do with me," she said.

"Do you think they will draw such fine distinctions?" he retorted. "I can tell you, when once the march has begun, they won't stop to ask whose fences they are tearing down ; and a shot or two fired through your windows is about the least you can expect.   And that is what comes of coddling people : they think they can terrorise over you whenever they choose—they welcome any kind of agitator, and think they're going to have it all their own way.   And can't you see who suggested the Twelfth to them?   I'll bet it was that fellow Ross—a clever trick !—either we lose the opening day of the shooting—and that would make him laugh like a cat—or else we leave the place free for those parading blackguards to plunder at their will."

"At all events, Miss Stanley," interposed Frank Meredyth, in a calmer manner, "there can be no harm in

postponing our grouse shooting until the Tuesday. I think
it will be better for Fred and myself to be about the
premises—and the keepers too—until this little disturbance
has blown over."

"Who are those people?" she said, taking back the
paper and regarding it. "Mr. Ogden I know something
of—mostly from pictures of him in *Punch ;* but I thought
it was strikes and trade unions in the north of England
that he busied himself with. What has brought him to
Scotland?"

"Why, wherever there is mischief to be stirred up
—and notoriety to be earned for himself—that is enough
for a low Radical of that stamp!" her brother said. He
was a young man, and his convictions were round and
complete.

"And Miss Ernestine Simon—who is she?"

"Oh, you don't know Ernestine?" said Frank Meredyth,
with a smile. "Oh yes, surely! Ernestine, the famous
pétroleuse, who fought at the Buttes Chaumont and got
wounded in the scramble through Belleville? You must
have heard of her, surely! Well, Ernestine is getting
old now; but there is still something of the sacred fire
about her—a sort of *mouton enragé* desperation : she can
use whirling words, as far as her broken English goes."

"And Mrs. Noyes?" Mary continued. "Who is Mrs.
Jackson Noyes, from Connecticut?"

"There I am done," he confessed. "I never heard of
Mrs. Jackson Noyes in any capacity whatever. But I
can imagine the sort of person she is likely to be."

"And what do those people know about the Highlands?" Mary demanded again.

"What they have been told by the Land League, I suppose," was his answer—and therewithal Miss Stanley led
the way back to the drawing-room, to carry these startling
tidings to Kate Glendinning.

But she was very silent and thoughtful all that evening ;
and when the two gentlemen, after dinner, had gone out on
the terrace to smoke a cigar, she said—

"Käthchen, I am going to confide in you ; and you
must not break faith with me. You hear what is likely
to happen next Monday. Very well : Mr. Meredyth and

Fred both want to remain about the house, along with the keepers, in case there should be any disturbance, any injury done to the place. Now I particularly wish that they should not ; and you must back me up, if it is spoken of again. Why, what harm can the people do ? I don't mind about a broken window, if one of the lads should become unruly in going by. And if they drive the sheep off Meall-na-Fearn, the sheep can be driven back the next day. I will warn Mr. Watson that he must not allow his men to show resistance. But, above all, I am anxious that Fred and Mr. Meredyth should leave in the morning for their shooting, as they had arranged. For the truth is, Käthchen, I mean to go to this meeting ; and I mean to go alone."

"Mamie ?" Käthchen exclaimed, with dismay in her eyes.

"There are many reasons," Mary Stanley went on. "If those strangers know anything about the condition of the Highlands that I do not know, I shall be glad to hear it. If they have merely come to stir up mischief, I wish to make my protest. But there is more than that : perhaps the people about here have their grievances and resentments that they would speak of more freely at such a meeting ; and if they have, I want to know what they are ; and I want to show that I am not afraid to trust myself among my neighbours, and to listen to what they have got to say. For, after all, Käthchen, the more you think of it, the more that emigration scheme—the drafting of a lot of people from their own homes—seems such a complete confession of failure. I would rather try something else first—or many things—rather than have the people go away to Canada or Queensland."

"Mamie," said Käthchen, rising to her feet, "I will not allow you to thrust yourself into this danger. You don't know what an excited crowd may not do. You are the representative here—the only representative—of the very class whom these strangers have come to denounce."

"That is why I mean to go and show them that the relations between landlord and tenant need not necessarily be what they imagine them to be," Mary said, with a certain dignity and reserve. "Why, if there is any risk of a serious disturbance, is it not my place to be there, to do what I can to prevent it ?"

"I will appeal to Mr. Meredyth," said Käthchen.

"You cannot," said Mary, calmly. "I have entrusted you with my secret—you cannot break faith."

Käthchen looked disconcerted for a second.

"It is quite monstrous, Mamie, that you should expose yourself to such a risk. Is it because you are so anxious Mr. Ross should not take away a lot of the people to Canada—and you want them to declare openly that they are on good terms with you ? At all events, you shall not be there alone. I will go with you."

"It is quite needless, Käthchen !"

"I don't care about that," said Kate Glendinning ; and then she added, vindictively: "and when I get hold of that Mr. Pettigrew, I will give him a bit of my mind ! The man of peace—always sighing and praying that people should live together in *ahmity*—and here he goes and lends his church to these professional mischief-makers. Wait till I get hold of Mr. Pettigrew !"

CHAPTER XVI.

"KAIN TO THE KING THE MORN !"

THE night was dark and yet clear ; the sea still ; not a whisper stirred in the birch-woods nor along the shores ; the small red points of fire, that told of the distant village, burned steadily. And here, down near the edge of the water, were Coinneach and Calum-a-bhata, hidden under the shadow of the projecting rocks.

"Oh, yes, Calum," the elder sailor was saying in his native tongue—and he spoke in something of an under-tone—"maybe we will get a few sea-trout this night ; and a good basket of sea-trout is a fine thing to take away with us to Heimra ; and who has a better right to the sea-trout than our master ? Perhaps you do not know what in other days they used to call *Kain* ; for you are a young man, and not hearing of many things ; but I will tell you now. It was in the days when there were very good relations between the people and the proprietors—"

"When the birds sang in Gaelic, Coinneach !" said Calum.

"Oh, you may laugh; for you are a young man, and ignorant of many things; but I tell you there was that time; and the tenants and the people at the Big House were very friendly. And the tenants they paid part of their rent in things that were useful for the Big House—such things as hens, and butter, and eggs, and the like; but it was not taken as rent; not at all; it was taken as a present; and the people at the Big House they would have the tenant sit down, and drink a glass of whisky, and hear the news. And now do you understand that there's many a one about here knows well of that custom; and they may pay their money-rent to the English family; but they would rather send their *Kain* to the old family, that is, to our master; and that is why the Gillie Ciotach and the rest of them are very glad when they can take out a hare or a brace of birds or something of that kind to Heimra. And why should not the sea pay *Kain* to Donald Ross of Heimra?—I will ask you that question, Calum. If the sea about here belongs to any one, it belongs to the old family, and not to the English family——"

"But if they catch us with the scringe-net, Coinneach?" said the younger man, ruefully. "Aw, *Dyeea*, I was never in a prison."

"The scringe-net!—a prison!" said Coinneach, with contempt. "How little you know about such things! Do they put the dukes and the lords in prison that come round the coast in their big yachts? and in nearly every one of the yachts you will see a scringe-net hung out to dry, and no one concealing it. Do you think I have no eyes, Calum? When the *Consuelo* came round to Camus Bheag, and the master was sending to us for his other clothes before he went away to the south, did I not see them taking down a scringe-net from the boom? It is very frightened you are, Calum, whether it is putting a few kegs into a cave, or putting a scringe-net round a shore. Now if there was something really to frighten you—like the card-playing the young man saw——"

"What was that, Coinneach?" said Calum quickly.

Coinneach paused for a second or two, and his face became grave and thoughtful.

"That was enough to frighten anyone," he continued

presently—in this mysterious chillness, while he kept his eyes watching the vague, dark plain that lay between him and the distant lights of the village. "And if I tell you the story, Calum, it is to show you there are many things we do not understand, and that it is wise not to speak too confidently, in case some one might overhear—someone that we cannot see. For sometimes they show themselves; and at other times they are not visible; but *they may be there.* Now I must tell you it happened in a great castle in the north; I am not remembering the name of it; maybe it was up in Caithness; I am not remembering that; but the story is well·known, and I was hearing that someone was putting it in a book as well. Now I must tell you that the owner of the castle is the head of the clan, and of a very old and great family; and it is the custom, whenever he goes away from home, that one of the other gentlemen of the clan goes to the castle to keep watch. It is not needful in these days, as you can guess for yourself; but it is a compliment to the head of the clan, and an old custom; and maybe it is kept up to this present time—though I am not swearing that to you, Calum. What I am telling you took place a good many years ago; that is what I have heard; maybe sixty years, maybe fifty years, maybe a hundred years; I am not swearing to that. But the chief had to go away from home; and according to the custom, one of the gentlemen went to keep watch; and he took with him a young country lad, one of his own servants. Now I must tell you there was a fire put in the great hall of the castle; for it was in the winter time; and they had to sit up all night, the one keeping the other awake—for no one likes to be left alone in a strange place like that, in the night-time, and not knowing what things have been experienced by others."

"You are not needing to tell me that, Coinneach," the other assented.

"Very well. But as I was saying, the master he sate close to the fire in the great hall; and the young man he remained some distance away, by one of the windows, and there was no speaking between them. So one hour after another hour went by; and there was nothing happening; and it was not until the dead of the night, or towards the morning, that the young man noticed that his master had fallen asleep. He did not like that, I can tell you, Calum ; for if you are left alone, the evil beings may appear and come upon you ; and there is no question about it. Very well. The young man he thought he would go over to the fire and waken his master ; but what do you think of this now, Calum, that when he tried to rise from his seat he could not do that—something was holding him back—he tried seven times over and seven times more, as I have heard, for he was trembling with the fear of being held. And then—what do you think of this, Calum ?—and it is the truth I am telling you—he saw what few men have ever seen, and what few would ever wish to see : the folding-doors at the end of the hall were opened wide ; and there were two footmen bringing in lights ; and then there was a procession of ladies and gentlemen all dressed in a way that was strange to him ; and they came into the hall so that you could not hear a sound. They took no notice of him or his master ; and he could see everything they were doing, for all that his eyes were starting out of his head with fright ; and I tell you he was so terrified he could not cry out to wake his master. But he was watching—oh, yes, he was watching with all his eyes, you may be sure of that ; and he saw the footmen bring forward the tables ; and those people in the strange clothes sate down and began to play at cards ; and they were talking to each other—but never any sound of their talking. He could see their lips moving ; but there was no sound. What do you think of that now, Calum ?—was it not a dreadful thing for a young man to see ?—even if they were not doing him any harm, or even knowing he was there ? There's many a one would have sprung up and shrieked out ; but as I tell you, there was no strength in his bones and he could not move ; and his master was fast asleep ; and all those people—the gentlemen with their small swords by their side, and the ladies in their silks— they were playing away at the cards, and talking to each other across the table, and not a sound to be heard. He watched and watched—aw, God, I suppose he was more dead than alive with trembling, and not being able to call on his master—until the windows began to grow grey with the morning light; and then he saw that the people were sometimes looking at the windows, and sometimes at each other, and they were talking less. Then they rose; and he could not see the candles any more because of the light in the hall; and they were going away in that noiseless manner, when one of them happened to spy the young man; and he came along and looked at him. He looked at him for a moment—and seemed to breathe on him—so that it was like a cold air touching him—and the young man knew that the hand of death had been put upon him. There was no sound; the strange person only looked; and the young man felt the cold air on his forehead, so that he was for sinking to the floor; for he thought that death was on him already, and that he must go with them wherever they were going. Calum, I have told you what I felt when I was coming back from Ru-Gobhar, and when the Woman came behind me; it was like that with the young man, as I have heard. And then all of a sudden a cock crew outside; and his master woke up and looked round; and there was no one in the hall but their two selves."

"Did he cry out then?—did he tell his master what he had seen?" Calum asked, in a low voice.

"He was not caring much to tell any one," Coinneach replied. "It was what he felt within him that concerned him; and he knew that the touch of death had been put upon him. Oh, yes, he told the story, though they found him so weak that he could not say much; and they put him to bed—but he was shivering all the time; and he had no heart for living left in him. He was not caring to speak much about it. When they asked him what the people were like, he said the gentlemen had velvet coats, and white hair tied with black ribbons behind; and the ladies were rich in their dresses; but he could not say what language they were speaking, for he could see their lips moving, but there was no sound. He was not caring to speak much about it. The life seemed to have been taken out of his body; he said he would never rise again from his bed. He said more than once, 'It was that one that breathed on me; he wanted me to go with them to be one of the servants; and if the cock had not crowed 1

would have gone with them. But now I am going.' And
he got weaker and weaker, until about the end of the third
day; and then it was all over with the poor lad; and
there was no struggle—he knew that the death-touch had
been put upon his heart."

"And I suppose now," said Calum, meditatively, "they
will have him bringing in the tables for them every time
they come to play cards in the middle of the night. Aw,
Dyeea, I know what I would do if I was the master of
that place: I would have the keepers hidden, and when
those people came in I would have three or four guns go
off at them all at once: would not that settle them?"

"You are a foolish lad, Calum, to think you can harm
people like that with a gun," said Coinneach. "No, if it
was I, I would say the Lord's Prayer to myself, very low,
so that they could not hear; and if they did hear, and
still came towards me, I would cry out, 'God on the
cross!' and that would put the people away from me, as
it made the Woman take her hands from my throat the
dreadful night I was coming by the Black Bay."

"Ay, but tell me this, Coinneach," said the younger of
the two men. "I have heard that in great terror your
tongue will cleave to your mouth; and you cannot cry out.
And what is to happen to you then, if one of those people
came near to put a cold breath on you?"

Coinneach did not answer this question: for the last
few seconds he had been carefully scanning the darkened
plain before him.

"The boat is coming now, Calum," he whispered. "And
it is just as noiseless as any ghost she is." And with
that the two men got up from the rock on which they
had been sitting, and went down to the water's edge,
where they waited in silence.

There was a low whistle; Coinneach answered it. Presently a dark object became dimly visible in the gloom.
It was a rowing-boat; and as she slowly drew near the
prow sent ripples of phosphorescence trembling away into
the dusk, while the blades of the muffled oars, each time
they dipped, struck white fire down into the sea. It looked
as if some huge and strange creature, with gauzy silver
wings, was coming shoreward from out of the unknown

deeps. Not a word was uttered by anyone. When the bow of the boat came near Coinneach caught it and checked it, so that it should not grate on the shingle. Then he and his companion tumbled in; two other oars, also muffled, were put in the rowlocks; and silently she went away again, under the guidance of a fifth man, who sate at the helm. Very soon the lights of Lochgarra were lost to view; they had got round one of the promontories. Out to seaward there was nothing visible at all; while the "loom" of the land was hardly to be distinguished from the overhanging heavens that did not show a single star.

And yet the steersman seemed to be sufficiently sure of his course. There was no calling a halt for consultation, nor any other sign of uncertainty. Noiselessly the four oars kept measured time; there were simultaneously the four sudden downward flashes of white—followed by a kind of seething of silver radiance deep in the dark water; then, here and there on the surface, a large and lambent jewel would shine keenly for a second or two, floating away on the ripples as the boat left it behind. Not one of the men smoked: that of itself showed that something unusual was happening. They kept their eyes on the sombre features of the adjacent shore—of which a landsman could have made next to nothing; or they turned to the dimly-descried outline of the low range of hills, where that could be made out against the sky. It was a long and monotonous pull—with absolute silence reigning. But at length a whispered "Easy, boys, easy!" told them that this part of their labour was about over; and now they proceeded with greater caution—merely dipping the tips of their oars in the water, while all their attention was concentrated on the blurred and vague shadows of the land.

They were now in a small and sheltered bay, the stillness of which was so intense that they could distinctly hear the murmur of some mountain burn. On the face of the hill rising from the sea there were certain darker patches—perhaps these were birch-woods: also down by the shore there were spaces of deeper gloom—these might be clumps of trees. No light was visible anywhere: this part of the coast was clearly uninhabited, or else the people were asleep.

And yet, before venturing nearer, they ceased rowing altogether; and watched; and listened. Not a sound: save for that continuous murmur of the stream, that at times became remote, and then grew more distinct again—as some wandering breath of wind passed across the face of the hill. The world around them lay in a trance as deep as death: the bark of a dog, the call of a heron, would have been a startling thing. Meanwhile two of the oars had been stealthily shipped; the remaining two were sufficient to paddle the boat nearer to the rocks, when that might be deemed safe.

And at last the steersman, who appeared to be in command, gave the word. As gently as might be, the boat was headed in for the shore, until Coinneach, who was up at the bow, whispered "That'll do now;" the rowing ceased; there was a pause, and some further anxious scrutinising of that amorphous gloom; then two black figures stepped over the side into the water, taking with them the lug-line of the net that was carefully arranged in the stern. They were almost immediately lost sight of; for the boat was again noiselessly paddled away, until the full length of the line was exhausted; while he in the stern began to pay out the net—each cork float that dropped into the water sending a shower of tremulous white stars spreading from it, and all the meshes shivering in silver as they were straightened out. A wonderful sight it was; but not the most likely to procure a good fishing; for, of course, that quivering, lustrous, far-extended web would be visible at some little distance. However, out went the net easily and steadily—with just the faintest possible "swish" as each successive armful soused into the sea; and then, as quick as was consistent with silence, the boat was pulled ashore, and two of the men jumped out with the other lug-line. They, too, vanished in the impenetrable dusk. The solitary occupant of the mysterious craft, standing up at the bow, was now left to watch the result of these operations and to direct, in low and eager whispers, his unseen comrades. Slowly, slowly the semicircular net was being hauled in; as it got nearer and nearer the men at the lug-lines splashed the water with them, so as to frighten the fish into the meshes; the

sea glimmered nebulous in white fire; here and there a
larger star burned clear on the black surface for a moment,
and then gradually faded away. The commotion increased
—in the water and out of it; it was evident from the
fluttering and seething that there was a good haul; and in
their excitement the scringers who were ashore forgot the
danger of their situation—there were muttered exclamations in Gaelic as the net was narrowed in and in. And
then, behold!—in the dark meshes those shining silver
things—each entangled fish a gleaming, scintillating wonder
—a radiant prize, here in the deep night. If this was
Kain for Donald Ross of Heimra, it was *Kain* fit to be
paid to a king.

It was at this moment that three men came across the
rocky headland guarding the bay on its northern side.
.They had just completed a careful inspection of the neighbouring creek—as careful as the darkness would allow;
they had followed the windings of the coast, searching
every inlet; and so far their quest had been in vain.
Now they stood on this promontory, peering and listening.

"No, sir, I do not see or hear anything," said Hector,
the tall keeper, who had a gun over his shoulder; and
he seemed inclined to give up further pursuit.

"But I tell you they must be somewhere," said Fred
Stanley, in an excited fashion. "There was no mistake
about what they were after. What would they be going
out in a boat for at this time of the night, if it wasn't for
scringeing?"

"Maybe they would be for setting night-lines," said the
keeper, evasively.

"Not a bit of it!" the young man retorted, with impatience. "I know better than that. And I know who is
in that boat—I know perfectly well. It isn't for nothing
that the *Sirène* is lying in Camus Bheag: I know who is
out with those poaching nets—and I'm going to catch
him if I can. I want to have certain things made public:
I want an explanation: I want to have the Sheriff at
Dingwall called in to settle this matter."

"Are you quite sure you saw the boat, sir?" said the
keeper—all this conversation taking place in lowered tones,
except when Fred Stanley grew angry and indignant.

"Why," said he, turning to his friend Meredyth, "how far was she from the steam-launch when she passed—not half a dozen yards, I'll swear! It was a marvellous stroke of luck we thought of going out for that draught-board; they little thought there would be any one on the launch at that hour; and I tell you, if the punt had been a bit bigger, I would have given chase to them there and then. Never mind, we ought to be able to catch them yet—catch them in the act—and I mean to see it out——"

"Yes, but we haven't caught them," said Frank Meredyth, discontentedly; for he had stumbled again and again, and knocked his ankles against the rocks; and he would far rather have been at home, talking to Mary Stanley. "And it's beastly dark: we shall be slipping down into the water sooner or later. What's the use of going on, Fred? What about a few sea-trout? Everybody does it——"

"But it's against the law all the same; and I mean to catch this poaching scoundrel red-handed, if I can," was the young man's answer. "Come, Hector, you must know perfectly well where they put out the scringe-nets. What's this place before us now?"

"It's the Camus Mhor, sir," said Hector, "in there towards the land."

"Well, is it any use scringeing in this bay?" the young man demanded.

"There's the mouth of the burn that comes down by the plantation," was the reply.

"Very well, take us there!" Fred Stanley said impatiently. "Those fellows must be somewhere; and I'll bet you they're not far off. I must say, Hector, you don't seem particularly anxious to get hold of them. Are there any of them friends of yours?"

Hector did not answer this taunt. He merely said—

"It is a dark night, sir, to make any one out."

And then they went on again, but with caution; for besides the danger of breaking a leg among the rocks, they knew that the yawning gulfs of the sea were by their side. Hector led the way, Fred Stanley coming next, Meredyth—with muttered grumblings—bringing up the rear. In this wise they followed the inward bend of the bay, until the keeper leapt from the rocks into a drifted mass of seaweed: they were at the corner of the semi-circular beach.

Suddenly Fred Stanley caught Hector's arm, and held him for a second.

"Do you hear that?" he said, in an eager whisper. "They are there—right ahead of us—fire a shot at them, Hector!—give them a peppering—give their coats a dusting!"

"Oh, no, sir," said the serious-mannered keeper, "I cannot do that. But I will go forward and challenge them. When you get to know who they are, then you will apply for a summons afterwards."

"Come on, then!—come along!" the young man said, and he began to run—stumbling over seaweed, stones, and shingle—but guided by the subdued commotion in front of him.

All at once that scuffle ceased. There was another sound—slight and yet distinct: it was the hurried dip of oars. Nay, was not that the "loom" of a boat, not twenty yards away from them—the dark hull receding from the land?

"Here, Hector!" the young man cried—furious that his prey had just escaped him. "Fire, man!—give them a charge!—give the thieving scoundrels a dose of shot amongst them!"

Hector made no answer to this appeal. He called aloud—

"Who are you? Whose is that boat?"

There was no word in reply—only the slight sound of the dipping oars. Fred Stanley caught at the gun; but the keeper held it away from him.

"No, sir, no," he said gravely. "We must keep within the law, whatever they do."

"Yes—and now they're off—and laughing at us!" the young man angrily exclaimed. And then he said: "Do you mean to tell me you don't know who these men are? Do you mean to tell me you don't know quite well that it is Ross of Heimra who is in that boat?"

"I am not thinking that, sir," Hector answered slowly.

"You took precious good care not to find out!" Fred

Stanley said, for he was grievously disappointed. "If you had come up with me you might have compelled them to stop and declare themselves: even if you had fired in the air, that would have brought them to reason fast enough. When shall we get such another chance? I knew things like this were going on—knew it quite well. And it's your place to stop it—it's your business. It is a monstrous thing that the fishing in the rivers should be destroyed by those thieves."

He continued looking out to sea; but the boat had disappeared in the dark.

"No, we shall not get another chance like that," said he, turning to his friend Meredyth. "And it is a thousand pities—for I would have given anything to have caught that fellow red-handed: I hate to think of my sister being imposed upon."

"Well, I suppose we'd better be getting back," said Frank Meredyth, who had displayed no great interest in this expedition. "And I dare say Hector can show us some inland way—I don't want to go round those infernal rocks again."

"Hector?" said Fred Stanley, in a savage undertone. "I'm pretty sure of this—that when Hector took us all round those rocks, he knew precious well where the scringers were!"

And very indignant was he, and sullenly resentful, when he carried this story home to Lochgarra House and to his sister. He roundly accused the keepers of connivance. They could put down the scringeing if they chose; but it was all part and parcel of the poaching system that existed for the benefit of Donald Ross. He it was who had the fishing and shooting of this estate. A fine condition of affairs, truly!

"I am afraid," said Mary Stanley, who seemed to take this stormy complaint with much composure, "that Mr. Ross has not quite enough skill to make much of a poacher, even if he were inclined that way. If you had been here yesterday, you would have heard himself say that he was a very indifferent shot, and a very poor fisherman also——"

"And you believed him, of course!" her brother said,

with contempt. "Of course he would say that! That is
the very thing he would profess——"

"But, you see, Fred," she continued, without taking any
offence, "he gave us a very good reason why he should be
but a poor sportsman. There is neither fishing nor shooting
on Heimra Island."

He laughed scornfully.

"Fishing and shooting on Heimra Island?" he repeated.
"What need has he of them, when he has the fishing and
shooting of Lochgarra?"

"You may be mistaken, Fred," Frank Meredyth interposed—careful to be on Miss Stanley's side, as usual.
"You may be going too much by what Purdie said that
evening at Inverness. At the same time, I quite know
this, that when once you suspect any one of poaching, it is
desperately difficult to get the idea out of your head. All
kinds of small things are constantly happening that seem
to offer confirmation——"

"I will bet you twenty pounds to five shillings," said the
young man hotly, "that if we go out to Heimra to-morrow,
and stay to luncheon, we shall find sea-trout on the table.
There may be no fishing on the island—that is quite
possible ; but I tell you there will be sea-trout in Ross's
house. I dare you all to put it to the proof. It is a fair
offer. We can run out in the steam-launch if the sea is as
calm as it is now—Mamie, you can come too, and Miss
Glendinning ; and my bet is twenty pounds to five shillings
that you will find sea-trout produced."

"Surely it would be rather shabby to go and ask a man
to give you lunch in order to prove something against
him?" she made answer. "And even then that would not
show he had been himself in the boat. As for any of the
people about here using a scringe-net now and again to
pick up a few fish—well, that is not a very heinous
offence."

"If it is," said Meredyth (still siding with her), "it is
committed every summer by a large number of highly
respectable persons. Why, only the other day the Fishery
Board had to issue a circular reminding owners of yachts
that netting in territorial seas wasn't allowed."

"Oh, very well," said Fred Stanley, with a sort of

affected resignation. "Very well. It is no concern of mine. The place does not belong to me. And of course, Mamie, you are only following out the programme which will be laid before the free and independent—the very free and independent—natives of this parish, on Monday. No doubt they will be told they have the right to take salmon and sea-trout wherever they can find them, either in the rivers, or round the mouths of the rivers, or in the sea. *They* have that right, you understand, but *you* haven't; if *you* try to catch a salmon, you will have a stone hurled into the pool in front of you! And what will be the rest of the programme when the English demagogue, and the French anarchist, and the Yankee platform-woman, come to set the heather on fire? How much more are you going to surrender, Mamie? You've cut down the rents everywhere—given up more pasture—given up more peat-land. What next? Don't you think it's an awful shame you should be living in a great big house like this, when those poor people are living in thatched hovels——"

"Well," said Mary, with an honest laugh, "if I must tell you the truth, I do sometimes think so. Sometimes, when I go outside, and look at the contrast, it does seem to me too great——"

"Oh, very well!" he said ironically. "When these are your sentiments, I don't wonder that the place is considered ripe for a general riot. But whatever your theories may be, I'm going to draw the line at personal violence and destruction of property. I shall have my six-chambered Colt loaded on Monday; and if any impudent blackguard dares to come near this place——"

"You are going up the hill on Monday," said she briefly. "Both you and Mr. Meredyth. I want some grouse for the kitchen; and as many more to send away as you can get for me."

"Pardon me, Miss Stanley," Meredyth said, and he spoke with a certain quiet decision, "you are asking a little too much. It is impossible for us to go away shooting and leave you at the mercy of what may turn out to be a riotous mob. It is quite impossible: you have no right to ask it."

" Yes, but I do ask it ?" she said, somewhat petulantly—
for she wished to be left free to follow her own designs on
that fateful Monday. "You are my guest; you are here
for the Twelfth; and I particularly want you—both you
and Fred—to go away after the grouse; and never mind
about this—this lecture, or whatever it is——"

" I for one, cannot," he said, firmly; " and I know Fred
will not."

Mary glanced half-imploringly at Käthchen. But Käthchen sate mute. Perhaps she was considering that, whether
Mary went to the meeting or not, it was just as well the
two gentlemen were to be within hail. Besides, before
then it was just possible Mary might be induced to confess
to them her mad resolve : in which case it would become
their duty to reason and remonstrate, seeing that Käthchen's protests had been of no avail. Or would they insist
on accompanying her to the meeting, if she was determined
to go ? For one thing, Käthchen did not at all like Fred
Stanley's reference to his Colt's revolver ; if there was going
to be any serious disturbance, that was not likely to prove
a satisfactory means of quelling it.

CHAPTER XVII.

A REVOLUTION THAT FAILED.

But at first the two young men—especially when they
were in the society of the young women—professed to make
light of the threatened invasion. What harm could come
of allowing a parcel of notoriety-hunting adventurers to
air their eloquence—and their ignorance? The crofters
would at once perceive that Ogden, M.P., knew no more
about them and their ways of life than he knew about
the inhabitants of the moon. As for Mademoiselle
Ernestine—the fiery Ernestine would find it difficult
to set the Highland peat-bogs in a blaze with her little
tin can of paraffin. And as for Mrs. Jackson Noyes of
Connecticut—but here the young men had to confess that
they knew nothing of Mrs. Jackson Noyes ; and so, to
amuse themselves, at dinner, they set to work to con-
struct an imaginary Mrs. Noyes out of a series of guesses.

"She is a passionate sympathiser with all suffering races—especially married women," said Mr. Meredyth, confidently.

"Men are brutes," observed Fred Stanley.

"She will denounce the hideous cruelty of landlords stalking grouse with express rifles," said Meredyth, keeping the ball rolling.

"She will call on the crofters to arise in their wrath and demand that of every stag killed two haunches must be delivered over to them, the remaining two to be retained by the landlord."

"But doesn't that sound reasonable!" said Käthchen, innocently—whereat there was a roar.

"Miss Glendinning," said Meredyth, apologetically, "you forget: the haunches of a stag are limited in number. It was Mrs. Jackson Noyes's idea of a stag we were dealing with. Well, Fred, what next?"

"Any landlord or farmer," continued the younger man, with a matter-of-fact air, "found guilty of killing a sheep without the aid of chloroform to be sent to jail for twenty-five years. No lamb to be taken away from its mother without the mother's consent—in writing, stamped, sealed, and delivered before the Sheriff of Dingwall."

"A compulsory rate," suggested Frank Meredyth, "levied on landlords, of course—for the relief of bed-ridden peat hags——"

"Oh, stop that nonsense!" Mary interposed, laughing in a shamefaced kind of way. "They can't be as ignorant as all that."

"Oh, can't they?" said he, coolly. "I've seen lots of worse things—accompanied by eloquent, if occasionally ungrammatical, denunciations of the brutal landlords. You are a landlord, Miss Stanley; and you have taken the wages of blood and sin. If I were you I should feel inclined to throw down the thirty pieces of silver and depart and go and hang myself."

"She won't do that," said her brother. "But what she is more likely to do is to give up the pasture of Meall-na-Fearn that those people demand. And then Mrs. Jackson Noyes will telegraph to the *Connecticut Radiator* that a great triumph has been achieved, and that the American banner has begun to wave over the benighted Highlands."

"I wish the American banner didn't wave over so many Highland deer-forests," said Meredyth, briefly; and there an end for the moment.

But the talk of the two young men when they were by themselves was very different.

"What ought to be done, and done at once," said Fred Stanley, "is to send over to Dingwall for a body of police. Indeed, the meeting should be suppressed altogether: it is a clear instigation to riot. I don't see how a riot can be avoided—if those howlers are allowed to rave. But my sister won't hear of it. Oh, no! Everything is to be amiable and friendly and pleasant. She is quite sure that the crofters are grateful to her for their lowered rents and all that. Grateful!—they don't know what gratitude is!"

"But at all events you must remember this," said Meredyth, "that your sister has been here a much longer time than you; and she has been doing her best to get to understand these people and their wants and their habits of thinking. She may be a little too confident: in that case it is for you and me to see that she is kept out of harm's way. And as far as I can judge, the main event of the day is to be a raid into Glen Orme forest——"

"By the Lord, they'll get a warm reception if they try that!" young Stanley broke in. "I can tell you, from what I've heard of him, Colonel Tomlins isn't the sort of man to let a lot of vagabonds march past Glen Orme Lodge and take possession of the forest—I should think not. The ragged army will find a sufficient force awaiting them —keepers, foresters, gillies, and the guns of the house-party: there may be driving—but it won't be the deer that will be driven off."

"That as it may be," said Meredyth, with much calmness. "But even if there is a scrimmage up there, what has that got to do with us? I don't care a brass farthing about the Glen Orme deer; I want to see your sister safe. And if the torrent of revolution flows peacefully past this house, and goes to expend itself in Glen Orme—let it, and welcome!"

"Yes, but that is too much to expect," Fred Stanley said, gloomily. "It is my sister who will be preached

against by those fanatics.   It is she who is the representative here of the landlord interest.   Gratitude !—it's precious
little gratitude they'll show, when they have this fellow
Donald Ross secretly egging them on.   Of course, he is
annoyed that you and I should have come up to interfere
with him ; he thought he would only have a woman to
deal with ; and that the keepers could make all kinds of
excuses to her.   But now he finds it different.   I imagine
he knows very well that he is suspected and watched,
and that there is a chance of his being caught at any
moment—a chance that I mean to make a certainty of
before I leave this place !"

"My young friend," said Meredyth, dispassionately,
"I'm afraid you are becoming *entêté* about this Donald
Ross.   And yet I don't wonder at it.   I've seen a similar
state of affairs, many a time before now.   The fact is,
when once you suspect poaching, the suspicion becomes a
sort of mania, and all your comfort in the shooting is
gone.   It is precisely the same on board a yacht.   If
you once suspect your skipper or your steward of drinking,
it's all over with you ; you are always looking out—
mistrusting—imagining ; you may as well go ashore at once,
or get another skipper or steward.   Of course, the poaching
is still more vexatious ; for you feel you are being defied
and cheated at the same time ; and you want revenge ;
and the poacher is generally a devil of a clever fellow.
But, after all, Fred, your sister is right : even if you are
convinced that there is poaching going on—as there has
certainly been some little ill-will shown against us now
and then—still, you have nothing to prove that Donald
Ross is the culprit—nothing."

"I will catch him yet," said Fred Stanley under his
breath.

Next morning being Sunday morning, they all went to
church. In going down through the village they could
perceive no sign of excitement, anticipatory of the next day :
on the contrary all was decorous quiet.   Shutters were
shut ; in some cases the blinds were drawn down ; the
few people they saw were dressed in black, and were certainly not breaking the Lord's day by idle or frivolous conversation.   But here was John the policeman.

" Well, John," said Mary, to the plump and placid Iain, who smiled good-naturedly when she addressed him, "are we to have civil war to-morrow ?"

" Mem ?" said John—not understanding.

" Is there going to be a riot to-morrow ?" she repeated.

" Aw, no, mem," said John, in a mildly deprecating way. " I am not thinking that. The meeting it will be in the church, and there is the Minister."

" And what are you going to do ?" said she. " I suppose you know they threaten to drive the sheep off Meall-na-Fearn, and there is a proposal to go into Glen Orme forest. Well, what are you going to do ?"

"I am not sure," said Iain, with a vague, propitiatory grin.

" You have taken no steps to preserve the peace then ?" she demanded—but, indeed, she was well aware of John's comfortable, easy-going optimism.

" Aw, well," said the round-cheeked representative of the law, "mebbe the lads will no do anything at ahl; and if they go into the forest, mebbe they will no do mich harm."

" But I suppose you have heard that Colonel Tomlins's keepers and foresters mean to stop them, if they should attempt any such thing; and it isn't at all likely that Mr. Watson's shepherds will let them drive the sheep off Meall-na-Fearn without some kind of resistance. What then ? What are you going to do ?"

" Aw, well," said John—letting his eyes rove aimlessly away towards Heimra Island, and then to the little white Free Church beyond the bay, and then back to the ground in front of Miss Stanley's feet, "mebbe there will be no mich harm; and the Minister will be in charge what-ever——"

"Look here, John," Fred Stanley broke in, peremptorily, " it is quite clear to me that you mean to stand by and let anything happen that is likely to happen. Very well, I wish to give you notice—and I wish the people about here to understand—that if there's any demonstration made against Lochgarra House, we've got a gun or two there —half a dozen of them—and we don't mean to stand any nonsense."

"Fred!" said she, and she drew her head up : he was put to silence in a moment. Then she turned to the phlegmatic Iain. "You must do what you can to give good advice to any of the young men you may hear talking. These strangers that are coming—what do they know about Lochgarra ? They only wish to stir up strife, for their own purposes. And it would be a very bad thing for any of the men about here to be sent for trial to Edinburgh, merely because these strangers were bent on making mischief."

"Yes, mem," answered Iain, obediently—but in a vague way : perhaps he did not quite comprehend.

"John," said Fred Stanley, coming to the front again, "do you know anything about the scringeing that goes on about here ?"

This time John did understand.

"Me, sir ?" he replied—as if such a question were an insult to the dignity of his office. And perhaps he would have gone on to protest as earnestly as his good-humoured laziness would allow, that he had no knowledge of any such illegal practices, but that Mary Stanley intervened, and carried her party off with her to church.

Of course it was the English portion of the day's services that they attended, in the little, plain, ill-ventilated building. The sermon was so severely doctrinal that they could not follow it very well ; while the occasional appeals to the heart, uttered in that high falsetto sing-song, fell with a somewhat unnatural note on the ear. Yet the small congregation listened devoutly—with an occasional sigh. Mary Stanley's attention was not occupied much with the pulpit : she was looking rather at the sad, withered, weather-worn faces of certain of the older people —and thinking what their lot in life had been. She recalled a saying she had heard somewhere in the Black Forest—"The world grows every day harder for us poor folk that are so old ; " and she was wondering when her modest, but at least assiduous and sincere, efforts to somewhat better their condition and introduce a measure of cheerfulness into their surroundings would be accepted with a little goodwill. As for the middle-aged and younger men, she was less concerned about them. If they meant to break the windows of Lochgarra House next day, or pillage the garden, or set fire to the kennels, she would stand by and let them do their worst. But she did not think she had deserved such treatment at their hands.

When they came out of church again Miss Stanley and her friends lingered awhile, for she wished to intercept the Minister; and eventually Mr. Pettigrew made his appearance. As he approached them, Mr. Pettigrew's gaunt and grey-hued face wore a certain look of apprehension, and he was nervously stroking his long and straggling beard. But Mary received him pleasantly enough.

"How do you do, Mr. Pettigrew?" said she. "I thought I should like to know whether you are going to the gathering to-morrow. If these placards that are scattered about mean anything, it may be necessary for someone who is well acquainted with the people to be present to speak a quieting word; and as you have lent the church for the purposes of the meeting, I suppose you accept a certain responsibility——"

"Oh, no, Miss Stanley, I would not say that," the Minister responded, rather anxiously, "I would not say that. I think it is a wise thing and a just thing that the people should have an opportunity of conferring one with another about their temporal interests; but it is not for me to be a partisan. I would fain see all men's minds contented as regards their worldly affairs, so that they might the more readily turn to their spiritual requirements and needs. Ay. It is hardly for me to give counsel— either the counsel of Ahitophel or the counsel of Hushai the Archite—"

"And so," said Käthchen, striking in (for she had not yet had a chánce of opening her mind to Mr. Pettigrew), "you invite these strangers to come here and stir up contention and mischief—you give them your pulpit to preach from—and then you step aside, and wash your hands of all responsibility! I should have thought a minister of the gospel would have been on the side of peace, not on the side of disturbance and riot——"

"Dear me—dear me—it is all a mistake!" the bewildered Minister exclaimed. "I assure ye it is all a mistake. I did not invite them—Mr. Fraser wrote to me—and I thought I was justified in giving them permission—so that all men's minds might be leeberated. Is not that on the side of peace? Let the truth be spoken, though the heavens fall!—it's a noble axiom—a noble axiom. If the message that these people bring with them have not the truth in it, it will perish; if it have the truth in it, it will endure——"

"Yes, that's all very well," said the intrepid Käthchen. "But in the meantime? What's going to happen in the meantime? And if there is a general riot to-morrow, and property destroyed, and people injured—the truth of the message won't mend that. And what do those people know about Lochgarra? How can they know anything? They are coming here merely to incite a lot of ignorant crofters and cottars to break the law; and you lend them your pulpit, so that the people about here will think the church is on their side, even if they should take it into their heads to set fire to Lochgarra House!"

"Dear me!" said the Minister—who had not expected any such attack from this amiable and rather nice-looking young lady, "I hope nothing of the kind will happen."

"At all events, Mr. Pettigrew," said Mary, interposing, "I understand you don't mean to be present at this meeting? You will let those strangers talk whatever inflammatory stuff they choose without any word of protest or caution. Well, I suppose you have the right to decide for yourself. But I mean to go. If they have anything to say against me, I want to hear it. If I have no one to defend me, I must defend myself——"

"Oh, but I beg your pardon, Miss Stanley?" Frank Meredyth broke in. "You are not quite so defenceless—not at all! For my own part, I don't think you ought to go to this meeting—I think it will be unwise and uncalled for; but if you do go, you sha'n't go alone—I will see to that."

And again, after they had left the Minister, and were on their way back to Lochgarra House, he urgently begged her to abandon this enterprise; and her brother joined in, and quite as warmly.

"Why, you are the very person they have come to

denounce ! " Fred Stanley exclaimed. " You are the representative of the landlords. And what will they think of your appearing at the meeting ? They will take it as an open challenge ? "

" I mean it as an open challenge," she said, proudly. " I want to know what I am accused of. I want to ask what more I could have done—with my limited means. For of course my means are limited. I can't build breakwaters, and buy fleets of fishing-boats, and make railways; for I haven't the money. And I can't change the soil, or alter the climate, or even alter the habits of the people."

" What did I tell you, Mamie, at Invershin Station ? " said Käthchen ; but Mary Stanley went on unheeding—

" If there are grievances still to be redressed, I want to hear of them."

" Their real grievance is that they haven't got the land for nothing," observed her brother, who had a short and summary way of dealing with such questions.

" Well, if you must go, at least we can promise you a bodyguard," said Frank Meredyth, as they were ascending the wide stone steps. " At the same time, I think you would be very much better advised to stay at home."

That afternoon the ordinary dull somnolence of a Lochgarra Sunday gave way to a quite unusual, if subdued, excitement. To begin with, about half-past three a waggonette came rattling into the silent little village, and drew up at the inn ; while its occupants—the three apostles of Land Liberation—descended and disappeared from view. They were not gone long, however. The cottagers, furtively peeping from behind door or window-blind, beheld the strangers come out again and set off for a walk along the sea-front, scanning every object on each hand of them as they passed. The central figure of the three was a large and heavily-built man, pale and flabby of face, with small, piggish, twinkling eyes, close-cropped and stubbly yellow hair, and a wide but thin-lipped and resolute mouth. He wore a loose-flapping frock-coat, and a black felt wideawake ; his hands were clasped behind him ; he waddled as he walked. On his right was a tall and elderly woman, spare, and rather elegant of figure ; with a thin, sharp face which, either from constitutional acridity of blood or perhaps from driving in the sun, was distinctly violent in colour : this was Ernestine—the fiery Ernestine—who had no doubt brought with her her torch and can of paraffin. As for the lady who had come all the way across the Atlantic to enlighten these poor souls of crofters, no one could say what she was like ; for she was entirely enveloped in a brown dust-coat and a blue veil. But she was shorter than either of her companions.

"There are only three of them—there ought to be four," said Frank Meredyth, as the Lochgarra House party were regarding these passing strangers from the drawing-room window. "The big man is Ogden—he is easily recognisable—I'm afraid he has puffed himself out with too much tea-drinking ; but where is the Highland Land Leaguer ? "

"Why, you don't suppose the vice-president of a branch of the Highland Land League would travel on a Sunday ? " said Käthchen. "He will be coming along to-morrow morning—even if he has to walk or drive all night."

Mary was also regarding the strangers.

"If the American woman, whichever she is," said she, quietly "is going to denounce me to-morrow, she has not left herself much time to get information about this place. She will have to begin at once, if she wishes to ascertain the facts."

"The facts ! " said Meredyth. "She won't have to search about for them. She has brought them with her—from Connecticut."

Truly this was an afternoon of surprises. For while on a rare occasion it might happen that someone arrived at Lochgarra on Sunday by road, it was almost an unheard-of thing that anyone should come in by sea. Boating of any description was quite unknown on the sacred day ; there was no ferry—no Queen's highway to be kept open ; while as for going on the water for pleasure, such sacrilege never entered the brain of a native of Lochgarra. And yet here, unmistakably, was a small, black-hulled lugger, with a ruddy brown sail, coming steadily in before the light westerly breeze ; and when, having at length gained the shelter of the quay, she was rounded into the wind, and yard and sail lowered, her occupants presently got into the little dinghy astern, and came ashore. From the drawing-room of Lochgarra House they were easily distinguishable ; they were Big Archie, Donald Ross of Heimar, and the young lad who was usually in charge of the lugger. When they landed, young Ross left his companions, and went directly up to the inn.

"Ha ! didn't I tell you ?" Fred Stanley cried, with an air of triumph. " Before the storm the petrel !—I thought we should see him somewhere about, when this affair was coming off. Only he has missed his confederates. I wonder if they have gone far. I suppose Mr. Ogden has taken his American friend up Minard way to show her what a crofter's cottage is like—or perhaps she wants to look at the bed-ridden peat-hags. We shall find Ross following them in a moment—only he won't know which way they have gone." Of a sudden he rose from his seat, as if struck by some new idea. "I've a great mind to go down to the inn. What do you say, Frank ? I should like to step up to him and tell him that he'll find his friends if he goes up the Minard road."

" You shall do nothing of the kind ! " said Mary, angrily.

" I should like to see the expression of his face ! " her brother observed.

"If they are friends of Mr. Ross, he can find them for himself," said she. " It is none of our business. And —and—if they are not—I won't have him insulted by any-one going from this house ! "

He looked at her : she did not often talk in this indignant and vehement way.

" Oh, very well," he said. "Very well. It doesn't matter to me. You may have cause to change your opinion to-morrow."

All that evening very little mention was made of the subject about which everyone was secretly thinking.. Frank Meredyth, finding it was of no use to try to move Mary from her purpose, thought the best thing he could do was to reassure her : he said he hoped Ernestine would prove amusing. And next morning, too, he professed to treat the whole affair as a jest ; but all the same he kept going to the window from time to time, to have a look at the little groups of twos and threes who were congregated here and there, talking amongst themselves. For there was clearly some small commotion prevailing; the people were not attending to their ordinary affairs; the most trifling occurrence—a dog-fight in the street—attracted all eyes.

Mary insisted on setting out early; she wished everyone to see that she was going to attend the meeting. And hardly had they left the house—they were going round by the end of the quay—when Fred Stanley said in an undertone to his neighbour Meredyth—

"I don't know what's going to happen; but if they try on any games, I've got a little friend in my pocket here that can bark—and bite."

Mary overheard, and turned on him at once.

"What is that?" said she. "Your revolver? Let me see it."

He looked round : there was no one by.

"Oh, it is an elegant little companion to have with you," he said, bringing forth the silver-mounted weapon from his pocket, and regarding it quite affectionately.

She took it from him—he thinking that she merely wished to look at it—and, without more ado, she pitched it over the low sea-wall : there was a splash in the clear green water, and a bubble or two of air.

"Things of that sort are not fit for children," she said— and she took no heed of the angry flush that at once rose to his forehead : anger more probably caused by the reference to his youth than to the loss of his revolver. However, he said nothing; and so they went on again; and eventually arrived at the church.

When they entered the little building and modestly took their places in the nearest of the pews, there ensued a rather awkward moment; for they had come early; and, on looking round, they found that the only other persons present were they who had summoned the meeting; so that the hostile camps had a good opportunity of contemplating each other. The pulpit (like the body of the church) was empty; but in the precentor's box was a serious-visaged, brown-bearded man, who was no doubt Mr. Fraser, of the Stratherrick Branch of the Highland Land League; while underneath him, in the square space partitioned off

for the pews of the elders, sate the three persons who were
to address the meeting. They were all gravely silent, as
was fit and proper ; but their eyes were alert; and it was
as clear as daylight to Mary's friends that the strangers
had recognised in her the lady of Lochgarra House, whom
they had come to impeach as the representative in these
parts of the iniquitous landlord interest. It was indeed
an awkward moment ; and Mr. Ogden's glances of scrutiny
were furtive, until he turned away altogether; but the
thin and feverish-faced Mlle. Ernestine took a more confident survey ; and her bold black eyes went from one to
the other of the group, but were most frequently fixed
on Mary Stanley. The lady from Connecticut, also, was
obviously curious : most probably she had never beheld
before any of those people whose malevolent turpitude had
brought the Highlands to such a pass.

The time went slowly by, in this constrained silence.
The vice-president of the Stratherrick Branch, from his
seat in the precentor's box, began to look rather anxiously
towards the door. Mr. Ogden glanced at his watch.
Frank Meredyth did likewise—it was ten minutes after
one. And yet there had been no sign of any human being
—except for a small boy who had thrust his shock head in
for a second, and gazed wonderingly around the empty
church, and then withdrawn with a scared face. At
length the chairman leaned over the edge of the precentor's
box, and in an audible whisper said—

"Mr. Ogden, I'm thinking ye'd better go out and
tell them ?"

Mr. Ogden hesitated for a moment, and then made
answer—

"Don't you think we should begin the proceedings ?—
that will be the best announcement."

"Very well," said Mr. Fraser ; and he rose in his place
with a heavy sigh of preparation. "Ladies and gentlemen," he began, "before coming to local matters, I will
ask Mrs. Jackson Noyes to read a paper that she has prepared. Mrs. Noyes has recently completed a two days'
trip round the West Highlands in the steamer *Dunara
Castle ;* and where she has been unable to land—for the
steamer does not give ye much time at any place—she has

used her eyes, or her opera-glass, impartially; and what she has seen she has put down. The title of the paper is: '*The Horrible Desolation of the Highlands, as Descried from the Deck of the Dunara.*' Would ye get up on the bench, mem?"

This last murmured invitation was addressed to Mrs. Noyes, who rose to her feet, but seemed to shrink from taking up any more prominent position. Indeed, the poor woman looked dreadfully embarrassed; her face was all aflame; instead of proceeding with her paper, she kept glancing helplessly towards the door, whither Mr. Ogden had gone to reconnoitre; and it was clear she could not bring herself to begin without an audience, or, rather, with that small audience that was a hundred times worse than none. And presently Mr. Ogden came back—his face black as thunder. He went up to the precentor's box, and muttered something to the chairman. He returned to the elders' enclosure, and said something to the two ladies—who seemed entirely bewildered. The next moment the four of them had filed out of the church, without a word.

"Well, this is the most astounding thing!" Frank Meredyth exclaimed, when his party had also left their places, and got into the open air. "What is the matter with the people? Not a living soul has come near the place! No wonder the big Parliament-man was in a furious rage!"

But Mary had turned to Kate Glendinning, who had fallen a step or two behind.

"Käthchen," she said, in an undertone, "what is the meaning of all this? I can see perfectly well you know something about it."

For indeed Käthchen was all tremblingly triumphant, and joyous, and also inclined to tears—half-hysterical, in short.

"Mamie—Mamie," she said, between that laughing and crying, "I knew he could do it if he liked—and—and— I thought he would—for your sake—"

"What are you talking about?" said Mary: but a sudden self-conscious look showed that she had guessed.

"You needn't be angry, Mamie," said Käthchen, her

wet eyes thining with a half-concealed pride and delight;
"but—but I was terribly frightened about what might
happen to you; and yesterday I sent Big Archie out to
Heimra—I told him to go as soon as the people had got
into church—and I gave him a note. For I knew he
would answer the message at once—and that he would see
you came to no harm—"

"Do you mean Donald Ross?" said Mary, rather breathlessly.

"Who else could have done it?" said Käthchen, with
something of reproach. "And I knew he would do that—
or anything—for your sake. Oh, do you think I can't
see?—do you think I have no eyes?"

Mary did not answer: she walked on in silence for a
little while. But by and by she said—

"Käthchen, don't you think I ought to see Mr. Ross—
before he goes back to Heimra?"

CHAPTER XVIII.

SMOKE AND FLAME.

But that was not at all the view that Fred Stanley took
of this amazing and incomprehensible incident.

"There's some trick in it, Frank," he said vehemently,
as he hurried his friend along with him, on their way back
to the house. "There's some underhand trick in it, and
I want to know what it means. I tell you, we must get
the keepers, and go up the hill at once, and see what is
going on. There's something at the bottom of all this
jugglery."

"Jugglery or no jugglery," his companion said, with
much good-humour, "it has come in very handy. If a
riot had been started, who knows what the end might have
been? It wasn't the raid into the Glen Orme forest that
concerned me, nor yet the driving of the sheep off Meall-
na-Fearn; but I confess I was anxious about your sister.
If she had been denounced before an angry and excited
meeting——"

"Oh, we should have been able to take care of ourselves !" the younger man said, dismissing that matter contemptuously.

"And if it was Ross of Heimra who stepped in to prevent all this," Meredyth continued, "I, for one, am very much obliged to him."

"Oh, don't be an ass, Frank !" the other said with angry impatience. "If it is Donald Ross who has done all this, I'll swear he has done it for his own purposes. And I want to know. I want to find out. I want to see what the trick means. And of one thing I am absolutely certain, and that is, that Donald Ross is up on the moor at this very moment. Oh, yes," the young man went on, seeing that his wild suspicions received no encouragement from his more cautious companion, "a fine stratagem, to keep us idling and kicking our heels about here all the morning—and on the Twelfth, too ! I thought it was odd that the meeting should be fixed for the Twelfth ; but now I begin to see. Now I begin to understand why Donald Ross came over from Heimra yesterday afternoon."

"Well, what do you imagine ?" Meredyth asked.

"Why, it's as clear as daylight !" the younger man exclaimed—jumping from vague surmises to definite conclusions. "Here have we been hanging about all the morning, like a couple of simpletons, waiting for a general riot or some nonsense of that kind, while Ross and his gang of poachers have been up on the moor, sweeping the best beats clean of every bird ! That has been the little programme !—and a fine consignment of game to be sent away to Inverness to-night, as soon as the dark comes down. But they may not be off the hill yet ; and we'll hurry up Hector and Hugh, and have a look round." And then he added, vindictively : "I'd let the Twelfth go—I shouldn't mind a bit having had the Twelfth spoilt—if only I could catch those scoundrels—and the chief of them—red-handed."

"All I have to say is," observed the more phlegmatic Meredyth, "that if we are going up the hill we may as well take our guns with us and a brace of dogs. We can have an hour or two. The fag-end of the Twelfth is better than no Twelfth ; and your sister says she wants some birds."

" Birds ? " the other repeated. " What do you expect to find on the ground after those poaching thieves have been over it ? "

However, in the end he consented; and as they found that Hector—undisturbed by all those alarming rumours of riot and pillage—had kept everything in readiness for them, the two young men snatched a hasty sandwich and set forth. It was not a very eager shooting party. There was a sensation that the great possibilities of the Twelfth had been ruined for them. Nevertheless, there would be some occupation for the afternoon, and the mistress of the household wanted some grouse.

But, indeed, it soon became evident that it was not shooting that was uppermost in Fred Stanley's mind. He overruled Hector's plan for taking the nearest beats. He would have his companions hold a way up the Corrie Bhreag, which leads to the Glen Orme forest ; and ever he was making for the higher ranges—scanning the ground far ahead of him, and listening intently in the strange silence ; while he was clearly unwilling to have the dogs uncoupled.

" Look here, man," at length said Meredyth, who, though new to the place, had a trained eye for the features of a moor ; " surely we have come down wind far enough ? It will take us all our time to get back before dinner, even if we pick the beats on the way home——"

The answer was unexpected—a half-smothered exclamation of mingled anger and triumph.

" Didn't I tell you so ? " young Stanley exclaimed, with his eyes fixed on a small, dark object a long distance up the glen. " Didn't I tell you we should find him here ? Don't you see him—away up yonder ? My lad, when you come poaching, you shouldn't put on sailor's clothes ; they're too conspicuous. What do you say, Hector : can you make him out ? Well, whether you can or not I will tell you his name. That is Mr. Donald Ross, if you want to know—and I guessed we should find him here or hereabouts ! "

" I am not sure," said Hector, slowly, also with his eyes fixed on the distant and dark figure.

" But I am ! " Fred Stanley went on. " And perhaps you can tell me what he is doing up on our shooting ? "

"Mebbe," said the serious-visaged keeper, with a little hesitation, "mebbe he was waiting to see that none of the lads would be for going into the forest. Or mebbe he was up at Glen Orme."

"Oh, stuff and nonsense!" the young man cried, scornfully. "Do you think we are children! I tell you, we have caught him at last; and wherever the rest of the gang have sneaked off to, he is bound to come along here, and face it out. Yes, he *is* coming: I can see he is moving this way. Very well, Frank, you have the dogs uncoupled now, and begin to shoot back home: I'm going to meet my gentleman—and I will take my gun with me, just to keep a wholesome check on insolence."

"You will not," said Meredyth, with decision—for he knew not whither this young man's obvious wrath and enmity might not lead him. "I will wait here with you: whoever that is, he is clearly coming this way."

"Why, of course he must!" was the rejoinder. "He sees he is caught: what else is there left for him but to come along and try to put some kind of face on it?" Then presently he exclaimed: "Well, of all the effrontery that I ever beheld! He is carrying a gun under his arm! how's that for coolness?"

"I am not thinking it is a gun, sir," said the tall, brown-bearded keeper; "it is more like a steeck."

"Yes, it is a stick, Fred," Meredyth put in, after a moment.

"Oh, why should he have a gun? What does he want with a gun?" the young man said, without being disconcerted for a moment. "He has only to direct the operations of his confederates. A stick?—very likely!—the master-poacher doesn't want to be encumbered with a gun!"

And so they waited. It was a singular scene for the Twelfth of August on the side of a Highland hill: no ranging of dogs, no cracking of breechloaders, no picking up of a bird here and there from the thick heather, but a small group, standing silent and constrained, and dimly aware that pent-up human passions were about to burst forth amid these vast and impressive solitudes. Young Ross of Heimra—for it was unmistakably he—came leisurely along; his intention was evidently fixed on the sportsmen; perhaps he was wondering that they did not let loose the dogs and get to work. But as he drew nearer he must have perceived that they were awaiting his approach; and so—with something of interrogation and surprise in his look—he came up to them.

"I hope you have had good sport," said Fred Stanley.

Donald Ross stared: there was something in the young man's tone that seemed to strike him.

"I—I don't quite understand," said he.

"Oh, well, it's only this," replied the other, striving to keep down his rising rage, and speaking in a deliberately taunting fashion, "that when you find anyone on a Highland moor on the Twelfth of August you naturally suppose that he has come for grouse. And why not? I am sorry we have interrupted you. When you have the fishing and the stalking, why shouldn't you have the shooting as well? I am sorry if we have disturbed you——"

They formed a curious contrast, those two: the tall, handsome, light-haired youth, with his fair complexion and his boyish moustache causing him to look almost effeminate, and yet with his nostrils dilated, his haughty grey eyes glistening with anger, a tremor of passion about the lines of his lips; the other, though hardly so tall, of more manly presence, his pale, proud, clear-cut features entirely reticent, his coal-black eyes, so far, without flame in them, an absolute self-possession and dignity governing his manner.

"I hardly know what you mean," said he, slowly, fixing those calmly observant black eyes on the young lad. "What is it all about? Do I understand you to accuse me of shooting over your moor—here—now?—do you imagine——"

"Oh, it isn't that only!—it is half-a-dozen things besides!" the young man exclaimed, letting his passion get entirely the mastery of him. "Who has this place? Not those who bought it! It is you who have the shooting and fishing and everything; and not content with that but you play dog-in-the-manger as well—heaving stones into the pools when anyone else goes down to the river. And who does the scringeing about here ?—answer me that !—do you think we don't know well enough ? Let us have an end to hypocrisy——"

"Let us have an end of madness " said Donald Ross, sternly ; and for a second there was a gleam of fire in his black eyes. But that sudden flame, and a certain set expression of the mouth, almost instantly vanished ; this young fellow, with the girlish complexion, was even now so curiously like his sister. "I do not answer you," Donald Ross went on, with a demeanour at once simple and austere. "You have chosen to insult me. I do not answer you. You are in my country : it is the same as if you were under my roof."

"Your country ! " the hot-headed young man cried, in open scorn, "What part of the country belongs to you ! That rock of an island out there !—and I wish you would keep to it ; and you'd better keep to it ; for we don't mean to have this kind of thing going on any longer. We mean to have an end of all this scringeing and poaching ! We have been precious near getting hold of those scringe-nets : we'll make sure of them the next time. And I want once for all to tell you that we mean to have the fishing for ourselves, and the shooting, too ; and we want you to understand that there is such a thing as the law of trespass. What right have you to be here, at this moment, on this moor ? " he demanded. "How can you explain your being here ? What are you doing here—on the Twelfth ? Do you know to whom this moor belongs ? And by what right do you trespass on it ? "

"Fred," interposed Frank Meredyth, who was painfully conscious that the two keepers—though they had discreetly turned away—must be hearing something of this one-sided altercation, "enough of this : if there is any dispute, it can be settled another time—not before third persons."

"One moment," said Donald Ross, turning with a grave courtesy to this intervener. "You have heard the questions I have just been asked. Well, I do not choose to account for my actions to any one. But this I wish to explain. I have no right to be where I am, I admit ; I have trespassed some dozen yards on to this moor, in order to come up and speak to you. When you saw me first I was on the old footpath—there it is, you can see for yourself—that leads up this corrie, and through the Glen Orme forest to Ledmore ; it is an old hill road that everyone has the right of using."

"Oh, yes, thieves' lawyers are always clever enough !" Fred Stanley said, disdainfully.

Donald Ross regarded him for a moment—with a strange kind of look, and that not of anger : then he quietly said, "Good afternoon ?" to Meredyth, and went on his way. Hector got out of the prevailing embarrassment by uncoupling the dogs ; and Frank Meredyth put cartridges in his gun. This encounter did not augur well for steady shooting.

Meanwhile Donald Ross was making down for the coast, slowly and thoughtfully. What had happened had been a matter of a few swift seconds ; it had now to be set in order and considered ; the scene had to be conjured up again—with all its minute but vivid incidents. And no longer was there any need for him to affect a calm and proud indifference ; phrases that he had seemed to pass unheeded began to burn ; the rapid glances and tones of those brief moments, now that they were recalled, struck deep. Indeed, the first effect of a blow is but to stun and bewilder—the pain comes afterwards ; and there are words that cause more deadly wounds than any blows. Taunt and insult : these are hard things for a Highlander to brook—and yet—and yet—that handsome, headstrong boy, even in the white-heat of his passion, had looked so curiously like his sister.

"Ah, well," said Ross, aloud, and there was a kind of smile on his face, "it is, perhaps, a wholesome lesson. Hereafter I'd better mind my own business. And if I have been ordered off the mainland—sent back to my little island—very well : the sea-gulls and gannets won't accuse me of trespass."

In time he drew near the village. But as he went down the hill from Minard, and had to pass Lochgarra House, he did not turn his eyes in that direction. He held straight on ; and at length encountered a small boy who had just been engaged in hauling a dinghy up on the beach.

"Alan," said he, "have you seen Big Archie anywhere about ?"

"Ay," said the boy, "he was at the inn to look at the people driving aweh."

"What people ? The strangers who were at the church this morning ?"

"Ay, chist that. There was many a one laughing at them," said Alan, with a bit of a grin.

"Well, run along now, and see if you can find Big Archie, and tell him I am going out to Heimra. Then you can come back with him, and pull us out to the lugger."

And away went Alan, with a will, eager to earn the sixpence that he foresaw awaiting his return, while the young laird of Heimra, having nothing else to do until Big Archie should put in an appearance, seated himself on the gunwale of the dinghy, with his eyes turned towards the sea. Not once had he glanced in the direction of Lochgarra House.

But Lochgarra House had taken notice of him. Mary Stanley chanced to be passing one of the windows, when of a sudden her face grew animated, and her eyes—those liquid grey-green eyes that were at all times so clear and radiant—those bland, good-humoured, kind eyes—shone with a quick interest and delight.

"Käthchen ! Käthchen !" she called. "There is Mr. Ross just gone by—tell Barbara to run after him—quick ! quick !—and—and my compliments—and I want to see him most particularly. He must not go out to Heimra before I have seen him—tell her not to lose a minute— I'm afraid he may be going along now to get Big Archie's boat."

But at such a crisis Kate Glendinning did not choose to wait for any servant. She flew into the hall, snatched a straw hat from the table, tripped down the wide stone steps, and made her way as quickly as might be round the sea-wall and along the beach. He did not hear her approach ; he seemed plunged in a profound reverie.

"Mr. Ross !" she said, rather breathlessly and timidly, to attract his attention.

He started to his feet ; and, when he saw who this was,

his naturally pale, dark face grew suddenly suffused—an almost school-boyish constraint visible there for a moment! Käthchen was surprised; but she made haste to deliver Miss Stanley's message.

"She happened to see you from the window; and she is most anxious you should not go back to Heimra before she has a chance of thanking you for your great kindness. For she quite understands it was you who prevented all the mischief that might have arisen from those people coming here; and she is very grateful; and wishes to say so to yourself. And I was to give you her compliments, and say that she wished particularly to see you—if you wouldn't mind coming along for a few moments."

This time he did throw a brief glance in the direction of Lochgarra House—perhaps thinking of what otherwise might have been. But now, how could he ever again be under that roof?

"Will you tell Miss Stanley," said he—and though that temporary confusion had gone, there was still a curious reserve in his manner—"that I am very glad if I have been of any service to her—very glad that she should think so, I mean; but it isn't worth speaking about; and she must not say anything more about it."

"But she wishes to see you!" exclaimed Käthchen, who naturally had expected an instant acquiescence. "Surely she is the best judge as to whether she ought to thank you, or not. And that was the message I was to take to you, that she wished most particularly to see you, before you went out to Heimra. A few moments only— she will not detain you——"

"If you will excuse me, I would rather not go along," said he, looking uneasily towards the cottages and the inn. "I have just sent for Big Archie."

Käthchen was astounded. What kind of a young man was this, to refuse the invitation of a beautiful young woman—one, indeed, who had shown herself singularly interested in him, even as he had gone out of his way to render friendly little services to her? Käthchen's secret conjectures, founded on what she had recently observed as between these two, seemed to have been suddenly and rudely stultified. What was the key to this enigma?

Jealousy? Was it the presence of Frank Meredyth that interposed? Would he decline to visit the house until that possible rival had been removed? She could not understand; she was bewildered; but still she had her commission to execute; and the faithful Kate was staunch.

"Miss Stanley will be disappointed," said she. "She is most anxious to see you. A couple of minutes would be enough. And surely you could let Big Archie wait."

"Thank you," said he—and it was clear that it was with the greatest reluctance he was forcing himself to refuse—"but I would rather not. I am very sensible of Miss Stanley's kindness; but—but she must not make too much of this trifling thing."

Käthchen paused irresolute. But, after all, she had no more to say. She could not appeal to him, she could not beg of him, as a favour, to accept Miss Stanley's invitation: Käthchen also had a little pride; so she civilly bade him good afternoon, and hoped he would have a pleasant voyage home; and set out on her way back to the house.

"Well?" said Mary, when Käthchen came into the room. But she had already seen, from the window, that her messenger was returning alone.

"Oh," said Käthchen, in an indifferent sort of fashion—and she began to gather up some samples of homespun that were strewn on the table—"he says he is going out to Heimra at once. He has sent for Big Archie. He says—he says—that he is glad if he has rendered you any little service—but you are not to think of it."

Mary's eyes had grown full of wonder. For out of these windows she could plainly see that he was still waiting on the beach: the fact being that the boy Alan had failed to find Big Archie at the inn, and had gone off to seek him throughout the cottages.

"But did you tell Mr. Ross that I wished to speak with him?" she asked.

"I said that you most particularly wished to speak with him."

"Yes—and then?"

"Then he—he begged to be excused," said Käthchen, bluntly.

Mary turned sharply away from the window, and for a second or two she was silent.

"Why did you say 'most particularly'? What right had you to give him any such message?" she demanded, with something of a cold and dignified air, but not looking towards Käthchen.

"Those were your very words, Mamie!" Käthchen protested.

"I may have said something like that—in the hurry of calling to you," Mary said, with flushed face. "But you ought to have known. You might have known it was not a message I wanted given to anyone—not to anyone. However, it is of little consequence." She advanced to the table—her head somewhat erect. "I suppose," she said, in a matter-of-fact way, "you will be writing about those samples to the Frasers, in Inverness?"

"Yes, Mamie—you told me to."

"Very well," she continued, still with that air of unconcern; "you might say to them at the same time that we can get patchwork quilts made for them at from ten to twelve shillings the piece, if they send us the materials. That is the price I promised to the women here. And if they prefer the stockings made longer, I will have them made longer; only they must give me a little more for them—there is so much more wool and so much more work."

She glanced furtively over her shoulder: it was only now that Big Archie had made his appearance—coming down the beach to the spot at which young Ross was idly walking about.

"Käthchen," she said of a sudden, with something of piteous vexation in her tone, "are you certain you said 'most particularly'?—are you quite certain?—I—I did not mean it—I was in a hurry—you did not say 'most particularly,' did you? At the same time," she went on, with an abrupt affectation of carelessness, "it is of very little consequence—no consequence whatever: the only thing is that the Highlanders appear to have odd manners —and that again, as I say, is a matter of perfect indifference. Don't forget to mention the patchwork quilts and the stockings."

But Kate Glendinning rose and went to the window.

By this time Donald Ross, Big Archie, and the young lad were all in the dinghy, on their way out to the lugger.

"There is something strange, Mamie," Käthchen said, thoughtfully. "I cannot imagine what made him refuse to come along to this house—and refuse with such embarrassment. And these are not Highland manners at all. But sometimes a Highlander is too proud to speak."

They were soon to learn what all this meant. When the two young men returned from their afternoon expedition, it appeared that they had got thirteen and a half brace of grouse, and a few odds and ends—a very fair bag, considering the size of the moor and the length of time they had been out. But it was not the success of the shooting that caused Fred Stanley to come into the drawing-room with something of a gay and triumphant air.

"Well, we have caught your poaching friend at last," he said to his sister, "and I think we have sent him home with a flea in his ear. I knew we should corner him sooner or later, in spite of his cunning. And a very pretty trick it was—to plan this insurrectionary meeting for the Twelfth, so that we should be kept away from the hill, keepers and all. But it didn't work, you see ; for we lost no time in getting up to the Corrie Bhreag, and there he was, sure enough. And very little he had to say for himself—not a word !—but I had something to say to him ; and I don't think we shall be troubled with his presence about Lochgarra for some little time to come."

"Are you speaking of Mr. Ross?" said Mary, with a certain calmness of manner that did not quite conceal her alarm.

"I should think I was !"

"And what did you find him doing?"

"I found him on the moor—where he had no right to be ; and if the rest of the gang managed to hide themselves or to get safe away, well, I did not care much about that ; he was there to answer for them ; and so we had it out. Yes, I may say we had it out."

Mary turned to Frank Meredyth.

"Mr. Meredyth, what is all this about? What happened? Did you find Mr. Ross shooting on the moor?"

"Well, no," said Meredyth, with something of disquiet,

for he was now placed in a most unenviable position. " The fact is, it would be difficult to bring any definite charge against him; for he was coming down from the direction of the Glen Orme forest, and when we first saw him he was following an old hill-path that everybody has the right to use—so he says. No, he wasn't shooting— not then, certainly; nor did we see any one with him : but as regards Fred's suspicions—well, you know, I have said before, that when you imagine there is poaching going on, you see it in every circumstance."

" What was he doing up there at all ? " the younger man broke in. " Why, he had no defence to make. He had not a word to say for himself. It's all very well to be high and mighty : you won't account for your actions to anybody—no, of course not, when you can't without convicting yourself ! "

" I suppose he had a gun with him ? " said she, still addressing Frank Meredyth.

" Well, no; he had not," Meredyth confessed, looking somewhat anxious and disconcerted.

" A game-bag, at least ? and a dog ? " she went on; " or something that entitled you to suspect him ? "

" Oh, no, not at all. The truth is, he was simply coming down the strath, and he had nothing under his arm but a walking-stick."

" Oh, indeed," said she; and she drew herself up a little proudly. " Very well. You meet a stranger—no, not a stranger—but one of my friends, whom you have seen under my roof, and he is walking along a public footpath carrying a stick in his hand. Well, and then ? I want to know what happens then ? "

Meredyth was grievously embarrassed.

" I am afraid there were a few hard words said—and— and I must say for Mr. Ross that he showed great for- bearance and self-control. Yes, I must admit that; and also that Fred was rather too—too outspoken. I must say I rather admired Mr. Ross because of his composure; for, indeed, I thought at one time—well, it was a very awkward meeting. When there is bad blood, you see— when one suspects poaching—everything points that way."

" Oh, I am responsible for everything that occurred ! "

Fred Stanley broke in again, impetuously. "Meredyth had nothing to do with it—nothing at all! And I tell you I spoke plainly. I thought the time for pretence and hypocrisy had gone by; I thought it was time my gentleman-poacher should understand we weren't going to be made fools of any longer. Oh, I spoke plainly enough, if that is what you want to find out!" continued this confident lad, who seemed to be rather vain of his achievement. "I told him we had had quite enough of him about Lochgarra—quite enough of him, and his scringe-nets, and his thieving of salmon, and heaving of stones into the pools. I told him we wanted this place to ourselves now. I recommended him to keep to that small island out there——"

"It is infamous—it is shameless!" said Mary Stanley—and the beautiful, proud face had grown suddenly pale, and there was a curious indignant vibration in her voice. "Do you know what that man has done for me, this very day? What does he value most in the world—what remains to him of all the possessions which his family used to hold—what but the devotion and affection with which these people about here regard him? And he risked it all—for my sake! He took my side—against his own people! They were appealed to by everything that could tempt them; and they had been taught to regard me as their enemy; and who knows what might have happened if he had not stepped in, and confronted them, and said—'No.' He has forgiven the injuries, the irreparable injuries, my family have done him and his; he has met me with friendliness at every turn—and always keeping out of the way and claiming no thanks for it; and now the return he gets is—insult!—and insult that he would scorn to answer." She went on with increasing indignation: "Shooting and fishing! What do I care for the shooting and fishing! I would rather have every fish in the river and every bird on the hill destroyed than that the disgrace of such ingratitude should have fallen on this house!" She paused—hesitated—her lips began to quiver. "I—I beg your pardon, Mr. Meredyth—I am sorry you should have met with any annoyance to-day." And the next second, and in despite of herself, she had burst into a passionate fit of weeping; while with the proud head bent, her handkerchief covering her eyes, and her frame shaken with sobbing, she left the room. Instantly Käthchen went with her—leaving silence behind.

It was about half an hour thereafter that the dinner-gong sounded upward from the big, empty, echoing hall. Käthchen came down to the drawing-room.

"Miss Stanley would rather that you did not wait for her," said she to the two gentlemen. And therewith Käthchen also withdrew.

CHAPTER XIX.

A SUMMONS.

"WHAT can I do, Käthchen? What can I do?" she was saying, in accents almost of despair; and in her agitation she was walking up and down before the windows, glancing out from time to time towards the far island that was now shining in the morning sunlight, while the driven blue sea was springing white along its rocky shores. "What can I do? What atonement can I make? Or is it quite hope-less? Is he to be sent away as a stranger, without a word of excuse, or apology, or appeal?" And then she said: "Käthchen, surely there is some fatality in it, that this young man, who has heaped kindness on me since ever I came to this place—but always keeping aloof in a strange, proud way, as if to avoid the possibility of thanks—surely there is some fatality that he should receive nothing but insult and wrong at our hands. First, my uncle—now, my brother——"

"At all events," said Kate Glendinning, boldly, "I don't see why you should torture your mind about it, Mamie. It has been none of your doing. You are not responsible for what your uncle may have done; and if Fred has spoken in a moment of anger, well, I don't suppose Mr. Ross will prove to be so unforgiving."

"It is the whole family he must think of, Käthchen!" Mary broke in bitterly. "I shouldn't wonder if he hated the very name of Stanley! What a despicable race he must think us! But I suppose there is an end now. He has borne too much already: this puts a climax to it.

Unforgiving? Why, even if I could persuade Fred to go out to Heimra and offer him an apology, he would treat it with scorn—and rightly too. I know he would!"

The shrewd Käthchen, though she did not say so, had her doubts on this score. In the dim recesses of her consciousness there was an echo of two lines from 'Maud'—

> 'Peace, angry spirit, and let him be!
> Has not his sister smiled on me?'

And she fancied, for reasons of her own, that if the headstrong lad could be brought to ask for pardon, the somewhat haughty features of the young owner of Heimra would not long remain stern and implacable. But she dared not reveal those reasons, even as she dared not repeat those two lines. She was a prudent lass; and careful not to presume unwarily.

Of a sudden Mary said, in her impetuous way—

"Käthchen, I will take the sheep off Meall-na-Fearn!"

Kate Glendinning looked up, startled.

"Yes," the young proprietress said, with decision. "After breakfast you and I must drive away out and see Mr. Watson. If he will give up Meall-na-Fearn on the same terms as Meall-na-Cruagan, good and well; the sheep must go; and the crofters can have the pasturage divided amongst them. I suppose," she added, with something of embarrassment in the clear-shining eyes, "some one would be sure to—to carry the news—out to Heimra? Or a line, perhaps—you might have occasion to send out to him——"

"Mamie!" said Käthchen, in warm protest. "What are you thinking of? Is that the atonement you want to make? Do you mean to cut down Mr. Watson's farm still further just to please Donald Ross? Why, it is madness! To begin with, it would not please him—not in the least; he has told you that you have already been far too generous; and I don't know what he would think of such a needless and useless sacrifice."

"Oh, you think he would not approve?" said Mary, slowly. She was now standing at one of the windows, looking out towards the distant island beyond the wide blue plain of the sea.

"I am pretty sure he would not," Käthchen responded, "especially if he fancied it was done to propitiate him : it would put him in a very awkward position. But I'll tell you what I should do if I were in your place, Mamie———"

"Yes," she said, instantly turning from the window. "What is it ? Is there anything I can do, Käthchen ? It seems so terrible—and so shameful; and here am I helpless. And then he is so proud—yes, proud and disdainful; I have said it before; only this time he has an ample right to be."

"Well, Mamie, if I were you, I would simply take no notice of what happened yesterday afternoon;" this was Käthchen's advice. "I would assume that the friendly relations between him and you were precisely as they always had been."

"Yes, but how to let him know that that is what I am thinking ?" said Mary eagerly—and rather piteously withal.

"I would send him a note," said the intrepid Käthchen.

"About what ?"

"About anything !"

"Shall I ask him to come over and dine with us ?" Mary asked, rather nervously.

"Well, no : that would be useless ; he would not accept —at present," Käthchen made answer. "But indeed, Mamie, I would not send him any invitation, nor would I say anything that needed an answer : I should write so that he might answer or not just as he pleased."

"Yes, yes," said Mary, with some animation. "Your advice is excellent, Käthchen, I will write at once. And about what ? Oh, about kelp. I have got all the information I wanted about the burning of kelp ; and I will tell him that any time he comes over to the mainland I should like to show him the report." And then as abruptly she discarded this idea. "No. Kelp is too commonplace. It would be like asking for his advice about something connected with the estate ; and I want him to understand that I can get on by myself. Oh, I'll tell you, Käthchen !— the photographs !—the photographs I promised to send to Mrs. Armour. You know how proud he was of the old woman's coming all the way from Canada to have but a glimpse of Young Donald; and I could see how he was pleased by the little attentions I was able to show her—quite grateful he seemed—though you know he doesn't say much."

She was all excitement now, and as happy and sanguine as hitherto she had been despondent. She went and got writing materials forthwith, and hastily, and yet with some consideration, penned this note :—

"Lochgarra House, Tuesday Morning.

"DEAR MR. ROSS,—I do not know whether I told you that, before Mrs. Armour left to return to Canada, I promised to send her a series of photographs of Lochgarra and the neighbourhood. I am arranging to have a photographer come through from Inverness, and any time that you happen to be over here I should be exceedingly obliged if you would spare me a few minutes to let me know what places would be likely to prove most interesting to her.

"Yours sincerely,
"MARY STANLEY."

"Now, you see," she said, as she rather triumphantly handed the letter to Käthchen, "that demands nothing. He does not need to reply unless he happens to have plenty of time and nothing else to do. It merely shows that, as far as I am concerned, I don't consider that anything has occurred to disturb our friendly relations. It was so clever of you to think of it, Käthchen. And I must send word to Big Archie that I shall want him and his boat. I'm afraid it's too rough to try the steam-launch. I'm so much obliged to you, Käthchen, for thinking about it!"

Indeed, she was quite joyous and radiant. Her keen remorse, and shame, and piteous despair seemed wholly to have fled; she was possessed with an audacious confidence; a sort of gratitude towards all the world shone in her eyes. And Käthchen, who had studied this young woman closely, and who was capable of drawing conclusions, knew perfectly the origin of this buoyancy of spirit: the letter Mary had just written demanded no answer, it is true, but none the less was she in her heart convinced that an

answer—an answer confirming all her best anticipations—
would be forthcoming, and that without delay. Big
Archie was bidden to haste and get his lugger ready : he
was to set out for Heimra at once.

Kate Glendinning was not the only one in this house
who could draw conclusions, or at least form suspicions.
When the two gentlemen returned that evening from the
hill, they found the letters and newspapers that had
arrived by the mid-day post spread out on the hall-table;
and they began to glance at addresses and tear open
envelopes. Fred Stanley was soon satisfied ; he went off to
his room to change for dinner; but his elder companion
remained—holding a letter in his hand, and apparently
much concerned about something. At this moment Käthchen appeared, passing across to the door leading out into
the garden ; and the instant he caught sight of her his·
eyes seemed to light up with interest. Here was a friend
in need.

"Miss Glendinning," said he, in something of an anxious
undertone, "could you give me a couple of minutes ? Are
you going into the garden ? May I come with you ? I
want to ask you to do me a great service—how great I can
hardly tell you."

Käthchen was surprised ; for this trim, brisk, bronze-
cheeked, shrewd-eyed sportsman generally took things in
a very happy-go-lucky, imperturbable fashion. But her
instant conjecture was a natural one : "Be sure this is
about Mamie ! " she said to herself.

Well, he accompanied her down the stone steps and into
the garden, where she began to employ herself in cutting
flowers for the dining-room table, while she listened attentively enough.

"The fact is," said he, "I have just had a letter from
home, with no very good news. My father, who is an old
man, has been an invalid for a great many years, varying
in health from time to time ; but now it seems he has had
a very bad attack of asthma along with his other ailments,
and the doctors have ordered him off to Bournemouth——

"I am very sorry," said Käthchen, as in duty bound.

"And—I have received an intimation that I may be
telegraphed for—I might have to leave here at a moment's

notice almost." He hesitated for a second or so. "Miss Glendinning," he said, "you see how I am situated : I may be called away at any moment—with something that is of great importance to me left unsettled. I have been living in a fool's paradise ; I thought there was plenty of time. And then, again, I did not care to confide in any one. But now I am going to appeal to you. Will you tell me something in strictest confidence—something you are likely to know ? It might save your friend—you can guess whom I mean—much embarrassment, even pain ; and it would be the greatest favour you could possibly confer on me."

And now Käthchen knew her surmise was correct ; and perhaps she may have been inclined to think that there was something incongruous, something even humorous, in this ordinarily cool and firm-nerved person appearing to be afflicted by the hesitation of an anxious lover, only that she was also aware of the gravity of the situation. For tragic things may happen even to the steeled.

"Miss Glendinning," said he, "I want you to tell me if there is anything between Mr. Ross and Miss Stanley ? "

Well, this was a frank challenge ; and she answered it as frankly.

"I do not think there is," she said ; "but I think there might be at any moment. That is only my impression ; and I may be quite wrong ; and indeed I have no right to say so——"

"But I have appealed to you as a friend, to do me this great favour," said he ; and then he paused for a second. "The fact is," he went on, as if with some unwillingness, "I have noticed one or two odd things—Miss Stanley's indignation with her brother if he said anything against Mr. Ross—and the painful scene of yesterday evening— these things might lead one to conjecture——"

"Oh, but I'm sure there is nothing between them— nothing at present, at least," said Käthchen, with some earnestness ; for this assurance she could honestly give him ; and when did a perplexed and troubled lover ever appeal in vain to a woman's heart ? "There is nothing between them at present, I am certain of that ; and whether there ever may be, who can tell ? Both of them have peculiar natures. Both of them are proud; and she, besides that, is wilful and impulsive; while he is reserved —and—and you might almost think cold—only that I imagine his studiously keeping away from her, and treating her with a kind of distant civility, has some meaning and intention in it. I don't think he would like to become the slave of any woman; and she—well, she is very independent, too. And then both of them are very peculiarly situated: there is the old-standing feud between the two families; it must have been hard on him and on his mother to have strangers coming into the neighbourhood, tearing down the old landmarks. There are things that the Highland nature can never forget; and Mary knows that well; more than once she has said to me, 'Käthchen, there are wrongs that can never be undone; I can never rebuild Castle Heimra.' "

" Yes, yes, I quite understand," said he, rather absently; "and yet Ross does not seem to bear any resentment—not against her. No, nor against any one belonging to her. I must say for him that his forbearance yesterday towards Fred Stanley was most remarkable: that was another thing that struck me as peculiar. And yet you say there is nothing between him and Miss Stanley ?"

" Nothing, I am certain," Käthchen assured him again.

" I am so awfully obliged to you !" he said, with some little expression of relief; and yet he was thoughtful and silent as they walked back to the house—Käthchen having got all the flowers she wanted.

That night, after dinner, when the two young ladies retired to the drawing-room, Mary seemed somewhat disturbed.

" Don't you think it rather strange, Käthchen," she said, "that Big Archie brought no message back from Heimra ? I don't mean an answer. I don't mean an answer to my note. That was not necessary—it was hardly to be expected. But why has he not come to say he delivered my letter ?"

She went to one of the windows, and pulled aside part of the blind. The night had turned out rather dark and squally; and there were spots of rain on the glass that caught the light of the lamps within.

" I should like to see Big Archie," said she, with a vague restlessness. And then of a sudden she made this abrupt proposal; "Käthchen, won't you come down with me into the village? Barbara says the gentlemen have gone into the billiard-room, for there is a threatening of rain; but we could put on waterproofs, and run away down there and back, without anything being known of it."

" Is it worth while, Mamie?" Käthchen remonstrated. " He must have delivered your note!"

" Yes; but it is so strange there should be no message of any kind!" said Mary. And then she instantly added, changing her tone: " Of course, it is not at all strange. Only—only, Big Archie sometimes takes a glass of whisky, you know; and he might have got some answer that he has forgotten—perhaps a note that he has left in his pocket——"

" Oh, if you like, I will go with you," said Käthchen at once, rather welcoming a little bit of adventure; and forthwith both of them hurried away to get their waterproofs.

The night was dark and blustering; the ordinarily clear twilight of these northern regions was obscured by heavy clouds; and the wind that blew in from the sea brought with it a sense of moisture that promised to become actual rain. The two black figures made their way with little difficulty in the direction of the orange lights of the village, the unseen sea washing up on the beach close by them. Neither spoke; but both walked quickly; perhaps they wanted to be back at Lochgarra House before their absence should be known.

Then, just as they were getting near to the inn, Kate suddenly put her hand on her friend's arm. Ahead of them were two other figures, as black as themselves, but looming larger through the dusk.

" That is Big Archie," said Käthchen, in a whisper, " and isn't the other Hector?—yes, I am sure that is Hector!"

At this moment the two men disappeared.

" I know where they have gone," Mary said promptly. " They have gone into the tap-room behind. Well, we will follow, in case the people in the inn should deny them. Come along, Käthchen, I know the way."

The two young women left the main street, crossed a

stable-yard, and, guided by the dull glow of a window, went up to a door, which Mary entered. The next moment they were gazing into a small sanded parlour, where Gilleasbuig Mòr and his friend the keeper were standing: indeed, the two men had not had time to sit down nor yet to order anything to drink. The oil-lamp on the table shed a feeble light, but it was quite sufficient to show that Hector, thus caught, was looking terribly guilty; while the great, heavy-shouldered fisherman, whose deep-set grey eyes under the bushy eyebrows seemed to say that he had already had a glass, instantly came to his companion's help.

"Aw, well now," Archie said, in his plaintive Argyll-shire accent, "iss it Miss Stanley herself that would be coming in here —indeed, indeed !—and Hector, the honest lad, chist feenished up with ahl his work—oh, aye—the guns ahl cleaned, and the dogs fed, and everything ready for the chentlemen to-morrow—and me coming bye from the Camus Bheag, and says I, 'Hector, will you come along with me and hef a dram when your work is feenished ?' And Miss Stanley need not be thinking there wass any more in our minds than that ; for Hector is a fine laad, and fine keeper, and what harm will a dram do to anyone when ahl the work is done ?"

"Sit down, Archie—sit down, Hector !" said Mary, quite good-naturedly. "I saw you come in this way, Archie, and I merely wished to ask you what happened at Heimra."

"Aw, Heimra," said Archie, collecting his thoughts—and his English. "Iss it at Heimra ? Aw, well now, Martha is a ferry nice woman, and she wass giving me some bread and cheese, ay, and a glass of spirits the like of it is not ahlways—a good woman Martha——"

"Yes, but my note, Archie," said Mary. "The note you took out : I suppose you gave it to Mr. Ross ? And he did not say anything ? Well, there was no need for an answer—none in the least——"

"Aw, the letter ?" said Archie. "Well, I wass not seeing Mr. Ross at ahl, for he wass aweh up on the north side of the island, setting snares for the rabbits."

"Oh, you did not see Mr. Ross ?" said Mary, quickly. "He could not possibly have sent any answer ?" She seemed greatly pleased—as Käthchen observed. "No, of course, he could not send an answer if he was away at the other end of the island." Then she turned to Hector; and the tall, swarthy, brown-bearded keeper perceived that the fair young Englishwoman—the Baintighearna—had no mind to rebuke him or to be in any way angry with him. "Why, Hector," she said, quite pleasantly, "that is a very strange thing, that he should go snaring rabbits: why doesn't he shoot them?"

"Mr. Ross, mem," said Hector, in his grave and respectful fashion, "he does not care much about shooting. And the rabbits, if they are not kept down, would do a dale of mischief on a smahl island like that."

"He is not fond of shooting, then! No; I think he told me so himself." Then, with one of her sudden impulses, she said—"Come, Hector, let me know what all this is about poaching on this place. Ever since I came here I have heard of all kinds of rumours and charges and suspicions; and I want to know the truth. I shan't blame anybody. I want to know the actual truth. Tell me frankly. It isn't such an important thing, after all. I only want to know what is happening around us."

The tall keeper looked concerned—not to say alarmed: the violent scene of the day before was fresh in his mind. But the big, good-natured giant from Cantire broke in.

"Aw, he is a fine lad, Hector, Miss Stanley may be sure of that; and there's no mich poaching going on about this country side—at least, not about Lochgarra whatever. It's myself that wass hearing Hector seh that if he wass catching the Gillie Ciotach with a gun, he would brek the gun over his head."

"Gillie Ciotach?" said Mary. "I know him—a wild-looking young fellow, with a mark across his forehead. Well, is he a poacher, Hector?"

"It is in this way, mem," Hector said, slowly and carefully; "there's very little poaching about Lochgarra, as Archie says, and Hugh and myself we know it well; but there's some of the young lads, ay, and some of the older men too, that if they came across a salmon, or a few sea-trout, or a hare, they would be for taking it out to Heimra, and slipping round by the back-door, and Martha there to take the present. Mr. Ross, he does not pay attention to such things; for he is ahlways having a salmon, or a capercailzie, or a box of grouse sent him by the big families that he knows, when their friends are up for the shooting; and he will believe anything that Martha says, and he pays no more heed to such things."

"Yes, but, Hector, what I want you to tell me is this," she interposed—and she spoke with a certain air of proud confidence—"what I want you to tell me distinctly is this: do you mean to say that Mr. Ross himself would take a gun or a fishing-rod and go where he had no right to go, either fishing or shooting?"

It was a challenge; and Hector met it unflinchingly. He said, in his serious way—

"Oh, no, mem—no, no: there is not anyone about here that would think such a thing of Mr. Ross."

Mary turned to Käthchen, with a quick, triumphant glance. Then she addressed herself again to Hector.

"Well, sit down, and have a chat with your friend, Hector," said she, very pleasantly. "We shan't interrupt you any longer. And if now and again one of the lads about here should be taking out a little present of fish or game to old Martha, for the housekeeping, well, that is a trifling matter; and I dare say she gives them a glass of whisky for their trouble. And, Archie, any other time you go out to Heimra with a message from me, mind you come back and tell me whether there is an answer or not, even when I am not expecting an answer, because that makes everything certain and correct. So good-night to you both—good-night!—good-night!" And therewith the two young ladies, who, even in the dull light of this little sanded parlour, had formed such a curious contrast to those two big, swarthy, heavily-bearded men, withdrew, and shut the door after them, and set out for home through the darkness and the drizzling rain.

Next morning Mary said, with a casual glance out towards Eilean Heimra—

"Käthchen, don't you think, if you lived on that island, you would rather have a good-sized steam-launch than any sailing-boat? It would be so much more handy—ready at a moment's notice almost—and taking up so much less time, if you wanted to send a message to the mainland. I suppose Mr. Ross has to think twice before telling his men to get the yacht ready, or even that big lugsail boat."

But as the day wore on there was no sign of either yacht or lugger coming away from Heimra; the grey and squally sea remained empty; indeed, towards the afternoon, the wind freshened up into something like half a gale, and it grew to be a matter of certainty that Donald Ross would not seek to communicate with the shore. Mary was not disheartened. On the contrary, her face wore the same happy look—that Frank Meredyth could not quite understand. He had become observant and thoughtful: not about grouse.

The following morning broke with a much more cheerful aspect.

"Käthchen," said Mary, before they went down to breakfast together, "don't you think that any time Mr. Ross comes across to the mainland he might as well walk along here for lunch, instead of going to the inn? Talking to us should interest him as much as talking to that soft-headed John, the policeman, or to the sulky Peter Grant, or even to the sing-song Minister. And it would be very pleasant for us, too, with the gentlemen away on the moor all day."

But again the slow hours of the day passed; and, whatever may have been her secret hopes, her anxious fears, or even, at times, her disposition to be proudly resentful, that width of rough blue water gave no answer to her surreptitiously questioning gaze. There was a fresh westerly breeze blowing; either the smart little cutter or the more cumbrous lugger could have made an easy and rapid passage. However, neither brown sail nor white sail appeared outside the distant headland; and so the afternoon drew on towards evening; and here were the sportsmen come down from the hill, and the dressing-bell about to sound.

After dinner, when the two young ladies were alone together, Mary said—with a curious affectation of indifference—

"I did not ask for an answer, Käthchen. Oh, certainly not. There was no answer needed—but still—it seems to me he might have acknowledged the receipt of my note.

Of course I am rather anxious to know on what terms we are—naturally—and—and naturally I should like to know whether he absolves me——" She was silent for a moment. When she spoke again she was more honest: there was something of a proud, hurt feeling in her tone. "I do think he might have sent me a message. Don't you, Käthchen? Either yesterday morning or to-day—the whole of to-day has been fine weather. I went out of my way to make the first overtures—after—after what happened. I held out the olive-branch. It seems to me that common courtesy would suggest some little acknow-ledgment: one is not used to being treated in this way——"

"Perhaps to-morrow——" suggested Käthchen, vaguely.

"Oh, if he is not in a hurry, neither am I," said she, with a sudden air of haughty unconcern; and she would have no more said.

Nay, from this moment she seemed to dismiss Donald Ross from her mind. When, on the following day, Eilean Heimra remained as mute and unresponsive as before, she made no remark to Käthchen; she resolutely dismissed an involuntary habit she had formed of scanning the space of sea intervening between the island and the coast; and if Käthchen mentioned Mr. Ross's name, she would either not reply at all, or reply with a cold indifference, as much as to say, "Who is the stranger whom you speak of?" All the day long she busied herself with her multifarious duties, and was particularly cheerful; in the evening she showed herself most complaisant towards the two young men who were her guests. She talked of giving a ball to the keepers, the gillies, and their friends; and won-dered whether there was anywhere a barn big enough for the purpose.

So time went by; and these four young people occupying Lochgarra House appeared to be as merry and happy as though they had belonged to a certain little band of Floren-tines of the fourteenth century. For Mary was not always deep-buried in her industrial schemes. Sometimes she and Kate Glendinning would go away up to join the sportsmen at lunch-time; and thereafter, perched high on these sterile and lonely altitudes, she would set to work to add to a series she was forming of sea-views and coast-views— drawings in most of which the horizon-line was close up to the top of the sheet. It is true that in these spacious sketches she had sometimes to include the island of Heimra; but no mention was made of Donald Ross; it was as if he had gone away, and for ever, into some unknown clime. Even Fred Stanley was almost ready to believe that the poaching had ceased; and so there was peace in the land.

But there came a thunder-clap into this idyllic quiet. One evening, when the two young men returned from their long day on the hill, there was a telegram among the letters on the hall-table. It was for Frank Meredyth. He tore open the envelope.

"I was afraid of it," he said to his companion. "I must be off, Fred, by the mail-car to-morrow morning. Very sorry, old chap, to have to leave you."

"I hope it is nothing serious," young Stanley put in, with his grey eyes grown grave.

"They don't say anything very definite," was the reply. "Only I am summoned, and I must go."

"Then I will go with you," said the other promptly, "as far as London. This just decides it. I'll accept Nugent's invitation, after all; and if he has started, I'll pick him up at Marseilles. We've seen pretty well what the moor is like; and perhaps some other time my sister asks us down, we may wait on and have a try for a stag or two. Very sorry, though, you must go."

Dinner that evening, in view of this summons, was rather a sombre affair: it was Käthchen who, when the young men subsequently made their appearance in the drawing-room, suggested they should all go out for a stroll up to the top of the Minard road. She thought this little excursion would remove some of the prevailing constraint. Besides, it promised to be a beautiful moonlight night; and from the summit of the hill they would have a view of the wide southern seas, with the black headlands running out into the shimmering pathway of silver.

Well, the expedition, so far as pictorial effects were concerned, was entirely successful; but it was not moonlight that was in Frank Meredyth's mind. He was going away on the morrow; he did not know what might happen in his absence; and he thought his departure was a fair and reasonable excuse for his revealing to Mary Stanley certain hopes and aspirations that had gradually, and for some long time back, been taking possession of him. On their way back to the house Fred and Käthchen were walking on in front; the night was still, so that half-murmured words were enough; the surroundings lent a certain charm. And so it came about that Frank Meredyth asked Mary to become his wife.

Now it cannot be said that the language in which this proposition was couched was quite in accordance with these poetical accessories of moonlit vale, and larchwood, and hill; for the average young Englishman, however honest and sincere he may be, does not express himself fluently on such occasions; probably he would be ashamed of himself if he could and did. Nevertheless, a proposal of marriage, however stumblingly and awkwardly conveyed, is a very serious thing to a young woman; and Mary, startled and frightened, had only the one immediate and overwhelming desire—to postpone the terrible necessity of giving a definite answer. For it was all too bewildering. She wanted to think. To tell the truth, Frank Meredyth's wooing had not been too open and avowed. A man of the world in other things, in this he had been a little shy—one touch of nature among a thousand conventionalities. Then, again, was not a refusal a very cruel thing, that should be administered gently?

"Oh, Mr. Meredyth," she said, in a very low and rather breathless voice, "I think—I think—this is hardly the time——"

"But surely it is!" said he. "For I am going away to-morrow morning. And I don't know when I may see you again. And I should like to take with me some little word of hope—something to remember——"

"Did you see that hare?" Fred Stanley called to them, looking back for a moment.

Meredyth did not pay much heed to the hare.

"Perhaps I have asked you too abruptly," he went on, in the same hurried and confused undertone. "Perhaps I am asking too much—that you should say something definite all at once. Very well: I will not press for an answer—I will wait—I will wait——"

They were emerging from the shadow of the larch trees; before them was an open space of gravel, white in the moonlight, and beyond that rose the grey walls and turrets of Lochgarra House.

"Only tell me this," said he, in a still lower voice, "tell me if there is any one before me. I have hesitated about speaking earlier because I imagined certain things—perhaps I was mistaken—at least you will tell me that—tell me if there is some one else——"

"No," said Mary, as they crossed that space of white moonlight, and perhaps she spoke a little proudly. "That —at least—I can assure you——"

"No one?" he said eagerly, in the same undertone.

But here they were at the house—with Fred and Käthchen waiting for them on the grey stone terrace: these two had turned to look at the wonderful beauty of the night.

CHAPTER XX.

A FORECAST.

Now, among the numerous undertakings on which the young proprietress of Lochgarra had set her heart was the establishment of a Public Reading-room and Free Library; and to that end she had planned and built—employing local labour only—a large, long, one-storeyed erection, of a solid and substantial cast, fit to withstand the buffetings of the western storms. The interior was as simple and unpretentious as the exterior; there was nothing beyond a strip of platform, a series of plain wooden benches, a few deal tables and chairs, and a small space partitioned off as kitchen. The rules and regulations, of her own sketching out, were likewise of an artless nature. The place was to be open to the whole community. Tea and coffee at cheap rates were to be procurable between five and seven a.m., and from seven till nine in the evening: the morning hours were for the benefit of bachelor workmen on their way to work, or of fishermen coming in cold and wet after a night at sea. Although reading was the ostensible aim, women were free to bring their knitting or sewing: good lamps would be provided, and a good fire in winter. There were to be no set entertainments of any kind; but on certain evenings such of the young people as could sing or play on any instrument would be expected to do their best for the amusement of their neighbours. Thus far only had she drawn out her simple code; she wished to get the opinions of the villagers themselves as to minor details; and so, all being ready, there one day appeared the following modest little handbill—"On Tuesday next, at six o'clock in the evening, Miss Stanley will open the Public Reading Room for the use of the inhabitants of Lochgarra. Everyone is invited to attend."

It was on the Monday afternoon that she and Kate Glendinning went along to have a final look. Apparently all was in order; though, to be sure, the supply of books, magazines, and newspapers was as yet somewhat scanty. But it was something else that was uppermost in Mary's mind at this moment.

"You don't think me really nervous, Käthchen?" said she, in a half-laughing and yet concerned way.

"No, I do not," her friend said explicitly. "Why, you, of all people!—you have courage for anything——"

"Look at that platform," Mary went on. "It is only a few inches raised above the floor. Yes, but those few inches make all the difference. Standing here I might perhaps be able to say something; but I declare to you, Käthchen, that the moment I set foot on that platform I shall be frozen into a voiceless statue. Why, I am trembling now, even to think of it! I feel the choking in my throat already. And to have all those eyes fixed on you—and your brain going round—and you unable to say a word; I know I shall tumble down in a faint—and the ignominy of it——"

"It is very unfortunate," Käthchen admitted, as they left the building and set out for home again, "that Mr. Meredyth was called away so suddenly. He could have done it for you. Or even your brother. But if you are so terrified, Mamie, why don't you ask the Minister?—he is accustomed to conduct all sorts of meetings."

"No, I could not do that either," Mary said. "You see,

I want the people thoroughly to understand that they are not going to be lectured or preached at. They are not even to be amused against their will. The whole place is to be their own: I have no educational fad to thrust on them. Do you remember Mrs. Armour talking about the *Ceilidh* of the old days?—well, I want to revive the *Ceilidh;* and I am not sure that Mr. Pettigrew would approve. No; I suppose I must get up on that platform, even if my knees should be knocking against each other. And if my tongue cleaves to the roof of my mouth, well, you must come forward, Käthchen, and make an apology, and tell them that I give them the use of the building and its contents, and that there's no more to be said."

Now Kate Glendinning, during these last few seconds, seemed to be occupied with something far ahead of them, on which she was fixing an earnest gaze. The afternoon around them was clear and golden, with an abundance of light everywhere; but the sun was getting over to the west, so that the larches threw a shadow across the Minard highway, whither her eyes were directed. Presently, however, she seemed to have satisfied herself.

"Well, Mamie," said she, "I have never tried to address a meeting, so I don't know what it is like; but I should have thought you had nerve and courage for anything."

"It isn't nerve, Käthchen; it isn't courage!" she exclaimed, in a kind of mock despair. "Why, at the Lord Mayor's dinner, I have seen one of the bravest soldiers that England possesses—I have seen him with his hands shaking like a leaf as he stood up to answer to a toast."

"Very well, then, Mamie," said her companion, calmly, "if you are so frightened, why don't you get Mr. Donald Ross to take your place? I am sure he would do it for you at once. And as for asking him, there can be no trouble about that; because if you look along there you will see him at the foot of the Minard road, and he is coming this way."

For one startled second Mary stood stock still, her eyes filled with alarm; perhaps some wild notion that escape might even yet be possible had flashed through her brain. But that was only for a moment. Käthchen had just been complimenting her on her courage: she could not show the white feather the very next minute. So instantly she resumed her onward walk, and that with something of an air of proud confidence. She was 'more than common tall,' and there was a certain freedom and dignity in her gait: how could any bystander have told that under that brave demeanour her heart was going like the heart of a captured hare?

"Oh, what were you saying, Käthchen?" she resumed, with a fine assumption of carelessness. "The Mansion House dinner—oh, yes, I assure you—a very famous soldier —and his hand was shaking—you see, I happened to be sitting next him——"

"Mamie, are you going to ask Mr. Ross about the photographs?" Käthchen asked, in a low voice, for young Donald of Heimra was drawing nearer.

But what could she say in reply? This encounter was altogether too abrupt and unexpected a thing. She had not even time to recall what she had decided was her position with regard to this solitary neighbour of hers. If he had wronged her by neglect, she had vehemently professed to Käthchen that that was of no consequence. If, on the other hand, he was still haughtily indignant over the insults that had been heaped upon him by her brother, how could she make him any fit apology? In fact, she hardly knew whether to treat him as friend or foe; and yet here he was approaching them—every moment coming nearer—and her heart going faster than ever.

As for him, he kept his eyes fixed on her, with a calm and even respectful attention. He, at least, was not embarrassed; and Mary, in a desperate kind of way, was conscious that it was for her to decide; she was aware, without looking, that he was expectant; she was mortified to think that her face was flushed and confused, while he was tranquilly regarding her. Then of a sudden she rebelled angrily against this calm superiority; and just as he came up she glanced towards him and coldly bowed. He raised his cap. Was he going on—without a word?

"Oh, Mr. Ross," said she, stammering and embarrassed, and yet affecting to treat this meeting as quite an everyday affair, "it is strange we should just have been talking about you—you—you haven't been much over to the mainland of late, have you ?—perhaps you haven't seen the reading-room since it was finished—no, I suppose not—do you think it will be of any use ?—do you think it will be of any service ?—do you think the people will care for it ?"

"They ought to be very grateful to you," said he. "I wonder what you are going to do for them next ?"

The sound of his voice seemed immensely to reassure her.

"Grateful ?" she said, quite cheerfully, and despite her conscious colour she managed to meet his eyes. "Well, I, for one, should be exceedingly grateful to you if you would do me a very particular favour with regard to this same reading-room. Miss Glendinning was talking about you only a moment or two ago—and—and the fact is, I propose to hand over the building to-morrow afternoon——"

"I saw the little handbill," said he, with a smile.

"Then I hope," said she, with an answering smile, "that you haven't come over to turn away my audience, as you did in the case of the people who wanted to create a disturbance."

"Oh, no," said he, "I hope you did not suspect me of any such intention. Oh, no ; it was quite the other way, indeed—if any one had asked me——"

"But I want more than that from you," said she—and all her confusion seemed to have fled : she was regarding him in the most friendly way, and talking with a happy confidence. "I want far more than that, Mr. Ross, if you will be so kind. Do you know, I was telling Käthchen here that the moment I put my foot on the platform to-morrow evening I should expire, or faint, or do something terrible ; for what experience have I in addressing a meeting ? I assure you I am in an absolute fright about it ; I tremble when I think of it ; when I try to imagine what I am going to say, my throat seems to gasp already. Now would you do this speechmaking for me—what little is needed ? Would it be too much of a favour ? Is it asking too much ?"

This was her brief prayer ; and Käthchen, standing by, a not uninterested spectator, was saying to herself, "Well, Mamie, you have the most extraordinary eyes, when they choose to be friendly and interested, and appealing ; I wonder what mortal man could resist them?" It was not Donald Ross, at all events.

"Oh, yes, certainly; I will do that for you with pleasure," said he at once. "I have never in my life addressed a meeting; but I don't suppose there can be any trouble about it—especially when one knows the people. Only, you must tell me what I am to say: if I am to be your counsel, you must give me instructions——"

"Oh, yes, yes," said she, quite eagerly. "I will tell you all the regulations I mean to propose; and the points on which I want to have the public opinion. Are you very busy just now? Will you come along and have tea with us? Then I could tell you all I wish to have said."

He hesitated; and the least tinge of colour appeared in the pale, keen, resolute face. He had not expected to be asked so soon to cross the threshold of Lochgarra House. Nevertheless, after that momentary indecision, he said—

"Thank you, yes, I will go with you and get my brief. Though it does seem a little impertinent in me to presume to be your spokesman."

"Oh, don't say that," she remonstrated, warmly. "I cannot tell you how much I am obliged to you. Why, Käthchen will assure you that I was just about dying with fear."

And all this had taken place so rapidly that even Käthchen was a little bewildered. How had such a mighty revolution come about within the space of two or three swift seconds? A few minutes before, and Mary Stanley would not have allowed this young man's name to have passed her lips; and now she was regarding him with the most obvious favour, and smiling and talking with an eager delight; while his keen, dark face and expressive eyes answered her in kind. Kate Glendinning, as they walked on towards the house, did not seek to interfere in this conversation: to watch the demeanour of those two was of far greater interest to her than any question connected with the Free Library. And Käthchen, if she did not talk to them, could commune with herself. "Mamie," she was saying, in this secret fashion, "you should not show yourself so anxious to please. It isn't like you.   If you are overjoyed to be on friendly terms with him again, don't make it so manifest.   You shouldn't seek him ; let him seek you.   And don't allow your eyes to say quite so much : do you know that they are just laughing with gladness ? "   And then, as they were passing into the hall, the door leading out on to the garden-terrace recalled a certain little incident.   " Poor Mr. Meredyth ! " said Käthchen to herself.

In the drawing-room, again, Mary plied this guest of hers with every kind of pretty attention ; and seemed very pleased and happy ; while she grew almost reckless in her philanthropic schemes.   Indeed, it was Donald Ross himself who had to interpose to put a check on her generous enthusiasm.

" No, no," he said, with a smile, and yet with a certain quiet and masterful air that was habitual with him, " you must not do anything of the kind.   Giving them Meall-na-Cruagan was quite enough.   You must not think of giving up Meall-na-Fearn as well.   You would be crippling Mr. Watson to no purpose.   The crofters have quite enough pasture now for their stock."

" Yes, but I want to do everything," she insisted, " I want to try everything that can be thought of—every-thing—before coming to the last confession of failure : and you know what that is ? "

" What ? "

" Why, emigration.   Oh, I haven't forgotten your threat," she said, with some little touch of confusion in her smiling eyes, " to take the people away with you to Canada or New South Wales, or some such place.   And—and I don't want that.   That seems to me ignominious.   That seems to me simply a confession of failure."

" At all events," said he, " it was not as a threat that I made the suggestion.   I thought it would help you."

" Oh," said she, with her face flushing a little, " but I don't want anybody to go away.   Surely something else should be tried first.   There are many things to be done. I want to have many more looms going ; and the fishing developed ; and several new industries started—perhaps even kelp-burning, if there are sufficient beds of seaweed. Why, I consider I am only beginning now.   I have been simply clearing the way—getting fair rents fixed—and all that ; and—and I don't want to be interfered with, in that rude fashion. Give me time. Let me have my chance first. Then if I fail——"

"Oh, but we shan't talk of failure," said he, good-naturedly. "Failure would be too cruel a return for all your kindness to these people."

He stayed till very near dinner-time : those two seemed to have so much to say to each other—and not about the Lochgarra estate only. Directly he had gone, Mary said, in quite an eager and excited fashion—

"Käthchen, if I had had the courage of a mouse, I'd have asked him to dine with us ! Why shouldn't I ? Don't you think I might—the next time ? Don't you think I might ? It is so pleasant for neighbours to be on neighbourly terms. And just imagine what his life must be out in that little island, seeing no one. It seems to me that, situated as we are, it is almost a duty to ask him to come to the house. And why not to dinner ? If he comes in, and has tea with us, why not dinner ? What is the difference between tea and dinner ?"

"He has very eloquent eyes," said Käthchen, demurely. "He seemed much pleased with his visit this evening."

"Käthchen," said Mary, and she seemed a little restless, and yet very happy withal : she went to the window occasionally to look at nothing, and appeared quite oblivious of the fact that the dinner-gong had just sounded—"Käth-chen, do you remember the blue and gold embroidered scarf that I told you could be so easily turned into a hood for the opera ?"

"I'm sure I do !" said Käthchen, little dreaming of what was coming.

"Then I'm going to give you that—yes, I will—now, don't protest——"

"Indeed I must, though, Mamie," said Käthchen, warmly. "Why, what use would it be to me ? And you know how admirably it suited your complexion and the colour of your hair. What mania for giving has seized you this afternoon ? I thought you were going to throw away the whole of the Lochgarra estate ; and I was glad to see Mr. Ross put some curb on your wildness. And I must say you were very amenable, Mamie. You're not quite so self-willed when Mr. Ross is talking to you——"

"I'm going to be self-willed enough to make you take that scarf, Käthchen," said Mary, with a gay impetuosity. "Yes, I am. I will send for it to-morrow. Why, you know it is a pretty thing, Käthchen—the Albanian needle-work is so quaint—and I remember perfectly that you admired it——"

"But what use would a hood for the theatre be in a place like this!" Käthchen exclaimed.

"Don't I tell you it is a pretty thing to look at, here or anywhere else?" was the imperious rejoinder. "And I want to give it to you, Käthchen—and that's all about it—and so not another word!"

When at length they went in to dinner, Mary sate silent and thoughtful for a little while : then she said—

"Käthchen, did you ever hear a voice that gave you such a curious impression of sincerity?"

"Do you mean Mr. Ross's?" said Käthchen, gravely.

"Yes," said Mary, with a bit of a start : she had been forgetting. "I mean quite apart from the quality of the voice, and that of itself seems to me remarkable. For you know most men's voices are repellent—unnecessarily harsh and grating—you are not interested—you would rather keep away. But his voice, quiet as it is, thrills; it is so clear, and soft, and persuasive ; I don't know that you can say of a man that he has a musical voice iñ talking, but if you can, then his is distinctly musical. Only that is not what you chiefly think of. It is the honesty of his tone that is so marked. He never seems to talk for effect; he does not want to impress you, or make any display ; it is the truth he aims at, and you feel that it is the truth, and that you can believe down to the very depths every word he is uttering. And you seem to feel that he makes you honest too. It is no use trying any pretence with him. He would laugh at you if you did—and yet not cruelly. He is so direct, so simple, so manly, not a grain of affecta-tion to be discovered. I wonder, now, when he is called to the Bar, if he will practise in the courts? For don't you think I rather effectually stopped the emigration scheme— didn't I, Käthchen? Oh, yes, I don't think he will talk any more about Canada or Australia—not, at least, until I have had my chance. But on the other hand, if he were to remain in this country, and practise at the Bar, don't you think he would succeed? I know if I were a judge, and Mr. Ross were pleading before me, I should have little difficulty in deciding who was speaking the truth."

"Counsel are not paid to speak the truth: quite the reverse," said Käthchen.

"And when he laughs, there is nothing sarcastic in his laugh—nothing but good-nature," continued the young lady, who was not paying much attention to Barbara's ministrations. "Is there anything so horrid as a cackling laugh—the conceited laugh of a small nature? Yes, it is a very good thing he has so pleasant and good-humoured a laugh—for—after all—yes, perhaps he is just a little blunt and peremptory. What do you think, Käthchen? Did you think he was a little dictatorial? And you said something— that I was amenable? But was I too amenable, Käthchen? I hope he did not imagine that I was subservient—especially if he was rather masterful and plain-spoken——"

"Come, come, Mamie, don't quarrel with him when he has hardly had time to get out of the house," Käthchen interposed, with a smile. "I consider that the manner of both of you was quite perfect, if what you wanted to convey was that you were both highly pleased to meet in this way and have a confidential and friendly chat. Dictatorial? Not in the least! Of course he knows a good many things about this place; and it was to save you yourself from being excessive in your generosity that he spoke plainly. And speaking plainly—why, wasn't it that very thing you were praising only a moment ago, when you spoke of the simplicity and sincerity of his speech?"

"Because," said Mary, drawing up her head a little, "if —if I thought he considered me too complaisant and sub- missive—if I thought so—well, I would show him some- thing different."

"Now, are you determined to quarrel?" Käthchen exclaimed, with laughing eyes. "Here is this poor young man who meets you in the road, and he is as respectful and distant as could possibly be, waiting to see how you mean to treat him; and you seem a little doubtful; then of a sudden you resolve to make the first advances ; and the next thing is that you appear so glad to find that both of you are on friendly terms, that nothing will do but he must come away home and have tea with you ; and you are exceedingly kind to him, and he is exceedingly grateful —as those black eyes of his showed. What is there in all that ? Yet now you must alarm yourself by thinking you have been too complaisant ! "

" No, Käthchen, no ; not that I think so ; what I dread is that he may have been thinking so."

" If I were to tell you, Mamie," said Käthchen, " what I imagine to have been in Donald Ross's mind when you and he were sitting talking together, eyes fixed on eyes, with never a thought for anything or anybody else in the whole wide world, well, I suppose you would be indignant, and would probably tell me to attend to my own affairs. Which I mean to do—only I am not blind." For a second Mary regarded her friend with a scrutinizing glance ; but she had not the courage to speak ; she changed the subject —and hardly mentioned Donald Ross's name for the rest of that evening.

Next day, and especially towards the afternoon, there was quite a commotion in the village, for small things become great in a remote little community like Lochgarra ; and when it drew near to six o'clock there were various groups of people scattered around the new building, walking about and chatting, sometimes peeping in at the door with a vague curiosity.

" I wonder if he expects us to go along and meet him there ? " said Mary, rather anxiously to Käthchen.

" You mean Mr. Ross ? " said Käthchen, though well she knew to whom the " he " referred. " I should think he would call for us. The *Sirène* is not in the bay ; she must be round in the Camus Bheag ; so Mr. Ross will be coming down from Minard."

Käthchen's anticipations proved correct ; young Ross, in passing Lochgarra House, stopped for a moment to ask if the ladies had gone on ; and, finding that they were just about ready to set out, he waited for them. And thus it was that the inhabitants of Lochgarra again witnessed a strange sight—something far more wonderful than the opening of a Free Library : they beheld young Donald of Heimra acting as escort to this Englishwoman—this alien—this representative of the family that had drained the waters out of Heimra Loch, and torn down the walls of the old Castle. And not only that, but when they came along, he seemed to manage everything for her. He drove the people into the large, long room, and got the benches filled up ; he had two chairs placed on the platform, one for Miss Stanley and one for Miss Glendinning ; and then, standing by the side of the Baintighearna, proceeded to speak for her, and to explain the conditions attaching to this bequest.

And here once more Mary, sitting there silent and observant, may have been struck by the curious directness and simplicity of his speech. Concise, explicit sentences : they seemed to accord well with his own bearing, which was distinctly straightforward, intrepid, resolute. Indeed, so little of effort, so little of talking for effect was there about this address, that once or twice, and in the most natural way in the world, he turned to Miss Stanley and asked her for information on certain points. Finally, he told them that Miss Stanley wished for no ceremony, opening or otherwise ; they were merely to take possession ; and they would now be left to examine the resources of the building, including the duplicate catalogues of the library.

"Three cheers for Donald Ross of Heimra !" called out a voice—and a cap was twirled to the roof.

"Don't make a fool of yourself, Gillie Ciotach !" said Ross, with a quick frown ; and then he went on calmly : "It is Miss Stanley's express wish that there should be no formalities whatever, otherwise I should have proposed a vote of thanks to her for her very great kindness and thoughtfulness. However, that is not to be ; and the best way you can show what you think of her munificent gift is by making a good use of it and taking every care of it." He turned to the Baintighearna. "I suppose that is about all I have to say, Miss Stanley?"

"Yes, I think so : thank you so much !" she said, in rather a low voice—for she was a trifle self-conscious before all those people.

Then she rose. He stepped down from the platform,

and led the way along the hall. There was some covert clapping of hands and stamping of feet; but the Gillie Ciotach had been snubbed into silence; and, indeed, the majority of those sad and weather-worn countenances remained stolidly indifferent, as if they hardly knew what was happening around them. Ross opened the door for his two companions, and followed them out into the golden-clear afternoon; the villagers were left to overhaul at their leisure this new possession, and to become familiar with its opportunities.

But no sooner were those three out in the open, and by themselves, than Mary Stanley's manner underwent a complete change. She had thrown off that platform constraint; she was profuse in her expressions of gratitude; her eyes were shining with pleasure.

"How can I ever sufficiently thank you?" said she. "I could never have got through it by myself—never! And of course they will remember everything you said: any word of yours is all-important with them. I am a stranger. I am suspected. But when you are on my side all goes well. And now that this serious business has been got over, I feel as if we had earned a holiday for the rest of the day," she continued, in a very radiant and light-hearted fashion. "What shall we do, Käthchen? Can't you devise something? Can't you devise some wild escapade —something terrible—something unheard of?"

"The Lady Superior of Lochgarra," said Donald Ross, "is much too distinguished a person to indulge in wild escapades."

"At least," said she, turning to him—and they were now on their way to Lochgarra House—"it would be very hard if we three, having so successfully got through the solemn duties and labours of the day, were to separate now. Don't you think we are entitled to a little relaxation? Now, tell me, Mr. Ross, where you are going at this moment. Back to the *Sirène*, are you not? And you will be dining alone? And after that a book and a pipe in the solitary saloon—isn't that about how you will pass the evening?"

"You have guessed pretty near the truth, Miss Stanley," said he, with a smile.

"Then," said she, boldly, "why should we separate ?
Come in and dine with us. Give up your book, and let
two frivolous creatures talk to you. We will allow you
to go away at ten ; and it will be a clear starlight night—
you will have no difficulty in finding your way round to
the Camus Bheag. Now, will you ?"

"Indeed, I shall be most happy," said he, without an
instant's hesitation ; and again Miss Stanley's clear grey-
green eyes thanked him—as they could, when she had a
mind.

And really this proved to be a most joyous and careless
evening without an atom of restraint or reserve ; the
little group of friends, brought together in that far-away
corner of the world, developed a very frank and informal
intimacy ; the time sped swiftly. Mary was in especial
merry-hearted and audacious ; occasionally betraying new
moods of wilful petulance ; and then again becoming suddenly honest, as much as to say, "No, don't believe that
of me ; it was only mischief." Even Käthchen was less
demurely observant than usual ; she had become a little
more accustomed to the flame of those coal-black eyes ;
moreover, the young man had a winning smile. He was
no longer the proud and austere person whom she had
regarded with a little anxiety and even awe. Implacable
she was no longer ready to call him : surely one who
could laugh in that frankly good humoured way was not
likely to prove revengeful and unforgiving ? As for his
being haughty and imperious, she noticed one small circumstance—that ever and again, amid this familiar and sprightly
intercourse, he checked himself a little, and would address
Miss Stanley with something almost of deference. It was
as if he were saying, ' It is exceedingly kind of you to treat
me in so very friendly a fashion ; but still—still—you are
the Lady Superior of Lochgarra—and I am your guest.'
And sometimes he seemed to veil his eyes a little—those
burning eyes that might unawares convey too much.

The lightning moments fled ; ten o'clock came ere he
knew. Indeed, it was half-an-hour thereafter before he
chanced to look at his watch : and instantly he rose, with
a quite boyish confusion on his clear, finely-cut face.

"When do you go back to Heimra ?" said Mary to

him—the two young ladies having accompanied him out
into the hall.

"I hardly know," said he.   "I am waiting for a rather
important letter that I must answer at once."

"Not to-morrow, then?"

"Perhaps not."

"For I have sent for the photographer," said she, "and
he may be here the day after."

"But I will stay over," said he; "oh, yes, certainly: I
should be so pleased if I can be of the least service to
you."

"Oh, thank you."   And then she hesitated.   "To-
morrow—to-morrow you will simply be waiting for the
mid-day mail?"

"Yes—is there anything that I can do for you in any
way?"

"Oh, no," she made answer, with still further hesitation.
"Some day—I am going to ask you to let me have a peep
at the *Sirène*.   She seems such a pretty little yacht."

"Won't you come along and look over her to-morrow
morning, if the weather is fine?" said he, quickly.

"Would you like to go, Käthchen?" asked Mary, with a
little shyness.

"Oh, I should be delighted," answered the useful Käthchen, divining what was wanted of her.

"If you are sure it is not troubling you," said Mary to
her departing guest.

"Why, it will give me the greatest possible pleasure,"
said he.   "Come as early as ever you like.   It will be
quite an event: it is many a day since I had the honour of
receiving visitors on the little *Sirène*."

"Then about eleven," said Mary; and therewith he took
his leave.

When they got back to the drawing-room, Kate Glendinning threw herself into the chair she had recently
quitted.

"Well, I think he is simply splendid!" said she, as if
she had some difficulty in finding words to express her
enthusiasm.   "That's all I can say—just splendid.   He is
so curiously straightforward, outspoken, independent; and
yet all the time he is so careful to treat you with marked

respect. If his eyes laugh at you, it is in such a good-natured way that you can't take offence. And he never agrees with you for courtesy's sake—never—oh, not a bit; but yet, as I say, to you he is always so respectful—in so many little ways—didn't you notice? Ah, well, Mamie," continued the observant but nevertheless cautious-tongued Käthchen, "it's a curious world, the way things happen in it. Do you remember, when you first came here, your distress about the destruction of Castle Heimra? You said nothing could ever atone for that; and I was of your opinion then. But I am not so sure now. I should not be so surprised, after all, if there were to be some atonement for the pulling down of Castle Heimra."

Mary did not answer : she had gone to put some Japanese water-colours into a large portfolio. Nor could the expression of her face be seen; if there was any indignant colour there, any proud, maidenly reserve and resentment, it was invisible; for she remained standing by the portfolio for some time, turning over the leaves.

CHAPTER XXI.

SLOW BUT SURE.

THE next morning was the very perfection of a September morning, clear, and crisp, and still; there was just enough wind to lift away the lazy blue smoke from the cottage chimneys, and to stir the smooth waters of the bay with a shimmering ripple. And here was the carriage in front of Lochgarra House, waiting for the two young ladies to come down.

"Käthchen," said Mary, in an undertone, as they took their seats and were driven off, "supposing I should get a chance of speaking to Mr. Ross privately—for a minute or two—do you think I should venture to apologise to him for Fred's outrageous conduct? What would you do if you were in my place?"

"Not that—oh, no, Mamie, not that!" Käthchen said at once. "Don't you see how he wishes to ignore it altogether? And surely you remember what he himself said about the pulling down of Castle Heimra ? 'There are some things that are best not spoken of.'"

"It is very generous of him," said Mary, absently.

They drove away up the Minard road ; and when they had got some distance past the top of the hill, they dismissed the carriage, and left the highway, striking across the rough high ground by a worn footpath. Presently they found far beneath them the sheltered waters of the Camus Bheag ; and the first thing they saw there was the *Sirène* at her moorings, with all her sails set and shining white in the morning sun. The next thing they perceived was that the two sailors, Coinneach and Calum, were on the beach, by the side of the yacht's boat ; while standing some way apart was Donald Ross. And who was this who was talking to him ?—a young girl, whose light brown curly hair was half hidden by her scarlet shawl.

"It is Anna Chlannach !" said Mary. "Now I have got her at last ! She is always escaping me—and I want to convince her that I will not allow Mr. Purdie to lock her up in any asylum. Käthchen, couldn't we get down some other way, so that she may not see us ?"

But at this very moment the girl down there happened to catch sight of them ; and instantly she turned and fled, disappearing from sight in an incredibly short space of time. For one thing, the face of this hill was a mass of tumbled rocks, intermingled with long heather and thick-stemmed gorse, while skirting it was a plantation of young larch : most likely Anna Chlannach had made good her escape into this plantation.

"Why did you let her go ?" said Mary, reproachfully, when she had got down to the beach. "You knew I wanted to talk to her."

"It isn't easy reasoning with Anna Chlannach," said Donald Ross, with his quiet smile. "She still associates you with Purdie ; she is afraid of you. And this time she was on other business ; she was pleading with me to take her out to Heimra—offering me all the money she has got —her shells, you know—if I would take her out."

"And why does she want to go out there ?" Mary asked—her eyes still searching that rocky hill-side for the vanished fugitive.

"To bring back her mother. Sometimes she forgets her fancy about the white bird, and thinks if she could only get out to Heimra she would bring back her mother alive and well. And it is no use trying to undeceive her."

The men were waiting. Mary and Käthchen got into the stern of the boat; the others followed; and presently they were on their way out to the yawl.

"How much bigger she is than I had imagined!" Mary said, as they were drawing near.

And again when they were on deck, looking around with the curiosity that an unknown vessel invariably arouses, she could not but express her high approval: everything looked so trim and neat and ship-shape—the spotless decks, the gleaming brass, the snow-white canvas. And these cushions along the gunwale?

"The fact is," young Ross confessed—with some look of timid appeal towards Mary, "I got the sails up this morning just in case I might be able to induce you to take a bit of a run with us. There is a nice breeze outside, and nothing of a sea. What do you say, Miss Stanley? The *Sirène* feels proud enough that you should have come on board—but if you would like to see how she takes to the water——"

If he was at all anxious, the quick glance of pleasure in Mary's eyes must have instantly reassured him.

"Oh, yes, why not?" said she, rather addressing herself to Kate Glendinning; "I am sure we shall be delighted—if it isn't taking up too much of your time, Mr. Ross——"

"We can slip the moorings and be off at once," said he, and he gave a brief order to the men, himself going to the tiller. In a few minutes the *Sirène* was under way, gliding along so quietly that the two visitors hardly knew that they were moving.

But their departure had not been unnoticed elsewhere. Suddenly, into the absolute silence prevailing around, there came a piteous wail—a wail so full of agony that immediately all eyes were directed to the shore, whence the sound proceeded. And there the origin of it was visible enough. Anna Chlannach had come down from her hiding-place to the edge of the water; she was seated on a rock, her hands clasped in front of her and her head bent down in an attitude of indescribable anguish, her body swaying to and fro, while from time to time she uttered this heart-rending cry, of despair and appeal.

"Poor Anna!" said Mary, with tears starting to her eyes. "Let us go back, Mr. Ross! Never mind us. We can go home. You must take her out to Heimra."

"What would be the use?" he said. "She would only be more miserable, searching about and finding no mother anywhere. And Anna does not keep very long in one mood. She will soon lose sight of us—and then she'll be off again searching for wild strawberries."

And perhaps it was to distract their attention from this melancholy setting out that he now called one of the men to the tiller, and would have his guests go below, to have a look at the ladies' cabin and the saloon. Of course they were much interested and pleased—admiring the cunning little contrivances for the utilisation of space; while Mary arrived at the conclusion that, if these rooms were kept in order by Calum, Calum was a very handy youth to have in one's service, whether afloat or ashore. They spent some time over these investigations; and when they came on deck again, they found they were well out at sea, with a far-extending view of the high and rocky coast, Lochgarra itself appearing as merely a thin grey-white line along one of those indented bays.

And still, and carelessly, and joyously, they kept on their course, the light breeze holding steady, the wide plain of water shining with a summer blue. Young Donald had not returned to the tiller; he was devoting himself assiduously to his two guests—their conversation, whatever its varying moods, accompanied by the soft, continuous murmur of these myriad-glancing ripples, for waves they could scarcely be called. And on this occasion Mary was not nearly so nervous, and excited, and wayward as she had been on the previous day; a placid, benign content reigned in her eyes; a sort of serious, bland sweetness in her demeanour. Küthchen thought to herself that she had never seen Mary Stanley look so beautiful, nor yet wearing so serene an air.

And still they held on, in this fair halcyon weather, alone

with the sky, and the fresh wind, and the slumberous main ; and so entirely and happily engrossed with themselves that they had no thought for the now distant land. But at last Käthchen said—

"Mr. Ross, how far are we going? I thought you were expecting an important letter."

"There are things of equal importance," said he, pleasantly. He cast a glance forward. "Soon we shall be getting near to Heimra, Miss Stanley. I have never had the chance of receiving you in my poor little bungalow : will you go ashore for a while?"

"Oh, yes," she replied, cheerfully. "I should like to renew my acquaintance with Martha ; she was exceedingly kind to us when Käthchen and I called."

"And perhaps," said he, "when we get round the point, you wouldn't mind standing up for a few seconds—you and Miss Glendinning?—then Martha will see I have visitors, and will have time to put on her best gown. Otherwise I should get into serious trouble."

And so they sailed into the small, quiet harbour, and eventually got ashore at the little slip, and made their way up to the house. Martha had seen them ; here she was in the porch, smiling a welcome, with her grey Highland eyes, to the young master, and also to his guests. These she took possession of—with suggestions of tea.

"No, no, Martha," said Donald Ross, "we are not going to have tea at this time of the day. The young ladies will stay for lunch ; and you must do the best you can for us. We will go for a stroll about the island, and be back in an hour or thereabouts."

"Oh, yes, indeed," said the old Highland woman, "but it is a peety I was not knowing before——"

"Martha," said Mary Stanley, interposing, "I dare say Mr. Ross does not understand much about housekeeping. Now, you must put yourself to no trouble on our account. A glass of milk will be quite sufficient."

"Aw, but there will be more than that," the old woman said, and she regarded this beautiful, tall, shining-eyed young creature with a most favouring look, and her speech was soft and propitiating ; "it would be strange if there was not more than that in the house, and Mr. Ross bringing his friends with him." And therewith she went away; and presently they heard her sharply calling on the lad Calum, who had come up from the slip, and was hanging about, to be in readiness if he were wanted.

And now as the proud young host led forth his fair guests on an exploration of these winding shores, and tumbled crags, and steep precipices, this island of Heimra looked infinitely more cheerful than it had done on Mary's previous visit, in the bleak April weather. There was an abundance of rich colour everywhere. The silver-grey rocks, and ruddy-grey rocks, and black-grey rocks were interspersed with masses of purple heather; and other masses there were of tall foxgloves, and bracken, and juniper, and broom. Their progress, it is true, was something of a scramble for there was no road nor semblance of a road; the sheep tracks, he explained, were up on the higher slopes and plateaus; down here by the shore they had to get along as best they could, though sometimes they had the chance of a space of velvet-soft sand—with the clear green water breaking in crisp white ripples and sparkling in the sun. A solitary, if a picturesque, island, facing those wide western seas; there was no sign of human existence or occupation after they had got out of sight of the single house and its small dependencies; and at last Mary said:

"One would think that no living creature had ever been round this coast before. But it cannot be so wild and lonely to you, Mr. Ross, as it seems to us; you have discovered all the secrets of it; and so I want you to take me to your grotto. In such an island of Monte Cristo, you must have the grotto of Monte Cristo: where is it?"

"How did you guess?" said he, with a smile.

"Guess what?"

"For there is a grotto," he said, regarding her. "Your surmise is quite correct. There is a grotto; only it isn't filled with sacks of jewels and coins—all that there is in it is some smuggled brandy."

"Oh, really?" she said, with her eyes showing a sudden attention. "Brandy?—smuggled brandy?—and how did it come there?—did you bring it?"

"Indeed I did," said he, without a moment's hesitation

—and he was standing in front of her now, for she had sate down on a smooth grey rock. "I suppose I must let you into my dark and terrible secret, and give you the power of sending the Supervisor over, and haling me off to Dingwall. It is not a grotto, however, it is a cave; and very few people know of its existence. In fact, you can't get to it by the shore at all; you must go by water; and I hope to show it to you some day, if you would care to go round in a boat. But then there are no wonders—no hasheesh— no heaps of diamonds and rubies—only little casks of spirits : perhaps they wouldn't interest you ? "

"Oh, but I think they would," she said—and yet with a little caution, for she did not quite know how to take this confession.

He observed her face for a moment.

"I see I must begin and justify myself," said he, lightly, "if justification is possible. For of course it's very wrong and wicked to evade the customs duties of your native land; only in my case there are two or three qualifying circumstances. For one thing, I am a Highlander; and smuggling comes natural to a Highlander. Then I have the proud consciousness that I am circumventing Mr. Purdie—and that of itself is a praiseworthy achievement. You may have heard, Miss Stanley, that Purdie plumes himself on having routed out the very last of the illicit stills from this country-side—and it was done merely out of ill-will to the people; but he forgot that it is difficult to watch a rough coast like this. I can put a counter-check on Mr. Purdie's zeal. But my real excuse is simply this— the old people about here are too poor to buy spirits of any kind, but especially of a wholesome quality ; and it is the only little bit of comfort they have when they are cold and wet, just as it is the only medicine they believe in ; and really I think the Government, that gives lavish grants here, there, and everywhere—except here, by the way—I think the Government can afford to wink at such a small trifle. Am I convincing you ? " he went on, with a laugh. "I'm afraid you look very stern. Is there to be no palliation ? "

Then up and spoke Kate Glendinning, valiantly—

"I consider you are perfectly justified, Mr. Ross ; yes, I do, indeed," said she.

"You see I have Miss Glendinning on my side," he pointed out, still addressing Mary.

"Ah, but you are both Highlanders," Mary said, as she rose from the rock; "and how can I argue one against two?"

"Shall I be quite honest," said he, as they were setting out for home again, "and confess that there is a spice of adventure in going away to the south for the cargo, and running it safely here? It is a break in the monotony of one's life on the island."

"Yes, I shouldn't wonder if that had something to do with all those fine reasons," she observed, with demure significance.

"And then," he continued, frankly, and perhaps not noticing her sarcasm, "I like to be on friendly terms with the old people who knew our family in former days. I like them to speak well of me; I like to think that they have some trifle of affection for me. And this is about the only way I can keep up the old relationship that used to exist between them and the 'big house'; it's very little kindness I am able to show them : they've got to take the will for the deed nowadays." He turned to her. "What, not convinced yet?" he said, laughing again. "What is to be the verdict? Not acquittal?"

She shook her head doubtfully : the Lady Superior of Lochgarra did not choose to say.

They found an excellent lunch awaiting them ; and after that, in his eager desire to entertain these rare visitors in every possible way, he showed them the heirlooms of the family, along with a heap of antiquities and curiosities that for the most part had been put away in cabinets and chests, as being out of keeping with these plain rooms. Naturally the old armour interested Mary less than the silks and embroideries, the porcelain and pottery ; and in particular was she struck by a Rhodian dish, the like of which she had never seen before. It was of coarse material, and of the simplest design—a plain draught-board pattern, with a free-handed scroll running round the rim ; but the curious pellucid green colour was singularly beautiful, and the glaze extraordinarily luminous.

"Where could that have come from?" said she, reluctantly laying it down, and still regarding it with admiration. "I have never seen one like it in England."

"My father sent it home from Smyrna," he said, simply, "to my mother. He could not live in the West Islands: the climate did not suit him. He travelled a great deal."

Donald Ross seemed to speak without any restraint or embarrassment; but there was some strange misgiving in Mary's mind; she was glad when Käthchen changed the subject—calling her attention to some exquisite lace.

And at last this wonderful and memorable visit had to come to an end; but when they went out to the little porch Mary said she could not go without saying good-bye to Martha, and so she turned and went through the passage into the kitchen.

"Martha," said she, in her most winning way, and with smiling eyes, "you have been very good to us, and I shall never forget your kindness on our first visit to Heimra, when we were quite strangers to you. And this is a little present I want you to take, as a souvenir, you understand——"

She had unclasped the châtelaine from her belt; and there it was, in antique silver, with all its ornaments and housewifely implements complete, pressed upon the old dame's acceptance. But Martha hung back—shyly—and yet looking at the marvellous treasure.

"Oh, no, mem," she said. "I thank ye; I'm sure I thank ye; but Mr. Ross would not be liking me to tek it."

"Mr. Ross!" said Mary impatiently. "What does Mr. Ross know about such things? Why, it is necessary for your housekeeping, Martha!—and, besides, you must take it to please me; and it will remind you of our visit until we come back again—for I hope to come back and see you some day."

"Yes, yes, and soon, mem," said the grateful Martha, who had been forced into compliance. "And I will be showing it to Mr. Ross, mem——"

"Good-bye, then, Martha, and thank you for all your kindness," said Mary, as she was going.

"No, no, mem, it is my thanks and service to you, mem," said Martha, and she timidly extended her hand. Mary had learnt the ways of this country. She shook hands with the old dame; and said good-bye again; and went her way.

Then once more over the shining sea, with the light northerly breeze providing them a steady and continuous passage. Mary turned once or twice to look at the now receding island.

"I suppose you get very much attached to a solitary home like that?" she said absently.

"But I like a few days on the mainland very well," said he, with much cheerfulness, "if there is anything to be done. When do you expect your photographer?"

"To-morrow or next day."

"I will wait for him," said he, promptly.

"That will be very kind of you," said she; "for what would pictures of Lochgarra be to Mrs. Armour if you were not in them?"

"And Saturday is Miss Stanley's birthday," put in Käthchen. "You should stay over for that."

"Saturday?" said he. "Oh, indeed. Oh, really." And then he added: "Why, they must get up a big bonfire on the top of Meall-na-Fearn."

"No, no," said Mary, with an odd kind of look; "that is not for me. I must wait a little for anything of that sort. It must come spontaneously, if ever it comes." And then she suddenly changed her tone. "Well, Mr. Ross, since you are remaining on the mainland for a day or two, I hope you will come and see what I have been doing. I have started a few things——"

"I know more about your work than you think," said he. "But I should be glad to go with you."

"And then perhaps the people won't treat me as a stranger," she said, with a touch of injury in her tone.

"It is very ungrateful of them if they do," said he with some emphasis.

And so it came about, on the next day, that Lochgarra again beheld the spectacle of Young Donald of Heimra acting as escort to the English lady, while she was taking him about and showing him all she was doing or trying to do. And to Käthchen it was clear as daylight that those people began to be a great deal more friendly—more willing to answer questions—more sympathetic in their looks. Why, when the two girls returned home that evening, they found the hall-door open, and Barbara in the act of lifting up two huge stenlock that had been laid on the stone slab.

"Why, what's this, Barbara?" Mary inquired.

"Oh, it's just that foolish lad, the Gillie Ciotach," said Barbara, with a smile of apology, "and he was leaving them here instead of taking them round by the back. He was saying the people are thanking Miss Stanley for the new building and the papers; and he and Archie MacNicol they had a big catch of stenlock, and would Miss Stanley take one or two."

"Do you mean that the Gillie Ciotach brought me those fish as a present?" said Mary, with a delighted surprise— and she was looking at those big, coarse lythe as if she had just received an Emperor's gift.

"Yes, ma'am," said Barbara.

"But of course you gave him something all the same?"

"Oh, no, ma'am."

"A glass of whisky, at least?" Mary demanded.

"Oh, no, ma'am," said the soft-spoken Barbara, "there is no whisky in the house."

"Then it is a shame there should be no whisky in a Highland house!" Mary exclaimed indignantly. "Why could you not have run over to your brother's cottage and got some?"

"The Gillie Ciotach was not giving me time, ma'am," answered Barbara, in her pleasant way. "May be he was thinking of something of that kind, and he went away quick after leaving the message."

"I'll make it up to the Gillie Ciotach—you will see if I don't!" she said to Käthchen, as they passed through the hall and went upstairs. And all that evening she appeared to be greatly pleased by this little incident; and spoke of it again and again: why, to her it seemed to presage the pacification of this lawless land—she was going to meet with some return at last.

Moreover, when the photographer at length made his appearance and set to work, it must have appeared to the people about that Donald Ross of Heimra had become the chosen ally and companion of the young Baintighearna;

while to Donald Ross himself it seemed as if Mary were bent on representing him—in these views, at least—as the owner of the whole place. And she was wilful and imperative about it, too ; though Käthchen, standing by as a spectator, perceived that she had to deal with a nature which, however quiet, was a good deal firmer than her own. For example, one of the first views was the front of Lochgarra House. The artist, having a soul above bare stone and lime, suggested that there should be some figures standing at the open hall-door, on the terrace above the steps.

"Oh, yes, certainly," said Mary at once. "You go, Mr. Ross, and stand there—will you be so kind ? "

"I ? " said he, in amazement—for it was clear she meant herself and Kate Glendinning to remain out of the picture —"What should I do there ? That is your place, surely— in front of your own house."

"Oh, what does Mrs. Armour want with me ! " she protested. "It is you she wants, naturally. Of course she associates Lochgarra House with you, not with me at all. Who am I ? A stranger—an interloper. What does Mrs. Armour care about me ? No, really, I must insist on your going and standing on the terrace."

" But indeed I cannot ; what right have I to be there ? " said he, with the faintest touch of colour coming to the keen, pale, dark face.

"Mrs. Armour would tell you you had a better right to be there than I have ! " said Mary, rather ruefully. " I knew what she was thinking, if she was kind enough to say nothing. Now, go, Mr. Ross, to please me ! I must not appear in this picture at all—indeed, I will not."

"And I cannot," he said, simply.

"Very well, then," said the shifty Käthchen, cheerfully stepping into the breach, "it is evident that I, at least, can't be expected to take up a position as owner of Lochgarra House ; but figures are wanted ; and so, if you are both resolved to remain out, I will go and get the keepers and gillies and servants, and range them along the front there, at the foot of the steps. I dare say Mrs. Armour will recognise some of them."

"Then you positively refuse me ? " Mary said to him.

"You ought to understand why," he answered her—and then she was silent.

But on the following morning she was deeply impressed by his thoughtful forbearance and consideration. They wished to get a view of the little hamlet of Cruagan, Mrs. Armour having lived there formerly; and, as the place was some distance off, they drove thither—the artist and his camera up beside the coachman. Now, it was inevitable they should pass the desert plain that used to be Loch Heimra, with the tumbled stones of the ancient keep ; and on coming in sight of these the photographer, recognising a subject, and yet a little puzzled, called on the coachman to stop.

"That, sir—what is that, sir ?" he asked of Donald Ross, whom he generally consulted.

"Oh, that is nothing," said Ross (and this time it was Mary who looked distressed and embarrassed). "Never mind ; go on."

"Isn't that an old ruin, sir ?" said the photographer, with professional instinct. Subjects did not abound in this neighbourhood, and he wished to do his best.

"That is of no use : that would not make a picture—a heap of stones like that," said young Donald ; and so the artist gave way ; and the carriage went on again. There was a space of silence thereafter.

But Mary was none the less grateful to him. And when they came to a stretch of the Connan, where there were some rocks in mid-stream and a bit of a waterfall, with some birches by the side of the river, she said :

"Now, Mr. Ross, Mrs. Armour is sure to remember this place ; and it is very pretty ; and since you want me to come into some of the pictures, I will come in this time, and the three of us can sit on the bank as if we were a pic-nic party. And if it turns out well, mightn't we have it enlarged and some copies printed for our own friends ? We will send on the carriage a bit, so that there shall be nothing but ourselves in this solitude."

"Let me go on with the carriage, Mamie !" interposed Käthchen at once.

"Don't be silly, Käthchen !" Mary made answer, with quickly lowered lashes. "We are supposed to be a pic-nic party, or a fishing party, taking a rest—anything you please; but of course we must all be together."

So that group also was taken, with the Highland river-scene for its background; and then they went forward and overtook the carriage. Mary was much more cheerful now, after getting away from that reproachful sight of Castle Heimra.

"Do you know, Mr. Ross," she was saying, ' I am about to encounter the bitterest enemy I have in the world?"

"I cannot believe you have any enemy," was his reply. "But who is this?"

"James Macdonald."

"Oh, Macdonald the crofter at Cruagan. Well, what have you been doing to him?"

"What have I been doing to him?" she said with some spirit. "You should rather ask what I have been doing for him. I have been doing far too much for him: I suppose that is why he hates me. What haven't I done for him? I took off the tax for the dyke; I handed over the pasturage of Meall-na-Cruagan; I lowered his rent; I forgave him arrears; I had the decree of removal quashed, and gave him back his holding after he had forfeited it; I stopped the action against him for deforcing the sheriff's officer. What more? What more? And yet he looks as if he would like to murder me if I try to speak to him."

"Have you any idea of the reason?"

"Yes," said Mary, a little proudly. "He says that you are his laird, and not I: he says I have nothing to do with the land or the people here."

"Macdonald is a foolish man—and stubborn: I will talk to him," he said; and he was thoughtful for a second or two.

Indeed, when they arrived at the scattered little hamlet of Cruagan, it was not the sun-pictures that occupied Mary Stanley's attention. The photographer was allowed to choose his subjects as he liked. For, in driving up, they had perceived the sullen-browed, Russian-looking crofter at work in his patch of potatoes; and as soon as the carriage stopped, young Ross left his companions, stepped over the bit of wire fence, and went along the potato drills. Macdonald ceased working, and respectfully raised his cap. Ross began speaking in a low voice, and yet with some emphasis, and increasing emphasis, as the ladies in the waggonette could gather. It was impossible for them to overhear the words, even if they had been able to understand; but as he proceeded it was clear enough that he was becoming angry and indignant, the man with the shaggy eyebrows and the determined jaw having answered once or twice. Then almost suddenly there came a strange termination to this fierce encounter. Young Ross remained behind, glancing around him as if merely wanting to know whether the crop promised well; but Macdonald came down the drills, in the direction of the carriage.

"Käthchen," said Mary in an eager whisper, "he is coming to speak to me! Let me get out—quick!"

She stepped into the roadway. As Macdonald came slowly towards her, he raised his eyes and regarded her for a second, in silence. He took off his cap—and forgot to put it on again. He was thinking what to say.

"I—not mich English. It is thanks to you—for many things. The young laird says that. And I—am to ask your pardon—and sorry I am if there is not goodwill— and there is goodwill now—and it is sorry I am——"

"Not at all—not at all; we are going to be quite good friends, Mr. Macdonald—and there's my hand on it," said she in her frank, impetuous way. "And you are going to ask me into your house; and will you give me a little bit of oatcake, or something of the kind?—and when you are next over at Lochgarra you must not forget to come and see me. And at any time, mind you, if you have anything to complain of come to me first; come direct to me; don't go to Mr. Purdie, or anybody; for perhaps I might be able to settle the matter for you at once."

And with that she called on Mr. Ross, and told him they were going into the cottage to get a bit of oat-cake; for Macdonald was already leading the way thither. When they came out of Macdonald's cottage, they found that the photographer had quite completed his work; so they at once set out for home again. Mary was in an extraordinary state of delight over this vanquishment of her obdurate enemy, and said she should take means to remind him of their compact of goodwill. But young Ross only laughed.

"'Wherefore he called that place Beersheba,'" he said, "'because there they sware both of them.'"

The following Saturday was Mary Stanley's birthday. Early in the morning she and Kate, in fulfilment of a long-standing engagement, drove away out to Craiglarig to pay a visit to Mr. Watson, and talk over some matters connected with his farm; and as they stayed for lunch, they did not get back till the afternoon. By that time the mail had come in, and there was an astonishing number of letters and parcels addressed to Miss Stanley, for she had a large number of friends in the south, who held her in kindly remembrance. She was looking at these and guessing at the senders, when she came to one that was larger and heavier than the others; moreover, it had not come by post but by hand. Something impelled her to tear off the brown wrapper, and behold, here was the Rhodian dish she had so particularly admired when they were out at Heimra Island.

"I saw he noticed how long you looked at it," said Käthchen, with smiling eyes.

Well, she did not look at it long now, beautiful as it was. She had turned again to the wrapper, and she seemed to take a curious interest in studying her own name as she found it there.

"It is an unusual handwriting, don't you think so, Käthchen?" she said, slowly, and almost as if she were talking to herself. "Firm and precise. . . . How odd one's own name appears when you see it written for the first time by some one you know! . . . Do you think character can be read in handwriting, Käthchen? . . . firmness—yes, apparently; and precision—well, I don't object to that so much, . . . but don't you think he is a little too—a little too confident in himself . . . careless of what others may think . . . . a little too independent. . . and proud in his own domain?"

"I don't know about that at all. But I am going to tell you something now, and you may be angry or not as you please," said Käthchen; and she went up to her friend, and put her hand on her arm: perhaps she wanted to watch the expression of her face : "Mamie," she said, "that man loves you."

CHAPTER XXII.

A PIOUS PILGRIMAGE.

ALL things appeared to be going well at Lochgarra: Mary was radiant and jubilant, and would pay no heed to Käthchen's underhand jibes and warnings. Her numerous schemes were thriving all along the line; she had orders for homespun webs and hand-knitted stockings far beyond what she could execute in the coming winter; she had been guaranteed two fishing-boats, with their furnishing of nets, for the next season; she was in treaty for more looms, for which there would be abundant employment; and to add to all this, the as yet ungarnered harvest—that poor, scattered, patchwork harvest, among the sterile rocks—promised a fair return if only the weather would leave it alone. But it was the attitude of the people towards her that warmed her heart. Since her open association with young Donald of Heimra, a miracle had been wrought in this neighbourhood; the dumb could speak; men and women who had sulkily turned away from the *ban-sassunnach*, shaking their heads, now managed to find quite sufficient English to answer her, and would ask her into their cottages, and offer her of their litte store. Even the sad-faced, silent, morose Peter Grant, of the inn, had been brought to see that there might be something in Miss Stanley's proposals. If he were to take the April fishing on the Garra at an annual rental of £15, she providing a water-bailiff, and if, by advertising in the sporting papers, he were to find two gentlemen who would pay him £25 for the month's salmon-fishing, and use the inn at the same time, would not that serve? Peter (committing one illegal act in order to prevent another) could give an occasional glass of whisky to the rosy-cheeked policeman: the placid and easy-going Iain, having little else to do, could now and again stroll down to the bridge of a morning or evening—there would be no fear of poachers at that end of the water.

But it was over the terrible rascal and outlaw, Gillie Ciotach, that she obtained (as she thought) her most signal triumph. She sent for that notorious scamp to thank him for the couple of lythe he had presented to her; and one evening the Gillie Ciotach sauntered along towards Lochgarra House, his fisherman clothes as clean as might be, and a brand-new Balmoral set jauntily on his short brown curls. When he arrived at the house, he dismissed a quid of tobacco he had been chewing, wiped his mouth with the back of his hand, and ascended the steps. Barbara received him, and went and told her mistress, who directed her to bring some whiskey into the hall. Then Mary came down.

"Good-evening!" said she, rather nervously, to this young fellow with the bold brown eyes and the heavy scar across his forehead, who stood twirling his Balmoral in his fingers. "Won't you be seated? I hope I have not put you to any inconvenience. The fact is, I wished to thank you for your kindness in leaving the two stenlock for me—I am sorry I was out—and—and perhaps you will take a glass of whiskey—will you help yourself?"

For Barbara had brought in a little tray, and placed it on the hall-table, and retired. Now, when the Gillie Ciotach received this invitation, which he had no thought of refusing, he went to the table; and finding there a tumbler, a wineglass, a decanter, and a carafe of water, and being far too polite to think of drinking by himself, he filled the wineglass with whisky, and half-filled the tumbler with the same fluid, and brought the former, as being the more elegant of the two, to Miss Stanley.

"Oh, no, thank you," said she, with an involuntary shudder.

"No, mem?" said he, in great surprise. "Well, well, now!" but not to waste good liquor he poured the contents of the wine-glass into the tumbler, and took that between his hands as he sate down, nursing it, as it were, while he listened respectfully.

"But first of all," she said, with a fine effort at jollity and good-comradeship, "I ought to know your real name, you know; I don't consider nicknames fair—even although they may not be meant to be nicknames. And I wish to be good friends with everybody in the place—and to get to know all about them——"

"Aw, my own name?" said the Gillie Ciotach, after

having, with careful manners, sipped a little of the whiskey, " Aw, it's just Andrew Mac Vean."

" Very well, then, Andrew, I am very pleased to see you ; and I am sure we shall be friends ; and I wished to say, besides, that I hope everything will go peaceably here, and that there will be no more riotous proceedings, like the assault on the lobster-fishermen at Ru-Minard——"

" Aw, God, that was a fine thing ! " cried the Gillie Ciotach, with a loud laugh that led Mary to suspect he must have had a glass, or even two, before coming along. " Aw, it was a fine thing, that ! And Miss Stanley has only to send us word, as she did before, and we'll drive the squatters into the sea—them and their traps, and their huts, ahltogether into the sea ! Never mind where they settle !—you send to me, mem, and we will drive the duvvles into the sea, and let them tek their chance of swimming the Minch !——"

" But what do you mean ? " she said, angrily.   " What word did I send you ? Do you imagine I authorized those mad and cruel proceedings ? I bade Big Archie tell those men what the Fishery Board had said—that they had no right there ; I did not ask you to drive the poor men out with sticks and stones, and set fire to their huts with petroleum. I don't want any such on-goings : why, it is monstrous that the people should take the law into their own hands, and get the neighbourhood a bad name for rioting."

" It's the God's truth, mem, and many's the time I was telling them that," said the Gillie Ciotach, solemnly.   " But ye see, mem, there's some wild duvvles about here ; and they're neither to hold nor to bind ; but I'll tell them what Miss Stanley says, that there's to be no more fighting ; and if a man is determined to fight, then we'll chist fell him with a chair, and fling him below the table until he gets sober. It's a peaceable neighbourhood : why should there be any fighting in it ?—but for these duvvles !——"

" I am glad you think so," said Mary, very gratefully. " And then there's another thing—the poaching. Now, is it fair ? I ask you if it is fair——"

" It's a b——y shame ! " said the Gillie Ciotach to himself, as he bent his head to sip a little more whiskey.

" Because look what I am doing, Andrew," she went on,

probably not having heard the penitent exclamation. "I want you to understand. I am having the ground shot over, moderately, by the keepers, and the game sent to Inverness and sold there to pay wages, and the cost of the kennels, and so on; and in that way I can afford to keep the gillies in employment. And I do think it is hardly fair that there should be poaching. *I* get no good out of the game—except a bird or two now and again for the house, or a brace or two to send away. Of course, I don't believe that there is very much poaching—for the keepers know their business too well; but it is disgraceful there should be any——"

"I declare to ye, mem," said the Gillie Ciotach, in tones of the most earnest conviction, "that if I was to come across one of them d——d scoundrels—I beg your pardon, mem—I meant to say there was one or two bad men about here, that mebbe would tek a hare if they found her sitting in her form—or—or a salmon; and as sure's death, mem, if I was to catch one of them scoundrels, I would bind him hand and foot with a heather rope, and I would fling him down in front of Hector's cottage, and I would say 'Hector, off with him to Dingwall!'"

This was almost too much of zeal.

"Andrew," said she, slowly, and she looked at him, "I have heard it said that even you yourself——"

"Me, mem?" he exclaimed, quick to repel this unspoken accusation. "Me, mem? Aw, Miss Stanley is not going to believe that! There's a great many liars about here, mem, and there's not one of them I would believe myself; and tekking away any one's character like that! I would just like to brek the bones of any one that I heard talking like that about me—begooh, I would shove his teeth down his throat!"

"Well, I won't detain you any longer, Andrew," said she—and he drained off the whiskey, and smoothed out the ribbons of his Balmoral. "I am glad to hear that there is to be no more fighting or poaching; for I want the neighbourhood to have a good name; and there are plenty of other and better occupations for the young men."

She went with him to the door. Suddenly something seemed to occur to the Gillie Ciotach.

"Would Miss Stanley be caring for two or three sea-trout now and again?" said he, in a casual kind of way.

Instantly she fixed her eyes on him.

"Sea-trout?—where are you getting sea-trout, Andrew?" she demanded. "Do you mean to say you have a scringe-net?"

For one brief moment the Gillie Ciotach looked disconcerted and guilty; but only for a moment.

"Aw, no, mem. A scringe-net? Is it a scringe-net? Aw, I'm sure there's no one would use a scringe-net about here!" he declared, assuming further and further an air of innocence as he went on. "The sea-trout?—well, mebbe they would be in the herring-nets—and mebbe a happening one would come on to the bait-lines—and—and mebbe the one way or the other; but if Miss Stanley not wishing to have them——"

"Why, isn't this the very time they go up the rivers to spawn!" she exclaimed. "And what a shame it would be to take them now!"

"Indeed, indeed, and that's the God's truth, mem," said the Gillie Ciotach, with a serious air. "It's at this very moment. And who would tek them? Who would put a scringe-net round the mouth of the ruvvers at a time of the year like this? Not a man about here, anyway. Aw, sea-trout?—who would think of tekkin sea-trout now? Well, good evening, mem; and I am thanking Miss Stanley for her kindness—yes, yes, indeed."

And therewith the Gillie Ciotach went down the steps, fumbling in his pocket for his pipe; while Mary returned to relate the story of this momentous interview to Käthchen—perhaps with some few judicious reservations. For if all that the Gillie Ciotach professed was not quite to be believed, at least it was something that so desperate a dare-devil had the grace to affect being on the side of virtue; and Mary chose to flatter herself that, now he had shown himself in a measure amenable, she would sooner or later complete his conversion—to the general quieting of the country-side.

And of course an account of this, her latest conquest, had to be written out forthwith and despatched to Heimra. Indeed, it was remarkable how constant had become the

communication between the island and the shore, now that
Donald Ross had returned for a few days to his own home.
Big Archie's lugger was continually being requisitioned, to
take out a note and wait for an answer; while Coinneach
and Calum, when they came to meet the mail, would be
intercepted by the swift-footed Barbara, and entrusted
with a message.   Käthchen was convinced that the replies
that came back from Eilean Heimra were kept and secretly
pondered over : more than once she had seen Mary thrust
a paper into her pocket when someone had suddenly come
upon her.   And she noticed that when they two were
walking along the shore, her companion's attention would
sometimes be so steadily and wistfully fixed on the distant
island—which sometimes was dark and misty under trailing
clouds of rain, and sometimes shining fair amid a wonder
of blue seas and sunlight—that when she was spoken to
she would look startled, as if summoned out of a dream.

One day there arrived, addressed to Miss Stanley, a
wooden box that had the name of a well-known London
florist printed on the label.   The contents were a mass of
flowers, all of them white; and Mary herself saw them
taken out and carefully placed in water—for the pale
wax-like buds of the tuberoses were hardly yet opened.
Then she went to Kate Glendinning.

"Käthchen," she said, rather diffidently, "don't you
think it is rather a sad thing, the lonely grave out there?"

"Do you mean at Heimra, Mamie?"

"Yes.   It seems so hard that no one has ever a chance
of showing sympathy—either with the dead or living.   I
have sent for some flowers; do you think we could go out
and place them on the grave—without being seen?"

Käthchen was silent : it did not appear a very feasible
project.

"I have been thinking it over," Mary continued, in the
same humbly apologetic, almost shamefaced way—though
what there was to be ashamed of Käthchen could not
make out.   "And, you see, if we landed at the little bay,
he would be sure to come down to meet us, and—and we
should have to tell him—and—and there are things you
can't speak of.   I would rather have this done quite
unknown—as if it were by the hand of a stranger : perhaps

I should like it better if Mr. Ross himself never knew. However, I was wondering if we could not get out to the west coast of the island without being seen, and then if there was a chance of our being able to get up to the top of the cliff that way. What do you think, Käthchen ? "

"Let us go along and ask Big Archie," said Käthchen, with promptitude : and that suggestion commending itself to her friend, both of them at once went off and got ready, and proceeded to walk down through the village.

Big Archie they found on the beach, screwing the nails into a lobster-box. Käthchen put the matter briefly before him—telling him frankly the object of the expedition, and explaining their reasons for secrecy. The huge, heavy-shouldered fisherman listened attentively, stroking his voluminous beard the while.

"Well, mem," said he, in his plaintive Argyllshire intonation, "I am thinking it would be easy enough to get out to the island, for we could go round by the norse side. If the wind wass holding as it is now, we would lie aweh up the coast there, and if anyone on Heimra wass seeing the lugger, they would think I wass mekkin for the Eddrachilles fishing-banks; and then, when we were far enough we would put about and run down to the back of the island, and mek in for the shore. I am thinking there would be no diffeekwulty about that—aw, no, mem ; we could get round to the back of the island ferry well ; but it is the next thing that would be the sore thing for leddies to try——"

"You mean climbing up to the top of the cliff ? " said Käthchen.

"Chist that ! It's a terrible rough place the west side of Heimra," said Gilleasbuig Mòr. "And where the big white stone is, it is fearful high."

"Mamie," said Käthchen, turning to her friend, "wouldn't it be better for you to send Archie out with some young lad who is used to the coast, and they could put the flowers on the grave for you ? "

"I wish to place them there with my own hand," said Mary, simply. "But you needn't come, Käthchen."

"Of course I will, though ! "

"Well, mem," said Big Archie, "I am not sure whether

you will be able to get to the top that way, but we can go out and see whatever. And if the wind would hold till to-morrow morning, it would be a very good wind, both for going and coming."

"Very well, then, Archie," said Mary; "to-morrow morning we shall be ready to start between nine and ten."

The wind did hold, as it proved; and long before the young ladies made their appearance Big Archie and his assistant had the lugsail hoisted and the cumbrous craft smartened up as much as might be. Then he sent the lad along to Lochgarra House to see if there was anything to be fetched; but there was only a couple of waterproofs; when Mary and her friend came out, the former was herself carrying a small basket, containing the freshly-sprinkled flowers.

And so they set forth—making away in a north-westerly direction, which would have led anyone to imagine they were either going to certain well-known fishing-banks, or that they intended to pay some visit not at all in the Heimra direction. But when at length they had got well out beyond the most northerly spur of the island, Big Archie altered his course, and bore down south, until they were quite near to these giant ramparts facing the Atlantic main. And already it appeared to the two girls that this expedition of theirs was a quite hopeless one. They were, it is true, under the lee of the island, and the water was smooth, so that they could get ashore wherever they wished; but who could scale those sterile and sombre precipices that, further to the south, rose sheer from water, and seemed to afford not even foothold for a goat? Even Big Archie was discouraged.

"No, mem," he said to Miss Stanley, "it is no use going aweh down there to where the big white stone is. There's no luvvin crayture could get up—it's far worse than I wass remembering it. But if we went ashore here where we are, and tried to get up one of them corries, then mebbe we could get along the top. Will ye try that, mem?"

"Whatever you like, Archie," said she—the aspect of that frowning, lonely, precipitous coast seemed to have overawed her.

And indeed when they did eventually choose a landing-place, and when they began to look around them, the arduous nature of their task became abundantly apparent. First of all there were the tumbled rocks on the shore to be got over or avoided; then they proceeded up a narrow watercourse that here cleaved the land into a deep ravine; and this they ascended for some distance, scrambling up the loose wet shingle and stones. Big Archie led the way, and also he carried the little basket, for the two girls had frequently need of both hands to help them along, especially when they left the water-course, and began to force a path through the stunted birches that lined the sides of the chasm. It was a thicket of short trees, with intertwisted branches; while underfoot the long heather and bracken concealed loose, angular stones perilous to the ankles. Sometimes they had to pause, from absolute want of breath; and Big Archie, looking back, would also stop. But no one made any suggestion of giving up: there must be light and open space somewhere, if only one could win to the summit.

So they toiled and toiled on, in silence, starting now a fox, and now a rabbit, until, at length, the stunted trees gave way to bushes, and these in turn gave way to knee-deep heather. It was still difficult to get along; but at least they had reached the open, and were presumably approaching the high plateaus: turning, they could look abroad over the wide Atlantic, the vast plain not showing one single ship. Their own boat, far below, was out of sight, so steep was this ascent they had made.

Here they rested for a minute or two, after their long and breathless struggle.

"One thing is quite certain, Mamie," said Käthchen, in rather a low voice, so that the big fisherman should not overhear, "When Mr. Ross finds these flowers on the grave, he will know very well who put them there."

"I am not sure that I want him to know," Mary answered, in an absent way. "I think I almost wish he were not to know. If he were to consider it merely a little kindness from some stranger—that would be better, it seems to me—it would be quite disinterested——"

"Why, what stranger could have managed to land on Heimra without being seen?" Käthchen asked; and as there was no answer to the question, they resumed their difficult progress, getting momentarily higher as they went along the summit of the cliffs.

But all at once Big Archie, who was some distance in front, halted, ducked his head, and immediately turned and came back.

"Miss Stanley, mem, Mr. Ross himself is there," said he.

"Mr. Ross!" said she, with frightened eyes.

"Ay. He is sitting on the heather, not far from the big white stone, and he is reading a book," said Big Archie. "He is often up there, mem. I am seeing him often and often when I am going by in the boat."

Mary turned to her companion, with her face aghast.

"We must go away back, Käthchen, and at once," she said, in a hurried undertone. "The embarrassment would be too dreadful. If he could image it was some stranger brought the flowers, that would be all right; but to go up to him—before his face—to make a parade—he would wonder what kind of creatures we were."

Käthchen hardly knew what to say. She had no more mind to go forward than her friend had; and yet she guessed with what a heavy heart, with what regretful lookings-back, Mary would set out on her voyage home again.

"Let us sit down and rest awhile," she said, at a venture.

But at this very instant Big Archie returned.

"Mr. Ross, mem, he has got up, and he is going aweh down the hill," he said, in an eager whisper.

"You are sure he is not coming this way?" she said quickly.

"No, no, mem—come a bit forrit, and you will see."

So they followed, with rather timorous steps and anxious glances, the big fisherman; and at last they just caught a glimpse of Donald Ross making his way down the hill by the winding pathway leading up to this little plateau. And here was the large white block of marble, with its deep-graven letters of gold shining in the sunlight. Mary regarded this inscription with some curious fancies in her mind.

"I wish I had known her," she murmured, apparently to herself, as she took the white flowers out of the basket and reverently placed them on the stone. It was a simple ceremony—up here on the lofty crest of this solitary island, between the wide, over-arching sky and the far-extending plain of the sea.

Then they went back along the silent and lonely cliffs, and got down to the boat in safety; returning to the mainland, as they hoped, unobserved. Mary Stanley was unusually absorbed and thoughtful during the rest of that day; and only once did she refer to their visit to Heimra.

"It seems strange, Käthchen, does it not," she said, musingly, "that he should go away up there to read? . . . Do you think it is perhaps for some sense of companion-ship? . . . That would be strange, wouldn't it, in a young man?..." And Käthchen did not venture to reply: she could not even conjecture what secret influences, what mysterious cogitations, might not have prompted such a question.

But Kate herself grew to wonder whether Donald Ross had become aware of that thoughtful little act of kindness and sympathy; and whether, and in what way, he would make recognition of it. This was what happened. Some two days after their visit to the island Mary chanced to be standing at one of the windows, when she suddenly called to her companion—

"Käthchen, there's a boat coming out from Heimra."

She went quickly and got her binocular telescope, and returned to the window.

"It's the *Sirène !*" she exclaimed.

"He has seen those flowers," Kate Glendinning said quietly.

Mary turned to her friend, with something of concern in her look.

"And if he has, Käthchen, I hope he won't speak of them. Don't you think it would be better—if nothing were said? Besides, you don't know that he is coming here at all."

But there was little doubt; and, in fact, on getting ashore, young Ross made straight for the house. When he was announced in the drawing-room, Mary happened to be standing near the door—perhaps with the least touch of conscious colour in the beautiful face. He, on the contrary, was pale, and calm, and self-possessed as usual;

only, when he took her hand in his, he held it for a second. "I thank you," he said, in rather a low voice: that was all—and it was enough.

But presently it appeared that his visit had some other aim; for when he sate down they saw that he had brought a small parcel with him; and presently he said—

"I am going to ask a favour of you, Miss Stanley; and I hope you won't refuse. I have brought a little present, if you will be so kind as to accept it: you may look on it as a souvenir of your visit to Heimra—for perhaps you remember the piece of lace you looked at——"

She remembered very well; it was the exquisite Spanish mantilla to which Käthchen had drawn her attention. And it was not because this sumptuous piece of work was of great value that she hesitated about accepting it: would it not look like despoiling the dead woman? Instantly he appeared to divine her thought.

"If my mother were alive," he said, simply, "she would ask you to take it—and from her, not from me.'

So there was no alternative. Mary silently accepted the gift. Nor was there any further word or hint on either side about that pious and secret pilgrimage to Heimra Island; but Donald Ross knew whose hand it was that had placed those flowers on the white grave.

One evening, about this time, two men were dining together in the Station Hotel, Inverness, in a corner of the long coffee-room; and these two were Mr. David Purdie, solicitor and agent, and Mr. James Watson, who was on his way through to his sheep farm of Craiglarig. But if they were dining together, their fare was very different; for while the fresh-complexioned, twinkling-eyed farmer was content with such simple vegetarian dishes as an ordinary hotel could devise at short notice, the Troich Bheag Dhearg was attacking an ample plateful of boiled beef and carrots, while a decanter of port stood near to his elbow.

"Man, Watson," said the factor, with an expression of impatient disgust on his harsh, ill-tempered features, "I wonder to see ye swallowing that trash! It's not food for human beings. Have ye been so long among sheep that ye must imitate their very eating?"

"It's live and let live, each in his own way," said the well-contented sheep-farmer; and then he added: "But tell me this, friend Purdie: if ye object to my eemitating a sheep, what kind o' animal is't you eemitate? For there's only kind one o' crayture I've heard o' that would eat a dead cow—and that's a hoodie crow."

But this was an incidental remark: presently they returned to their main object, which was the condition of Lochgarra.

"It's just terrible to think of," said the Little Red Dwarf, with his mouth as vindictive as the process of eating would allow; "it's just terrible to think of, the waste and extravagance going forward, on what used to be a carefully-ordered, carefully-kept estate. And the pampering o' they idle, whining, deceitful, ill-thrawn wretches, that would be the better of a cat-o'-nine tails to make them work! Work? Not them!—if they can get money out o' the proprietors, or out o' the Government, or out o' the rates. And what could ye expect to happen wi' a silly, ignorant woman coming into such a nest of liars, and believing everything she hears? What could ye expect? Born liars every one o' them—ay, from end to end of the West Highlands: there's not a man o' them that would not lie the very soul out o' his body for a dram of whiskey!"

"That's an old contention o' yours, friend Purdie," said the farmer; and then he proceeded, with a twinkle of humour in his eyes: "But I'll just tell ye this, man, that's it's a mercy there's one thing in the West Highlands that will not lie. One thing at least, I tell ye. Among the universal lying, isn't it a mercy there's one thing will *not* lie—and that's the snow. It's a blessing for the sheep —and for the sheep-farmers."

"And what am I? Where am I?" resumed Mr. Purdie, paying no heed to this little jocosity, for his small, piggish eyes had grown heated with anger and indignation. "What is my poseetion? I ask ye that. What have I to do wi' the estate except to collect what rent there is left? It's this fashionable young dame that must come in to manage the place, snipping off here and snipping off there, ordering this and ordering that, building byres and sheds for nothing, and putting advertisements in the papers about druggets and blankets to sell, as if Lochgarra House was a warehousemen's shop. I tell ye, it's enough to make her uncle turn in his grave. *He* knew better how to dale wi' they ill-thrawn paupers ! And what will she not give them, after giving them Meall-na-Cruagan ?—and that without consulting any one—no ' by your leave ' or ' with your leave,' but ' this is what I have decided ' and ' you can carry it out like a clerk.' Man, Watson, ye were a silly creature to consent to that Meall-na-Cruagan business ! That was but a beginning—where is to be the end ? Well, I'll tell ye the end ! She'll snip here, and snip there, until she has divided every acre of ground among the crofters ; and then, when they've resolved among themselves to pay no more rent, I suppose they'll be happy. No, d——n them if they will !—they'll want her to sell Lochgarra House, and give them the money to buy more stock." And here Mr. Purdie poured himself out a glass of port, and gulped it as a dog grabs at a rat.

"Ye've never forgiven the folk out there," said Mr. Watson, with an amused and demure air, " since the procession and the burning in effigy. Dod, that was a queer business !—I heard of it away up in Caithness. But I'm thinking ye might let bygones be bygones ; ye've had them under your thumb a good while now—and—and—well, ye might consider that ye've paid off that score. But as for the young leddy—well, I tell ye, friend Purdie, it's just wonderful what she has done since she cam' to the place. A busy, industrious creature ; ay, and she has a way of talking folk over to her way of thinking ; she seems to get on famously wi' them, though they cannot have too friendly recollections of her uncle. Yes, I will say that for her : an active, well-meaning creature ; and light-hearted as a lintie ; dod, she takes her own way, and gets it too ! But I'm thinking there's a great deal owing to young Mr. Ross— he goes about wi' her just conteenually."

"Ay," said the factor, with a malignant scowl, " I'm told my young gentleman doesna shut himself up as much wi' his brandy-drinking as he used to do. So he comes over to the mainland sometimes, and goes about wi' her, does he ?"

"Faith, ye may say that," Mr. Watson made answer,

with a laugh. "Theyre just insayperable, as ye might say, any time that he comes over from Heimra, and that's often enough." He regarded the factor curiously. "Purdie, my man, that's going to be a match."

For a second Purdie looked startled and incredulous, but instantly he lowered his eyes again.

"It's a match, Purdie, depend on't," Mr. Watson proceeded, still looking at his companion with an odd sort of scrutiny. "And I have been thinking, if such a thing were to come about, it might be a wee bit difficult for you—with young Ross the master at Lochgarra, eh? What d'ye think? Dod, ye'd have to make friends with him and keep a civil tongue besides, or he might be for bringing up old scores."

Mr. Purdie's dinner did not seem to interest him much after that. He remained plunged in a profound reverie, with his truculent mouth drawn down, the shaggy red eyebrows shading the small irascible eyes that were now grown intent and thoughtful. And when at length Mr. Watson haled him off to the smoking-room he did not speak for some considerable time. But by and by he said—

"Are ye off by the early train to-morrow, Watson?"

"Yes, indeed."

"And you go right through?"

"Just that."

"Well, I think I'll bear ye company," said the Troich Bheag Dhearg, with the heavily down-drawn mouth expressing something more than mere decision. "There's a few things I want to see to. And I havena been out to Lochgarra for some time."

CHAPTER XXIII.

ΠΑΒΕΤ !

MARY went singing through the house : her step free and agile, her face radiant, her eyes shining with good humour and the delight of life.

"Käthchen," she said, one morning, "the proofs of the photographs should come to-day, and if they turn out well

I mean to have the whole of them enlarged, every one of them, to make a handsome series for Mrs. Armour. Don't you think they should be very interesting to those people away over there—'where wild Altama murmurs to their woe'? Woe, indeed!   I wish we could import some of their woeful circumstances into this neighbourhood. Forty bushels of wheat to the acre : what do you say to that? A hundred and sixty acres of land for two pounds! I don't like to think of it, Käthchen : to tell you the truth, I just hate to hear Mr. Ross begin and talk about emigration : it all sounds so horribly reasonable, and practicable and right. Sometimes I lie awake convincing myself that the very next day or the next again he will make his appearance with the announcement that he has decided to go back to his original intention, and then—then he will say good-bye to Lochgarra—he and half the people from about here—and be off to the Gilbert Plains or the Lake Dauphin District——"

"You need not be afraid," said Käthchen, quietly. "It is neither wheat-fields nor gold-fields that are likely to allure Mr. Ross. There's metal more attractive nearer home. By the way, Mamie," she continued, with a certain significance, "you remember there was a group taken on the banks of the Connan—and you and Mr. Ross are standing together. When you get the pictures enlarged, are you going to send any copies of that one to your friends in the south?"

"Why not?" said she, boldly.

"They may draw conclusions," said Kate Glendinning, looking at her.

"They are welcome to draw a cart-load of conclusions!" she retorted ; but all the same she changed the subject quickly.

"Do you know, Käthchen, it is quite wonderful how easily things go forward when Donald Ross is helping me. Look at the wood-carving class—started in a moment, almost ; and that left-handed rascal turning out the cleverest of any of them. And then he is quite of a mind with me about corrugated iron——"

"You mean Mr. Ross, Mamie?" said Kate demurely.

"Of course. Quite of a mind with me as to corrugated

iron; and I won't have a square yard of it in the place.
If, as he says, thatch takes too much time and labour,
then they may have slates for their roofs, in place of the
turf that I hope to see the last of before I have done
with them; but not an inch of corrugated iron—not an
inch. Oh, I tell you we will have Lochgarra smartened
up in course of time, and Minard and Cruagan too. And
I will never rest, Käthchen, I tell you I will never rest
until Lochgarra has taken the first prize at the Inverness
Exhibition—I mean for the best suit of men's clothes
made from the wool of. sheep fed on the croft, and carded,
dyed, spun, hand-loom woven, and cut and sewn in the
family. There! It may be a long time yet, but I mean
Lochgarra to have it in the end."

"Oh, but you must not stop at that point," said
Käthchen. "There are a whole heap of things to be done
before you have finally established your earthly paradise.
You must banish all sickness and illness—but especially
rheumatism. You must abolish old age. You must control
the climate to suit the crops. Perhaps you could magnetise
the herring-shoals, and bring them round this way, and
ward off storms at the same time?"

"Käthchen," said Mary abruptly, "why does he keep
harking back on Manitoba? Don't you think there is a
curious tenacity about his mind?—he does not change
plans or opinions quickly. And I know he was resolved
on that emigration scheme. Why does he still talk about
Manitoba? If he really has abandoned that project, why
does he still keep thinking about Portage, and La Prairie,
and Brandon? Of course, I admit that a hundred and
sixty acres for two pounds is very tempting; and forty
bushels of wheat to the acre sounds well; and I have no
doubt the emigrants have better clothes, and better food,
and better cottages, and that they don't run such risks
from floods and rain. But still—still there's something
about one's own country——"

"You need not be afraid, Mamie," said Kate Glendinning
again.

Mary went to the window, and remained there for a
minute or two, looking absently across the wide plain of
the sea.

"After all," she said, "it is a very pleasant and comfortable thing to have a neighbour. Heimra is a good way off; but all the same, if you knew there was no one living on the island, Lochgarra would be a very different place, wouldn't it, Käthchen? And Manitoba! Why, I have seen it stated that there is a most serious scarcity of water in a great many of the districts; and that often they have summer frosts that do incalculable mischief to the grain. So you see it isn't a certainty!"

"No, it is not," said Käthchen; "but I will tell you what is, Mamie. It is a certainty, an absolute certainty, that Donald Ross of Heimra will not go to Manitoba, or to any other corner of Canada, so long as Mary Stanley is living in Lochgarra."

"Käthchen," rejoined Mary, a little proudly, "you will go on talking like that until you believe what you say."

This same afternoon, shortly after luncheon, Mary left the house alone, which was unusual. She passed down through the village, greeting everyone, right and left, with a fine cheerfulness; for the weather still held good, and there was a fair chance for the harvest; while her individual schemes and industries were doing as well as could be expected. In fact, the only idle person in the place, apart from the aged and infirm, appeared to be John the policeman, and him she found by the bridge that crosses the Garra—no doubt he had been amusing himself by watching for some lively salmon or sea-trout on its way up the river. Iain seemed to have grown plumper and more roseate than ever in these piping times of peace; and the smile with which he greeted the young proprietress was good-nature itself.

"John," said she, "I want you to tell me something."

"Aw, yes, mem," said the amiable John; and then he added: "but the lads hef been keeping very quiet."

"So I hear," she answered him. "The Gillie Ciotach says he will smash the head of anyone that wants to fight; and I suppose that is one way to stop quarrelling."

John laughed, showing his milk-white teeth.

"A very good weh, too, mem. There's not many would like to hef their head brokken by the Gillie Ciotach."

"It is not about that I want you to give me some

information," said Miss Stanley. "I want you to tell me
if you have been long in this place. I mean, do yon
remember the old castle, up there in the loch, before it was
pulled down?"

"Aw, yes, mem, yes, indeed," he made answer. "Who
does not remember Castle Stanley?"

"Oh, nonsense with your Castle Stanley!" she said,
angrily. "It never was Castle Stanley, and never will be
Castle Stanley. It was Castle Heimra; and if I could
have my way it would be Castle Heimra again——"

"Aw, yes, mem," said John, anxious to please, "who
would be for calling it Castle Stanley? It is not Castle
Stanley at ahl; it's just Castle Heimra, as it always was—
ay, before any one can remember."

"Well, tell me; what size of a place was it before it
was pulled down? Was it a big place?"

"Big!" repeated John, doubtfully, for he did not know
which way she wished to be answered.

"Yes, was it a great ruin?" she went on. "Some of
those old castles are mere towers, you know; and others
are great strongholds. What was Castle Heimra like?
Was it as big as Ardvreck?"

Now John had jumped to the conclusion that she wished
to have the ancient glories of Castle Heimra magnified.

"Aw, far bigger nor Ardvreck!" he asserted confidently.
"Aw, yes, yes; far bigger nor Ardvreck. A fearful big
place, Castle Heimra—if you had seen the dingeons, and
the towers, and the windows, and everything——"

"Oh, bigger than Ardvreck?" Mary said, with fallen
face. And instantly John perceived that he had erred.

"Aw, no, mem," said he quickly. "Mebbe it was bigger
nor Ardvreck at one time—that is a long time ago, before
any one about here can remember; but Castle Heimra?—
aw, no!—a smahl place, a smahl place, indeed! There
was nothing but the road out to it, when the loch was not
too high flooded; and then the archway, and the dingeon,
and the tower. Castle Heimra!—aw, it's a smahl place
was Castle Heimra."

"And do you suppose it could be built up again!" she
asked—but rather to see how far his complaisance would
carry him.

"Quite easy !" said John, without a moment's hesitation.

"Why, how do you know ?" she demanded. "Are you a builder ?"

"The stons are there," John pointed out. "And if they were pulled down, it is easy to put them back. What has been done once can be done twice."

"Ah, but it would not be Castle Heimra," Mary said to herself, rather sadly, as she went on her solitary way.

In course of time she came within view of the desolate expanse of mud and stones and rushes that had once been Heimra Loch ; and when she chose out for herself a seat on a heathery hillock close to the road, there before her were the tumbled ruins of the stronghold that had withstood the storms of centuries only to fall before the withering blast of one man's spite. And as she sate there, alone, in the absolute silence, a kind of desperation came into her mind. In all other directions there was hope for her ; but here there was none. Elsewhere she could labour, and patiently wait for fruition ; but how was she to drag back the past ! The future had abundant and fair possibilities within it ; and she was naturally sanguine ; her happiness consisted in action ; and perhaps she was looking forward to the time when she could say to her lover, "See, this is what I have striven to do—for your people : is it well or ill ?" But as between him and her, would there not be ever and always the consciousness of this black deed that could in no wise be recalled or atoned for, that could never be forgiven or forgotten ? She was not even allowed to speak ; he had declined to hear her shamefaced expressions of sorrow. Nay, she began to think he was too proud, too implacable, that he would have no word uttered. And if she went to him and said : 'Donald, do not blame me !—I had no part in it : I would give my right hand to undo what has been done'—would not his looks still remain haughty and cold, telling her that she had not ceased to be the *ban-sassunnach*—a stranger—the enemy of his race and name ?

There was a sound of wheels. She started to her feet, for there were tears in her eyes that she had to hide. The approaching vehicle turned out to be the mail-car ; and on it were Mr. Purdie and Mr. Watson, seated beside the driver. Both of them raised their hats to her, and would doubtless have driven on, but that she called to the factor; whereupon the mail-car was stopped, and Mr. Purdie descended.

"Leave my bag at the inn, Jimmie," he said to the driver, who sent his horses on again: then the Troich Bheag Dhearg came along to the spot at which Mary awaited him.

"I wish to speak to you about one or two things, Mr. Purdie," she said, in a curiously reserved and frigid fashion. "You told me it was under your direction that the loch here was drained. I do not know whether my uncle was acting on the advice or suggestion of any one; I can hardly believe that so insensate a piece of malice could have entered his head without instigation. And if there was instigation, if this thing was done out of ill-will towards the Rosses of Heimra, then I say it was a cowardly blow— a mean, shameless, and cowardly blow!" Her lips were a little pale; but she was apparently quite calm.

"It was just the thrawn nature of the people about here that brought it on themselves," said the Little Red Dwarf, sullenly. "The Rosses of Heimra had no further concern with the loch and the castle, once the property was sold. They belonged to your uncle: surely it was for him to say what they should be called? Surely he had the right to do what he liked with his own?"

"In this instance," said Mary, still preserving that somewhat cold and distant demeanour, "what he did has got to be undone as far as that is now possible. I suppose it would be useless to try and rebuild the castle. Even if the stones were put up again, it would hardly be Castle Heimra. But Loch Heimra can be restored to what it used to be; and since the mischief was done under your direction, Mr. Purdie, you can now take steps to repair it."

"Bless me, Miss Stanley," the factor protested, "it would be quite useless—perfectly useless! The loch was never worth anything to anybody. Salmon cannot get up; and there was nothing in it but a wheen brown trout——"

"It is not the value of the loch I am considering," she rejoined. "I wish to make some reparation, as far as I can. And I suppose if those channels you had cut were partially blocked up, the water from the hills would soon fill the lake again. Or you could bring the Connan round in this direction with very little trouble, and let it find its way down to the Garra after going through the loch——"

"The expense, Miss Stanley!—the expense!"

"I tell you I will have this done, if I have to sell Lochgarra House to do it!" she said—forgetting for a moment her austere demeanour. The factor had no further word. Mary went on "It cannot be a difficult thing to do, any more than the draining was difficult; and it will give employment to some of the people, when the harvest is in and the fishing season over. So you'd better see about it at once, Mr. Purdie; and make arrangements. And there is to be no more talk of Loch Stanley or of Castle Stanley either; this is Loch Heimra; and if Castle Heimra has been pulled down—shamefully and wickedly pulled down —at least there are the ruins to show where it stood."

The factor remained darkly silent, his vindictive mouth drawn down, his small eyes morose. And little did she know what gall and wormwood she had poured into his heart, in directing him to employ those very Lochgarra people in this work of restoration. However, he made no further protest: indeed, he endeavoured to assume an air of hopeless acquiescence—it was his business to obey orders, even if she should bring the whole estate to waste and ruin.

But as they together set out to return to the village, and as she was talking over general business affairs with him, explaining what she had done and what she meant to do, he could not quite conceal his bitter resentment.

"It seems to me, Miss Stanley, that I am hardly wanted here. A strange condeetion of affairs. The factor the very last one to be consulted. And when I think of the way ye allow these people to impose on ye—well, maybe, I'm not so much astonished; for what could one expect?—you come here an absolute stranger, and you wish to do without them that have experience of the place, and of course you believe every tale that is told ye. Though I say it who maybe should not, Lochgarra was a well-managed estate;

everything actually valued, and in order; and the tenants, large and small, knowing fine that they had to fulfil their contracts, or take the consequences. But what prevails now? A system of wholesale charity, as it seems to me. It is giving everything, and getting nothing. I hope, Miss Stanley," he went on, "ye will not mind my speaking warmly; for I've done my best for my employers all my life through; and I cannot be supposed to like other ways and means—which were never contemplated by the law of the land. If the other proprietors were to go on as you are doing, there's three-fourths o' them would be in beggary——"

"It might do them good to try a little of it," said she—which was an odd speech for the owner of a considerable estate.

"And what has been the result?" he demanded. "What has been gained by so much sacrifice?"

"Well," said she, "for one thing, the people are more contented. And they are more friendly towards me. When I came here at first, I was hated; now I am not so much so. Quite friendly most of them are—or, at least, they appear to be."

"Ay, trust them for that!" said the Little Red Dwarf, scornfully. "Trust them for that—the cunningest mongrels that ever whined for a bone! Well they know how to fawn and beslaver, when they're expecting more and more. I tell ye, Miss Stanley, ye do not understand these creatures, and it angers me to think that ye are being cheated and imposed on right and left. Getting more boats and nets?—they'll laugh at ye, they'll just laugh at ye when ye ask them to pay up the instalments! And who is your adviser?—a young man who is in secret league with them—an underhand, conspiring ne'er-do-weel, as cunning as any one of them, and as treacherous——"

"Mr. Purdie," she said—with a sudden change of tone he did not fail to note, "what do you mean? I—I beg you to be a little more respectful in your language."

"It's the old story," said the factor, with affected resignation. "Ye may work and work, and do the best for your employers; and then some stranger is called in, new advice is taken, and all you have done is destroyed. And

I wonder if the people will be any the better off. I wonder what change in their condeetion it will make—what permanent change, when once you stop putting your hand in your pocket. Improvements? Oh, yes, yes; improvements are all very fine. But I'm thinking that spending money on free libraries and the like o' that will not help them much in getting in their crops."

"As for that," she retorted—but with no displeasure, only a little quiet confidence, "I can merely say that I am trying to do my best, in a great many different ways; and the result, whatever it may be, is a long way off yet. And I live in hope. Of course, there is much more that I should like to do, and do at once; but I cannot; for I haven't sufficient money. I don't deny that there is a great deal still to be amended: I can't work miracles. The people are very poor—and many of them not too industrious; the soil is bad; the fishing is uncertain; and communication difficult. I dare say there is even a good deal of wretchedness—or rather, what a stranger would regard as extreme wretchedness and misery; but all that cannot be changed in a moment, even if it turns out that it can be changed at all. And at least there is little sickness; the poorest cottages have the fresh air blowing around them— they're better than the London slums, at all events. And one must just do what one can; and hope for the best."

"I tell ye, ye are going entirely the wrong way to work wi' these people, Miss Stanley," said he, as they were crossing the bridge and about to enter the village. "It's my place to tell ye. It's my bounden duty to tell ye. And I say they are just making sport wi' ye. They are born beggars; work of any kind is an abomination to them; and you'll find they'll be like leeches—give, give always; and when you've ruined the estate on their behalf, what then?"

"I don't see any such prospect—not at present," said Mary, cheerfully.

"Who is likely to know most about them, you or me?" he went on with dogged persistence. "Who has had most experience of them? Who has had dealings with them for years and years, and learned their tricks? A whining, cringing, useless set, cunning as the very mischief, and having not even an idea of what speaking the truth is. Plausible enough—oh, ay—plausible with a stranger —especially when they expect to get anything."

"Mr. Purdie," said Mary, interrupting him, "I presume from your name you belong to the south of Scotland. Well, I have been told that the Scotch—the people in the southern half of Scotland—do not understand the Highland character at all; and cannot understand it, for they have no sympathy with it. I have been told that the English have far more sympathy with the Highland nature. And I am English."

"Ay, and who told ye that about the Scotch and the Highlanders?" he said, suddenly and sharply.

She hesitated for a second.

"It is of little consequence," she answered him. "But I would like to add this—that denunciations of the inhabitants of a whole country-side do not seem to me of much value. I suppose human nature is pretty much the same in Lochgarra as it is elsewhere. And—and—besides, Mr. Purdie—I do not wish to hear evil spoken of a people amongst whom I have many friends."

She spoke with some dignity.

"Evil speaking?" said he, with lowering eyebrows, "I for one am not given to evil speaking—or the truth might have been told you ere now."

"The truth?—what truth?" she demanded.

"The truth about one that is too much at your right hand, Miss Stanley, if I may make bold to say so." At this moment they arrived at the door of the inn; and she paused, expecting him to leave her; but he said: "No, I will go on with you as far as Lochgarra House. It is time I should open my lips at last. I have been patient. I have stood by. I have heard what has been going on— and I have held my tongue. And why?—because there are things that it is difficult to speak of to an unmarried young woman."

Mary was a trifle bewildered. They were walking along through the village, on this quiet afternoon, with nothing to interrupt the peaceful stillness save the recurrent plash of the ripples on the beach: it was hardly the time or the place to be associated with any tragic disclosure. Moreover, had she heard aright? Was it of Donald Ross he was speaking?

"And I will say this for myself," the factor continued, "that I warned ye about the character of that young man, as plainly as I dared—ay, the very first day ye set foot in the place——"

"You mean Mr. Ross?" said she, lightly. "Pray spare yourself the trouble, Mr. Purdie. You forget I have had some opportunities of studying Mr. Ross's character. I know him a little. What did you say?—that you had something to tell? Oh, no; don't give yourself the trouble. I know him a little."

"You do not know him at all!" he said, with a vehemence that startled her. "I tell ye there is not one in this place who would dare to tell ye the story; and would I, unless I was bound to do it? If there was a married woman at Lochgarra House, it's to her I would go; and she would tell ye; but I say it is my bounden duty to speak—and to speak plainly——"

"Mr. Purdie, I do not wish to hear," she said, with some touch of alarm.

"But ye must hear," he said, with set lips and slow, emphatic utterance. "Ye are bound to hear—and to understand the character of the man ye are publicly associating yourself with. A scoundrel of that kind has no right to be going about with a virtuous and respectable young woman——"

"Mr. Purdie," she said, hurriedly, "I don't want to know—I don't believe—I wouldn't believe——"

"Miss Stanley," he said, with measured deliberation, "ye have some knowledge of that poor half-witted creature they call Anna Chlannach. But did it never occur to ye to ask how she came to lose her reason? Ay, but if ye had asked, they would not have told ye; there's not one o' them about here but would lie through thick and thin to screen that scapegrace; and what then would be the use o' your asking? But I can tell ye; and I say it's my bounden duty to speak, if there's none else here to warn ye. And there is my witness—there is the living witness to that scoundrel's licentiousness and wicked cruelty: go to her—ask herself—ask her what makes her wander about the shore watching for him, looking out to Heimra, as if the ill he has done her could now be repaired. The poor lass, betrayed, deserted: no wonder she lost her reason—ay, and it's a good thing the currents along this coast are strong, or I'm thinking there might have been a trial for infanticide as well——"

Mary heard no more: she did not know that he was still talking to her; she did not know that he accompanied her almost to the house, where he left her. For—after the first fierce and indignant denial that involuntarily rushed to her mind—what she saw before her burning eyes was a series of visions, each of them of the most terrible distinctness, and all of them related in some ghastly way to this story she had just been told. What were these things then that seemed to sear her very eye-balls? She saw the little harbour of Camus Bheag; she saw the figure of a young girl rocking herself in an utter abandonment of misery and despair; she saw piteous hands held out; she heard that heart-broken wail piercing the silence as the boat made slowly away for Eilean Heimra. And then again she was on the heights above the Garra, and looking down upon the bridge. Those two there?—she had taken them for lovers—she had called Käthchen's attention—it was a pretty scene. Then the sudden, swift disappearance of the girl into the woods; and the young man's easy, confident professions: all those things grew manifest before her with an appalling clearness; a blinding light burned upon them. Nay, her very first interview with Anna Chlannach came back to startle her: she remembered the poor demented girl wandering among the rocks, all her intelligible talk being about Heimra: she remembered her being easily persuaded to walk towards the house; she remembered, too, how Anna Chlannach fled in terror the moment she came in sight of the stranger who knew her history. What hideous tale was it that seemed to summon up these scenes, appealing to them for corroboration? What was it they seemed to say was true—true as if written up before her in letters of fire?

There was no time for her to reason or think. For here, as it chanced, was this very man—this Donald Ross— coming down the wide steps from her own door. And all her soul was in revolt. Her wounded pride—her sense of humiliation—scorched her like flame. How had this man dared to lift his eyes to her? Unabashed he had come into the same room with her—he had breathed the same air—he had touched her hand—a contamination that was a poisoned sting. And the people of Lochgarra, who had seen him and her walking together: were they cognisant of his low amours? They had wagged their heads, perhaps? They had looked the one to the other?

"I half-expected to meet you," said Donald Ross.

There was no answer. But Mary Stanley did not lower her head, or avert her face; she was too proud for that; her heart might be beating as though it would burst its prison, but to all outward appearance she was quite unmoved. She passed him, pale and cold and silent; and he stood on one side looking at her, without a word. She went into the house; she took no notice of Käthchen, who was still in the hall; she made for her own room, and locked herself in there—voiceless, tearless, with all the fair fabric of her life, its aims, and dreams, and ideals, its still more secret and trembling hopes, become suddenly and at one blow a tragic desolation of wreckage and ruin.

CHAPTER XXIV.

"'TWAS WHEN THE SEAS WERE ROARING."

IT was early morning out at Heimra; the sky comparatively clear as yet, though there was a squally look about the flying rags of cloud; the sea obviously freshening up, and already springing white along the headlands. And here at the little landing-slip were Coinneach Breac and Calum, waiting by the side of the yacht's boat, and from time to time conversing in their native tongue.

"I am not liking the look of this morning," said Coinneach, "with the glass down near half-an-inch since last night. But if the master wishes me to go, then it is I who am ready to go, and I do not care where it is that I may be going. For who knows the anchorages better than himself, and the tides, and the currents, and the navigation?"

And then presently he said in a more sombre tone:

"There is something that I do not understand. Did you look at the master when he was coming away from the mainland last evening? There has a trouble fallen on him: mark my words, Calum; for you are a young man and not quick to see such things. And do you know what Martha was telling me when I went up to the house this morning?—she was telling me that the master was not coming near the house all the night through; and it is I myself that saw him coming slowly down the hill not more than half-an-hour ago. And if he was up by the white grave all the night through, that is not a good thing for a young man. A grave without a wall round it is not a good thing."

And then again he said:

"It is I who would like to know who brought the trouble on the young master; and last night, as I was lying in my bunk, thinking over this thing and that thing, and wondering what it was that had happened, I was remembering that the Little Red Dwarf came to Lochgarra yesterday—yes, and he the only stranger that came to Lochgarra yesterday."

"I wish the Little Red Dwarf were with his father the devil," said Calum, with calm content.

"And if I thought it was the Little Red Dwarf that was the cause of the master's trouble," said Coinneach, with his deep-set grey eyes full of a dark hatred, "do you know what I would do, Calum? I would put the *orra-an-donais* on him. That is what I would do, ay, this very night. This very night I would take two branches of hawthorn, and I would nail them as a cross, and at twelve o'clock I would put them against his door; and then I would say this: '*God's wrath to be set against thy face, whether thou art drowning at sea or burning on land; and a branch of hawthorn between thy heart and thy kidneys; and for thy soul the lowermost floor in hell, for ever and ever.*' He is a powerful man, the Little Red Dwarf, and he has wide shoulders; but how would he fare with the *orra-an-donais* on his wide shoulders?"

But Calum shook his head.

"No, no," said the long, loutish, good-humoured-looking

lad, "I do not think well of such things. They are dangerous things. They are like the bending of a stick; and who knows but that the stick may fly back and strike you? But this is what I have in my mind, Coinneach : if the master wishes, then I would just take the Little Red Dwarf and I would put him in a pool in the Garra, ay, and I would hold his head down until he was as dead as a rat. Aw, *Dyeea*, there would be no trouble with the Little Red Dwarf after that!"

"The master!" said Coinneach—and there was silence.

Young Donald appeared somewhat pale and tired; but otherwise did not seem out of spirits.

"Well, Coinneach," he said, cheerfully enough, as he came up—and he spoke in the tongue that was most familiar to them—"what do you think of taking the world for your pillow—as they say in the old stories; and would you set out at this very moment?"

"But with you, sir?" said Coinneach, quickly.

"Oh, yes, yes—in the *Sirène*."

"I am willing to go wherever Mr. Ross wishes, and at any time, and for any length of time—it is Mr. Ross himself knows that," Coinneach made answer.

"And you, Calum?"

"It is the same that I am saying," responded the younger lad, with downcast eyes.

"And where would you like to go, Coinneach, if you have all the world to choose from?" the young master asked.

"That is not for me to say—that is for Mr. Ross to say."

"And if you were never to see Eilean Heimra again?"

"That also to me is indifferent," said Coinneach, with dogged obedience.

Donald Ross stepped into the boat, and took his seat in the stern.

"Come away, then, lads; for if we are to set out on our travels, we must make a hasty start. Did you look at the glass this morning, Coinneach? And there is a thick bank of cloud rising in the west: we shall not want for wind, I'm thinking, when we get outside. And as for getting under way at a moment's notice, well, we can put in stores and everything else that is wanted when we are safe in Portree Harbour, with a little time to spare. For there is wild weather coming, Coinneach, if I am not mistaken; but anything is better than being storm-stayed at Heimra, when it is to the south you wish to be going."

And he himself helped the two men to get the vessel in readiness when they had got on board—ordering them, as a preliminary precaution, to take down a couple of reefs in the mainsail. For even here in this sheltered little bay, the omens were inauspicious; the sky had grown dark and the wind had risen; there was a low and troubled and continuous murmur from the out-jutting spur on the north.

"It is an angry-looking day to be leaving Heimra," young Ross said; "but perhaps there is no one wishing us to remain at Heimra; and you and I, Coinneach, have been companions before now. And if I am asking you to go away in a hurry, well, there will be time to get all we want at Portree."

"And what do I want," said Coinneach, "except tobacco? And it is not even that would hinder me from going wherever Mr. Ross wishes to be going."

The young master went aft to the tiller. As the yacht slowly crept forward he turned for a moment and glanced towards the island they were leaving.

"Poor old Martha," he said to himself; "I must try to find another place for her somewhere and get her away; it would be the breaking of her heart if she were to see strangers come to take possession of Eilean Heimra."

On Eilean Heimra he bestowed this single farewell glance; but on Lochgarra none. When they got outside into the heavily-running seas he did not turn once to look at the distant bay and its strip of cottages, nor yet at the promontory where the sharp gusts of the gale were already ploughing waves along the tops of the larchwoods surrounding Lochgarra House. The affected cheerfulness with which he had addressed the two sailors on setting forth was gone now; his face was pale and worn; the mouth stern; the eyes clouded and dark. But he had his hands full; for every moment the weather became more threatening.

"Calum," he called out, "go below and fetch me up

my oil-skins. We are going to catch something pretty soon."

And so—amid this wild turmoil of driven skies and black-rolling seas—the *Sirène* bore away for the south.

And meanwhile at yonder big building among the wind-swept larches? All the long and terrible night Mary Stanley had neither slept nor thought of sleeping; she had not even undressed; she had kept walking up and down her room in a fever of agitation; or she had sate at the table, her hands clasped over her forehead, striving to shut out from her memory that dire succession of scenes, those haunting visions that seemed to have been burned into her brain. And if they would not go?—then blindly and stubbornly would she refuse to admit that they lent any air of credibility to this tale that had been told her. Nay, she abased herself; and overwhelmed herself with re-proaches; and called herself the meanest of living creatures in that she could have believed, even for one frantic moment, that base and malignant fabrication. Why, had she not known all along of the deadly animosity that Purdie, for some reason or another, bore towards young Ross and all his family? Had she not herself discovered that previous charges against Donald Ross owned no foundation other than a rancorous and reckless spite? And she had taken the unsupported testimony of one who appeared to be out of his mind with malice and hatred against the man who was her lover, as he and she knew in their secret hearts? In one second of unreasoning impulse she had destroyed all those fair possibilities that lay within her grasp; she had ruined her life; and wounded to the quick the one that was dearest to her in all the world. And well she knew how proud and relentless he was: he had forgiven much, to her and hers; but this he would never forgive. It was more than an insult; it was a betrayal: what would he think of her, even if she could go to him, and make humble confession, and implore his pardon? How could she explain that instant of panic following her first indignant repudiation—then the hapless chance that brought him face to face with her—then the fierce revolt of a maiden soul against contamination— alas! all in a sudden bewilderment of error, that could

never be atoned for now. What must he think of her?—
she kept repeating to herself—of her, faithless, shameless,
who had spurned his loyal trust in her? If she went
and grovelled in the very dust before him, and stretched
out her hands towards him, he would turn away from her,
remorseless and implacable. She was not worthy of his
disdain.

And nevertheless, upbraid herself as she might, she
still beheld before her aching eyes those two figures on
the Garra bridge, followed by the swift disappearance of
the girl into the woods; and again she saw her down at
the shore, entreating to be taken out to Heimra Island,
and piercing the silence with her despair when she was left
behind. It was not Purdie who had shown her these
things; it was of her own knowledge she knew them; they
had started up before her, in corroboration of his im-
peachment, even as he spoke. But what if she were to
accept his challenge? What if she were to go to Anna
Chlannach herself? He had declared she was his witness
—his living witness. If there were any foundation for
this terrible story, she would confess the truth: if, as
Mary Stanley strove to convince herself, the charge was
nothing but a deliberate and malevolent invention, she
would be able to hurl the black falsehood back in his teeth.
He had challenged her to go to Anna Chlannach: to Anna
Chlannach she would go.

And then (as the blue-grey light of the dawn appeared
in the window-panes) a sense of her utter helplessness
came over her. That poor, half-witted creature knew no
word of English. And how was she to appeal to any
third person, asking for intervention? How could she
demean herself by repeating such a story, and by admitting
even the possibility of its being true? Nay more: might
not her motives be misconstrued? What would the third
person, the interpreter, think of these shamefaced inquiries?
That the mistress of Lochgarra House was moved by an
angry jealousy of that poor wandering waif? That Mary
Stanley and Anna Chlannach were in the position of rivals?
Her cheeks burned. Not in that way could she find the
means of hurling back Purdie's monstrous accusation.

The white daylight broadened over land and sea; and

away out yonder was Heimra Island, shining all the fairer because of the black and slow-moving wall of cloud along the western horizon.   What had happened since yesterday, then? She hardly knew : she knew only that her heart lay heavy within her bosom, and that despair instead of sleep seemed to weigh down her eyelids.   Was it only yesterday that she had been away up at Loch Heimra, imagining it once more a sheet of water, and pleasing herself with the fancy that some afternoon she would bring her lover along the road with her, to show him what she had done to make meek amends? Yesterday, when she thought of him, which was often enough, joy had filled her whole being, and kindness, and gratitude, and well-wishing to the universal world. Yesterday he and she were friends ; and to look forward to their next meeting was to her a secret delight which she could dwell upon, even in talking with strangers. But now—this new day : what had it brought her, that she was so numb, and cold, and hopeless ? And what was this that lay so heavy in her breast ?

Suddenly she sprang to her feet—her eyes staring. A boat was creeping out from the southernmost headland of Eilean Heimra. It was a small vessel with sails : it was the *Sirène*, she made sure. And was he coming ashore now—coming straight to Lochgarra House, as was his wont—coming, in open and manly fashion, to demand an explanation from her ? And even if he were to upbraid her, and shower anger and scorn upon her, what then ?— so long as he showed himself not wholly unforgiving, so long as he allowed her to speak. But as she stood at the window there, intently watching the distant ship, a shuddering suspicion seemed to paralyse her. The *Sirène* was not coming this way at all ; it was slowly, gradually, unmistakably making for the south. And no sooner had this fear become a certainty than the world appeared to swim around her. There was to be no explanation, then ?— not even that torrent of bitter and angry reproach ? He was going away—silent, stern, inexorable ? This was his answer ? He would not stoop to demand explanations : he would simply withdraw ? It was not fit that he should mate or match with such as she.

And at the same moment she caught sight of Big Archie, who was pulling out to his boat. In her terror, and despair, and helplessness, she did not think twice; her resolution was formed in a moment; she threw a shawl over her head and shoulders, and fled dowstairs, and out into the open. Quickly she made her way along the beach.

"Archie!" she called, in the teeth of the wind. "Archie! Archie! I want you!—come ashore, quick!"

The heavy-shouldered and heavy-bearded fisherman, who was still in the smaller boat, paused on his oars for a second; and then, probably understanding more from her gestures than from her words what she wished, he headed round and made for the beach. And before he had reached the land she had called to him again.

"Archie, that is the *Sirène*—going away from Heimra?"

"Yes, indeed, mem," said Archie.

"You must take me out in your lugger, Archie," she said, in a frenzied sort of way. "There's not a moment to be lost; even if you can't sail as quick as they can, never mind—we will get some distance after them—they will see us—we can signal to them——"

The bow of the small boat rose on the shingle and seaweed; Big Archie stepped out and pulled it up a bit further. He did not quite understand at first what was demanded of him; perhaps he was a trifle scared by the unusual look on Miss Stanley's face—the pallid cheeks, the piteous and anxious eyes; but when he did comprehend, his answer was a serious and earnest remonstrance.

"Aw, *Dyeea*, do you not see what it is threatening out there?" said he, quite concerned.

"I do not care about that," she answered him. "If the *Sirène* can go out, so can you. And you have the sail up, Archie!"

"Ay, ay, indeed," he explained, "bekass I was thinking of going round to Ru Gobhar, to hef a look at the lobster-traps. But when I was seeing the bad weather threatening, and the glass down, then I was just going out to the boat to get the sail lowered again and the young lad brought ashore. It is just anything I would do to please Miss Stanley; but it is looking very, very bad; and we could not catch up on the *Sirène* whatever—aw, no!—it is no

use to think my boat could get near to the *Sirène*, and her
a first-class yat and a fine sailer.   And Miss Stanley
getting very wet, too, for there's a heavy sea outside——"

"Archie," she said, in an imploring voice, "if you are a
friend of mine, you will try! You will try to stop the
Sirène—cannot we make some signal to her? And you
said the young lad was in the boat?—and the sail is up—
we could get away at once——"

"Oh, if you wish it, mem, that is enough for me," he
said ; and presently he had got her into the stern of the
small boat, had shoved off, and was pulling out to the
big, brown-sailed lugger.

Archie had moorings in the bay, so that they lost no
time in setting forth. And at first everything went well
enough ; for they had merely to beat out against the swirls
of wind that came into the sheltered harbour ; and the
water was comparatively smooth. But when they got into
the open they found a heavy sea running ; and the lugger
began to dip her bows and fling flying showers of spray
down to the stern ; while the bank of black cloud in the
west was slowly advancing, heralded by torn shreds of
silver that chased each other across the menacing sky.
Big Archie took off his jacket and offered it to Miss
Stanley, to shield her from the wet ; but she obstinately
refused, and bade him put it on again : her sole and whole
attention was fixed on the phantom-grey yacht down there
in the south, that was every other moment hidden from
view by the surging crests of the waves. She had to cling
to the gunwale, to prevent her being hurled from her seat ;
for the lugger was labouring sorely, and staggering under
these successive shocks ; but all the same her eyes, though
they smarted from the salt foam, were following the now
distant *Sirène* with a kind of wild entreaty in them, as
though she would fain have called across the waste of
waters.

"Can they see us, Archie?—can they see us?" she cried.
"Could not the boy climb up to the mast-head and wave
something?"

"Aw, no, mem," said Archie, "they are too far aweh.
They are far, too far aweh. And they are not knowing we
are looking towards them."

"But if we keep right on to Heimra?" said she, in her desperation. "Surely they will see we are making for the island—they will come back——"

"They would just think it was the Gillie Ciotach going out to look after the lobster-traps," said Archie.

"Not in this weather!" she urged. "Not in this weather! They must see it is something of importance. They will see the boat going out to Heimra—they are sure to come back. Archie —they are certain to come back!"

"We will hold on for Heimra if you wish it, mem—but there's a bad sea getting up," said Archie, with his eye on those tumultuous swift-running masses of water, the crashing into which caused even this heavy craft to quiver from stem to stern. By this time the heavens had still further darkened around them—a boding gloom, accompanied, as it was, by a fitful howling of wind; while rain was falling in torrents. Not that this latter mattered very much, for they were all of them drenched to the skin by the seas that were leaping high from the lugger's bows; only that the deluge thickened all the air, so that it became more and more difficult to catch a glimpse of the now fast-receding *Sirène*. Archie paid but little attention to the yacht; he seemed to have no hope of attracting her notice; but he was greatly distressed about the condition of the young mistress of Lochgarra.

"If I had known, mem—if I had known early in the moarning I would hef brought something to cover you," said he, in accents of deep commiseration. "It is a great peety——"

"Never mind about that, Archie," said she. "Don't you think they must know now that we are making for Heimra?"

"They are a long weh aweh," said Big Archie, shaking the salt water from his eyebrows and beard. "And they will be looking after themselves now. It was a stranche thing for Mr. Ross to put out with a storm coming on."

"Is there any danger, Archie?" she said, quickly. "Are they going into any danger?"

Archie was silent for a second.

"I am not knowing what would mek Mr. Ross start out on a moarning like this," said he. "And where he is going

I cannot seh. But he is one that knows the signs of the weather—aw, yes, mem!—and it is likely he will make in for Gairloch, or Loch Torridon, or mebbe he will get as far down as the back of Rona Island——

"No, no, Archie, he must see us—he cannot help seeing us!" she exclaimed. "When we are getting close to Heimra, then he cannot help seeing us—he will understand —and surely he will come back!"

And meanwhile the gale had been increasing in fury: the wind moaning low and whistling shrill alternately, the high-springing spray rattling down on the boat with a noise as of gravel. The old lugger groaned and strained and creaked—burying herself—shaking herself—reeling before the ponderous blows of the surge ; but Archie gave it her well ; there was no timorous shivering up into the wind. His two hands gripped the sheet—the tiller under his arm ; his feet were wedged firm against the stone ballast ; his mouth set hard ; his eyes clear enough in spite of the driving rain and whirling foam. And now this island of Heimra was drawing nearer—if the *Sirène* far away in the south had almost vanished.

"Look now, Archie!—look now, for I can see nothing," she said, piteously.

He raised himself somewhat ; and scanned the southern horizon, as well as the heaving and breaking billows would allow.

"Aw, no, mem, the *Sirène* is not in sight at ahl—not in sight at ahl now," he said.

She uttered a stifled little cry, as of despair.

"Archie," she said, "could you not follow down to Loch Torridon?"

"Aw, God bless us, mem, the boat would not live long in a sea like this—it is getting worse and worse every meenit——"

"Very well," said she, wearily, "very well. You have done what you could, Archie : now there is nothing but to get away back home again."

But that was not at all Big Archie's intention.

"Indeed no, mem," said he, with decision, "I am not going aweh back to Lochgarra, and you in such a state, mem, when there is a good shelter close by, ay, and a house. It is into Heimra Bay that I am going; and there is the house ; and Martha will hef your clothes dried for you, mem, and give you warm food and such things. And mebbe the gale will quiet down a little in the afternoon, or mebbe to-morrow it will quiet down, and we will get back to Lochgarra ; but it is not weather for an open boat at ahl."

She made no answer. She did not seem to care. She sate there with eyes fixed and haggard : perhaps it was not the cliffs of Heimra she saw before her, but the wild headlands of Wester Ross, and a lurid and thundering sea, and a small phantom-grey yacht flying for shelter. She appeared to take no notice as they rounded the stormy point with its furious boiling surge, and as they gradually left behind them that roaring waste of waves, escaping into the friendly quietude of the land-locked little bay. She was quite passive in Archie's hands—getting into the small boat listlessly when the lugger had been brought to anchor ; and when she stepped ashore she set out to walk up to the house, he respectfully following. But she had miscalculated her strength. For one thing, she had not tasted food since the middle of the previous day ; nor had she once closed her eyes during the night. Then she was dazed with the wind and the rain ; her clothes clung to her and chilled her to the bone ; the feverish anxiety of the morning had left her nerves all unstrung. Indeed, she could not drag herself up the beach. She went a few steps— hesitated—turned round as if seeking for help in a piteous sort of way—then she sank on to the rocks, and abandoned herself to a passion of grief and despair, from sheer weakness.

"I cannot go up to the house, Archie," she said, in a half-hysterical fashion, amid her choking sobs, "and—and why should I go—to an empty house? It—it is empty —you—you let the *Sirène* sail away—but—but never mind that—it is all my fault—more than you know. And I want you to leave me here, Archie—go away back to Lochgarra—there is no one cares what becomes of me— what does it matter to anyone ? I do nothing but harm —nothing but harm—there is no need to care what becomes of me——"

The huge, lumbering, good-hearted fisherman was in a sad plight; he knew not in the least what to do; he stood there irresolute, the deepest concern and sympathy in his eyes, himself unable or not daring to utter a word. But help was at hand. For here was Martha, hurrying along as fast as her aged limbs would allow, and bringing with her a great fur rug.

"Dear, dear me!" she exclaimed, as she came up. "What could mek Miss Stanley venture out o' the house on a day like this?'

And therewith she put the rug round the girl's shoulders, and got her to her feet, and, with many encouragements and consolatory phrases, assisted her on her way up from the shore.

"I will get a nice warm bed ready for you at once, mem," said the old dame, "with plenty of blankets; and I will bring you something hot and comfortable for you, for you hef got ferry, ferry wet. Dear, dear me!—but we'll soon hef you made all right; for Mr. Ross would be an angry man, ay, indeed, if he was hearing that Miss . Stanley had come to Heimra, and not everything done for her that could be done."

But when, after struggling through the blinding rain, they reached the porch, and when Martha had opened the front-door, Miss Stanley did not go further than the hall: she sank exhausted into the solitary chair there.

"Martha," she said, "do not trouble about me. I want to ask you a question. Did Mr. Ross say where he was going when he left in the *Sirène* this morning?"

"No, mem—not a word," Martha answered her, "about where he was going, or when he was coming back. It was a strange way of leaving—and in the face of such weather; but young people they hef odd fancies come in their head. Think of this, mem, that he never was near the house last night; he was aweh up the hill; and I'm feared that he was saying good-bye to his mother's grave, and that it will be long ere we see him back in Heimra again. For he is a strange young man—and not like others. But you'll come aweh now, mem, and get off your wet things: it is Mr. Ross himself would be terrible angry if you were not well cared for in this house."

The day without was sombre and dark; and the light entering here was wan: perhaps that was the cause of the singular alteration in Mary Stanley's appearance. She— who had hitherto been always and ever the very embodiment of buoyant youth, and health, and high spirits—. now looked old. And her eyes were as if night had fallen upon them.

CHAPTER XXV.

A MISSION.

ALL that day the gale did not abate in fury; nor yet on the next; and even on the third day Gilleasbuig Mòr still hesitated about trying to get back to Lochgarra, for the sea was running high, and the wind blew in angry gusts and squalls. But on the morning of this third day communication with the mainland was resumed; for shortly after eleven o'clock a lug-sail boat made its appearance, coming round the point into the little bay; and at a glance Archie knew who this must be—this could be no other than that venturesome dare devil the Gillie Ciotach, who had doubtless been sent out by Miss Glendinning to gain tidings of her friend. Big Archie went down to the slip, to await the boat's arrival.

And when the Gillie Ciotach, whose sole companion was a little, old, white-headed man called Dugald MacIsaac, came ashore he was in a triumphant mood over his exploit, and had nothing but taunts and jeers for the storm-stayed Archie.

"Aw, God," said he (in Gaelic) as he fetched out the parcels that had come by the mail for Martha, "there is nothing makes me laugh so much as a Tarbert man when there is a little breeze of wind anywhere. A Tarbert man will hide behind a barn-door; and if a rat squeaks, his heart is in his mouth. For what is Loch Fyne? Loch Fyne is only a ditch. A Tarbert man does not learn anything of the sea; he runs away behind a door if there is a puff of wind blowing anywhere. And have you taken possession of Heimra, Archie? Are you going to stay here for ever? Are you never going back to Lochgarra?"

" Andrew," said Big Archie, quite good-naturedly, " you are a clever lad ; but maybe you do not know what the wise man of Mull said : he said : ' *The proper time is better than too soon.*' "

" Too soon ? And is it too soon, then, for me to come over ? " said the young man of the slashed forehead and the bold eye.

" You ! " said Big Archie. " But who is mindful of you or what becomes of you ? When I go over to Lochgarra, it is a valuable cargo I will have with me. That is what makes me mindful. You ?—who cares whether you and your packages of tea go to the bottom ? "

But the Gillie Ciotach was so elate over this achievement of his that, instead of bandying further words, he stood up to Big Archie, and began to spar, dancing from side to side, and aiming cuffs at him with his open hand. The huge, good-humoured giant bore this for a while, merely trying to ward off these playful blows ; but at last—the Gillie Ciotach unwarily offering an opportunity—Archie suddenly seized him by the breeches and the scruff of the neck, and by a tremendous effort of strength heaved him off the slip altogether—heaved him into a bed of seaweed and sand.

The Gillie Ciotach picked himself up slowly, and slowly and deliberately he took off his jacket. His brows were frowning.

" We will just settle this thing now, Archie," said he, stepping up on to the slip again. " We will see who is the better man, you or I. You can catch a quick grip— oh yes, and you have strength in your arms ; but maybe in an honest fight you will not do so well——"

" Oh, be peaceable !—be peaceable ! " said Big Archie. " If you want fighting, go and seek out some of the Minard lads—though that would be carrying timber to Lochaber, as the saying is."

" Andrew, my son," said the little old man in the boat, " there is the Baintighearna come to the door."

The Gillie Ciotach glanced towards the porch of the cottage ; and there, sure enough, was Miss Stanley—and also Martha.

" It is the luck of Friday that is on me," he said, with a

laugh; "for I am the one that was to stop all the fighting! Well, come away up to the house, Archie; you are a friendly man; and if she asks why I was taking off my jacket, you will swear to her that I was only searching for my pipe. For a lie is good enough for women at any time."

They got up to the house, and the Gillie Ciotach delivered his parcels, and the newspapers, and one or two letters, and said that Miss Glendinning had sent him over to take back assurances of their safety.

"But I was telling the lady there was no chance of harm," said he; "for we saw Miss Stanley go on board, and we saw Archie's lugger standing in for Heimra, and every one knew there would be good shelter from the storm——"

"And the *Sirène*, Andrew—have you heard anything of the *Sirène*?" Mary asked quickly—and her eyes were alert and anxious, if the rest of her features looked tired and worn.

"Aw, the *Sirène*, mem?" said the Gillie Ciotach, confidently. "I am sure the *Sirène* is just as safe as any of us. There's no harm coming to the *Sirène*, mem, as long as Mr. Ross himself is on board. It's the God's truth I'm telling ye, mem. Mr. Ross he would put in to Loch Broom or Loch Ewe; and he knows every anchorage to half a fathom; and, with plenty of chain out, and an anchor-watch, where would the harm be coming to him?"

"You have no doubt of it, Andrew?"

"It's as sure as death, mem!" said the Gillie Ciotach, with an almost angry vehemence.

She seemed a little relieved.

"And the sea outside, Andrew—is it very bad?"

"It's a bit wild," he admitted; and then he added, with a cool audacity: "but mebbe Miss Stanley would be for going back with me now, if Archie is too afraid to go out?"

"Oh, no, thank you," said she. "If Archie does not think it safe, I should not think of venturing. I will wait for him—thank you all the same."

Here there was an awkward pause. Mary left the little group, walking over to the edge of the plateau, to get a better view of the distant and troubled line of the sea. The Gillie Ciotach stood twirling his Glengarry bonnet. Then he said timidly to Martha—

" Are there any empty casks going back ? "

"None but yourself, Andrew, my lad," said Martha, with a dark smile in her eyes.

At this he plucked up spirit.

"There's a way of curing that, as you know, Martha," said he. " And it's many's the time I have come out to Heimra, and I never before had to complain of going away like an empty cask."

"And you need not complain of it now, Andrew, my son," said Martha. " Come away round to the kitchen, and I will get you something—ay, and you will take something down to old Dugald, too. For although the master of the house is not in his own home, I know his wish ; and it is I who would get the blame if any one went away hungry or cold from Eilean Heimra."

But it was not until the afternoon that Big Archie considered it prudent to cross to the mainland ; and a rough passage they had of it. Mary, however, was on this occasion provided with an abundance of wraps ; and was indifferent to wind, and spray, and rain. Possibly there may have been other reasons for her apathy.

Kate Glendinning was down at the slip beside the quay.

" Mamie," she exclaimed, when her friend landed, " what took you out to Heimra on that wild morning ? I could not believe it when I was told. And I sent over to know you were safe as soon as I could get any one to go. What is the meaning of all ? If you had seen the people watching the boat !—they did not know what might happen."

" I cannot explain ; and you must not ask, Käthchen, now or at any time," was her answer. " But tell me, has the gale done much damage ? The harvest was looking so well in those little patches——"

" Damage ? " said Käthchen. " It isn't damage, Mamie , it is destruction—devastation—everywhere. Oh, it is pitiable. The corn beaten down—the crofts flooded—well, well, the only thing to be said is that the poor people are not so disheartened as you might expect. Perhaps they are used to such bitter disappointments. I do believe this place is fit only for sheep—and hardly fit for them."

"What can I do, Käthchen," said Mary, with a curious listlessness, "beyond lowering their rent again? I suppose that is all I can do. They would not go to Manitoba with me: would they, Käthchen? Do you think they would? Would you, now?"

"Manitoba?" repeated Käthchen, looking at her. "What has happened, Mamie? I don't understand the way you speak. Why should you talk about Manitoba, when you were so set against it?"

"The climate appears to be so uncertain here," she said, rather wearily, as they were ascending the steps of Lochgarra House; "and—and the people have of late been more friendly towards me; and I would like to do what I could for them. There is nothing to keep me in this country. I would go away willingly with them—to Canada, or anywhere. But perhaps not you, Käthchen. I could not expect you. All your interests are in this country— or in England, at least. But if I were to sell Lochgarra, I could get money to take them all away to Canada, and buy good land for them, and see them comfortably established; and then I should have done my duty by them, as I intended to do when I came here at first. And—and I don't think I should care to come back."

She furtively wiped away the tears from her lashes: Käthchen did not notice. They were passing through the hall now.

"I cannot understand what you mean, Mamie. What is it? What has happened? Did you see Mr. Ross when you were at Heimra? I heard that the *Sirène* had left the morning you went out—and I took it for granted that Mr. Ross had gone with her——"

"Käthchen, to please me," she said, beseechingly, "will you never mention Heimra again? Mr. Ross is away—and— and I have been to the island for the last time; that is all."

When they went into the room, she threw herself down on a couch, and put her clasped hands on the arm of it, and hid her face. She was not crying; she merely seemed overcome with fatigue and lassitude. Kate Glendinning knelt down beside her, and with gentle fingers caressingly stroked and smoothed the beautiful golden-brown hair that had been all dishevelled by the wind.

" What is it, Mamie ? "

"Tell me about the farms, Käthchen," was the answer, uttered in a hopeless kind of way. " I don't know anything about farm work, except what I have been told since I came here. Are the crops so completely destroyed ? Would not fine weather give them another chance ? Surely entire ruin cannot have been caused by one gale—gales are frequent on this coast——"

"This one came at a bad time, Mamie," said her companion; " and a great part of the corn will have to be cut and given to the cows. But why should you distress yourself unnecessarily ? It was none of your fault. You have done everything for these poor people that could be devised. And, as I tell you, they seem used to misfortunes of this kind ; there is no bewailing ; their despondency has become a sort of habit with them——"

" Send for Mr. Purdie : I wish to see him "—this was what came from those closed hands. But the next moment she had thrown herself upright. " No ! " she said fiercely. " No, I will not see Mr. Purdie. With my consent, Mr. Purdie shall never enter this house again."

"Mr. Purdie left on the very day you went out to Heimra," said Käthchen, gently ; and then she went on : "You are hiding something from me, Mamie. Well, I will not ask any further. I will wait. But I am afraid you are very much fatigued, and upset, and I can see you are not well. Now will you be persuaded, Mamie ! If you will only go to bed you will have a far more thorough rest ; and I will bring you something that will make you sleep. Why, your forehead is burning hot, and your hands quite cold !—and if you were to get seriously ill, that would be a good deal worse for the crofters than the flattening down of their corn ! "

She was amenable enough ; she consented to be led away ; she was ready to do anything asked of her—except to touch food or drink.

And yet the next morning she was up and out of the house before anyone was awake, and she was making away for the solitude of the hills. She wished to be alone —and to look at the wide sea. She walked slowly, but yet her sick heart was resolute ; the arduous toil of getting up the lower slopes and corries, filled with bracken, and rocks, and heather, did not hinder her; she turned from time to time to look, absently enough, at the ever-broadening plain of the Atlantic, rising up to the pale greenish-turquoise of the sky. And in time she had got over this rough ground, and had reached the lofty and sterile plateaus of peat-bog and grass, where, if it was loneliness she sought she found it. No sign of life: no sound, except the plaintive call of a greenshank from a melancholy tarn: no movement, save that of the silver-grey masses of cloud that came over from the west. But away out yonder was the deserted island of Heimra; and far in the south were the long black promontories—Ru-Minard, Ru-Gobhar, and the rest—behind which a boat would disappear when it left for other lands. And had she heard of the Fhir-a-Bhàta? Did Kate Glendinning know of the song that is the most familiar, the greatest favourite of all the West Highland songs; and had she told her friend of the maiden who used to go up the cliffs, day by day, to watch for the coming of her lover?—

> 'I climb the mountain and scan the ocean,
> For thee, my boatman, with fond devotion:
> When shall I see thee?—to-day?—to-morrow?
> Oh, do not leave me in lonely sorrow!
>
> Broken-hearted I droop and languish,
> And frequent tears show my bosom's anguish:
> Shall I expect thee to-night to cheer me?
> Or close the door, sighing and weary.'

This, at least, Kate Glendinning soon began to learn —that nearly every morning now Mary left the house, entirely by herself, and was away by herself, in these desolate altitudes. It was clear she wished for no companionship; and Käthchen did not offer her services. Nor was any reference made to these solitary expeditions. The rest of the day Mary devoted herself to her usual work—increased, at this time, by her investigations into the extent of the injury done by the gale: as to the rest there was silence.

And thus it was that Käthchen remained ignorant of this curious fact—that day by day these excursions were gradually being shortened. Day by day Mary Stanley found that her strength would not carry her quite so far : she had to be content with a lesser height. And at last she had altogether to abandon that laborious task of breasting the hill ; she merely, and wearily enough, walked away up the Minard road—whence you can see a portion of the southern and western horizon ; and there she would sit down on the heather or a boulder of rock—with a strange look in her eyes.

"Mamie ! " said Käthchen, one evening—and there was grief in her voice. "Won't you tell me what has happened ! I cannot bear to see you like that ! You are ill. I tell you, you are seriously ill ; and yet you will not say a word. And there is no one here but myself ; I am in charge of you ; I am responsible for you ; and how can I bear to see you killing yourself before my eyes ? "

Mary was lying on the couch, her face averted from the light.

"You are right in one way, Käthchen," she said, rather sadly. "Something has happened. But no good would come of speaking about it ; because it cannot be undone now. And as for being ill, I know what will make me well. It is only sleep I want. It is the sleep that knows no waking that I wish for."

Käthchen burst out crying, and flung herself down on her knees, and put her arms round her friend.

"Mamie, I declare to you I will not rest until you tell me what this is ! " she exclaimed passionately.

Nor did she. And that very evening, after an unheard-of pleading and coaxing on the one side and despairing protest on the other, all those recent occurrences were confided to the faithful Käthchen. She was a little bewildered at first ; but she had a nimble brain.

"Mamie," she said, with a firm air, "I don't know what doubts, or if any, may still be lingering in your mind ; but I am absolutely convinced that that story of Purdie's is a lie—a wicked and abominable lie. And I can guess what drove him to it ; it was a bold stroke, and it was nearly proving successful ; but it shall not prove successful. I will make it my business to get Donald Ross back to Lochgarra—and then we shall have an explanation."

"Do you think he will come back to Lochgarra? Then you do not know him," Mary made answer, and almost listlessly. "Do you imagine I have not considered everything, night after night, ay, and every hour of the night all the way through? He will never come back to Lochgarra—if it is to speak to me that you mean. I have told you before: it seems a fatality that he and his should receive nothing but injury and insult at our hands, from one member of our family after another; and never has there been a word in reply—never a single syllable of reproach—but only kindnesses innumerable, and thoughtfulness, and respect. Well, there is an end of respect now. How can he have anything but scorn of me? If I were to confess to him that I had believed that story—even for one frightened moment—what could he think of me? Why, what he thinks of me now—as a base creature, ignoble, ungrateful, unworthy—oh! do you imagine I cannot read what is in that man's heart at this moment?"

"Do you imagine I cannot?" said Käthchen, boldly. "I have not been blind all these months. What is in that man's heart, Mamie, is a passionate love and devotion towards you; and there is no injury, and no insult, he would not forgive you if he thought that you—that you —well, that you cared for him a little. Oh, I know both you and him. I know that you are wilful and impulsive; and I know that he is proud, and sensitive, and reserved; but I think—I think—well, Mamie, no more words; but I am going to have my own way in this matter, and you must let me do precisely what I please."

And that was all she would say meanwhile. But next day was a busy day for Kate Glendinning. First of all she went straight to the Minister and demanded point-blank whether there were, or could be, any foundation for that story about Anna Chlannach; and the Minister—not directly, of course, but with many lamentations, in his high falsetto, over the wickedness of the human mind in harbouring and uttering slanders and calumnies—answered that he had known Anna Chlannach all her life, and that she had been half-witted from her infancy, and that the tale now told him was an entire and deplorable fabrication. Indeed, he would have liked to enlarge on the theme, but Kate was in a hurry. For she had heard in passing through the village that the Gillie Ciotach was about to go over to Heimra, with the parcels and letters that had come by the previous day's mail ; and it occurred to her that here was a happy chance for herself.

"Now, Andrew," she said, when she was seated comfortably in the stern of the lugger, "keep everything smooth for me. I haven't once been sea-sick since I came to Lochgarra, and I don't want to begin now."

"Aw, is it the sea-seeckness ? " said the Gillie Ciotach. "Well mem, when you feel the seeckness coming on, just you tell me, and I will give you something to mek you all right. Ay, I will give you a good strong glass of whiskey ; and in a moment it will make the seeckness jump out of your body."

"Whiskey ? " said Käthchen. "Do you mean to say you take a bottle of whiskey with you every time you put out in a boat ? "

"Aw, as for that " said the Gillie Ciotach—and he was clearly casting about for some portentous lie or another— "I was saying to Peter Grant that mebbe the young leddy might have the sea-seeckness ; and Peter he was saying to me, ' Tek a smahl bottle of whiskey with you, Andrew, and then she will hef no fear of the sea-seeckness.' And it was just for yourself, mem, I was bringing the whiskey."

"And a pretty character you seem to have given me at the inn ! " said Käthchen, as she contentedly wrapped herself up in her rugs.

Martha had seen the boat on its way into the harbour ; she had come out to the door of the cottage ; a visitor was welcome in this solitary island.

"Martha," she said, as soon as she had got within, "have you heard any news of late ?—can you tell me where the *Sirène* is now ? "

"Yes, indeed, mem," said the old Highland dame with wondering eyes. "But do you not know that the *Sirène* is at the bottom of the sea ? Was the master not writing to Miss Stanley about it ? "

"We have not heard a word," Käthchen exclaimed.

"Dear, dear me now ! " said Martha. "That is a stranche thing."

"But tell me—tell me about it," said Käthchen anxiously. "There was no one drowned?"

"No, no," said Martha, with much complacency. "There was plenty of time for them to get into the boat. And the master not writing to Miss Stanley at the same time he was writing to me—that is a stranche thing. But this was the weh of it, as he says; that it was an ahfu' dark night, the night of the first day of the gale; and they were mekkin for shelter between Scalpa and Skye, and they had got through the Caol-Mòr, and were coming near to an anchorage, when they ran into a trading schooner that was lying there without a single light up. Without a single light, and the night fearful dark: I'm sure the men should be hanged that would do such a thing to save a little oil."

"And where is Mr. Ross, now?" asked Käthchen.

"Just in Greenock. He says he will try to get a place for Coinneach and for Calum, and will not trouble with a yat any more for the present. Ay, indeed," Martha went on, with a bit of a sigh, "and I'm thinking he will not be coming back soon to Heimra, when he says he will not trouble with a yat, and when he could have a yat easy enough with the insurance money——"

"Is he at a hotel in Greenock?"

"Ay, the Tontine Hotel," the old woman said. "And I am not liking what he says—that he is waiting for a friend, and they are going away from Greenock together. I am not liking that at ahl. There's many a one sailed away from the Tail of the Bank that never came back again. And he says, if it is too lonely here for me and the young lass Maggie, we are to go over to Lochgarra and get lodgings; but how could I be leaving the house to the rain and the damp? Ay, lonely it is, except when Gillie Ciotach comes out to look after the lobster traps——"

"Well, Martha," said her visitor, "this time the Gillie Ciotach is going straight back again; for I'm rather in a hurry. And don't you move over to the mainland until you hear further. I will come and see you sometimes if you are so lonely." And therewithal the industrious Kate hied her back to the lobster boat, and set out for Lochgarra again.

Mary was lying on a sofa, her head half hidden by the

cushion. She had been attempting to read; but her arm had fallen supinely by her side, and the book was half closed.

"Mamie," said Kate Glendinning, entering the room noiselessly, and approaching the sofa, "I have a favour to beg of you; but please to remember this; that I have waited on you—and worried you—all this long time; and I have never asked you for an hour's holiday. Now I am going to ask you for two or three days; and if you give me permission I mean to be off by the mail-car to-morrow morning. May I go?"

The pale cheek flushed—and the fingers that held the book trembled a little. But she affected not to understand.

"Do as you wish, Käthchen," said she, in a low voice.

Well, this was an onerous, and difficult, and delicate task that Kate had undertaken; but she had plenty of courage. And her setting-forth was auspicious: when the mail-car started away from Lochgarra the dawn was giving every promise of a pleasant and cheerful day for the long drive. It is true that as they passed the Cruagan crofts her face fell a little on noticing here and there traces of the devastation that had been wrought by the gale; but she had heard that things were mending a little in consequence of the continued fine weather; and she was greatly cheered to hear the driver maintain that the people about this neighbourhood had little cause to grumble; matters had been made very easy for them, he declared, since Miss Stanley came to Lochgarra. And so on they drove, hour after hour, by Lednore, and Oykel Bridge, and Invercassley, and Rosehall, until the afternoon saw her safely arrived at Lairg. Then the more tedious railway journey—away down to Inverness; on through the night to Perth; breakfast there, and on again to Glasgow; from Glasgow down to Greenock. It was about noon, or something thereafter, that she entered the dismal and rainy town.

Fortune favoured her. The Tontine Hotel is almost opposite the railway station, so that she had no difficulty in finding it; and hardly had she got within the doorway when she met Donald Ross himself crossing the hall, and apparently on his way into the street. When he made out

who this was (her face was in shadow, and he did not at
first recognise her) his eyes looked startled, and he threw
an involuntary glance towards the door to see if there was
any one accompanying her.   But the girl was alone.

"Mr. Ross," said Käthchen, rather nervously—for she
had not expected to encounter him just at once—"I wish
to speak with you——"

"Oh, come in here, then," said he, with a certain coldness
of manner, as if he were about to face an unpleasant
ordeal that was also useless ; and he led the way into the
coffee-room, where, at this time of the day, there was no
one, not even a waiter.

Nervous Käthchen distinctly was ; for she knew the
terrible responsibility that lay on her ; and all the fine
calmness she had been calculating on in her communings
with herself in lonely railway-carriages seemed now to
have fled.   But perhaps it was just as well ; for in a somewhat incoherent, but earnest, fashion, she plunged right
into the middle of things, and told him the whole story—
told him of the factor's circumstantial and malignant
slander, of Mary's momentary bewilderment, of the luckless
meeting, and of her subsequent bitter remorse and despair.
At one portion of this narrative his face grew dark, and
the black eyes burned with a sullen fire.

"I have a long account to settle with Purdie," said he,
as if to himself, "and it is about time the reckoning was
come."

But when she had quite finished with her eager explanations, and excuses, and indirect appeals, what was his reply?
Why, not one word.   She looked at him—in blank dismay.

"But, Mr. Ross !—Mr. Ross !——" she said piteously.

There was no response ; he had received her communication—that was all.

"I have told you everything ; surely you understand ;
what—what message am I to take ? " Käthchen exclaimed,
in trembling appeal.

"I have heard what you had to say," he answered her,
with a studied reserve that seemed to Käthchen's anxious
soul nothing less than brutal, "and of course I am sorry
if there has been any misunderstanding, or any suffering,
anywhere.   But these things are past.   And as for the

present, I do not gather that you have been commissioned by Miss Stanley to bring one solitary word to me—one expression of any kind whatsoever. Why should I return any reply?—she has not spoken one word."

"Oh, you ask too much!" Käthchen exclaimed, in hot indignation. "You ask too much! Do you think Mary Stanley would send for you? She is as proud as yourself—every bit as proud! And she is a woman. You are a man: it is your place to have the courage of yielding—to have the courage of offering forgiveness, even before it is asked. If I were a man, and if I loved a woman that I thought loved me, I would not stand too much on my dignity, even if she did not speak. And what do you want—that she should say she is sorry? Mr. Ross, she is ill! I tell you, she is ill. Come and judge for yourself what all this has done to her!—you will see only too clearly whether she has been sorry or not. And that superstition of hers, about there being a fatality attending her family—that they cannot help inflicting injury and insult on you and yours—who can remove that but yourself? No," she said, a little stiffly, "I have no message from Mary Stanley to you; and if I had, I would not deliver it. And now it is for you to say or do what you think best."

"Yes, yes; yes, yes," he said, after a moment's deliberation. "I was thinking too much of the Little Red Dwarf; I was thinking too much of that side of it. I will go back to Lochgarra, and at once. And this is Thursday; the steamer will be coming down from Glasgow to-day; that will be the easiest way for us to go back."

There was a flash of joy and triumph—and of gratitude—in Käthchen's sufficiently pretty eyes.

CHAPTER XXVI.

THE BANABHARD.

THE big steamer was slowly and cautiously making in for Lochgarra Bay—slowly and cautiously, for though the harbour is an excellent one after you are in it, the entrance is somewhat difficult of navigation; and Donald Ross and

Kate Glendinning were seated in the after part of the boat, passing the time in talking. And of course it was mostly of Miss Stanley they spoke.

"For one thing, you ought to remember," said Käthchen, "the amount of prejudice against you she has had to overcome. If you only knew the character she received of you the very first evening we arrived here! I wonder if you would recognise the picture—a terrible outlaw living in a lonely island, a drunken, thieving, poaching ne'er-do-well, a malignant conspirator and mischief-maker: Mr. Purdie laid on the colours pretty thickly. By the way, I wish you would tell me the cause of that bitter animosity Mr. Purdie shows against you and all your family——"

"It is simple enough—but it is not worth speaking about," he said, with a certain indifference. It was not of Purdie, nor of Purdie's doings, that he was thinking at the moment.

"But I want to know—I am curious to know," Käthchen insisted.

"It is simple enough, then," he repeated. "When the old factor died—old MacInnes—I hardly remember him, but I fancy he was a decent sort of man—when he died, my father appointed this Purdie, on the recommendation of a friend, and without knowing much about him. Well, Purdie never did get on at all with the people about here. He was an ill-tempered, ill-conditioned brute, to begin with; spiteful, revengeful, and merciless; and of course the people hated him, and of course he came to know it, and had it out with them whenever he got the chance. You see, my father was almost constantly abroad and Purdie had complete control. My mother tried to interfere a little; and he resented her interference; I think it made him all the more savage. And at last the discontent of the people broke out in open revolt. Purdie happened to have come over to Lochgarra; and when they heard of it, the whole lot of them—from Minard, and Cruagan, and everywhere—came together in front of the inn, and there was no end of howling and hooting. Purdie escaped through the back-garden, and took refuge with the Minister; but the crowd followed him to the Minister's cottage, and burnt his effigy in front of the door—oh, I don't know what they didn't do. Only, it got into the papers; it was a public scandal; and my father, coming to hear of it, at once deposed the two-penny-halfpenny tyrant. That is all the story. But no doubt his being ignominiously dismissed was a sore thing for a man of his nature—the public humiliation, and all the rest of it——"

"But how did he get back to his former position?" Käthchen demanded.

"Miss Stanley's uncle put him back when he bought the estate," Donald Ross said, quietly. "I fancy he had an idea that Purdie was the right kind of man for this place, especially as he himself had to be absent a good deal. Yes, I will say this for Purdie—he is an excellent man of business; he will squeeze out for you every penny of rent that is to be got at; and he has no sort of hesitation about calling in the aid of the sheriff. And of course he came back more malevolent than ever; he knew they had rejoiced over his downfall; and he was determined to make them smart for it. As for his honouring me with his hatred, that is quite natural I suppose. It was my father who sent him into disgrace; and then—then the people about here and I are rather friendly, you know; and they had a great regard for my mother; and all that taken together is enough for Purdie. We were in league with his enemies; and they with us."

"I can imagine what he thought," said Käthchen, meditatively, "when he saw the new proprietress taking you into her counsels, and adopting a new system, and interfering with him, overriding his decisions at every turn. He made a bold stroke to sever that alliance between her and you; but it failed; and now he is sorry—very sorry—exceedingly sorry, I should think."

"What do you mean?" he asked, fixing his eyes upon her.

"Perhaps I should leave Mary herself to tell you," she answered him. "But that is of little consequence; it cannot be a secret. Very well: she has ordered Mr. Purdie to prepare a statement of his accounts; and his factorship ceases at Michaelmas. It was the last thing she told me before I left Lochgarra."

Donald Ross laughed.

"I had intended to have a word with Purdie," said he, "but it seems the Baintighearna has been before me."

The arrival of the steamer is always a great event at Lochgarra; there were several well-known faces on the quay. Here were the Gillie Ciotach, and Big Archie, and the Minister, and Peter Grant, the innkeeper; and here also was Anna Chlannach. The poor lass was in sad distress; she was crying and wringing her hands.

"What is the matter, Anna?" said Donald Ross, in Gaelic, as he stepped from the gangway on to the pier.

"I am wishing to go out to Heimra," said the Irish-looking girl with the dishevelled hair and streaming eyes.

"Why so?" he asked.

"It is to find my mother," she made answer, with many sobs. "When I was sleeping my mother came to me, and said I was to come out to Heimra for her, and to brink her back, but when I offer the money to the men they laugh at me—— "

"Anna," said he, gently, "you must not think of going out to Heimra. If you were not to find your mother there, that would be great sorrow for you. If she is coming for you, you must wait patiently—— "

"But I am going out in the steamer?" said the girl, beginning to cry afresh.

"The steamer?" he said. "The steamer does not call at Heimra, not at any time."

"But it is Mr. Ross has the mastery," * she pleaded. "It is every one that must obey Mr. Ross; and the steamer will take me out to Heimra if he tells the captain."

"Now, Anna," he said, trying to reason with her, "listen to what I am telling you. How can a great boat like that go into the small harbour of Eilean Heimra? And I have no authority over the captain, nor has any one: it is to Stornoway he is going now, and to no other place. So you must wait patiently; and I think you should go and live with the Widow MacVean, and help to do little things about the croft. For it is not good for a young lass to be without an occupation."

Anna Chlannach turned away weeping silently, and

---

* *Tighearnas*—lordship, or dominion.

refusing to be comforted ; while young Ross was immediately tackled by the Minister who had a long tale to tell about some Presbytery case in Edinburgh.

What now occurred it is difficult to describe consecutively, for so many things seemed to happen at once, or within the space of a few breathless seconds. The captain had discharged his cargo (Kate Glendinning and Donald Ross, with their bodyguard of Coinneach and Calum, were the only passengers), and was getting under weigh again ; and to do this the more easily he had signalled down to have the engines reversed, while keeping the stern hawser on its stanchion on the pier, so that the bow of the boat should gradually slew round. It was to the man who was in charge of this massive rope that Anna Chlannach, seeing the steamer was beginning to move, addressed her final and frantic appeal—nay, she even seized him by the arm, and implored him, with loud lamentations, to let her go on the boat. The man, intently watching the captain on the bridge, tried to shake her off ; grew more and more impatient of her importunity ; at last he said savagely—

"To the devil with you and your mother !—I tell you your mother is dead and buried these three years ! "

At this Anna Chlannach uttered a piercing shriek—she seemed to reel under the blow, in a wild horror—then, with her hands raised high above her head, she rushed to the end of the quay, and threw herself over, right under the stern-post of the steamer. Donald Ross, startled by that despairing cry, wheeled round just in time to see her disappear ; and in a moment he was after her, heedless of the fact that the steamer was still backing, the powerful screw churning up the green water into seething and hissing whirlpools. But the captain had seen this swift thing happen ; instantly he recognised the terrible danger ; he rapped down to the engine room "Full speed ahead ! "— while the man in charge of the hawser, who had *not* seen, taking this for a sufficient signal, slipped the noose off the post, and let the ponderous cable drop into the sea.

" The raven's death to you, what have you done ! " Archie MacNichol cried, as he ran quickly to the end of the quay, and stared over, his eyes aghast, his lips ashen-grey.

The river, nothing visible but the seething and foaming

water, with its million million bells of air showing white in the pellucid green. Had the girl been struck down by the revolving screw? Had Donald Ross been knocked senseless by a blow from the heavy cable? Big Archie pulled off his jacket and flung it aside. He clambered over the edge of the quay, and let himself down until he stood on one of the beams below. His eyes—a fisherman's eyes—were searching those green deeps, that every moment showed more and more clear.

All this was the work of a second, and so was Archie's quick plunge into the sea when he beheld a dark object rise to the surface, some half-dozen yards away from him—the tangled black hair and the wan face belonging to a quite listless if not lifeless form. It needed but a few powerful strokes to take him along—then one arm was placed under the apparently inanimate body—while with the other he began to fight his way back again to the pier. Of course, bearing such a burden, it was impossible for him to drag himself up to his former position; he could only cling on to one of the mussel-encrusted beams, waiting for the boat that the people were now hurriedly pushing off from the shore. And if, while bravely hanging on there, he looked back to see if there was no sign of that other one, then he looked in vain : the corpse of the hapless Anna Chlannach was not found until some two days thereafter.

Meanwhile, this was what was taking place at Lochgarra House. Barbara had come to tell her young mistress, who was lying tired and languid on the sofa, of the arrival of the steamer.

"Go to the window, Barbara," said she, rather faintly, "and—and tell me who are coming ashore. Maybe you can make them out?"

"Oh, yes, indeed, mem," said Barbara, who had been famous for her eyesight, even among the keepers and stalkers, when she was parlour-maid up at Glen Orme.

She went to the window.

"There is Miss Glendinning, mem," said Barbara, in her soft-spoken way; "and glad I am of that : it is not good for Miss Stanley to be so much alone. Yes, and Mr. Ross coming ashore too—no, he is going back down the gangway—maybe he is going on to Stornoway?—no, no, I think he is only calling something to Coinneach Breac, and the lad Calum—and they are carrying a portmanteau. And there is Anna Chlannach going from the one to the other on the quay—yes, and Mr. Ross now speaking to her—and Miss Glendinning speaking to the Minister. And now Mr. Ross speaking to the Minister—and—and Miss Glendinning watching the steamer—ay, just waiting to see her go aweh . . . Oh, mem!—oh, mem!—there is something happening on the quay!" exclaimed Barbara, in terrified accents. "The people are running—and I am not seeing Mr. Ross anywhere—and they are shoving out a boat from the shore——"

"What is it!—what is it, Barbara! Tell me!—tell me!"

"Oh, mem, do not be afraid," cried Barbara, even amidst her own wild alarm. "There's a boat going out—oh, yes, they are pulling hard—they will be at the end of the quay in a moment or two—and the people are all looking over—oh, yes, yes, mem, if anyone is in the water, they have found him—and—and the boat—now the boat has gone by the end of the quay, and I am not seeing it any more—yes, yes, it is there now—and they are coming this way, mem—they will be coming into the slip—oh, yes—I am sure they have got the one that was in the water—and Big Archie in the stern of the boat, mem—and the people now running to meet them at the slip—now it is Big Archie that is lifting the one out of the stern of the boat——" Suddenly Barbara uttered a plaintive cry, "Oh, *Dyeea*, it is the young master himself!"

"What do you say? Mr. Ross? What has happened, Barbara?" She struggled to her feet, pale and shuddering; and Barbara was at her side in at instant. "Quick, Barbara!—come with me!—help me!—I must go down to the slip—your arm, Barbara—help me!—quick, quick——"

And so, with trembling limbs and dazed eyes—dazed by the fear of some dread unknown thing—she managed to cross the hall dand get down the steps and across the road. It was but a short distance to the slip. The little crowd made way on her approach: and there, lying extended on the stone, she beheld the senseless body of her lover, while the big fisherman, kneeling, was making such examination as was possible. Big Archie rose at once.

"Oh, he will be ahl right directly, mem—I'm sure of it!—he has been struck on the back of the head—mebbe by the keel of the steamer——"

She paid no heed to him—no, nor to any who were standing there. She threw herself on her knees beside the prostrate figure; with her warm hands she pushed back the coal-black tangled hair; she bent down close to him; she spoke to him, almost in a whisper—but with a passionate tenderness that might have thrilled the dead.

"Donald!—speak to me!—tell me I have not killed you!—I sent you away—yes—but my heart has cried for you to come back—speak to me!—speak to me!—Donald! —do you not hear me?—Donald——"

Was it the touch of her warm, trembling fingers about his face, or was it the low-breathing, piteous cry of her voice that seemed to stir his pulses and call him slowly back to life? The eyelids opened wearily—to find this wonderful vision hanging over him, and they seemed to rest there and understand.

"*Mo-lua!*" * he murmured.

She did not know the meaning of the phrase; but the look in his eyes was enough. She held his hand as they carried him up to the house.

*   *   *   *   *

It was on a clear and white-shining morning in the following spring that Donald Ross and his newly-wedded bride were walking arm in arm through the budding larch-woods, the sun warm on the green bracken, on the golden furze, and on the grey rocks. She was angry with him; though the anger did not show much in her dimpled and fresh-tinted cheeks, nor yet in her eyes, where the love-light lay only half-concealed by the modest lashes.

"It is a pestilent language!" she was saying, with frowning brows. "I do believe the heavens and the earth shall pass away before I become thoroughly acquainted with that awful grammar; and unless, as Barbara says, I 'have the Gaelic,' how am I to get into proper relation·

---

* *Mo-luaidh*—My dearest one, or my most-prized one.

ship with the people about here?—yes, and how am I to be sure that you are not stealing away their hearts from me? Oh, it is a very pretty trick, the stealing away of hearts—you are rather clever at it," said she, with downcast and smiling eyes.

"*Mo-ghaol*," said he (and there were some Gaelic phrases, at least, of which she had by this time got to know the meaning well enough), "I thought you were going to let me be your interpreter."

"Why do you not begin, then? Where are the verses that Mrs. Armour sent?" she said. "You promised you would write out a translation for me."

"And so I have," he answered her—yet with some apparent unwillingness. "I have written out a translation, in a kind of way, because you insisted on it. But it is a shame. For the Gaelic is a most expressive language ; and all the subtlety and grace of the original escape when you come down to a literal rendering in English. Besides, what skill have I in such things? If you like, I will send it to the editor of the *Celtic Magazine*, and ask him to get it properly translated—he has printed some of Mrs. Armour's pieces before now—in Gaelic, of course——"

"I want your version—none other," she said, imperatively.

"Very well, very well ; I will read it to you," said he, taking a sheet of paper from his pocket. "Here is a seat for you."

It was a rock mostly covered by soft green moss ; and when she had seated herself, he threw himself down on the bracken by her side, leaning his head against her knee. And this is what the old dame out there in Canada had sent them as her humble wedding gift—perhaps, as to the form of it, with some recollection of the song of the Princess Deirdri influencing her unequal lines :—

> *I am far from the land of my fathers.*
> *I sit and mourn because of the great distance.*
> *My old age brings me no comfort,*
> *Since I am far from my own land.*
>
> *My eyes strain across the wide ocean.*
> *I see the lofty hills, and the peaks, and the glens ;*
> *I see the corries where the wide-antlered deer wander.*
> *Joyful to me was my youth there.*

I see the woods, deep·sheltered;
I see the rivers flowing by the rocks;
I see the sandy bays, and the headlands;
I see the sun [setting] behind Eilean Heimra.

Ru-Minard, O Ru-Minard!—
The promontory facing the great waves:
Often as a girl have I sate and watched the ships,
Singing to myself on Ru-Minard.

Loch-Heimra, O Loch-Heimra!—
Pleasant its shores, with the many birches;
Sweet were the youthful moments I spent watching
For one that I used to meet by Loch-Heimra.

Lochgarra, O Lochgarra!—
The fair town—the Town of the Big House—

" I wonder if the Americans know the meaning of Baltimore ? " he said ; and then he went on again—

Dear to me were my friends, happy the hours
We spent together at Lochgarra.

But to-day there is no more of mourning;
To-day my old age is comforted;
To-day I lift up my voice, I send a message
Across the sea to the dear one of my heart.

Well I remember him, the young boy fearless;
Fearless on the land, fearless on the sea;
Clinging the crags seeking the ravens' nests.
Proud was I of Young Donald——

"There are some more verses about me," he again interpolated. "I will skip them."

"You shall not," she said. "Not a single word."

" Oh, how can I read all this about myself !" he protested.

" Well, then, give me the paper," said she, and she leant over and took it from him. Nor did she return it. She read right on to the end—though not aloud—

My eyes have beheld him come to man's estate.
Proudly I name him: Donald, son of John, son of Roderick.
Of the ancient Clan Anrias, high he holds his head.
Joyful were my eyes when I beheld him.

Swift and alert, firm-sinewed as a man.
Laughing and light-hearted: dangerous to his foe.
Strong as an eagle to choose his mate,
Strong likewise to defend her.

Bold-eyed and resolute; confident at the helm;
Long-enduring; scornful of danger.
Small his possessions, but rich-chambered his mind:
Wealth has he other than Eilean Heimra.

I see the people as they go along the road:
Their regard is turned upon Young Donald;
There is deep love in their bosom for him;
They wish him many days and prosperity.

I see her whom he has chosen:
The lady of the Big House near to the trees:
The fair mistress, the beautiful one,
The generous daughter of the Saxon.

Mild of speech, smiling pleasantly:
My heart was warm towards her;
Much did I hear of the kindness
Of the generous, open-handed maiden.

Tall of stature, graceful in step as a young fawn;
Glad was I when I gazed on her;
I regarded her many beauties, and I said—
Well has young Donald chosen his mate.

Now I hear the sound of rejoicings;
I hear the festivities wide-echoing;
Across the ocean I hear the shouts of the wedding:
Hail to the young chief of Clan Anrias!

The wine-cup is lifted by many hands;
The bride and bridegroom are smiling among their friends;
To-night the bonfires will blaze on the hills;
I hear the loud sound of the pipes.

No gifts have I for the home-coming;
No amulet of secret virtue;
But the voice of the woman-bard is welcome to her chief;*
Young Donald will not despise what I send.

Salutations and blessings I send:
Happy may his days be with his love:
Long years, many friends, a warm hearth—
These are the things I wish for him.

For her also the same:
For her, the chosen one, the fair-haired one, the beautiful Saxon;
Many years, and love through all of them,
For the bride of Young Donald of Heimra!

She carefully folded the paper and put it in her pocket.

"This is to be mine," she said. "For if young Donald despises that message from across the sea, Young Donald's wife does not."

* Banabhard.

THE END.